MY
GRANDMOTHER
SENDS HER
REGARDS &
apologises

Fredrik Backman is a Swedish blogger, columnist and author. His debut novel *A Man Called Ove* was a number 1 bestseller across Scandinavia and has sold over one million copies worldwide. *My Grandmother Sends Her Regards and Apologises*, Fredrik's second novel, also went straight to number 1 in Sweden on publication in 2014.

MY
GRANDMOTHER
SENDS HER
REGARDS &
apologises

Translated from the Swedish
by Henning Koch

FREDRIK BACKMAN

SCEPTRE

First published in Great Britain in 2015 by Sceptre
An imprint of Hodder & Stoughton
An Hachette UK company

First published in paperback in 2016

5

Copyright © Fredrik Backman 2015
Translation © by Henning Koch 2015

The right of Fredrik Backman to be identified as the
Author of the Work has been asserted by him in accordance
with the Copyright, Designs and Patents Act 1988.

A CIP catalogue record for this title is available from the British Library

Paperback ISBN 978 1 473 62684 3
eBook ISBN 978 1 444 77586 0

Typeset in Sabon MT by Palimpsest Book Production Limited,
Falkirk, Stirlingshire

Printed and bound in Great Britain by Clays Ltd, St Ives plc

Hodder & Stoughton policy is to use papers that are natural, renewable
and recyclable products and made from wood grown in sustainable forests.
The logging and manufacturing processes are expected to conform
to the environmental regulations of the country of origin.

Hodder & Stoughton Ltd
Carmelite House
50 Victoria Embankment
London EC4Y 0DZ

www.sceptrebooks.co.uk

To the monkey and the frog. For an eternity of ten thousand tales.

1

TOBACCO

Every seven-year-old deserves a superhero. That's just how it is.

Anyone who doesn't agree needs their head examined.

That's what Elsa's granny says, at least.

Elsa is seven, going on eight. She knows she isn't especially good at being seven. She knows she's different. Her headmaster says she needs to 'fall into line' in order to achieve 'a better fit with her peers'. Other adults describe her as 'very grown-up for her age.' Elsa knows this is just another way of saying 'massively annoying for her age,' because they only tend to say this when she corrects them for mispronouncing 'déjà vu' or not being able to tell the difference between 'me' and 'I' at the end of a sentence. Smart-arses usually can't, hence the 'grown-up for her age' comment, generally said with a strained smile at her parents. As if she has a mental impairment, as if Elsa has shown them up by not being totally thick just because she's seven. And that's why she doesn't have any friends except Granny. Because all the other seven-year-olds in her school are as idiotic as seven-year-olds tend to be, but Elsa is different.

She shouldn't take any notice of what those muppets think, says Granny. Because all the best people are different – look at superheroes. After all, if superpowers were normal everyone would have them.

Granny is seventy-seven years old, going on seventy-eight. She's not very good at it either. You can tell she's old because

1

her face looks like newspaper stuffed into wet shoes, but no one ever accuses Granny of being grown-up for her age. 'Perky,' people sometimes say to Elsa's mum, looking either fairly worried or fairly angry as Mum sighs and asks how much she owes for the damages. Or when Granny's smoking at the hospital sets the fire alarm off and she starts ranting and raving about how 'everything *has to be* so bloody politically correct these days!' when the security guards make her extinguish her cigarette. Or that time she made a snowman in Britt-Marie and Kent's garden right under their balcony and dressed it up in grown-up clothes so it looked as if a person had fallen from the roof. Or that time those prim men wearing spectacles started ringing all the doorbells and wanted to talk about God and Jesus and heaven, and Granny stood on her balcony with her dressing gown flapping open, shooting at them with her paintball gun, and Britt-Marie couldn't quite decide if she was most annoyed about the paintball-gun thing or the not-wearing-anything-under-the-dressing-gown thing, but she reported both to the police just to be on the safe side.

Those are the times, Elsa supposes, that people find Granny perky for her age.

They also say that Granny is mad, but in actual fact she's a genius. It's just that she's a bit of a crackpot at the same time. She used to be a doctor, and she won prizes and journalists wrote articles about her and she went to all the most terrible places in the world when everyone else was getting out. She saved lives and fought evil everywhere on earth. As superheroes do.

But one day someone decided she was too old to save lives, even if Elsa quite strongly suspects what they really meant by 'too old' was 'too crazy.' Granny refers to this person as 'Society' and says it's only because everything has to be so bloody politically correct nowadays that she's no longer allowed to make incisions in people. And that it was really mainly about Society getting so bleeding fussy about the smoking ban in the operating theatres, and who could work under those sorts of conditions?

2

So now she's mainly at home driving Britt-Marie and Mum round the bend. Britt-Marie lives one floor down from Granny. And really Britt-Marie also lives one floor down from Elsa's mum, because Elsa's mum lives next door to Elsa's granny. And Elsa obviously also lives next door to Granny, because Elsa lives with her mum. Except every other weekend, when she lives with Dad and Lisette. And of course George is also Granny's neighbour, because he lives with Mum. It's a bit all over the place.

But anyway, to get back to the point: life-saving and driving people nuts are Granny's superpowers. Which perhaps makes her a bit of a *dysfunctional* superhero. Elsa knows this because she looked up 'dysfunctional' on Wikipedia. People of Granny's age describe Wikipedia as 'an encyclopaedia, but on the net!' Encyclopaedias are what Elsa describes as 'Wikipedia, but analogue.' Elsa has checked 'dysfunctional' in both places and it means that something is not functioning quite as it's supposed to. Which is one of Elsa's favourite things about her granny.

But maybe not today. Because it's half past one in the morning and Elsa is fairly tired and would really like to go back to bed. Except that's not going to happen, because Granny's been throwing turds at a policeman.

It's a little complicated.

Elsa looks around the little rectangular room and yawns listlessly and so widely that she looks like she's trying to swallow her own head.

'I *did* tell you not to climb the fence,' she mutters, checking her watch.

Granny doesn't answer. Elsa takes off her Gryffindor scarf and puts it in her lap. She was born on Boxing Day seven years ago (almost eight). The same day some German scientists recorded the strongest ever emission of gamma radiation from a magnetar over the Earth. Admittedly Elsa doesn't know what a magnetar is, but it's some kind of neutron star. And it sounds a little like 'Megatron,' which is the name of the evil one in *Transformers*, which is what simpletons who don't read enough quality literature call 'a children's programme.' In actual fact the Transformers are robots, but if you look at it academically they could also be counted as superheroes. Elsa is very keen on both *Transformers* and neutron stars and she imagines that an 'emission of gamma radiation' would look a bit like that time Granny spilled Fanta on Elsa's iPhone and tried to dry it out in the toaster. And Granny says it makes Elsa special to have been born on a day like that. And being special is the best way of being different.

Granny is busy distributing small heaps of tobacco all over the wooden table in front of her and rolling them into rustling cigarette papers.

'I said I told you not to climb the fence!'

Granny makes a snorting sound and searches the pockets of her much too large overcoat for a lighter. She doesn't seem to be taking any of this very seriously, mainly because she never seems to take anything seriously. Except when she wants to smoke and can't find a lighter.

'It was a tiny little fence, for God's sake!' she says breezily. 'It's nothing to get worked up about.'

'Don't you "for God's sake" me! You're the one who threw shit at the police.'

'Stop fussing. You sound like your mother. Do you have a lighter?'

'I'm seven!'

'How long are you going to use that as an excuse?'

'Until I'm not seven any more?'

Granny mumbles something that sounds like 'Not a crime to ask, is it?' and continues riffling through her pockets.

'I don't think you can smoke in here, actually,' Elsa informs her, sounding calmer now and fingering the long rip in the Gryffindor scarf.

'Course you can smoke. We'll just open a window.'

Elsa looks sceptically at the windows.

'I don't think they're the sort of windows that open.'

'Why not?'

'They've got bars on them.'

Granny glares with dissatisfaction at the windows. And then at Elsa.

'So now you can't even smoke at the police station. Jesus. It's like being in *1984*.'

Elsa yawns again. 'Can I borrow your phone?'

'What for?'

'To check something.'

'Where?'

'Online.'

'You invest too much time on that internet stuff.'

'You mean spend.'

'I beg your pardon?'

'What I mean is, you don't use "invest" in that way. You wouldn't go round saying, "I invested two hours in reading *Harry Potter and the Philosopher's Stone*", would you?'

Granny just rolls her eyes and hands her the phone. 'Did you ever hear about the girl who blew up because she did too much thinking?'

The policeman who shuffles into the room looks very, very tired.

'I want to call my lawyer,' Granny demands at once.

'I want to call my mum!' Elsa demands at once.

'In that case I want to call my lawyer first!' Granny insists.

The policeman sits down opposite them and fidgets with a little pile of papers.

'Your mother is on her way,' he says to Elsa, with a sigh.

Granny makes the sort of dramatic gasp that only Granny knows how to do.

'Why did you call *her*? Are you mad?' she protests, as if the policeman just told her he was going to leave Elsa in the forest to be raised by a pack of wolves. 'She'll be bloody livid!'

'We have to call the child's legal guardian,' the policeman explains calmly.

'*I* am also the child's legal guardian! I am the child's *grandmother*!' Granny fumes, rising slightly out of her chair and shaking her unlit cigarette menacingly.

'It's half past one in the morning. Someone has to take care of the child.'

'Yes, me! *I'm* taking care of the child!' she splutters.

The policeman makes a fairly strained attempt to gesture amicably across the interrogation room.

'And how do you feel it's going so far?'

Granny looks slightly offended.

'Well . . . everything was going just fine until you started chasing me.'

'You broke into a zoo.'

'It was a *tiny little* fence—'

'There's no such thing as a "tiny" burglary.'

Granny shrugs and makes a brushing movement over the table, as if she thinks they've stretched this out long enough. The policeman notices the cigarette and eyes it dubiously.

'Oh, come on! I can smoke in here, can't I?'

He shakes his head sternly. Granny leans forward, looks him deep in the eyes and smiles.

'Can't you make an exception? Not even for little old me?'

Elsa gives Granny a little shove in the side and switches to their secret language. Because Granny and Elsa have a secret language, as all grannies must have with their grandchildren, because by law that's a requirement, says Granny. Or at least it should be.

'Drop it Granny. It's, like, illegal to flirt with policemen.'

'Says who?'

'Well, the police for starters!' Elsa replies.

'The police are supposed to be there for the sake of the *citizens*,' Granny hisses. 'I pay my taxes, you know.'

The policeman looks at them as you do when a seven-year-old and a seventy-seven-year-old start arguing in a secret language in a police station in the middle of the night. Then Granny's eyelashes tremble alluringly at him as she once again

6

points pleadingly at her cigarette, but when he shakes his head, Granny leans back in the chair and exclaims in normal language:

'I mean, this political correctness! It's worse than apartheid for smokers in this bloody country nowadays!'

'How do you spell that?' asks Elsa.

'What?' Granny sighs as you do when precisely the whole world is against you, even though you pay tax.

'That *apartight* thing,' says Elsa.

'A-p-p-a-r-t-e-j-d,' Granny spells.

Elsa immediately Googles it on Granny's phone. It takes her a few attempts – Granny's always been a rubbish speller. Meanwhile the policeman explains that they've decided to let them go, but Granny will be called in at a later date to explain the burglary and 'other aggravations'.

'What aggravations?'

'Driving illegally, to begin with.'

'What do you mean, illegally? That's my car! I don't need permission to drive my own car, do I?'

'No,' replies the policeman patiently, 'But you need a driving licence.'

Granny throws out her arms in exasperation. She's just launched into another rant about this being a Big Brother society when Elsa whacks the phone sharply against the table.

'It's got NOTHING to do with that apartheid thing!!! You compared not being able to smoke with apartheid and it's not the same thing at all. It's not even CLOSE!'

Granny waves her hand resignedly.

'I meant it was . . . you know, more or less like that—'

'It isn't at all!'

'It was a metaphor, for God's sake—'

'A bloody crap metaphor!'

'How would you know?'

'WIKIPEDIA!'

Granny turns in defeat to the policeman. 'Do your children carry on like this?' The policeman looks uncomfortable.

'We . . . don't let the children surf the net unsupervised . . .'

Granny stretches out her arms towards Elsa, a gesture that seems to say 'You see!' Elsa just shakes her head and crosses her arms very hard.

'Granny, just say sorry for throwing turds at the police, and we can go home,' she snorts in the secret language, though still very expressly upset about that whole apartheid thing.

'Sorry,' says Granny in the secret language.

'To the police, not me, you muppet.'

'There'll be no apologising to fascists here. I pay my taxes. And *you're* the muppet.' Granny sulks.

'Takes one to know one.'

Then they both sit with their arms crossed, demonstratively looking away from each other until Granny nods at the policeman and says in normal language:

'Would you be kind enough to let my spoilt granddaughter know that if she takes this attitude she's quite welcome to walk home?'

'Tell *her* I'm going home with Mum and *she's* the one who can walk!' Elsa replies at once.

'Tell HER she can—'

The policeman stands up without a word, walks out of the room and closes the door behind him, as if intending to go into another room and bury his head in a large, soft cushion and yell as loud as he can.

'Now look what you did,' says Granny.

'Look what YOU did!'

Eventually a heavyset policewoman with piercing green eyes comes in instead. It doesn't seem to be the first time she's run into Granny, because she smiles in that tired way so typical of people who know Granny, and says: 'You have to stop doing this, we also have real criminals to worry about.' Granny just mumbles, 'Why don't *you* stop doing this?' And then they're allowed to go home.

Standing on the pavement waiting for her mother, Elsa fingers the rip in her scarf. It goes right through the Gryffindor emblem.

She tries as hard as she can not to cry, but doesn't make much of a success of it.

'Ah come on, your mum can mend that,' says Granny, trying to be cheerful, giving her a little punch on the shoulder.

Elsa looks up anxiously.

'And, you know . . . we can tell your mum the scarf got torn when you were trying to stop me climbing the fence to get to the monkeys.'

Elsa nods and runs her fingers over the scarf again. It didn't get torn when Granny was climbing the fence. It got torn at school when three older girls who hate Elsa without Elsa really understanding why got hold of her outside the canteen and hit her and tore her scarf and threw it down the toilet. Their jeers are still echoing round Elsa's head. Granny notices the look in her eyes and leans forward before whispering in their secret language:

'One day we'll take those losers at your school to Miamas and throw them to the lions!'

Elsa dries her eyes with the back of her hand and smiles faintly.

'I'm not stupid, Granny,' she whispers. 'I know you did all that stuff tonight to make me forget about what happened at school.'

Granny kicks at some gravel and clears her throat.

'I didn't want you to remember this day because of the scarf. So I thought instead you could remember it as the day your Granny broke into a zoo—'

'And escaped from a hospital,' Elsa says with a grin.

'And escaped from a hospital,' says Granny with a grin.

'And threw turds at the police.'

'Actually it was soil! Or mainly soil, anyway.'

'Changing memories is a good superpower, I suppose.'

Granny shrugs.

'If you can't get rid of the bad you have to top it up with more goody stuff.'

'That's not a word.'

9

'I know.'

'Thanks Granny,' says Elsa and leans her head against her arm.

And then Granny just nods and whispers: 'We're knights of the kingdom of Miamas, we have to do our duty.'

Because all seven-year-olds deserve superheroes.

And anyone who doesn't agree needs their head examined.

2

MONKEY

Mum picked them up at the police station. You could tell that she was very angry, but she was controlled and full of composure and never even raised her voice, because Mum is everything Elsa's granny is not. Elsa fell asleep almost before she'd fastened her seat belt. By the time they were on the motorway, she was already in Miamas.

Miamas is Elsa and Granny's secret kingdom. It is one of six kingdoms in the Land-of-Almost-Awake. Granny came up with it when Elsa was small and Mum and Dad had just got divorced and Elsa was afraid of sleeping because she'd read on the internet about children who died in their sleep. Granny is good at coming up with things. So when Dad moved out of the flat and everyone was upset and tired, Elsa sneaked out of the front door every night and scampered across the landing in her bare feet into Granny's flat, and then she and Granny crawled into the big wardrobe that never stopped growing, and then they half-closed their eyes and set off.

Because you don't need to close your eyes to get to the Land-of-Almost-Awake. That's the whole point of it, sort of thing. You only need to be *almost* asleep. And in those last few seconds when your eyes are closing, when the mists come rolling in across the boundary between what you think and what you just know, that's when you set off. You ride into the Land-of-Almost-Awake on the back of cloud animals, because that's the only way of getting there. The cloud animals come in through

11

Granny's balcony door and pick her and Elsa up, and then they fly higher and higher and higher until Elsa sees all the magical creatures that live in the Land-of-Almost-Awake: the enphants and regretters and the Noween and wurses and snow-angels and princes and princesses and knights. The cloud animals soar over the endless dark forests, where Wolfheart and all the other monsters live, then they sweep down through the blindingly bright colours and soft winds to the city gates of the kingdom of Miamas.

It's difficult to say for sure whether Granny is a bit odd because she's spent too much time in Miamas, or Miamas is a bit odd because Granny's spent too much time there. But this is the source of all of Granny's amazing, monstrous, magical fairy tales.

Granny says that the kingdom has been called Miamas for an eternity of at least ten thousand fairy tales, but Elsa knows that Granny made this up because Elsa couldn't say 'pyjamas' when she was small and used to say 'mjamas' instead. Except of course Granny insists that she never made up a bloody thing and Miamas and the other five kingdoms in the Land-of-Almost-Awake are not only real, but actually far *more* real than the world we're in now, where 'everyone is an economist and drinks lactose-free milk and makes a right carry-on.' Granny isn't particularly good at living in the real world. There are too many rules. She cheats when she plays Monopoly and drives Renault in the bus lane and steals those yellow carrier bags from IKEA and won't stand behind the line when she's at the conveyor belt at the airport. And when she goes to the toilet she leaves the door open.

But she does tell the very best fairy tales ever, and for that Elsa can forgive quite a few character defects.

All fairy tales that are worth something come from Miamas, says Granny. The other five kingdoms in the Land-of-Almost-Awake are busy doing other things: Mirevas is the kingdom where they stand guard over dreams, Miploris is the kingdom where they store all sorrow, Mimovas is where music comes from, Miaudacas is where courage comes from and Mibatalos is the kingdom where the bravest warriors, who fought against the fearsome shadows in the War-Without-End, were raised.

But Miamas is Granny and Elsa's favourite kingdom, because there storytelling is considered the noblest profession of all. The currency there is imagination; instead of buying something with coins you buy it with a good story. Libraries aren't known as libraries but as 'banks' and every fairy tale is worth a fortune. Granny spends millions every night: tales full of dragons and trolls and kings and queens and witches. And shadows. Because all imaginary worlds have to have terrible enemies, and in the Land-of-Almost-Awake the enemies are the shadows, because the shadows want to kill the imagination. And if we're going to talk about shadows, we must mention Wolfheart. He was the one who defeated the shadows in the War-Without-End. He was the first and greatest superhero Elsa ever heard about.

Elsa was knighted in Miamas; she gets to ride cloud animals and have her own sword. She hasn't once been afraid to fall asleep since Granny started taking her there each night. Because in Miamas no one says girls can't be knights, and the mountains reach up to the sky, and the campfires never go out, and no one tries to shred your Gryffindor scarf.

Of course, Granny also says that no one in Miamas closes the door when they go to the toilet. An open-door policy is more or less legally enforceable in every situation across the Land-of-Almost-Awake. But Elsa is pretty sure she is describing another version of the truth there. That's what Granny calls lies: 'Other versions of the truth.' So when Elsa wakes up in a chair in Granny's room at the hospital the next morning, Granny is on the toilet with the door open, while Elsa's mum is in the hall, and Granny is in the midst of telling another version of the truth. It's not going all that well. The real truth, after all, is that

Granny escaped from hospital last night and Elsa sneaked out of the flat while Mum and George were sleeping, and they went to the zoo together in Renault, and Granny climbed the fence. Elsa quietly admits to herself that it now seems a little irresponsible to have done all this with a seven-year-old in the middle of the night.

Granny, whose clothes are lying in a pile on the floor and still very literally smelling a bit monkey-ish, is claiming that when she was climbing the fence by the monkey cage and the guard shouted at her, she thought he could have been a 'lethal rapist', and *this* was why she started throwing muck at him and the police. Mum shakes her head in a very controlled way and says Granny is making all this up. Granny doesn't like it when people say that things are made up, and reminds Mum she prefers the less derogatory term 'reality-challenged'. Mum clearly disagrees but controls herself. Because she is everything that Granny isn't.

'This is one of the worst things you've done,' Mum calls out grimly towards the toilet.

'I find that very, very unlikely, my dear daughter,' Granny answers from within, unconcerned.

Mum responds by methodically running through all the trouble Granny has caused. Granny says the only reason she's getting so worked up is that she doesn't have a sense of humour. And then Mum says Granny should stop behaving like an irresponsible child. And then Granny says: 'Do you know where pirates park their cars?' And when Mum doesn't answer, Granny yells from the toilet, 'In a gAAARRRage!' Mum just sighs, massages her temples and closes the toilet door. This makes Granny really, really, really angry because she doesn't like feeling enclosed when she's on the toilet.

She's been in hospital for two weeks now, but absconds almost every day and picks up Elsa and they have ice cream or go to the flat when Mum isn't home and make a soap-sud slide on the landing. Or break into zoos. Basically whatever appeals to her, whenever. But Granny doesn't consider this to be an 'escape' in the proper sense of the word, because she believes there has to be some basic aspect of challenge to the whole thing if it's to count as an escape – a dragon or a series of traps or at least a wall and a respectably sized moat, and so on. Mum and the hospital staff don't quite agree with her on this point.

A nurse comes into the room and quietly asks for a moment of Mum's time. She gives Mum a piece of paper and Mum writes something on it and returns it, and then the nurse leaves. Granny has had nine different nurses since she was admitted. Seven of these she refused to cooperate with, and two refused to cooperate with her, one of them because Granny said he had a 'nice arse'. Granny insists it was a compliment to his arse, not to him, and he shouldn't make such a fuss about it. Then Mum told Elsa to put on her headphones, but Elsa still heard their argument about the difference between 'sexual harassment' and 'basic appreciation of a perfectly splendid arse'.

They argue a lot, Mum and Granny. They've been arguing for as long as Elsa can remember. About everything. If Granny is a dysfunctional superhero, then Mum is very much a fully operational one. Their interaction is a bit like Cyclops and Wolverine in *X-Men*, Elsa often thinks, and whenever she has those types of thoughts she wishes she had someone around who could understand what she means. People around Elsa don't read enough quality literature and certainly don't understand that *X-Men* comics count as precisely that. To such philistines Elsa would explain, very slowly, that X-Men are indeed superheroes, but first and foremost they are mutants, and there is a certain academic difference. Anyway, without putting too fine a point on it, she would sum it up by saying that Granny and Mum's superhero powers are in direct opposition. As if Spider-Man, one of Elsa's favourite superheroes, had an antagonist called Slip-Up Man whose superpower was that he couldn't even climb onto a bench. But in a good way.

Basically, Mum is orderly and Granny is chaotic. Elsa once read that 'Chaos is God's neighbour', but Mum said if Chaos had moved onto God's landing it was only because Chaos couldn't put up with living next door to Granny any more.

Mum has files and calendars for everything and her telephone plays a little jingle fifteen minutes before she has a meeting. Granny writes down things she needs to remember directly on the wall. And not only when she's at home, but on any wall, wherever she is. It's not a perfect system, because in order to remember a particular task she needs to be in exactly the same place where she wrote it down. When Elsa pointed out this flaw, Granny replied indignantly that 'There's still a smaller risk of me losing a kitchen wall than your mother losing that poxy telephone!' But then Elsa pointed out that Mum never lost anything. And then Granny rolled her eyes and sighed: 'No, no, but your mother is the exception, of course. It only applies to . . . you know . . . people who aren't perfect.'

Perfection is Mum's superpower. She's not as much fun as Granny, but on the other hand she always knows where Elsa's Gryffindor scarf is. 'Nothing is ever really gone until your mum can't find it,' Mum often whispers into Elsa's ear when she's wrapping it round her neck.

Elsa's mum is the boss. 'Not just a job, but a lifestyle,' Granny often snorts. Mum is not someone you go with, she's someone you follow. Whereas Elsa's granny is more the type you're dodging rather than following, and she never found a scarf in her life.

Granny doesn't like bosses, which is a particular problem at this hospital, because Mum is even more of a boss here. Because she is the boss here.

'You're overreacting, Ulrika, good God!' Granny calls out through the toilet door just as another nurse comes in and Mum again writes on a bit of paper and mentions some numbers. Mum gives her a controlled smile; the nurse smiles back nervously. And then things go silent inside the toilet for a long while and Mum suddenly looks anxious, as one does when things go quiet around Granny for too long. And then she sniffs the air

16

and pulls the door open. Granny is sitting naked on the toilet seat with her legs comfortably crossed. She waves her smouldering cigarette at Mum.

'Hello? A little privacy, perhaps?'

Mum massages her temples again, takes a deep breath and rests her hand on her belly. Granny nods intently at her, waving her cigarette at the bump.

'You know stress isn't good for my new grandchild. Remember you're worrying for two now!'

'I'm not the one who seems to have forgotten,' replies Mum curtly.

'Touché,' Granny mumbles and inhales deeply.

(That's one of those words Elsa understands without even having to know what it means.)

'Does it not occur to you how dangerous that is for the baby, not to mention Elsa?' she says, pointing at the cigarette.

'Don't make such a fuss! People have been smoking since the dawn of time and there have been perfectly healthy babies born the whole way through. Your generation forgets that humanity has lived for thousands of years without allergy tests and crap like that before you showed up and started thinking you were so important. When we were living in caves, do you think they used to put mammoth skins through a ninety-degree machine-wash programme?'

'Did they have cigarettes back then?' asks Elsa.

Granny says, 'Don't you start.' Mum puts her hand on her belly. Elsa is unsure if she's doing it because Halfie is kicking in there or because she wants to cover her-his ears. Mum is Halfie's mum but George is Halfie's dad, so Halfie is Elsa's half-sibling. Or she-he will be, anyway. She-he will be a proper full-sized human; a half-sibling, but not in any way half a person, Elsa has been promised. She had a couple of confused days until she understood the difference. 'Considering how smart you are, you can certainly be a bit of a thickie sometimes,' Granny burst out when Elsa asked her about it. And then they bickered for nearly three hours, which was almost a new bickering record for them.

17

'I only wanted to show her the monkeys, Ulrika,' mumbles Granny as she extinguishes the cigarette in the sink.

'I don't have the energy for this . . .' Mum answers with resignation, although she's absolutely controlled about it, and then goes into the corridor to sign a piece of paper covered in numbers.

Granny really did want to show Elsa the monkeys. They'd been arguing on the phone the night before about whether there was a certain type of monkey that slept standing up. Granny was wrong, of course, because it said on Wikipedia and everything. And then Elsa had mentioned the scarf and what had happened at school, which was when Granny decided that they were going to the zoo, and Elsa sneaked out while Mum and George were sleeping.

Mum disappears down the corridor, her head buried in her phone, while Elsa climbs into Granny's bed so they can play Monopoly. Granny steals money from the bank and, when Elsa catches her out, also steals the car so she can skip town. After a while Mum comes back looking tired and tells Elsa they have to go home now, because Granny has to rest. And Elsa hugs Granny for a long, long, long time.

'When are you coming home?' asks Elsa.

'Probably tomorrow!' Granny promises chirpily.

Because that is what she always says. And then she pushes the hair out of Elsa's eyes and when Mum disappears into the corridor again, Granny suddenly looks very serious and says in their secret language: 'I have an important assignment for you.'

Elsa nods, because Granny always gives her assignments in the secret language, only spoken by initiates of the Land-of-Almost-Awake. Elsa always gets them done. Because that is what a knight of Miamas has to do. Anything except buying cigarettes or frying meat, which is where Elsa draws the line. Because they make her feel sick. Even knights have to have certain principles.

Granny reaches down next to the bed and picks up a big plastic bag from the floor. There are no cigarettes or meat in it. Just sweets.

'You have to give the chocolate to Our Friend.'

It takes a few seconds before Elsa understands exactly what friend she is referring to. And she stares at Granny with alarm.

'Have you gone MAD? You want me to DIE?'

Granny rolls her eyes.

'Don't faff about. Are you telling me a knight of Miamas is too scared to complete a quest?'

Elsa gives her an offended glare.

'That's very mature of you to threaten me with that.'

'Very mature of you to say "mature".'

Elsa snatches up the plastic bag. It's full of small, crinkly packets of Daim chocolate. Granny says, 'It's important that you remove the wrapper from each piece. Otherwise he gets cross.'

Elsa peers sulkily into the bag.

'He doesn't know me, though . . .'

Granny snorts so loudly that it sounds as if she's blowing her nose.

'Course he knows! Good God. Just tell him your granny sends her regards and apologises.'

Elsa raises her eyebrows.

'Apologises for what?'

'For not bringing him any sweets for days and days,' Granny replies, as if this was the most natural thing in the world.

Elsa looks into the bag again.

'It's irresponsible to send out your only grandchild on a mission like this, Granny. It's insane. He could actually kill me.'

'Stop faffing about.'

'Stop faffing about yourself!'

Granny grins; Elsa can't help but grin back. Granny lowers her voice.

'You have to give Our Friend the chocolate secretly. Britt-Marie mustn't see. Wait till they have that residents' meeting tomorrow evening and then sneak over to him.'

Elsa nods, though she's terrified of Our Friend and still thinks it's pretty irresponsible to send a seven-year-old on such a perilous mission. But Granny grabs her fingers and squeezes them in her hands like she always does, and it's difficult to be afraid when someone does that. They hug again.

'See you, oh proud knight of Miamas,' Granny whispers in her ear.

Granny never says 'goodbye', only 'see you'.

While Elsa is putting on her jacket in the hall she hears Mum and Granny talking about 'the treatment'. And then Mum tells Elsa to listen to her headphones. And that's what Elsa does. She put the headphones on her wish list last Christmas and was very particular about Mum and Granny splitting the cost, because it was only fair.

Whenever Mum and Granny start arguing, Elsa turns up the volume and pretends they're both actresses in a silent movie. Elsa is the sort of child who learned early in life that it's easier to make your way if you get to choose your own soundtrack.

The last thing she hears is Granny asking when she can pick up Renault at the police station. Renault is Granny's car. Granny says she won it in a game of poker. It obviously should be 'a' Renault, but Elsa learned that the car was a Renault when she was small, before she understood that there were also other cars with the same name. So she still says 'Renault' as if it's a name.

And it's a very suitable name, because Granny's Renault is old and rusty and French and when you change gears it makes an ungodly racket, like an old Frenchman with a cough. Elsa knows that because sometimes when Granny is driving Renault while smoking and eating a kebab, she only has her knees to steer with, and then she stamps on the clutch and shouts 'NOW!' and then Elsa has to change gear.

Elsa misses doing that.

Mum tells Granny that she won't be able to go and pick up Renault. Granny protests that it's actually her car; Mum just reminds her that it's illegal to drive without a licence. And then Granny calls Mum 'young lady' and tells her she's got driving licences in six countries. Mum asks in a restrained voice if one of these countries happens to be the one they live in, after which Granny goes into a sulk while a nurse takes some blood from her.

Elsa waits by the lift. She doesn't like needles, irrespective of whether they're being stuck into her own arm or Granny's. She sits reading *Harry Potter and the Order of the Phoenix* on the iPad for about the twelfth time. It's the Harry Potter book she likes the least; that's why she's read it so few times.

Only when Mum comes to get her and they're about to go down to the car does Elsa remember that she's left her Gryffindor scarf in the hall outside Granny's room. So she runs back.

Granny is sitting on the edge of the bed with her back against the door, talking on the phone. She doesn't see her, and Elsa realises Granny is talking to her lawyer, because she's instructing him about what sort of beer she wants the next time he comes to the hospital. Elsa knows that the lawyer smuggles in the beer in large encyclopaedias. Granny says she needs them for her 'research', but in fact they are hollowed out inside with beer-bottle-shaped slots. Elsa takes her scarf from the hook and is just about to call out to Granny when she hears her voice fill with emotion as she says, into the telephone:

'She's my grandchild, Marcel. May the heavens bless her little head. I've never met such a good and clever girl. The responsibility must be left to her. She's the only one who can make the right decision.'

There's silence for a moment. And then Granny goes on determinedly:

'I KNOW she's only a child, Marcel! But she's a damn sight smarter than all the other fools put together! And this is my will and you're my lawyer. Just do what I say.'

Elsa stands in the hall holding her breath. And only when Granny says, 'Because I don't WANT TO tell her yet! Because all seven-year-olds deserve superheroes!' – only then does Elsa turn round to quietly slip away, her Gryffindor scarf damp with tears.

And the last thing she hears Granny say on the telephone is: 'I don't want Elsa to know that I am going to die because all seven-year-olds deserve superheroes, Marcel. And one of their superpowers ought to be that they can't get cancer.'

3

COFFEE

There's something special about a grandmother's house. You never forget how it smells.

It's a normal building, by and large. It has four floors and nine flats and the whole block smells of Granny (and coffee, thanks to Lennart). It also has a clear set of regulations pinned up in the laundry, with the heading **For Everyone's Well-Being** in which **Well-Being** has been underlined twice. And a lift that's always broken and rubbish separated for recycling in the yard, and a drunk, a very large animal of some sort and, of course, a granny.

Granny lives at the top, opposite Mum and Elsa and George. Granny's flat is exactly like Mum's except much messier, because Granny's flat is like Granny and Mum's flat is like Mum.

George lives with Mum and that's not always the easiest of things, because it means he also lives next door to Granny. He has a beard and a very small hat and is obsessed with jogging, during which he insists on wearing his shorts over the top of his tracksuit. He cooks in English, and so when he's reading the recipes he says 'cured pork' instead of the Swedish word for it, which is 'fläsk'. Granny never calls him 'George', just 'Loser', which infuriates Mum, but Elsa knows why Granny's doing it. She just wants Elsa to know she's on Elsa's side, no matter what. Because that's what you do when you're a granny and your grandchild's parents get divorced and find themselves new partners and suddenly tell your grandchild there's a half-sibling on its way. That it irritates the hell out of Mum is something Granny views purely as a bonus.

Mum and George don't want to know if Halfie is a boy-half or a girl-half, even though it's easy to find out. It's especially important for George not to know. He always calls Halfie she-he, so he doesn't 'trap the child in a gender role.' The first time he said it, Elsa thought he said 'gender troll.' It ended up being a very confusing afternoon for all involved.

Halfie is either going to be called Elvir or Elvira, Mum and George have decided. When Elsa told Granny this, she just stared at her.

'*ELV-ir*!?'

'It's the half-boy version of "Elvira".'

'*Elvir*, though? Are they planning to send him to Mordor to destroy the ring, or what?' (This was soon after Granny had watched all of the *Lord of the Rings* films with Elsa, because Elsa's mum had expressly told Elsa she wasn't allowed to watch them.)

Obviously Elsa knows that Granny doesn't dislike Halfie. Or even George, really. She just talks that way because she's Granny. One time Elsa told Granny she really did hate George, and that sometimes she even hated Halfie too. It's very difficult not to love someone who can hear you say something as horrible as that and still be on your side.

In the flat under Granny's live Britt-Marie and Kent. They like owning things, and Kent especially likes telling you how much everything costs. He's hardly ever at home because he's an entrepreneur, or a 'Kentrepreneur' as he likes to joke loudly to people he doesn't know. And if people don't laugh right away, he repeats it even louder. As if their hearing is the problem.

Britt-Marie is almost always at home, so Elsa assumes she is not an entrepreneur. Granny calls her 'a full-time nag-bag who will forever be the bane of my life.' She always looks a little like she just popped the wrong chocolate into her mouth. She's the one who put up the sign in the laundry with that **For Everyone's Well-Being** bit on it. Everyone's well-being is very important to Britt-Marie, even though she and Kent are the only people in the house with a washing machine and tumble-drier in their flat.

One time after George had done some laundry, Britt-Marie came upstairs and asked to have a word with Elsa's mum. She'd brought a little ball of blue fluff from the tumble-drier filter, which she held out towards Mum as if it was a newly hatched chick, and said: 'I think you forgot this when you were doing the laundry, Ulrika!' And then when George explained that actually he was in charge of their laundry, Britt-Marie looked at him and smiled, though she didn't seem very genuine about it. And then she said, 'How very modern,' and smiled well-meaningly at Mum and handed her the fluff and said: 'For *everyone's* well-being in *this* leaseholders' association we clear the tumbler filter when we've finished, Ulrika!'

It actually isn't a leaseholders' association yet. But it's going to become one, Britt-Marie is at pains to point out. She and Kent will see it done. And in Britt-Marie's leaseholders' association it's going to be very important to keep to the rules. That is why she is Granny's antagonist. Elsa knows what 'antagonist' means, because you do if you read quality literature.

In the flat opposite Britt-Marie and Kent lives the woman with the black skirt. You hardly ever see her except when she scurries between the front entrance and her door early in the morning and late at night. She always wears high heels and a perfectly ironed black skirt and talks extremely loudly into a white lead trailing from her ear. She never says hello and she never smiles. Granny says that her skirt is too well-ironed and 'if you were the cloth hanging off that woman you'd be terrified of getting yourself creased.'

Under Britt-Marie and Kent's flat live Lennart and Maud. Lennart drinks at least twenty cups of coffee per day and always looks triumphantly proud every time his percolator is turned on. He is the second nicest person in the world, and he's married to Maud. Maud is the nicest person in the world and she has always just baked some biscuits. They live with Samantha, who's almost always asleep. Samantha is a bichon frisé but Lennart and Maud talk to her as if she wasn't. When Lennart and Maud drink coffee in front of Samantha they don't say they're having 'coffee', they call it 'a drink for grown-ups'. Granny says they're soft in the head, but Elsa just thinks they're nice. And they always have dreams and hugs – dreams are a kind of biscuit; hugs are just normal hugs.

Opposite Lennart and Maud lives Alf. He drives a taxi and always wears a leather jacket under a layer of irascibility. His shoes have soles as thin as greaseproof paper because he doesn't lift his feet when he walks. Granny says he has the lowest centre of gravity in the entire bloody universe.

In the flat under Lennart and Maud live the boy with a syndrome and his mum. The boy with a syndrome is a year and a few weeks younger than Elsa, and never speaks. His mother loses things the whole time. Objects seem to rain from her pockets, like in a cartoon when the crook gets frisked by the police and the pile of stuff from his pockets ends up bigger than they are. Both the boy and his mother have very kind eyes, and not even Granny seems to dislike them. And the boy's always dancing. He dances his way through his existence.

In the flat next to theirs, on the other side of the lift that never works, lives The Monster. Elsa doesn't know what his real name is, but she calls him The Monster because everyone is afraid of him. Even Elsa's mum, who isn't scared of anything in the entire world, gives Elsa's back a little shove when they're about to walk past his flat. No one ever sees The Monster because he never goes out in the daytime, but Kent always says, 'People like that shouldn't be let loose! But that's what happens when the authorities go for the soft option. People in this bloody country get psychiatric care instead of prison!' Britt-Marie has written letters to the landlord, demanding that The Monster be evicted in view of her firm conviction that he 'attracts other substance abusers into the building.' Elsa is not sure what that means, and she's not even sure Britt-Marie knows. She asked Granny one day, but she just went a bit quiet and said, 'Certain things should be left well alone.' And this is a granny who fought in the War-Without-End, the war against the shadows in the Land-of-Almost-Awake, and who has met the most terrifying

creatures that have been dreamed up in an eternity of ten thous-
and fairy tales.

That's how you measure time in the Land-of-Almost-Awake: in
eternities. There are no watches in the Land-of-Almost-Awake, so
time is measured according to how you feel. If it feels like an
eternity, you say 'This is a lesser eternity.' And if it feels sort of
like two dozen eternities, you say 'An utter eternity.' And the
only thing that feels longer than an utter eternity is the eternity
of a fairy tale, because a fairy tale is an eternity of utter eternities. And the very longest kind of eternity in existence is the
eternity of ten thousand fairy tales. That's the biggest number
in the Land-of-Almost-Awake.

Anyway, to get back to the point: at the bottom of the house
where all these people live, there's a meeting room, where residents' meetings are held once every month. This is a bit more
than in most buildings, but the flats are rented, and Britt-Marie
and Kent really want everyone living there, by 'a democratic
process', to make a request to the landlord to sell them the
building so they can become flat-owners. And to do that, you
must have residents' meetings. Because no one else in the house
actually wants to be a flat-owner. The democratic bit of the
democratic process is the one Kent and Britt-Marie like the least,
you might say.

And the meetings are obviously terrifically boring. First
everyone argues about what they were arguing about in the
last meeting, and then they all look at their agendas and argue
about when to have the next meeting, and then the meeting
is over. But Elsa still goes there today because she needs to
know when the arguing starts, so no one notices when she
sneaks off.

Elsa arrives early. Kent hasn't got there yet, because Kent is
always late. Alf hasn't arrived either, because Alf is always
exactly on time. But Maud and Lennart are sitting at the big
table and Britt-Marie and Mum are in the pantry discussing the
coffee. Samantha is sleeping on the floor. Maud pushes a big
tin of dreams towards Elsa. Lennart sits next to her, waiting for

the coffee. Meanwhile he sips from a Thermos he has brought with him. It's important to Lennart to have stand-by coffee available while he's waiting for the new coffee.

Britt-Marie is by the kitchen counter in the pantry with her hands clasped together in frustration over her stomach, while she looks nervously at Mum. Mum is making coffee. This is making Britt-Marie nervous because she thinks it would be best if they waited for Kent. Britt-Marie always thinks it would be best to wait for Kent, but Mum is not so big on waiting. She is more about taking control. Britt-Marie smiles well-meaningly at Mum.

'Everything all right with the coffee, Ulrika?'

'Yes, thanks,' says Mum curtly.

'Maybe we should wait for Kent after all?'

'Oh, I think we can manage to make some coffee without Kent,' Mum answers pleasantly.

Again, Britt-Marie clasps her hands together over her stomach. Smiles.

'Well, of course, please yourself, Ulrika. You always do.'

Mum looks as if she's counting to some three-digit number and continues measuring the scoops of coffee.

'It's only coffee, Britt-Marie.'

Britt-Marie nods her understanding of the situation and brushes some invisible dust off her skirt. There is always a bit of invisible dust on Britt-Marie's skirt, which only Britt-Marie can see, and which she absolutely must brush off.

'Kent always makes very nice coffee. Everyone always thinks Kent makes very nice coffee.'

Maud sits at the table looking worried. Because Maud doesn't like conflict. That's why she bakes so many biscuits, because it's much more difficult to have conflict when there are biscuits around.

'Well it's lovely that you and your little Elsa are here today. We all think it's . . . lovely.'

There's a patient 'mmm' from Mum. A bit more coffee is measured out. A bit more dust is brushed off.

'I mean it must be hard for you to find time for little Elsa, we can appreciate that, what with you being so ambitious about your career.'

And then Mum spoons the coffee a little as if she's having fantasies of flinging it in Britt-Marie's face. But in a controlled way.

Britt-Marie goes to the window and moves a plant and says, as if thinking out loud: 'And your partner's so good, isn't he, staying at home to take care of the household. That's what you call it, isn't it? *Partner*? It's very modern, I understand.' And then she smiles again. Well-meaning. Brushes a little more and adds, 'Not that there's anything wrong with that, of course. Nothing at all.'

Alf comes in, in a very bad mood, wearing his creaking leather jacket with a taxi logo on its chest. He has an evening newspaper in his hand. Checks his watch. It's seven o'clock sharp.

'Bloody says seven on the note,' he grunts across the room at no one in particular.

'Kent is a little late,' says Britt-Marie and smiles and clasps her hands together over her stomach again. 'He has an important group meeting with Germany,' she goes on, as if Kent is meeting the entire population of Germany.

Fifteen minutes later Kent comes storming into the room, his jacket flapping like a mantle around him, and yelling, 'Ja, Klaus! Ja! We will dizcuzz it at ze meeting in Frankfurt!' into his telephone. Alf looks up from his evening newspaper and taps his wristwatch and mutters: 'Hope we didn't cause you any inconvenience by being here on time.' Kent ignores him and instead claps his hands excitedly towards Lennart and Maud and says, with a grin: 'Shall we kick things off, then? Eh? It's not like we're getting any babies made here, are we?' And then he turns quickly to Mum and points at her belly and laughs: 'At least no more than we've already got!' And when Mum doesn't immediately laugh, Kent points at her belly again and repeats 'At least no more than we've already got!' in a louder voice, as if his levels weren't quite right the first time.

Maud brings in biscuits. Mum serves coffee. Kent takes a gulp, pauses and announces that it's rather strong. Alf sweeps down the whole cup in one go and mutters, 'Just right!' Britt-Marie takes a tiny, tiny mouthful and rests the cup in the palm of her hand before offering her verdict: 'I do think it's a little strong, personally.' Then she throws a furtive glance at Mum and adds, 'And you're drinking coffee, Ulrika, even though you're pregnant.' And before Mum has time to answer, Britt-Marie immediately excuses herself: 'Not that there's anything wrong with that, obviously. Obviously not!'

And then Kent declares the meeting open and then everyone argues for two hours about what they argued about at the last meeting. Which is when Elsa sneaks out without anyone noticing.

She tiptoes up the stairs to the mezzanine floor. She peers at the door to The Monster's flat, but calms herself with the thought that there is still daylight outside. The Monster never goes outside while it's still light.

Then she looks at the door of the flat next to The Monster's, the one without a name on the letter box. That is where Our Friend lives. Elsa stands two metres from it, holding her breath because she's afraid it will smash the door and come charging out of the splintered remains and try to close its jaws round her throat if it hears her coming too close. Only Granny calls it 'Our Friend'; everyone else says 'the hound'. Especially Britt-Marie. Elsa doesn't know how much fight there is in it, but either way she's never seen such a big dog in her life. When you hear it barking from behind the door it's like being whacked in the stomach by a medicine ball.

But she has only seen it once, in Granny's flat, a few days before Granny got taken ill. She couldn't have imagined feeling more afraid, even if facing a shadow eye-to-eye in the Land-of-Almost-Awake.

It was a Saturday and Granny and Elsa were going to an exhibition about dinosaurs. That was the morning Mum put the Gryffindor scarf in the wash without asking and made Elsa take another scarf – a vomit-green one. Mum knows Elsa hates green. She really lacks empathy sometimes, that woman.

Our Friend had been lying on Granny's bed, like a sphinx outside a pyramid. Elsa stood transfixed in the hall, staring at that gigantic black head and terrifying, depthless eyes. Granny had come out of the kitchen and was putting on her coat as if it was the most natural thing in the whole universe to have the biggest thing ever lying on her bed.

'What is . . . that thing?' Elsa had whispered. Granny carried on rolling her cigarette and replied indifferently: 'This is Our Friend. He won't hurt you if you don't hurt him.'

Easy for her to say, Elsa thought – how was she supposed to know what would provoke one of those? Once, one of the girls at school had hit her because she had 'an ugly scarf'. That was apparently all Elsa had done to her, and she got hit for it.

And so Elsa stood there, her usual scarf in the wash and in its place an ugly scarf chosen by her mother, worrying that vomit-green might provoke the beast. In the end Elsa explained that it was her mum's scarf, not hers, and her mum had terrible taste, before backing away towards the door. Our Friend just stared at her. Or at least that was what Elsa thought, if she was right in thinking those were its eyes. And then it also bared its teeth, Elsa was almost sure of it. But Granny just muttered something about 'kids, you know' and rolled her eyes at Our Friend. Then she went to find the keys to Renault and then she and Elsa went to the dinosaur exhibition. Granny left the front door wide open, Elsa remembers, and when they sat in Renault and Elsa asked what Our Friend was doing in Granny's flat, Granny just answered: 'Visiting.' When Elsa asked why it was always barking behind its door, Granny answered cheerily, 'Barking? Ah, it only does that when Britt-Marie goes past.' And when Elsa asked why, Granny grinned from ear to ear and answered: 'Because that's what he likes doing.'

And then Elsa had asked who Our Friend lived with, and then Granny said: 'Not everyone needs to live with someone, good

31

God. For instance I don't live with anybody.' And even though Elsa insisted that this might have some connection with the fact that Granny was not a d-o-g, Granny never explained anything else about it.

And now here Elsa stands, on the landing, peeling off sweet wrappers from the Daim chocolate. She throws in the first one so quickly that that the letter box slams when she lets go of it. She holds her breath and feels her heart thumping in her whole head. But then she remembers Granny saying that this needs to be done quickly, so Britt-Marie doesn't get suspicious during the residents' meeting downstairs.

Britt-Marie really hates Our Friend. Elsa tries to remind herself that, in spite of it all, she is a knight of Miamas, and after that she opens the letter box with more courage.

She hears its breath. It sounds like there's a rockfall going on in its lungs. Elsa's heart thumps until she's sure Our Friend will feel the vibrations through the door.

'My granny sends her regards and apologises for not bringing you any sweets for such a long time!' she says diligently through the letter box, removing fistfuls of wrappers and dropping them on the floor.

Then she hears it moving and snatches back her hand, startled. There's a silence for a few seconds. She hears the abrupt crunch of Our Friend taking the chocolate in its jaws.

'Granny's ill,' Elsa explains while it's eating.

She isn't prepared for the way the words tremble as they come out of her. She convinces herself that Our Friend is breathing more slowly. She empties in more chocolate.

'She has cancer,' whispers Elsa.

Elsa has no friends, so she isn't quite sure of the normal procedure for these types of errands. But she imagines that if she did have friends, she'd want them to know if she had cancer. 'She sends her best and says sorry,' she whispers into the darkness and drops in the rest of the chocolate and gently closes the letter box.

She stays there for a moment, looking at Our Friend's door.

And then at The Monster's. If this wild animal can be hiding behind one of the doors, she doesn't even want to know what might be behind the other.

Then she jogs down the stairs to the front entrance.

George is still in the laundry. In the meeting room, they are all drinking coffee and arguing.

Because it's a normal house.

By and large.

4

BEER

The room in the hospital smells as bad and feels as cold as hospital rooms tend to when it is two degrees above zero outside and someone has hidden beer bottles under their pillow and opened a window to try to get rid of the smell of cigarette smoke. It hasn't worked.

Granny and Elsa are playing Monopoly. Granny doesn't say anything about cancer, for Elsa's sake. And Elsa doesn't say anything about death, for Granny's sake. Because Granny doesn't like talking about death, especially not her own. So when Elsa's mum and the doctors leave the room to talk in low, serious voices in the corridor, Elsa tries not to look worried. That doesn't really work either.

Granny grins secretively.

'Did I ever tell you about the time I fixed a job for the dragons in Miamas?' she asks in their secret language.

It's good to have a secret language in hospital, because hospitals have ears in their walls, says Granny. Especially when the walls have Elsa's mum as their boss.

'Duh – obviously!'

Granny nods as a courtesy and tells the whole story anyway. Because no one ever taught Granny how not to tell a story. And Elsa listens, because no one ever taught her how not to.

That's why she knows that one of the things people say about Granny most often when she's not around is, 'This time she's really crossed the line.' Britt-Marie is *always* saying it. Elsa

34

assumes this is why Granny likes the kingdom of Miamas so much; you can't cross the line in Miamas, because the kingdom is endless. And not like on television when people toss their hair about and say that they 'have no boundaries,' but properly, without any limits, because no one knows for certain where Miamas begins and ends. This is partly because unlike the other five kingdoms in the Land-of-Almost-Awake, which are mainly built of stone and mortar, Miamas is wholly made of imagination. It could also be slightly because the Miamas city wall has an insanely irascible temperament and may suddenly one morning have the idea of moving itself a couple of kilometres into the forest because it needs a bit of 'me-time'. Only to move twice as far back in the opposite direction the next morning, because it has decided to wall in some dragon or troll that for one reason or another it has decided to be grumpy with. (Usually because the dragon or the troll has been up all night drinking schnapps and weeing on the wall while sleeping, Granny suggests.)

There are more trolls and dragons in Miamas than in any other of the five kingdoms in the Land-of-Almost-Awake, you see, because the main export industry in Miamas is fairy tales. Trolls and dragons have excellent employment prospects in Miamas because stories need villains. 'Of course it hasn't always been like this,' Granny sometimes muses. 'There was a time when the dragons had been almost forgotten by Miamas's story-tellers, particularly the ones who'd grown a little long in the tooth.' Then she recounts the whole story about how the dragons were causing too much trouble in Miamas, drifting about without jobs, drinking schnapps and smoking cigars and getting involved in violent confrontations with the city wall. So in the end the people of Miamas begged Granny to help them come up with some kind of practical job-creation scheme. And that's when Granny had the idea that dragons should guard treasures at the end of the tales.

Up until that point, it had actually been a massive narrative problem, the fact that heroes in fairy tales looked for a treasure and, once they had located it in some deep cave, only had to nip inside to pick it up. Just like that. No epic closing battles or dramatic apexes or anything. 'All you could do was play worthless video games afterwards,' Granny said, nodding sombrely. Granny knows all about it, because last summer Elsa taught her how to play a game called World of Warcraft and Granny played it round the clock for several weeks until Mum said she was beginning to 'exhibit disturbing tendencies' and banned her from sleeping in Elsa's room from then on.

But anyway, when the storytellers heard Granny's idea the whole problem was solved in an afternoon. 'And that's why all fairy tales nowadays have dragons at the end! It's my doing!' Granny chortles. Like she always does.

Granny has a story from Miamas for every situation. One of them is about Miploris, the kingdom where all sorrow is kept in storage, and its princess who was robbed of a magical treasure by an ugly witch who she's been hunting ever since. Another story is about two princeling brothers, both in love with the princess of Miploris, practically breaking the Land-of-Almost-Awake into pieces in their furious battle for her love.

One story was about the sea-angel, weighed down by a curse that forced her to drift up and down the coast of the Land-of-Almost-Awake after losing her beloved. And another story was about the Chosen One, the most universally loved dancer in Mimovas, which is the kingdom where all music comes from. In the fairy tale the shadows tried to abduct the Chosen One in order to destroy Mimovas, but the cloud animals saved him and flew him all the way back to Miamas. And when the shadows came after them, all the inhabitants of the six kingdoms of the Land-of-Almost-Awake – the princes, princesses, knights, soldiers, trolls, angels and the witch – agreed to protect the Chosen One. And that was when the War-Without-End started. It raged for an eternity of ten thousand fairy tales, until the wurses and Wolfheart came out of the forest and led the good army into the last battle and forced the shadows back across the sea.

Of course, Wolfheart is a whole fairy tale in his own right, because he was born in Miamas but just like all other soldiers he grew up in Mibatalos. He has a warrior's heart but the soul of a storyteller, and he's the most invincible fighter ever seen in any of the six kingdoms. He had been living deep in the dark forests for many eternities of fairy tales, but he came back when the Land-of-Almost-Awake needed him most.

Granny has been telling these fairy tales for as long as Elsa can remember. In the beginning they were only to make Elsa go to sleep, and to get her to practise Granny's secret language, and a little because Granny is just about as nutty as one should be. But lately the stories have another dimension as well. Something Elsa can't quite put her finger on.

'Put Marylebone Station back,' says Elsa tersely.

'I bought it . . . ?' Granny tries.

'Mmm, sure you did. Put it back.'

'This is how it must have been playing bloody Monopoly with Hitler!'

'Hitler would only have wanted to play Risk,' mutters Elsa, because she's checked out Hitler on Wikipedia, after there were some rows between her and Granny about her use of Hitler as a metaphor.

'Touché,' mutters Granny.

And then they play in silence for about a minute. Because that is about the usual length of time they can be bothered to keep feuding.

'Did you give the chocolate to Our Friend?' asks Granny.

Elsa nods. But she doesn't mention how she told it about Granny's cancer. A little bit because she thinks Granny would be annoyed, and quite a bit because she doesn't want to talk about cancer. She checked it on Wikipedia yesterday. And then she checked what a 'will' is and then she was so angry that she couldn't sleep all night.

'How did you and Our Friend become friends?' she asks instead.

Granny shrugs. 'The usual way.'

Elsa doesn't know what the usual way is, because she has no other friends than Granny. But she doesn't say anything, because she knows Granny would be upset if she heard that.

'Anyway, the mission is done,' she says in a low voice.

Granny nods keenly and throws a searching look at the door, as if concerned someone could be watching them. Then she reaches under her pillow. The bottles clink against each other and she swears when she spills some beer on the pillowcase, but then she hauls out an envelope and presses it into Elsa's hand.

'This is your next mission, my knight Elsa. But you mustn't open it until tomorrow.'

Elsa looks at the envelope sceptically.

'Haven't you heard of email?'

'You can't email something this important.'

Elsa weighs the envelope in her hand, presses the lumpy bit at the bottom of it.

'What is it?'

'A letter and a key,' says Granny. And then she looks both serious and frightened, both of which are very rare emotions in Granny. She reaches out and grabs hold of Elsa's index fingers. 'Tomorrow I'm going to send you out on the biggest treasure hunt you've ever seen, my brave little knight. Are you ready for that?'

Granny has always loved treasure hunts. In Miamas, treasure hunting is considered a sport. You can compete in it, because it's an approved Olympic field event. But in Miamas it's not called the Olympic Games, it's actually known as the Invisible Games, because all the participants are invisible. Not exactly a spectator sport, as Elsa pointed out when Granny told her about it.

Elsa also loves treasure hunts, but not as much as Granny. No one in any kingdom in the eternity of ten thousand fairy tales could love them like she does. She can make anything into a treasure hunt: if they've been out shopping and Granny can't remember where she parked Renault; or when she wants Elsa to go through her mail and pay her bills because Granny finds this insanely boring; or when there's a sports day at school and Elsa knows the older children are going to lash her in the shower with rolled-up towels. Granny can make a parking area into magic mountains, and rolled-up towels into dragons that must be outsmarted. And Elsa is always the heroine.

This sounds like a different kind of treasure hunt altogether though.

'The one who's supposed to have the key will know what to do with it. You have to protect the castle, Elsa.'

Granny has always called their house 'the castle'. Elsa always just thought it was because she's a bit nutty. But now she's not so sure.

'Protect the castle, Elsa. Protect your family. Protect your friends!' Granny repeats determinedly.

'What friends?'

Granny puts her hands against Elsa's cheeks and smiles.

'They'll come. Tomorrow I am sending you out on a treasure hunt, and it's going to be a fairy tale of marvels and a grand adventure. And you have to promise not to hate me for it.'

Elsa blinks, and there's a burning sensation.

'Why would I hate you?'

Granny caresses her eyelids.

'It's a grandmother's prerogative never to have to show her worst sides to her grandchild, Elsa. Never to have to talk about what she was like before she became a grandmother.'

'I know loads of your worst sides!'

She's hoping to make Granny laugh with that one. But it doesn't work. Granny just whispers in a sad voice: 'It's going to be a grand adventure and a fairy tale of marvels. But it's my fault that you'll find a dragon at the end, my darling knight.'

Elsa squints at her. Because she has never heard Granny talking like this. She always claims credit for the dragons at the end. It's never her 'fault'. Granny sits before her, tinier and more fragile than Elsa can remember ever having seen her. Not at all like a superhero.

Granny kisses her forehead.

39

'Promise you won't hate me when you find out who I've been. And promise me you'll protect the castle. Protect your friends.'

Elsa doesn't know what any of this means, but she promises. And then Granny embraces her for longer than ever before.

'Give the letter to him who's waiting. He won't want to accept it, but tell him it's from me. Tell him your granny sends her regards and apologises.'

And then she wipes the tears from Elsa's cheeks. And Elsa points out that you're supposed to say 'to he who's waiting', not 'him'. And they argue a bit about that, as usual. And then they play Monopoly and eat cinnamon buns and talk about who'd win a fight between Harry Potter and Spider-Man. Bloody pathetic discussion, of course, thinks Elsa. But Granny likes nattering on about these types of things because she's too immature to understand that Harry Potter would have crushed Spider-Man.

Granny gets out some more cinnamon buns from large paper bags under another pillow. Not that she has to hide the cinnamon buns from Elsa's mum the way she has to hide the beer from Elsa's mum, but she likes keeping them together because she likes eating them together. Beer and cinnamon buns is Granny's favourite snack. Elsa recognises the name of the bakery on the bags; Granny only eats cinnamon buns from that one bakery, because she says no one else knows how to make real Mirevas cinnamon buns. In fact, it's the national dish of the Land-of-Almost-Awake. One very bad thing about it is that one can only have the national dish on the national day. But a very good thing about it is that in the Land-of-Almost-Awake every day is the national day. As Granny likes to put it, 'In the end the problem disappears, said the old lady who crapped in the sink.' Elsa hopes with all her might that this doesn't mean Granny is going to start using the kitchen sink with the door left open.

'Are you really going to get well?' Elsa asks with the reluctance of an almost-eight-year-old asking a question to which she already knows she doesn't want to know the answer.

'Course I will!' Granny says with complete confidence, although she can see well enough that Elsa knows she's lying.

'Promise,' Elsa insists.

And then Granny leans forward and whispers into her ear, in their secret language:

'I promise, my beloved, beloved knight. I promise that it will get better. I promise that everything will be fine.'

Because that is what Granny always says. That it will get better. That everything will be fine.

'But I still think that Spider-Man fellow would have wiped the floor with this Harry,' Granny adds with a grin. And, in the end, Elsa grins back at her.

They eat more cinnamon buns and play more Monopoly. And this makes it much more difficult to stay grumpy.

The sun goes down. Everything goes silent. Elsa lies very close to Granny in the narrow hospital bed. And they mainly just close their eyes, and the cloud animals come to fetch them, and they go to Miamas together.

And in an apartment block on the other side of town, everyone wakes up with a start when the hound in the first-floor flat, without any early warning, starts howling. Louder and more heart-rending than anything they have ever heard coming out of the primal depths of any animal. As if it was singing with the sorrow and yearning of an eternity of ten thousand fairy tales. It howls for hours, all through the night, until dawn.

And by the time the morning light seeps into the hospital room, Elsa wakes up in Granny's arms. But Granny is still in Miamas.

5

LILIES

Having a grandmother is like having an army. This is a grand-child's ultimate privilege: knowing that someone is on your side, always, whatever the details. Even when you are wrong. Especially then, in fact.

A grandmother is both a sword and a shield. When they say at school that Elsa is 'different', as if this was something bad; or when she comes home with bruises and the headmaster says she 'has to learn to fit in,' this is when Granny backs her up. Won't let her apologise. Refuses to let her take the blame. Granny never says to Elsa that she shouldn't let it get to her because 'then they won't enjoy teasing you as much'. Or that she should 'just walk away'. Granny knows better than that.

And the lonelier Elsa gets in the real world, the larger her army in the Land-of-Almost-Awake. The harder the lashes of rolled-up towels in the day, the more astounding the adventures she gets to ride into in the nights. In Miamas, no one says she has to learn to fit in. That's why Elsa wasn't especially impressed when Dad took her to that hotel in Spain and explained that it was 'all-inclusive' there. Because if you have a granny, your whole life is all-inclusive.

Her teachers at school say that Elsa is having 'concentration issues'. But it isn't true. She can recite more or less all of Harry Potter by memory. She can outline the exact superpowers of all the X-Men and knows exactly which of them Spider-Man could and could not take out in a fight. And she can draw a fairly

OK version of the map at the start of *The Lord of the Rings* with her eyes closed. Unless Granny is standing next to her, tugging at the paper and moaning about how this is insanely boring and how she'd rather take Renault out and 'do something'. She's a bit restless, Granny. But she has shown Elsa every corner of Miamas and the all the corners of the other five kingdoms in the Land-of-Almost-Awake. Even the ruins of Mibatalos, which was sacked by the shadows at the end of the War-Without-End. Elsa has stood with Granny on the rocks by the coast, where the ninety-nine snow-angels sacrificed themselves; she has looked out over the sea, where one day the shadows will come back. And she knows all about the shadows, because Granny always says one should know one's enemies better than oneself.

The shadows were dragons in the beginning, but they had an evil and a darkness of such strength within themselves that it made them into something else. Something much more dangerous. They hate people and their stories; they have hated for so long and with such intensity that in the end the darkness enveloped their whole bodies until their shapes were no longer discernible. That is also why they are so difficult to defeat, because they can disappear into walls or into the ground or float up. They're ferocious and bloodthirsty and if you're bitten by one you don't just die; a far more serious and terrible fate lies in store: you lose your imagination. It just runs out of your wound and leaves you grey and empty. You wither away year by year until your body is just a shell. Until no one remembers any fairy tales any more.

And without fairy tales, Miamas and the whole Land-of-Almost-Awake die a death without imagination. The most repellent kind of death.

But Wolfheart defeated the shadows in the War-Without-End. He came out of the forests when the fairy tales needed him most and drove the shadows into the sea. And one day the shadows will come back, and maybe that is why Granny tells her all the stories now, thinks Elsa. To prepare her.

So the teachers are wrong. Elsa has no problems concentrating. She just concentrates on the right things.

Granny says people who think slowly always accuse quick thinkers of concentration problems. 'Idiots can't understand that non-idiots are done with a thought and already moving on to the next before they have. That's why idiots are always so scared and aggressive. Because nothing scares idiots more than a smart girl.'

That is what she often says to Elsa when Elsa has had a particularly concentration-challenged day at school, and they lie on Granny's gigantic bed under all the black-and-white photographs on Granny's ceiling, and close their eyes until the people in the photographs start dancing. Elsa doesn't know who they are, Granny just calls them her 'stars', because when the street-light comes through the blinds they glitter like the sky at night. Men in uniforms stand there and other men in doctors' coats and a few men with hardly any clothes on at all. Tall men and smiling men and men with moustaches and four square men wearing hats, and they all stand next to Granny and they look as if she just told them a cheeky joke. None of them are looking into the camera, because none of them can tear their eyes away from her.

Granny is young. She is beautiful. And immortal. She stands by road signs whose letters Elsa can't read; she stands outside tents in deserts between men with rifles in their hands. And everywhere in the photos are children. Some of them have bandages round their heads and some lie in hospital beds with tubes inserted into their bodies, and one of them only has one arm and a stump where the other arm should have been. But one of the boys hardly looks hurt at all. He looks like he could run a hundred kilometres in his bare feet. He's about the same age as Elsa, and his hair is so thick and tangled that you could lose your keys in it, and there's something in his eyes as if he just found a secret stash of fireworks and ice cream. His eyes are big and perfectly round and so black that the surrounding white is like chalk on a blackboard. Elsa doesn't know who he is, but she calls him The Werewolf Boy, because that is what he looks like to her.

She always thinks about asking Granny more about The Werewolf Boy. But the minute the thought occurs to her, her eyelids start drooping and in the next moment she is sitting on a cloud animal and Granny is next to her on hers and they're gliding over the Land-of-Almost-Awake and landing by the city gates of Miamas. And then Elsa thinks that she'll ask Granny in the morning.

And then one morning there is no morning any more.

Elsa is sitting on the bench outside the big window. She's so cold that her teeth are chattering. Her mum is inside talking to the woman who sounds like a whale, or, at least, the way Elsa imagines a whale would sound. Which is difficult to know, admittedly, when you have never happened to run into a whale, but she sounds like Granny's gramophone player after Granny tried to build a robot out of it. It was slightly unclear what sort of robot she was intending to build, but whatever the case it wasn't a very good one. And then the gramophone sounded like a whale after that whenever you tried to play a record on it. Elsa learned all about LPs and CDs that afternoon. That was when she worked out why old people seem to have so much free time, because in the olden days until Spotify came along they must have used up almost all their time just changing the track.

She tightens her coat collar and her Gryffindor scarf round her chin. The first snow came in the night. Gradually, almost reluctantly. Now it's so deep you can make snow-angels. Elsa loves doing that.

In Miamas there are snow-angels all year round. But as Granny constantly reminds Elsa, they are not especially polite. They're quite arrogant and self-important, in fact, and always complain about the service when they're eating out at one of the inns. 'There's a right carry-on, smelling the wine and all that crap,' snorts Granny.

She holds out her foot and catches the snowflakes on her shoe. She hates sitting on benches outside, waiting for Mum, but she still does it, because the only thing Elsa hates more is sitting inside waiting for Mum.

She wants to go home. With Granny. It's as if the whole house is missing Granny now. Not the people living in it, but the actual building. The walls are creaking and whining. And Our Friend has been howling without pause in its flat for two whole nights.

Britt-Marie forced Kent to ring the doorbell of Our Friend's flat, but no one answered. It just barked so loudly that Kent stumbled into a wall. So Britt-Marie called the police. She has hated Our Friend for a long time. A couple of months ago she went round the house with a petition, to get everyone to sign it so she could send it to the landlord and demand 'the eviction of that horrendous hound.'

'We can't have dogs in the leaseholders' association. It's a question of safety! It's dangerous for the children and one *must* think of the children!' Britt-Marie explained this to everyone in the manner of someone who is concerned about children, although the only children in the house are Elsa and the boy with a syndrome and Elsa is pretty sure that Britt-Marie is not massively worried about Elsa's safety.

The boy with a syndrome lives opposite the terrifying dog, but his mother light-heartedly told Britt-Marie she believed the hound was more bothered by her son than the other way round. Granny couldn't stop herself laughing when she heard this, but it made Elsa worry about Britt-Marie trying to prohibit children as well.

Elsa jumps off the bench and starts traipsing around in the snow, to warm up her feet. Next to the big window where the whale-woman is working there's a supermarket with a sign outside: **MINCEBEEF 49:90.** Elsa tries to control herself because her mum is always telling her to control herself. But in the end she gets out her red felt-tip pen from her jacket pocket and adds a neat 'D' and a slash, to show that it should be two words.

She looks at the result and nods slightly. Then puts the pen back in her pocket and sits down again on the bench. Leans her head back and closes her eyes and feels the cold little feet of the snowflakes landing on her face. When the smell of smoke reaches her nostrils she thinks she's imagining it. At first it's even wonderful to feel that acrid smell at the back of her throat and, though Elsa can't think why, it makes her feel warm and secure. But then she feels something else. Something thumping behind her ribs. Like a warning signal.

The man is standing a distance away. In the shadow of one of the high-rise blocks. She can't see him clearly, only pick out the red glow of his cigarette between his fingers and the fact that he's very thin. As if he's lacking in contours. He stands partially turned away from her, as if he hasn't even seen her.

And Elsa doesn't know why she gets so scared, but she finds herself fumbling around the bench for a weapon. It's very odd; she never does that in the real world. In the real world, her first instinct is always to run. Only in Miamas would she reach for her sword, like a knight does when sensing danger. But there are no swords here.

When she looks up again the man is still turned away from her, but she could swear that he's moved closer. And he's still in the shade, although he's moved away from the high-rise. As if the shadow isn't cast by the house, but by the man himself. Elsa blinks and when she opens her eyes she no longer thinks the man has moved closer.

She knows he has.

She slips off the bench and reverses towards the big window, fumbling for the door handle. Stumbles inside. Stands there panting, gasping, trying to calm down. Only when the door closes behind her with a little friendly 'pling' does she understand what she found reassuring about the cigarette smoke.

The man smokes the same tobacco as Granny. Elsa would recognise it anywhere, because Granny used to let her help out with the cigarette-rolling, because Granny says that Elsa has 'such small fingers and they're perfect for these little sods.'

When she looks out of the window she no longer knows where the shadows begin and end. One moment she imagines the man is still standing there on the other side of the street, but then she starts wondering if she actually saw him at all.

She jumps like a startled animal when Mum's hands alight on her shoulders. She spins round with wide-open eyes, before her legs give way. Tiredness disarms all her senses once she is in her mother's arms. She has not slept for two days. Mum's distended belly is big enough to rest a teacup on. George says it is nature's way of giving a pregnant woman a break.

'Let's go home,' Mum whispers softly in her ear.

Elsa stares, forcing her tiredness away and sliding out of her grip.

'First I want to talk to Granny!'

Mum looks devastated. Elsa knows that because 'devastated' is a word for the word jar.

(We'll get to the word jar later in this story.)

'It's . . . darling . . . I don't know if it's a good idea,' whispers Mum.

But Elsa has already run past the reception desk and into the next room. She can hear the whale-woman yelling behind her but then she hears her mother's composed voice asking her to let Elsa go inside.

Granny is waiting for her in the middle of the room. There's a fragrance of lilies, Mum's favourite flower. Granny doesn't have any favourite flowers because no plant lives for longer than twenty-four hours in Granny's flat, and in a fairly rare instance of compliance, possibly also because of the enthusiastic encouragement of her favourite grandchild, Granny has decided it would be bloody unfair to nature for her to have any favourite flowers.

Elsa stands to one side with her hands pushed moodily into her jacket pockets. Defiantly she stamps snow from her shoes onto the floor.

'I don't want to be a part of this treasure hunt, it's idiotic.'

Granny doesn't answer. She never answers when she knows that Elsa is right. Elsa stamps more snow off her shoes.

'YOU are idiotic,' she says cuttingly.

Granny doesn't rise to that one either. Elsa sits on the chair next to her and holds out the letter.

'You can take care of this idiotic letter yourself,' she whispers.

Two days have gone by since Our Friend started howling. Two days since Elsa was last in the Land-of-Almost-Awake and the kingdom of Miamas. No one is being straight with her. All the grown-ups try to wrap it in cotton wool, so it doesn't sound dangerous or frightening or unpleasant. As if Granny hasn't been ill. As if the whole thing was an accident. But Elsa knows they're lying, because Elsa's granny hasn't ever been laid low by an accident. Usually it's the accident that gets laid low by Granny.

And Elsa knows what cancer is. It says all about it on Wikipedia.

She gives the edge of the coffin a shove, to get a reaction. Because deep down she's still hoping this could be one of those occasions when Granny is just pulling her leg. Like that time Granny dressed the snowman so he looked like a real person who'd fallen from the balcony, and Britt-Marie got so furious when she realised it was a joke that she called the police. And the next morning when Britt-Marie looked out of the window, she discovered that Granny had made another identical snowman, and then Britt-Marie 'went loopy', as Granny put it, and came charging out with a snow shovel. And then the snowman jumped up and roared, 'WAAAAAAAAH!!!' Granny told her afterwards that she'd lain in the snow for hours waiting for Britt-Marie and at least two cats had weed on her in the meantime, 'but it was well worth it!' Britt-Marie called the police again, of course, but they said it wasn't a crime to scare someone.

This time, though, Granny doesn't get up. Elsa bangs her fists against the coffin, but Granny doesn't answer, and Elsa bangs harder and harder as if it's possible to put right all the things that are wrong by banging. In the end she slips off the chair and sinks onto her knees on the floor and whispers:

'Do you know that they're lying, they say you've "passed away", or, that we've "lost you"? No one says "dead".'

49

Elsa digs her nails into her palms and her whole body trembles.

'I don't know how to get to Miamas if you're dead . . .'

Granny doesn't answer. Elsa puts her forehead against the lower edge of the coffin. She feels the cold wood against her skin and warm tears on her lips. Then she feels Mum's soft fingers against her neck, and she turns round and throws her arms round her, and Mum carries her out of there. When she opens her eyes again she's sitting in Kia, Mum's car.

Mum is standing outside in the snow talking to George on the telephone. Elsa knows she doesn't want her to hear them talking about the funeral. She's not an idiot. She's still got Granny's letter in her hand. She knows you're not supposed to read other people's letters but she must have read this one a hundred times these last two days. Granny must have known she'd do this, because she's written the entire letter in symbols that Elsa can't understand. Using the strange alphabet she saw on the road signs in Granny's photographs.

Elsa glares at it. Granny always said she and Elsa shouldn't have any secrets from each other, only secrets together. She's furious with Granny for the lie, because now Elsa sits here with the greatest secret of them all and she can't understand a crapping thing. And she knows that if she falls out with Granny at this point it will set a personal record that they can never beat.

The ink smudges over the paper when she blinks down at it. Although there are letters that Elsa doesn't know, Granny has probably misspelled things. When Granny writes, it's as if she is just scattering words over the page while she's already mentally on her way somewhere else. It's not that Granny can't spell, it's just that she thinks so fast that the letters and words can't keep up. And unlike Elsa, Granny can't see the point of spelling things correctly; anyway she was always better at science and numbers. 'You bloody understand what I mean!' she hisses when she passes Elsa secret notes while they're eating with Mum and George and Elsa adds the dashes and spaces in the right places with her red felt-tip pen.

It's one of the few things they really row about, Granny and Elsa, because Elsa thinks letters are something more than just a way of sending messages. Something more important.

Or used to. They used to row about it.

There's only one word in the whole letter that Elsa can read. Just one, which has been written in normal letters, tossed down almost haphazardly in the middle of the text. It's so anonymous that Elsa didn't notice it the first time she read it. She reads it again and again until she can't see it through all her blinking. She feels let down and angry for tens of thousands of reasons and probably another ten thousand she hasn't even thought of yet. Because she knows it's not a coincidence. Granny put that word right there so Elsa would see it.

The name on the envelope is the same name as the one on The Monster's letter box. And the only word Elsa can read in the letter is 'Miamas.'

Granny has always loved treasure hunts.

6

CLEANING AGENTS

She has three scratch marks on her cheek. As if from claws. She knows they'll want to know how it all began. Elsa ran, is the short answer. She's good at running. That's what happens when you get chased all the time.

This morning she lied to Mum about starting school an hour earlier than usual. And when Mum pulled her up on it, Elsa played the bad mother card. The bad mother card is like Renault: hardly a beauty but surprisingly effective. 'I've told you like a hundred times I start earlier on Mondays! I even gave you a slip but you never listen to me any more!'

Mum mumbled something about 'pregnant airhead' and looked guilty. The easiest way of getting her on the back foot is if you can manage to convince her she's lost control. There used to be just two people in the world who knew how to make Mum lose control. And now there's only one. That's a lot of power to put into the hands of someone who's not even eight yet.

At lunchtime, Elsa took the bus home, as she figured she had a better chance of dodging Britt-Marie during the day. She stopped and bought four bags of Daim in the supermarket. The house was as dark and silent as only Granny's house could be without the presence of Granny, and it felt as if even the house was missing her. Elsa hid carefully from Britt-Marie, who was on her way to the space where the bins are kept, although she didn't even have any bags of separated rubbish. After Britt-Marie had checked the contents of all the bins and pursed her mouth the way she does when she decides to raise some issue at the next residents' meeting, she set off down the street to the supermarket so she could walk about and purse her mouth in there for a while. Elsa sneaked in and went up the stairs to the mezzanine floor. There she stood, shaking with fear and anger outside the flat, still with the letter in her hand. Her anger was reserved for Granny. Her fear was of The Monster.

Not long after, she was running through the playground so fast she thought her feet were on fire. And now she sits in a small room with luminous red scratch marks on her cheek, waiting for Mum and fully aware that they'll demand to know what's happened.

She spins the globe at one end of the desk. The headmaster looks particularly vexed about it. So she keeps doing it.

'Well?' the headmaster asks, pointing at her cheek, 'Are you ready to tell me what happened?'

She doesn't even grace him with an answer.

It was smart of Granny, Elsa has to admit it. She's still insanely irritated about this stupid treasure hunt but it was smart of Granny to write 'Miamas' in normal characters in the letter. Because Elsa had stood there earlier on the landing, summoning her courage for at least a hundred eternities before she rang the doorbell. And if Granny hadn't known that Elsa would read the letter even though one mustn't read other people's letters, and if she hadn't written 'Miamas' in normal characters, Elsa would just have thrown the envelope in The Monster's letter box and run away. Instead, she stood there ringing the doorbell, because she had to press The Monster for some answers.

Because Miamas belongs to Granny and Elsa. It's only theirs. Elsa's fury at the thought of Granny bringing along some random muppet was bigger than any fear she might have of monsters.

OK, not *much* bigger than her monster fear, but big enough.

Our Friend was still howling in the flat next door, but nothing happened when she rang The Monster's doorbell. She rang again and banged the door until the wood was creaking and then peered inside through the letter box, but it was too dark to see anything. Not a movement. Not a breath. All she could feel was an acrid smell of cleaning agents, the sort of smell that rushes up your nasal membranes and starts kicking the back of your eyeballs when you breathe it in.

But no sign of a monster. Not even a little one.

Elsa took off her backpack and got out the four bags of Daim and emptied them through Our Friend's letter box. For a few brief, brief moments the creature stopped howling in there. Elsa had decided to call it 'the creature' until she had figured out what it really was, because, irrespective of what Britt-Marie says, Elsa is pretty damn sure that this is no mere dog.

'You have to stop howling; Britt-Marie will call the police and they'll come here and kill you,' she whispered through the letter box.

She didn't know if the creature understood. But at least it was being quiet and eating its Daim. As any rational creature does, when offered Daim.

'If you see The Monster tell him I have post for him,' said Elsa.

The creature didn't answer, but Elsa felt its warm breath when it sniffed at the door.

'Tell him my granny sends her regards and apologises,' she whispered.

And then she put the letter in her backpack and took the bus back to school. And when she looked out of the bus window she thought she saw him again. The thin man who'd been standing outside the undertaker's yesterday while Mum was talking to the whale-woman. Now he was in the shadows on the other side of the street. She couldn't see his face behind the cigarette smoke, but a cold, instinctual terror wrapped itself round her ribs.

And then he was gone.

Elsa reckons this may have been why she couldn't make herself invisible when she got to school. Invisibility is the sort of super-power you can train yourself to have, and Elsa practises it all the time, but it doesn't work if you are angry or frightened. When she got to school Elsa was both. Afraid of men turning up in the shadows without her knowing why, and angry at Granny for sending a letter to a monster, and both angry at and afraid of monsters. Normal monsters have the decency to live deep inside black caves or at the bottom of ice-cold lakes. Normal, terrifying monsters don't actually live in flats and get their post delivered.

And anyway Elsa hates Monday. School is always at its worst on Monday mornings, because people who like chasing you have had to hang about all weekend with no one to chase. The notes in her locker are always the worst on Mondays. Which could also be why the invisibility thing is not working.

Elsa starts fidgeting with the headmaster's globe again. Then she hears the door opening behind her and the headmaster stands up, looking relieved.

'Hello! Sorry I'm so late! It's the traffic!' Elsa's mum pants, out of breath, and Elsa feels her fingers brushing her neck.

Elsa doesn't turn round. She also feels Mum's telephone brushing against her neck, because Mum always carries it. As if she was a cyborg and it was a part of her organic tissue.

Elsa fingers the globe a little more demonstratively. The headmaster sits down in his chair, then leans forward and discreetly tries to move the globe out of her reach. He turns hopefully to Mum.

'Shall we wait for Elsa's father, perhaps?'

The headmaster prefers Dad to be present at these types of meetings, because he seems to find dads easier to reason with when it comes to this sort of thing. Mum doesn't look especially pleased.

'Elsa's father is away and unfortunately he won't be back until tomorrow.' The headmaster looks disappointed.

'Of course there's no intention on our part to create a sense of panic here. Especially not in your condition . . .'

He nods at Mum's belly. Mum looks like she needs to control herself quite a lot not to ask exactly what he's driving at. The headmaster clears his throat and pulls the globe even further from Elsa's reaching fingers. He looks as if he's going to impress on Mum that she should think of the child, which is what people try to impress on Mum when they're nervous that she may get angry.

'Think about the child.' They used to mean Elsa when they said that. But now they mean Halfie.

Elsa straightens her leg and kicks the waste paper basket. She can hear the headmaster and Mum talking, but she doesn't listen. Deep inside, she's hoping Granny will come storming in at any moment with her fists raised, like in a boxing match in an old film. The last time Elsa was called in to see the headmaster he only called Mum and Dad, but Granny came along all the same. Granny was not the sort of person you had to call.

Elsa had sat there spinning the headmaster's globe on that occasion too. The boy who'd given her a black eye had been there with his parents. The headmaster had turned to Elsa's father and said: 'There's an element of a typical boyish prank about this . . .' And then he had to devote quite a long time to explaining to Granny what a typical girlish prank might be, because Granny really wanted to know.

The headmaster had tried to calm Granny by telling the boy who'd given Elsa the black eye that 'only cowards hit girls,' but Granny was not the least bit calmed by that.

'It's not bloody cowardly to hit girls!' she had roared at the headmaster. 'This kid isn't a little arsewipe for hitting a girl, he's an arsewipe for hitting anyone!' And then the boy's father got upset and started being rude to Granny for calling his son an arsewipe, and then Granny had replied that she was going to teach Elsa how to 'kick boys on the fuse box' and then they'd see 'how much bloody fun it was fighting with girls!' And then the headmaster had asked everyone to compose themselves a little. And then they all tried that for a bit. But then the headmaster wanted the boy and Elsa to shake hands and apologise to each other, and then Granny sprang out of her chair asking, 'Why the hell should Elsa apologise?' The headmaster said that Elsa must take her share of the guilt because she had 'provoked' the boy and one had to understand that the boy had experienced difficulties in 'controlling himself'. And that was when Granny had tried to throw the globe at the headmaster, but Mum managed to catch hold of Granny's arm at the very last moment, so that the globe ended up hitting the headmaster's computer instead and smashing the screen. 'I WAS PROVOKED!' Granny had roared at the headmaster while Mum tried to drag her into the corridor. 'I COULDN'T CONTROL MYSELF!'

That's why Elsa always tore up the notes she got in her locker. The notes about how she is ugly. That she's disgusting. That they're going to kill her. Elsa ripped them into such tiny pieces that they could hardly be seen and then threw them into different waste paper bins all over the school. It was an act of mercy to those who wrote the notes, because Granny would have beaten them to death if she'd found out.

Elsa rises slightly from the chair and quickly reaches across the desk to give the globe another spin. The headmaster looks close to despair. Elsa sinks back into her chair, satisfied.

'My God, Elsa! What happened to your cheek!' Mum bursts out with exclamation marks at the end, when she sees the three red lacerations.

Elsa shrugs without answering. Mum turns to the headmaster. Her eyes are burning.

'What happened to her cheek!?'

The headmaster twists in his seat.

'Now, then. Let's calm ourselves down, now. Think about . . . I mean, think about your child.'

He isn't pointing at Elsa when he says that last bit, he's pointing at Mum. Elsa stretches her leg and kicks the waste paper bin again. Mum takes a deep breath and closes her eyes, then determinedly moves the waste paper bin further under the desk. Elsa looks at her, offended, sinks so deep into the chair that she has to hold onto the armrests to stop herself sliding out, and reaches out with her leg until her toe almost, almost, touches the rim of the waste paper bin. Mum sighs. Elsa sighs even louder. The headmaster looks at them and then at the globe on his desk. He pulls it closer towards him.

'So . . .' he begins at last, smiling half-heartedly at Mum.

'It's been a difficult week for the whole family,' Mum interrupts him at once and sounds as if she's trying to apologise.

Elsa hates it.

'We can all empathise with that,' says the headmaster in the manner of someone who doesn't know the meaning of the word. He looks nervously at the globe. 'Unfortunately it's not the first time Elsa has found herself in conflict at this school.'

'Not the last either,' Elsa mutters.

'Elsa!' snaps Mum.

'Mum!!!' Elsa roars with three exclamation marks.

Mum sighs. Elsa sighs even louder. The headmaster clears his throat and holds the globe with both hands as he says:

'We, and by that I mean the staff at this school, obviously in collaboration with the welfare officer, feel that Elsa could be helped by a psychologist to channel her aggressions.'

'A psychologist?' says Mum hesitantly, 'Surely that's a bit dramatic?'

The headmaster raises his hands defensively as if apologising, or possibly as if he's about to start playing an air tambourine.

'It's not that we think anything is w-r-o-n-g! Absolutely not! Lots of special-needs children benefit from therapy. It's nothing to be ashamed of!'

Elsa reaches out with the tips of her toes and pushes over the waste paper basket. 'Why don't you go to a psychologist yourself?'

The headmaster decides to make the globe safe by putting it on the floor next to his chair. Mum leans towards Elsa and exerts herself incredibly not to raise her voice.

'If you tell me and the headmaster which of the children are causing you trouble, we can help you solve the conflicts instead of things always ending up like this, darling.'

Elsa looks up, her lips pressed into a straight line.

The scratch marks on her cheek have stopped bleeding but they are still as bright as neon lights.

'Snitches get stitches,' she says succinctly.

'Elsa, please try to cooperate,' the headmaster says, attempting a grimace that Elsa assumes to be his way of smiling a little.

'Why don't you cooperate yourself!' Elsa replies without an attempt to smile even a little.

The headmaster looks at Mum.

'We, well, I mean the school staff and I, believe that if Elsa could just try to walk away sometimes when she feels there's a conflict about to happ . . .'

Elsa doesn't wait for Mum's answer, because she knows Mum won't defend her. So she snatches up her backpack from the floor and stands up.

'Can we go now, or what?'

And then the headmaster says she can go into the corridor. He sounds relieved. Elsa marches out, while Mum stays in there, apologising. Elsa hates it. She just wants to go home so it won't be Monday any more.

During the last lesson before lunch, one of their smarmy teachers told them their assignment over the Christmas holiday would be to prepare a talk on the theme of 'A Literary Hero I Look Up To'. And they were to dress up as their hero and talk about the hero in the first person singular. Everyone had to put up their hands and choose a hero. Elsa was going to go for Harry Potter, but someone else got him first. So when her turn came she said Spider-Man. And then one of the boys behind her got annoyed because he was going for that. And then there was an argument. 'You can't take Spider-Man!' shouted the boy. And Elsa said, 'Pity, because I just did!' And then the boy said: 'It's a pity for YOU, yeah!' And then Elsa snorted, 'Sure!' Because that is Elsa's favourite word in English. And then the boy shouted that Elsa couldn't be Spider-Man because 'only boys can be Spider-Man!' And then Elsa told him he could be Spider-Man's girlfriend. And then he pushed Elsa into a radiator. And then Elsa hit him with a book.

Elsa still thinks he should thank her for it, because that's probably the nearest that boy ever got to a book. But then the teacher came running and put a stop to it all and said that no one could be Spider-Man because Spider-Man only existed in films and so he wasn't a 'literary character'. And then Elsa got possibly a bit disproportionally worked up and asked the teacher if he'd heard of something called Marvel Comics, but the teacher hadn't. 'AND THEY LET YOU TEACH CHILDREN!?' Then Elsa had to sit for ages after the class 'having a chat' with the teacher, which was just a lot of teacher-babbling.

The boy and a few others were waiting for her when she came out. So she tightened the straps of her backpack until they hugged her tight like a little koala hanging on to her back, and then she ran.

Like many children who are different, she's good at running. She heard one of the boys roar, 'Get her!' and the clattering of footsteps behind her across the icy asphalt. She heard their excited panting. She ran so fast that her knees were hitting her ribcage, and if it hadn't been for her backpack she would have made it over the fence and into the street, and then they would never have caught up with her. But one of the boys got a grip on her backpack. And of course she could have wriggled out of it and got away.

But Granny's letter to The Monster was inside. So she turned round and fought.

As usual she tried to shield her face so Mum wouldn't get upset when she saw the damage. But it wasn't possible to shield both her face and the backpack. So things took their course. 'You should choose your battles if you can, but if the battle chooses you then you kick the sod in his fuse box!' Granny used to tell Elsa, and that is what Elsa did. Even though she hates violence, she's good at fighting because she's had a lot of practice. That's why there are so many of them now when they chase her.

Mum comes out of the headmaster's office after at least ten eternities of fairy tales, and then they cross the deserted playground without saying anything. Elsa gets into the back seat of Kia with her arms round her backpack. Mum looks unhappy.

'Please, Elsa—'

'It wasn't me that started it! He said girls can't be Spider-Man!'

'Yes, but why do you fight?'

'Just because!'

'You're not a little kid, Elsa. You always say I should treat you like a grown-up. So stop answering me like a little kid. Why do you fight?'

Elsa pokes at the rubber seal in the door.

'Because I'm tired of running.'

And then Mum tries to reach into the back and caress her gently across her scratch marks, but Elsa snatches her head away.

'I don't know what to do,' Mum sighs, holding back her tears.

'You don't have to do anything,' Elsa mumbles.

Mum backs Kia out of the parking area and drives off. They sit there in the sort of silent eternity that only mothers and daughters can build up between themselves.

'Maybe we should go to a psychologist after all,' she says at last.

Elsa shrugs.

'Whatever.' That's her second favourite word in English.

'I . . . Elsa . . . darling, I know what's happened with Granny
has hit you terribly hard. Death is hard for everyone—'

'You don't know anything!' Elsa interrupts and pulls so hard
at the rubber seal that, when she lets go, it snaps back against
the window with a loud noise.

'I'm sad as well, Elsa,' says Mum, swallowing. 'She was my
mother, not just your grandmother.'

'You hated her. So don't talk rubbish.'

'I did not hate her. She was my mother.'

'You were always fighting! You're probably just GLAD she's
dead!!!'

Elsa wishes she never said that last bit. But it's too late. There's
a silence lasting for all imaginable eternities and she pokes at
the rubber seal until its edge comes away from the door. Mum
notices, but she doesn't say anything. When they stop at a red
light she puts her hands over her eyes and says resignedly, 'I'm
really trying here, Elsa. Really trying. I know I'm a bad mother
and I'm not at home enough, but I'm really trying . . .'

Elsa doesn't answer. Mum massages her temples.

'Maybe we should talk to a psychologist anyway.'

'You talk to a psychologist,' says Elsa.

'Yeah. Maybe I should.'

'Yeah. Maybe you should!'

'Why are you so horrible?'

'Why are YOU so horrible?'

'Darling. I'm really sad about Granny dying but we have t—'

'No you're not!' And then something happens that hardly
ever, ever happens. Mum loses her composure and yells:

'YES I BLOODY AM! TRY TO UNDERSTAND THAT
YOU'RE NOT THE ONLY ONE WHO'S CAPABLE OF BEING
UPSET AND STOP BEING SUCH A LITTLE BRAT!'

Mum and Elsa stare at each other. Mum covers her mouth
with her hand.

'Elsa . . . I . . . darl . . .'

Elsa shakes her head and pulls off the entire rubber seal from the door in a single tug. She knows she's won. When Mum loses control Elsa wins every time.

'Cut it out. It's not good shouting like that,' she mumbles. And then she adds without so much as glancing at her mother: 'Think about the baby.'

7

LEATHER

It's possible to love your grandmother for years and years without really knowing anything about her.

It's Tuesday when Elsa meets The Monster for the first time. School is better on Tuesdays. Elsa only has one bruise today, and bruises can be explained away by saying she's been playing football.

She sits in Audi. Audi is Dad's car. It's the exact opposite of Renault. Normally Dad picks her up from school every other Friday, because that's when she stays with Dad and Lisette and Lisette's children. Granny used to pick her up on all the other days and now Mum will have to do it. But today Mum and George have gone to a doctor to look at Halfie, so today Dad is picking her up even though it's a Tuesday.

Granny always came on time and stood at the gate. Dad is late and stays in the Audi in the parking area.

'What did you do to your eye?' Dad asks insecurely.

He came back from Spain this morning, because he went there with Lisette and Lisette's children, but he hasn't caught the sun because he doesn't know how to.

'We played football,' says Elsa.

Granny would never have let her get away with the football story.

But Dad isn't Granny, so he just nods tentatively and asks her to be good enough to put on her seat belt. He does that very often. Nods tentatively. Dad is a tentative person. Mum is a perfectionist and Dad is a pedant and that was partly why their marriage didn't work so well, Elsa figures. Because a perfectionist and a pedant are two very different things. When Mum and Dad did the cleaning, Mum wrote a minute-by-minute breakdown of the cleaning schedule, but then Dad would sort of get caught up with descaling the coffee percolator for two and a half hours, and you really can't plan a life with a person like that around you, said Mum. The teachers at school always tell Elsa that her problem is her inability to concentrate, which is very odd, Elsa thinks, because Dad's big problem is that he can't stop concentrating.

'So, what do you want to do?' asks Dad, indecisively putting his hands on the wheel.

He often does that. Asks what Elsa would like to do. Because he very rarely wants to do anything himself. And this Tuesday was very unexpected for him: Dad is not very good at dealing with unexpected Tuesdays. That's why Elsa only stays every other weekend with him, because after he met Lisette and she and her children moved in, Dad said it was too 'messy' for Elsa there. When Granny found out she phoned him and called him a Nazi at least ten times in a minute. That was a Nazi record, even for Granny. And when she'd hung up she turned to Elsa and spluttered, 'Lisette? What sort of name is that?' And Elsa knew she didn't really mean it, of course, because everyone likes Lisette – she has the same superpower as George. But Granny was the sort of person you brought with you when you went to war, and that was what Elsa loved about her.

Dad's always late picking Elsa up from school. Granny was never late. Elsa has tried to understand exactly what 'irony' means and she's fairly sure it's that Dad is never late for anything other than picking up Elsa from school, and Granny was always late for everything except for that one thing.

Dad fiddles with the wheel again.

'So . . . where would you like to go today?'

Elsa looks surprised, because it sounds as if he really means they're going somewhere. He twists in his seat.

'I was thinking maybe you'd like to do . . . something.'

Elsa knows he's only saying it to be nice. Because Dad doesn't like doing things, Dad is not a doing type of person. Elsa looks at him. He looks at the steering wheel.

'I think I'd just like to go home,' she says.

Dad nods and looks disappointed and relieved at the same time, which is a facial expression that only he in the whole world has mastered. Because Dad never says no to Elsa, even though she sometimes wishes he would.

'Audi is really nice,' she says when they're halfway home and neither of them have said a word.

She pats the glove compartment of Audi, as if it was a cat. New cars smell of soft leather, the polar opposite of the smell of old split leather in Granny's flat. Elsa likes both smells, though she prefers living animals to dead ones that have been made into car seats. 'You know what you're getting with an Audi,' Dad says, nodding. His last car was also called Audi.

Dad likes to know what he's getting. One time last year they rearranged the shelves in the supermarket near to where Dad and Lisette live, and Elsa had to run those tests she had seen advertised on the television, to make sure he hadn't had a stroke.

Once they get home, Dad gets out of Audi and goes with her to the entrance. Britt-Marie is on the other side of the door, hunched up like a livid little house pixie on guard. It occurs to Elsa that you always know no good can come of catching sight of Britt-Marie. 'She's like a letter from the tax authorities, that old biddy,' Granny used to say. Dad seems to agree, because Britt-Marie is one of the few subjects on which he and Granny were in agreement. She's holding a crossword magazine in her hand. Britt-Marie likes crosswords very much because there are very clear rules about how to do them. She only ever does them in pencil, though – Granny always said Britt-Marie was the sort of woman who would have to drink two glasses of wine and feel really wild and crazy to be able to fantasise about solving a crossword in ink.

Dad offers a tentative hello, but Britt-Marie interrupts him.

'Do you know whose this is?' she says, pointing at a pram padlocked to the stair railing under the noticeboard.

Only now does Elsa notice it. It's odd that it should be there at all, because there are no babies in the house except Halfie, and she-he still gets a lift everywhere with Mum. But Britt-Marie seems unable to attach any value to this deeper philosophical question.

'Prams are not allowed in the entrance vestibule! They're a fire risk!' she declares, firmly clasping her hands together so that the crossword magazine sticks out like a rather feeble sword.

'Yes. It says on the notice here,' says Elsa, nodding helpfully and pointing at a neatly written sign right above the pram, on which it is written: **Do not leave prams here: they are a fire risk.**

'That's what I mean!' Britt-Marie replies, with a slightly raised – but still well-meaning – voice.

'I don't understand,' says Dad, as if he doesn't understand.

'I am obviously wondering if you put this sign up! That's what I'm wondering!' says Britt-Marie, taking a small step forward and then a very small step back as if to emphasise the gravity of this.

'Is there something wrong with the notice?' asks Elsa.

'Of course not, of course not. But it's not *common practice* in this leaseholders' association to simply put up signs in any old way without first clearing it with the other residents in the house!'

'But there is no leaseholders' association, is there?' asks Elsa.

'No, but there's going to be! And until there is, I'm in charge of information in the association committee. It's not common practice to put up signs without notifying the head of information of the association committee!'

She is interrupted by the bark of a dog, so loud that it rattles a pane of glass in the door.

They all jump. Yesterday Elsa heard Mum telling George that Britt-Marie had called the police to say that Our Friend should be put down. It seems to have heard Britt-Marie's voice now, and just like Granny, Our Friend can't shut up for a second when that happens. Britt-Marie starts ranting about how that dog needs to be dealt with. Dad just looks uncomfortable. 'Maybe someone tried to tell you but you weren't home?' Elsa suggests to Britt-Marie, pointing at the sign on the wall. It works, at least temporarily. Britt-Marie forgets to be upset about Our Friend when she gets re-upset by the sign. Because the most important thing for her is not to run out of things to be upset about. Elsa briefly considers telling Britt-Marie to put up a sign letting the neighbours know that if they want to put up a notice they have to inform their neighbours first. For instance by putting up a notice.

The dog barks again from the flat a half-stair up. Britt-Marie purses her mouth.

'I've called the police. I have! But of course they won't do anything! They say we have to wait until tomorrow to see if the owner turns up!'

Dad doesn't answer, and Britt-Marie immediately interprets his silence as a sign that he'd love to hear more about Britt-Marie's feelings on the topic.

'Kent has rung on the door of that flat lots of times, but no one even lives there! As if that wild animal lives there on its own! Would you believe it?'

Elsa holds her breath, but no more barking can be heard – as if Our Friend has summoned some common sense at last.

The entrance door behind Dad opens and the woman in the black skirt comes in. Her heels click against the floor and she's talking loudly into the white lead attached to her ear.

'Hello!' says Elsa, to deflect Britt-Marie's attention from any further barking.

'Hello,' says Dad, to be polite.

'Well, well. Hello there,' says Britt-Marie, as if the woman is potentially a criminal billposter. The woman doesn't answer. She just talks even louder into the white cable, gives all three of them an irritated look and disappears up the stairs.

There's a long, strained silence in the stairwell after she has gone. Elsa's dad is not so good at dealing with strained silences.

'Helvetica,' he manages to say, in the middle of a nervous bout of throat-clearing.

'Pardon me?' says Britt-Marie and purses her mouth even harder.

'Helvetica. The font, I mean,' says Dad skittishly, nodding at the sign on the wall.

'It's a good . . . font.'

Fonts are the sort of thing Dad finds important. One time when Mum was at a parents' evening at Elsa's school and Dad had called at the very last possible moment to say he couldn't make it because of something that had come up at work, Mum, as a punishment, signed him up as a volunteer to do the posters for the school's jumble sale. Dad looked very doubtful about it when he found out. It took him three weeks to decide what sort of font the posters should have. When he brought them in to school, Elsa's teacher didn't want to put them up because they'd already had the jumble sale – but Elsa's father had apparently not understood what this had to do with it.

It's a little like Britt-Marie not really comprehending what the Helvetica font has to do with anything at all right now.

Dad looks down at the floor and clears his throat again.

'Do you have . . . keys?' he asks Elsa.

She nods. They hug briefly. Relieved, Dad disappears out of the door and Elsa darts up the stairs before Britt-Marie has time to start talking to her again. Outside Our Friend's flat she stops briefly, peers back over her shoulder to make sure Britt-Marie is not watching, then opens the letter box to whisper, 'Please, be quiet!' She knows that it understands. She hopes that it cares.

She runs up the last flight of stairs with the keys to the flat in her hand, but she doesn't go into Mum and George's flat. Instead she opens Granny's door. There are storage boxes and a scouring bucket in the kitchen; she tries not to pay any attention to those, but fails. She hops into the big wardrobe. The darkness inside the wardrobe settles around her, and no one knows she is crying.

It used to be magic, this wardrobe. Elsa used to be able to lie full-length in it and only just reach the walls with her toes and fingertips. However much she grew, the wardrobe was exactly the right size. Granny maintained, of course, that it was all 'faffing about because this wardrobe has always been exactly the same size,' but Elsa has measured it. So she knows.

She lies down, stretching herself as far as she can. Touching both walls. In a few months she won't have to reach. In a year she won't be able to lie here at all. Because nothing will be magic any more.

She can hear Maud and Lennart's muted voices in the flat, can smell their coffee. Elsa knows Samantha is also there long before she hears the sound of the bichon frisé's paws in the living room and, shortly after, its snoring under Granny's sofa table. Maud and Lennart are tidying up Granny's flat and starting to pack up her things. Mum has asked them to help, and Elsa hates Mum for that. Hates everyone for it.

Soon she hears Britt-Marie's voice as well. As if she's pursuing Maud and Lennart. She's very angry. Only wants to talk about who's had the cheek to put up that sign in the vestibule, and who's been impudent enough to lock up that pram directly under the sign. It seems very unclear, also to Britt-Marie herself, which of these two occurrences is the most upsetting to her. But at least she doesn't mention Our Friend again.

Elsa has been in the wardrobe for an hour when the boy with a syndrome comes crawling in. Through the half-open door Elsa sees his mother walking about, tidying, and how Maud carefully walks behind her, picking up the things that are falling all around her.

Lennart puts a big platter of dreams outside the wardrobe. Elsa pulls them inside and closes the door, and then she and the boy with a syndrome eat them in silence. The boy doesn't say anything, because he never does. That is one of Elsa's favourite things about him.

She hears George's voice in the kitchen. It's warm and re-assuring; it asks if anyone wants eggs, because in that case he'll cook eggs. Everyone likes George, it's his superpower. Elsa hates him for that. Then Elsa hears her mum's voice, and for a moment she wants to run out and throw herself into her arms. But she doesn't, because she wants her mother to be upset. Elsa knows she has already won, but she wants Mum to know it too. Just to make sure she's hurting as much as Elsa is about Granny dying.

The boy falls asleep at the bottom of the wardrobe. His mother gently opens the door soon after, and crawls inside and lifts him out. It's as if she knew he had fallen asleep the minute he did. Maybe that is her superpower.

Moments later Maud crawls inside and carefully picks up all the things the boy's mother dropped when she was picking him up.

'Thanks for the biscuits,' whispers Elsa.

Maud pats her on the cheek and looks so upset on Elsa's behalf that Elsa gets upset on Maud's behalf.

She stays in the wardrobe until everyone has stopped tidying and stopped packing and gone back to their own flats. She knows that Mum is sitting in the hall of their flat, waiting for her, so she sits in the big deep window on the stairs for a long time. To ensure that Mum has to keep waiting. She sits there until the lights in the stairwell automatically switch off.

After a while the drunk comes stumbling out of a flat further down in the house, and starts hitting the banister with her shoehorn and mumbling something about how people aren't allowed to take baths at night. The drunk does this a few times every week. There's nothing abnormal about it.

'Turn off the water!' mutters the drunk, but Elsa doesn't answer.

Nor does anyone else. Because people in houses like this seem to believe that drunks are like monsters, and if one pretends they are not there they actually disappear.

Elsa hears how the drunk, in a passionate exhortation for water rationing, slips and falls and ends up on her arse with the shoehorn falling on her head. The drunk and the shoehorn have a fairly long drawn out dispute after that, like two old friends

71

at loggerheads about money. And then at last there's silence. And then Elsa hears the song. The song the drunk always sings. Elsa sits in the darkness on the stairs and hugs herself, as if it was a lullaby just for her. And then even that falls silent. She hears the drunk trying to calm down the shoehorn, before disappearing into her flat again. Elsa half-closes her eyes. Tries to see the cloud animals and the first, outlying fields of the Land-of-Almost-Awake, but it doesn't work. She can't get there any more. Not without Granny. She opens her eyes, absolutely inconsolable. The snowflakes fall like wet mittens against the window.

And that's when she sees The Monster for the first time.

It's one of those winter nights when the darkness is so thick it's as if the whole area has been dipped head first in a bucket of blackness, and The Monster steals out of the door and crosses the half-circle of light around the last light in the street so quickly that if Elsa had blinked a little too hard she would have thought she was imagining it. But as it is she knows what she saw, and she hits the floor and makes her way down the stairs in one fluid movement.

She's never seen him before, but she knows from his sheer size that it must be him. He glides across the snow like an animal, a beast from one of Granny's fairy tales. Elsa knows very well that what she's about to do is both dangerous and idiotic, but she runs down the stairs three steps at a time. Her socks slip on the last step and she careers across the ground-floor vestibule, smacking her chin into the door handle.

Her face throbbing with pain, she throws the door open and breathlessly churns through the snow, still only in her socks.

'I have post for you!' she cries into the night. Only then does she realise that her tears have lodged in her throat. She's so desperate to know who this person is that Granny secretly talked to about Miamas.

There's no answer. She hears his light footfalls in the snow, surprisingly agile considering his enormity. He's moving away from her. Elsa ought to be afraid, she should be terrified of what

The Monster could do to her. He's big enough to tear her apart with a single tug, she knows that. But she's too angry to be afraid.

'My granny sends her regards and apologises!' she roars.

She can't see him. But she no longer hears the creaking of his steps in the snow. He's stopped.

Elsa isn't thinking. She rushes into the darkness, relying on pure instinct, towards the spot where she last heard him put down his foot. She feels the movement of air from his jacket. He starts running; she stumbles through the snow and catapults herself forward, catching hold of his trouser-leg. When she lands on her back in the snow she sees him staring down at her, by the light of the last streetlight. Elsa has time to feel her tears freezing on her cheeks.

He must be a good deal more than two metres tall. As big as a tree. There's a thick hood covering his head and his black hair spills out over his shoulders. Almost his entire face is buried under a beard as thick as an animal pelt, and, emerging from the shadows of the hood, a scar zigzags down over one eye, so pronounced that it looks as if the skin has melted. Elsa feels his gaze creeping through her circulating blood.

'Let go!'

The dark mass of his torso sinks over Elsa as he hisses these words at her.

'My granny sends her regards and apologises!' Elsa pants, holding up the envelope.

The Monster doesn't take it. She lets go of his trouser-leg because she thinks he'll kick her, but he only takes a half-step back. And what comes out of him next is more of a growl than a word. As if he's talking to himself, not to her.

'Get lost, stupid girl . . .'

The words pulsate against Elsa's eardrums. They sound wrong, somehow. Elsa understands them, but they chafe at the passages of her inner ear. As if they didn't belong there.

The Monster turns with a quick, hostile movement. In the next moment he's gone. As if he's stepped right through a doorway in the darkness.

Elsa lies in the snow, trying to catch her breath while the cold stamps on her chest. Then she stands up and gathers her strength, crumpling the envelope into a ball and flinging it into the darkness after him.

She doesn't know how many eternities pass before she hears the entrance porch opening behind her. Then she hears Mum's footsteps, hears her calling Elsa's name. Elsa rushes blindly into her arms.

'What are you doing out here?' asks Mum, scared.

Elsa doesn't answer. Tenderly, Mum takes her face in her hands.

'How did you get that black eye?'

'Football,' whispers Elsa.

'You're lying,' whispers Mum.

Elsa nods. Mum holds her hard. Elsa sobs against her stomach.

'I miss her . . .'

Mum leans down and puts her forehead against hers.

'Me too.'

They don't hear The Monster moving out there. They don't see him picking up the envelope. But then, at last, burrowing into her mum's arms, Elsa realises why his words sounded wrong.

The Monster was talking in Granny and Elsa's secret language.

It's possible to love your grandmother for years and years without really knowing anything about her.

8

RUBBER

It's Wednesday. She's running again.

She doesn't know the exact reason this time. Maybe it's because it's one of the last days before the Christmas holidays, and they know they won't be able to chase anyone for several weeks now, so they have to get it out of their system. Or maybe it's something else altogether – it doesn't matter. People who have never been hunted always seem to think there's a reason for it. 'They wouldn't do it without a cause, would they? You must have done something to provoke them.' As if that was how oppression works.

But it's pointless trying to explain to these people, as fruitless as clarifying to a guy carrying round a rabbit's foot – because of its supposed good luck – that if rabbits' feet really *were* lucky they'd still be attached to the rabbits.

And this is really no one's fault. It's not that Dad was a bit late picking her up, it's just that the school day finished slightly too early. And it's difficult making oneself invisible when the hunt starts inside the school building.

So Elsa runs.

'Catch her!' yells the girl somewhere behind her.

Today it all started with Elsa's scarf. Or at least Elsa thinks it did. She has started learning who the chasers are at school, and how they operate. Some only chase children if they prove to be weak. And some chase just for the thrill of it; they don't even hit their victims when they catch them, just want to see the terror in their eyes. And then there are some like the boy Elsa fought about the right to be Spider-Man. He fights and chases people as a point of principle because he can't stand anyone disagreeing with him. Especially not someone who's different.

With this girl it's something else. She wants a reason for giving chase. A way of justifying the chase. 'She wants to feel like a hero while she's chasing me,' thinks Elsa with unfeasibly cool clarity as she charges towards the fence, her heart thumping like a jackhammer and her throat burning like that time Granny made jalapeño smoothies.

Elsa throws herself at the fence, and her backpack lands so hard on her head when she jumps down on the pavement on the other side that for a few seconds her eyes start to black out. She pulls hard on the straps with both hands to tighten it against her back. Hazily she blinks and looks left towards the parking area where Audi should show up at any moment. She hears the girl behind her screaming like an insulted, ravenous orc. She knows that by the time Audi arrives it'll be too late, so she looks right instead, down the hill towards the big road. The lorries are thundering by like an invading army on its way towards a castle still held by the enemy, but in the gaps between the traffic Elsa sees the entrance to the park on the other side.

'Shoot-up Park', that's what people call it at school, because there are drug addicts there who chase children with heroin syringes. At least that's what Elsa's heard, and it terrifies her. It's the sort of park that never seems to catch any daylight, and this is the kind of winter's day when the sun never seems to rise.

Elsa had managed just fine until lunchtime, but not even someone who's very good at being invisible can quite manage it in a lunch canteen. The girl had materialised before her so suddenly that Elsa was startled and spilled salad dressing on her Gryffindor scarf. The girl had pointed at it and roared: 'Didn't I tell you to stop going around with that ugly bloody scarf?' Elsa had looked back at the girl in the only way one can look back at someone who has just pointed at a Gryffindor scarf and said, 'ugly bloody scarf.' Not totally dissimilar to how one would look at someone who had just seen a horse and gaily burst out, 'Crocodile!' The first time the scarf caught the girl's attention Elsa had simply assumed that the girl was a Slytherin. Only after she'd smacked Elsa in the face, ripped her scarf and thrown it in a toilet had Elsa grown conscious of the fact that the girl hadn't read Harry Potter at all. She knew who he was, of course, everyone knows who Harry Potter is, but she hadn't read the books. She didn't even understand the most basic symbolism of a Gryffindor scarf. And while Elsa didn't want to be elitist or anything, how could one be expected to reason with a person like that?

Muggles.

So today when the girl in the lunch canteen had reached out to snatch away Elsa's scarf, Elsa decided to continue the discussion on the girl's own intellectual level. She simply threw her glass of milk at her and ran for it. Through the corridors, up to the second floor of the school, then the third, where there was a space under the stairs that the cleaners used as a storage cupboard. Elsa had curled up in there with her arms round her knees, making herself as invisible as possible while she listened to the girl and her followers run up to the fourth floor. And then she hid in the classroom for the rest of the day.

It's the distance between the classroom and the school gates that's impossible; even a seasoned expert can't be invisible there. So Elsa had to be strategic.

First she stayed close to the teacher while her classmates were crowding to get out of the classroom. Then she slipped out of the door in the general tumult and darted down the other flight of stairs, the one that does not lead to the main gates. Of course her pursuers knew she'd do that, they may even have wanted her to do it, because she'd be easier to catch on those stairs. But the lesson had finished early and Elsa took a chance that lessons on the floor below were still in progress, so she had perhaps half a minute to run down the stairs and through the empty corridor and establish a small head start while her pursuers got entangled with the pupils welling out of the class-rooms below.

She was right. She saw the girl and her friends no more than ten metres behind her, but they couldn't reach her.

Granny has told her thousands of stories from Miamas about pursuit and war. About evading shadows when they're on your tail, how to lay traps for them and how to beat them with distraction. Like all hunters, shadows have one really significant weakness: they focus all their attention on the one they're pursuing, rather than seeing their entire surroundings. The one being chased, on the other hand, devotes every scrap of attention to finding an escape route. It may not be a gigantic advantage, but it is an advantage. Elsa knows this, because she's checked what 'distraction' means.

So she shoved her hand into her jeans pocket and got out a handful of coins she kept in her pocket for emergencies. Just as the throng of children was starting to disperse and she was getting close to the second stair towards the main entrance, she dropped the coins on the floor and ran.

Elsa has noticed one odd thing about people. Almost none of us can hear the tinkling sound of coins against a stone floor without instinctively stopping and looking down. The sudden crush and eager arms blocked her pursuers and gave her another few seconds to get clear of them. She made full use of the moment and bolted.

But she hears them throwing themselves at the fence now. Trendy winter boots scraping against the buckled steel wire. Just a few more moments until they catch her. Elsa looks left, towards the parking area. No Audi. Looks right, down at the chaos of the road and the black silence of the park. She looks left again, thinks to herself that this would be the safe option if Dad turned up on time for once. Then she looks right, feels an abrasive fear in her gut when she glimpses the park between the roaring lorries.

And then she thinks about Granny's stories from Miamas, about how one of the princes once evaded a whole flock of pursuing shadows by riding into the darkest forest in the Land-of-Almost-Awake. Shadows are the foulest foulnesses ever to live in any fantasy, but even shadows feel fear, said Granny. Even those bastards are afraid of something. Because even shadows have a sense of imagination.

'So sometimes the safest place is when you flee to what seems the most dangerous,' said Granny, and then she described how the prince rode right into the darkest forest and the shadows stopped, hissing, at the edge. For not even they were sure what might be lurking inside, on the other side of the trees, and nothing scares anyone more than the unknown, which can only be known by reliance on the imagination. 'When it comes to terror, reality's got nothing on the power of the imagination,' Granny said.

So Elsa runs to the right. She can smell the burning rubber when the cars brake on the ice. That's how Renault smells almost all the time. She darts between the lorries and hears their blaring horns and her pursuers screaming at her. She's reached the pavement when she feels the first of them grab her backpack. She is so near the park that she could reach into the darkness with her hand, but it's too late. By the time she's being pulled down into the snow, Elsa knows that the blows and kicks will rain down on her quicker than her hands can shield her, but she pulls up her knees and closes her eyes and tries to cover her face so Mum won't be upset again.

She waits for the dull thuds against the back of her head. Often it doesn't hurt when they hit her; usually it doesn't hurt until the day after. The pain she feels during the actual beating is a different kind of pain.

But nothing happens.

Elsa holds her breath.

Nothing.

She opens her eyes and there's deafening noise all around her. She can hear them yelling. Can hear that they're running. And then she hears The Monster's voice. Something is booming out of him, like a primeval power.

'NEVER. TOUCH. HER!'

Everything echoes.

Elsa's eardrums are rattling. The Monster is not roaring in Granny and Elsa's secret language, but in normal language. The words sound strange in his mouth, as if the intonation of every syllable slips and ends up wrong. As if he hasn't spoken such words for a very long time.

Elsa looks up. The Monster stares down at her through the shadow of the upturned hood and that beard, which never seems to end. His chest heaves a few times. Elsa hunches up instinctively, terrified that his huge hands are going to grab her and toss her into the traffic like a giant flicking a mouse with a single finger. But he just stands there breathing heavily and looking angry and confused. At last he raises his hand, as if it's a heavy mallet, and points back at the school.

When Elsa turns round she sees the girl who doesn't read Harry Potter and her friends scattering like bits of paper thrown into the wind.

In the distance she sees Audi turning into the parking area. Elsa takes a deep breath and feels air entering her lungs for what seems like the first time in several minutes.

When she turns round again, The Monster has gone.

9

SOAP

There are thousands of stories in the real world, but every single one of them is from the Land-of-Almost-Awake. And the very best are from Miamas.

All six of the kingdoms have produced the odd fairy tale now and then of course, but none of them are anywhere near as good. In Miamas, fairy tales are still produced round the clock, lovingly handmade one by one, and only the very, very finest of them are exported. Most are only told once and then they fall flat on the ground, but the best and most beautiful of them rise from the lips of their tellers after the last words have been spoken, and then slowly hover off over the heads of the listeners, like small, shimmering paper lanterns. When night comes they are fetched by the enphants. The enphants are very small creatures with decorous hats that ride on cloud animals (the enphants, not the hats). The lanterns are gathered up by the enphants with the help of large, golden nets, and then the cloud animals turn and rise up towards the sky so swiftly that even the wind has to get out of the way. And if the wind doesn't move out of the way quickly enough, the clouds transform themselves into an animal that has fingers, so the cloud animals can give the finger to the wind. (Granny always bellowed with laughter at this; it was a while before Elsa worked out why.)

And at the peak of the highest mountain in the Land-of-Almost-Awake, known as the Telling Mountain, the enphants open their nets and let the stories fly free. And that is how the stories find their way into the real world.

At first when Elsa's granny started telling her stories from Miamas, they only seemed like disconnected fairy tales without a context, told by someone who needed her head examined. It took years before Elsa understood that they belonged together. All really good stories work like this.

Granny told her about the lamentable curse of the sea-angel, and about the two princelings who waged war on each other because they were both in love with the princess of Miploris. She also talked about the princess engaged in a fight with a witch who had stolen the most valuable treasure in the Land-of-Almost-Awake from her, and she described the warriors of Mibatalos and the dancers of Mimovas and the dream hunters of Mirevas. How they all constantly bickered and nagged at each other about this or that, until the day the Chosen One from Mimovas fled the shadows that had tried to kidnap him. And how the cloud animals carried the Chosen One to Miamas and how the inhabitants of the Land-of-Almost-Awake eventually realised that there was something more important to fight for. When the shadows amassed their army and came to take the Chosen One by force, they stood united against them. Not even when the War-Without-End seemed unlikely to end in any other way than crushing defeat, not even when the kingdom of Mibatalos fell and was levelled with the ground, did the other kingdoms capitulate. Because they knew that if the shadows were allowed to take the Chosen One, it would kill all music and then the power of the imagination in the Land-of-Almost-Awake. After that there would no longer be anything left that was different. All fairy stories take their life from the fact of being different. 'Only different people change the world,' Granny used to say. 'No one normal has ever changed a crapping thing.'

And then she used to talk about the wurses. And Elsa should have understood this from the beginning. She really should have understood everything from the beginning.

* * *

Dad turns off the stereo just before she jumps into Audi. Elsa is glad that he does, because Dad always looks very downhearted when she points out to him that he listens to the worst music in the world, and it's very difficult not pointing it out to him when you have to sit in Audi and listen to the worst music in the world.

'The belt?' Dad asks as she takes a seat.

Elsa's heart is still thumping in her chest.

'Well hi there, you old hyena!' she yells at Dad. Because that's what she would have yelled if Granny had picked her up. And Granny would have bellowed back, 'Hello, hello, my beauty!' And then everything would have felt better. Because you can still feel scared while you're yelling 'Well hi there, you old hyena!' to someone, but it's almost insane how much more difficult it is.

Dad looks unsure about it. Elsa sighs and straps herself in and tries to slow her pulse by thinking about things she isn't afraid of. Dad looks even more hesitant.

'Your mum and George are at the hospital again . . .'

'I know,' says Elsa, as you do when something has not succeeded in allaying one's fears.

Dad nods. Elsa throws her backpack between the seats and it lands lying across the back seat. Dad turns round and straightens it up very neatly.

'You want to do something?' he says, sounding slightly anxious when he says 'something'.

Elsa shrugs.

'We can do something . . . fun?'

Elsa knows he's only offering to be nice. Because he has a bad conscience about seeing her so seldom and because he pities Elsa because her granny has died and because this Wednesday thing was rather sudden for him. Elsa knows this because Dad would never usually suggest doing something 'fun', because Dad doesn't like having fun. Fun things make Dad nervous. One time when they were on holiday when Elsa was small, he went with Elsa and Mum to the beach, and then they had so much fun that Dad had to take two Anadin and lie down all afternoon for a rest at the hotel. He had too much fun at once, said Mum.

'A fun overdose,' said Elsa, and then Mum laughed for a really long time.

The strange thing about Dad is that no one brings out the fun in Mum as much as he does. It's as if Mum is always the opposite pole of a battery. No one brings out order and neatness in Mum like Granny, and no one makes her as untidy and whimsical as Dad. Once when Elsa was small and Mum was talking on the phone with Dad, and Elsa kept asking 'Is it Dad? Is it Dad? Can I talk to Dad? Where is he?' Mum finally turned round and sighed dramatically: 'No, you can't talk to Dad because Dad is in heaven now, Elsa!' And when Elsa went absolutely silent and just stared at her mum, Mum grinned: 'Good God, I'm only joking, Elsa. He's at the supermarket.'

She grinned just like Granny used to do.

The morning after, Elsa came into the kitchen with shiny eyes when Mum was drinking coffee with loads of lactose-free milk, and when Mum, looking worried, asked why Elsa was looking so upset, Elsa replied that she had dreamed that 'Dad was in heaven.' And then Mum went out of her mind with guilt and hugged Elsa hard, hard, hard and said sorry over and over and over again, and then Elsa waited almost ten minutes before she grinned and said: 'Good God, I was only joking. I dreamed he was at the supermarket.'

After that, Mum and Elsa often used to joke with Dad and ask him what it was like in heaven. 'Is it cold in heaven? Can one fly in heaven? Is one allowed to meet God in heaven?' asked Mum. 'Do you have cheese-graters in heaven?' asked Elsa. And then they laughed until they couldn't sit straight. Dad used to look really quite hesitant when they did that. Elsa misses it. Misses when Dad was in heaven.

'Is Granny in heaven now?' she says to him and grins, because she means it as a joke, and she imagines he'll start laughing.

But he doesn't laugh. He just looks *that way*, and Elsa feels ashamed of saying something that makes him look *that way*.

'Oh, never mind,' she mumbles and pats the glove compartment. 'We can go home, it's cool,' she adds quickly.

Dad nods and looks relieved and disappointed.

They see the police car from a distance, in the street outside the house. And Elsa can already hear the barking as they are getting out of Audi. The stairs are full of people. Our Friend's furious howling from inside its flat is making the whole building shake.

'Do you have . . . a key?' asks Dad.

Elsa nods and gives him a quick hug. Stairwells filled with people make Dad very tentative. He gets back into Audi and Elsa goes inside by herself. And somewhere beyond that ear-splitting noise from Our Friend she hears other things too. Voices.

Dark, composed and threatening. They have uniforms and they move about outside the flat where the boy with a syndrome and his mother live.

Eyeing Our Friend's door intently but clearly afraid of getting too close, they press themselves to the wall on the other side. One of the policewomen turns round. Her green eyes meet Elsa's – it's the same policewoman she and Granny met at the station that night Granny threw the turds. She nods morosely at Elsa, as if trying to apologise.

Elsa doesn't nod back, she just pushes past and runs.

She hears one of the police talking into a telephone, mentioning the words 'Animal Control' and 'to be destroyed'. Britt-Marie is standing halfway up the stairs, close enough to be able to give the police suggestions about what they should do, but at a safe distance in case the beast manages to get out of the door. She smiles in a well-meaning way at Elsa. Elsa hates her. When she reaches the top floor, Our Friend starts baying louder than ever, like a hurricane of ten thousand fairy tales. Looking down the shaft between the flights of stairs, Elsa can see that the police are backing away.

And Elsa should have understood it all from the beginning. She really should have.

There is an absolutely unimaginable number of very special monsters in the forests and mountains of Miamas. But none were more legendary or more deserving of the respect of every creature in Miamas (even Granny) than the wurses.

They were as big as polar bears, moved as fluidly as desert foxes and were as quick on the attack as cobras. They were stronger than oxen, with the stamina of wild stallions and jaws more ferocious than tigers'. They had a lustrous black pelt as soft as a summer wind, but underneath, their hide was thick as armour. In the really old fairy tales they were said to be immortal. These were the tales from the elder eternities, when the wurses lived in Miploris and served the royal family as castle guards.

It was the Princess of Miploris who banished them from the Land-of-Almost-Awake, Granny used to explain, a sense of guilt lingering in the silences between her words. When the princess was still a child she'd wanted to play with one of the puppies while it was sleeping. She tugged its tail and it woke in a panic and bit her hand. Of course, everyone knew that the real blame lay with her parents, who had not taught her never, ever to wake a wurse that's sleeping. But the princess was so afraid and her parents so angry that they had to put the blame on someone else, so they could live with themselves. For this reason the court decided to banish the wurses from the kingdom for ever. They gave a particularly merciless group of bounty-hunting trolls permission to hunt them with poison arrows and fire.

Obviously the wurses could have hit back; not even the assembled armies of the Land-of-Almost-Awake would have dared face them in battle, that was how feared the animals were as warriors. But instead of fighting, the wurses turned and ran. They ran so far and so high into the mountains that no one believed they would ever be found again. They ran until the children in the six kingdoms had grown up without seeing a single wurse in their entire lives. Ran for so long that they became legendary.

It was only with the coming of the War-Without-End that the Princess of Miploris realised her terrible mistake. The shadows had killed all the soldiers in the warrior kingdom of Mibatalos and levelled it with the ground, and now they pressed in with terrific power against the rest of the Land-of-Almost-Awake. When all hope seemed lost, the princess herself rode away from the city walls on her white horse. She rode like a storm into the mountains and there, after an almost endless search that had made her horse succumb to exhaustion and almost crushed her too, the wurses found her.

By the time the shadows heard the thunder and felt the ground shaking it was already too late for them. The princess rode at the front on the greatest of all wurse warriors. And that was the moment of Wolfheart's return from the forests. Maybe because Miamas was teetering on the edge of extinction and needed him more than ever. 'But maybe . . .' Granny used to whisper into Elsa's ear when they sat on the cloud animals at night, 'maybe most of all because the princess, by realising how unjust she had been to the wurses, proved that all the kingdoms deserved to be saved.'

The War-Without-End ended that day. The shadows were driven across the sea. And Wolfheart disappeared back into the forests. But the wurses remained, and to this day they are still serving as the princess's personal guard in Miploris. On guard outside her castle gate.

Elsa hears Our Friend barking quite madly down there now. She remembers what Granny said about how 'making a racket amuses it'. Elsa feels a bit unsure about Our Friend's sense of humour, but then remembers what Granny said about Our Friend not needing to live with anyone. Granny didn't live with anyone herself, of course, and when Elsa pointed out that perhaps she shouldn't compare herself to a dog, Granny rolled her eyes. Now Elsa understands why.

She should have got all this from the start. She really should have.

Because this is no dog.

One of the police fumbles with a big bunch of keys. Elsa hears the main door opening downstairs and between Our Friend's barks she hears the boy with a syndrome dancing up the stairs.

The police gently shove him and his mother into their flat. Britt-Marie minces back and forth with tiny steps on her floor. Elsa hates her through the banisters.

Our Friend is completely quiet for a moment, as if it has made a strategic retreat for a moment to gather its strength for the real battle. The police jingle the bunch of keys and talk about being 'ready in case it attacks'. They all sound fuller of themselves now, because Our Friend is no longer barking.

Elsa hears another door opening, and then she hears Lennart's voice. He asks timidly what's happening. The police explain that they have come to 'take charge of a dangerous dog'. Lennart sounds a bit worried. Then he sounds a little like he doesn't know what to say. Then he says what he always says: 'Does anyone want a cup of coffee? Maud just made some fresh.'

Britt-Marie interrupts, hissing at him that surely Lennart can understand that the police have more important things to get on with than drinking coffee. The police sound a little disappointed about this. Elsa sees Lennart going back up the stairs. At first he seems to consider staying on the landing, but then seems to realise this might lead to a situation of his own coffee getting cold and conclude that whatever is going on here, it could not possibly be worth a risk like that. He disappears into the flat.

The first bark after that is short and defined. As if Our Friend is merely testing its vocal cords. The second is so loud that all Elsa can hear for several eternities is a ringing sound in her ears. When it finally ebbs away, she hears a terrific thud. Then another. And one more. Only then does she understand what the noise means. Our Friend is launching itself with all its strength at the inside of the door.

Elsa hears one of the police talking on the telephone again. She can't hear most of what's being said, but she hears the words 'extremely large and aggressive'. She peers down through the railings and sees the police standing a few metres from the door of Our Friend's flat, their self-confidence dwindling as Our Friend throws itself at the door with increasing force. Two more police have turned up, Elsa notices. One of them has brought an Alsatian on a leash. The Alsatian doesn't seem to think it's a terrific idea to go wherever that thing, whatever it is, is trying to get out. It watches its handler a little like Elsa looked at Granny that time she tried to rewire Mum's microwave.

'Call in Animal Control, then,' Elsa hears the policewoman with green eyes saying, at last, with a disconsolate sigh.

'That's what I said! Exactly what I said!' Britt-Marie calls out eagerly.

The green eyes throw a glance at Britt-Marie that causes her to shut up abruptly.

Our Friend barks one last time, horrifyingly loud. Then grows silent again. There's a lot of noise on the stairs for a moment, and then Elsa hears the main entrance door closing. The police have clearly decided to wait further away from whatever is living in that flat, until Animal Control get there. Elsa watches through the window as they make off, something in their body language suggesting coffee. Whereas the Alsatian has something in its body language that suggests it is considering early retirement.

Everything is suddenly so quiet on the stairs that Britt-Marie's lone tripping steps further down are giving off an echo.

Elsa stands there in two minds. (She knows that 'in two minds' is a phrase for the word jar.) She can see the police through the window, and in retrospect Elsa will not be able to explain exactly why she does it. But no true knight of Miamas could stand and watch a friend of Granny's being killed without trying to do something about it. So she quickly sneaks down the stairs, taking extra care as she passes Britt-Marie and Kent's flat, and taking the precaution of stopping on every half-landing to listen and make sure the police are not coming back in.

Finally she stops outside Our Friend's flat and carefully opens the letter box. Everything is black in there, but she hears Our Friend's rumbling breath.

'It's . . . me,' Elsa stammers.

She doesn't know exactly how to start this type of conversation. And Our Friend doesn't answer. On the other hand it doesn't throw itself against the door either. Elsa sees this as a clear sign of progress in their communication.

'It's me. The one with the Daim bars.'

Our Friend doesn't answer. But she can hear its breathing slowing down. Elsa's words tumble out of her as if someone had toppled them over.

'Hey . . . I mean this might sound mega-weird . . . but I sort of think my granny would have wanted you to get out of here somehow. You know? If you have a back door or something. Because otherwise they'll shoot you! Maybe that sounds mega-weird but it's pretty weird that you've got your own flat as well . . . if you get what I mean . . .'

Only once all the words have fallen out of her does she realise that she's spoken them in the secret language. Like a test. Because if there's just a dog on the other side of the door, it won't understand. 'But if it does understand,' she thinks, 'then it's something quite different.' She hears a sound made by a paw the size of a car tyre, quickly scraping the inside of the door.

'Hope you understand,' Elsa whispers in the secret language.

She never hears the door opening behind her. The only thing she has time to register is Our Friend backing away from the door. As if preparing itself.

Elsa grows aware of someone standing behind her, as if a ghost has appeared behind her. Or a . . .

'Look out!' growls the voice.

Elsa throws herself against the wall as The Monster silently sweeps past with a key in his hand. In the next moment, she is caught halfway between The Monster and Our Friend. And this really is the biggest damned wurse and biggest damned monster Elsa has ever seen. It feels as if someone is standing on her lungs. She wants to scream, but nothing comes out.

Everything goes terribly fast after that. They hear the door opening at the bottom of the stairs. The voices of the police. And someone else, who, Elsa realises, must be Animal Control. Looking back, Elsa is not completely convinced that she's in control of her own movements. If she's been placed under a spell or something it wouldn't be so unlikely considering that even if it was unlikely, it would be far less unlikely than running into a flipping wurse. But when the door closes behind her she's standing in the hall in The Monster's flat.

It smells of soap.

10

ALCOHOL

The sound of splintering wood fills the stairwell as the police drive the crowbar into the door frame.

Elsa stands in the hall in The Monster's flat and watches them through the spyhole. Technically, her feet aren't touching the floor, though, because the wurse has sat down on the hall mat so that she's wedged between the rear end of the enormous animal and the inside of the door. The wurse looks extremely irritated. Not threatening, just irritated. As if there's a wasp in its bottle of lemonade.

It occurs to Elsa that she's more panicked by the police on the other side of the door than the two creatures in the hall with her. Maybe it doesn't seem so very rational, but she's decided to trust more in Granny's friends than Britt-Marie's. She rotates carefully by the door until she's facing the wurse, then whispers in the secret language:

'You mustn't bark now, please be good. Or they'll kill you!'

The wurse doesn't look entirely convinced that it would come off worse if she opened the door and let it out among the police, and turns away dismissively. It stays silent, though seemingly more for Elsa's sake than its own.

Outside on the landing, the police have almost forced the door open. Elsa hears them yelling command words at each other, about being 'ready'.

She looks around the hall and into the living room. It's a very small flat but the tidiest one of any description she has ever set foot in. There is hardly any furniture, and the few items that there are have been arranged face to face, looking as if they'll commit furniture hara-kiri if a single speck of dust lands on them. (Elsa knows that because she had a samurai phase about a year ago.)

The Monster disappears into the bathroom. The tap runs in there for a long time before he comes out again. He dries his hands elaborately on a small white towel, which he then folds neatly and goes to put in a laundry basket. He has to stoop to fit through the doorway. Elsa feels as Odysseus must have felt when he was with that giant, Polyphemus, because Elsa recently read about Odysseus. Apart from the fact that Polyphemus probably didn't wash his hands as carefully as The Monster. And apart from Elsa thinking she's not as high-and-mighty and self-righteous as Odysseus seems to be in the books. Obviously. But apart from that, sort of like Odysseus.

The Monster looks at her. He doesn't look angry. More confused, actually. Almost startled. Maybe that's what gives Elsa the courage to blurt right out:

'Why did my granny send you a letter?'

She says it in normal language. Because, for reasons not yet entirely clear to her, she doesn't want to talk to him in the secret language. The Monster's eyebrows sink under his black hair so that it's difficult to make out any facial expressions at all behind it, and the beard and the scar. He's barefoot, but wears those blue plastic shoe covers you get at the swimming pool. His boots are neatly placed just inside the door, very precisely in line with the edge of the doormat. He hands Elsa another two blue plastic bags, but jerks back his hand once she touches them, as if worried that Elsa might also touch him. Elsa bends down and puts the plastic bags over her muddy shoes. She notices that she has slightly stepped off the mat and left two halves of her footprints in melted snow on the parquet floor.

The Monster bends down with impressive fluidity and starts wiping the floor with a fresh white towel. When he has finished, he sprays the area with a small bottle of a cleaning agent that makes Elsa's eyes smart, and wipes it with another small white towel. Then he stands up and neatly puts the towels in the laundry basket, and places the spray-bottle very exactly on a shelf.

Then he stands for a very long time and stares uncomfortably at the wurse. It lies splayed across the hall, covering the floor almost in its entirety. The Monster looks like he's about to hyperventilate. He disappears into the bathroom and comes back and starts carefully arranging towels in a tight ring around the wurse while taking extreme care not to touch any part of it. Then he goes back to the bathroom and scrubs his hands so hard under the tap that the basin vibrates.

When he comes back he's got a little bottle of antibacterial Alcogel. Elsa recognises it, because she had to rub that sort of stuff into her hands every time she was visiting Granny at the hospital. She peers into the bathroom through the gap under The Monster's armpit when he reaches out. There are more bottles of Alcogel in there than she could imagine there would be in Mum's entire hospital.

The Monster looks infinitely vexed. He puts down the bottle and smears his fingers with Alcogel, as if they were covered in a layer of extra skin, which he had to try and rub off. Then he demonstratively holds up his two palms, each the size of a flatbed truck, and nods firmly at Elsa.

Elsa holds up her own palms, which are more tennis-ball-sized. He pours Alcogel on them and does his best not to look too disgusted. She quickly rubs the Alcogel into her skin and wipes off the excess on her trouser-legs. The Monster looks a little as if he's about to roll himself up in a rug and start yelling and crying. To compensate, he pours more Alcogel on his own hands and rubs, rubs, rubs. Then he notices that Elsa has knocked one of his boots out of position in relation to the other. He bends down and adjusts the boot. Then more Alcogel.

Elsa tilts her head and looks at him.

'Do you have compulsive thoughts?' says Elsa.

The Monster doesn't answer. Only rubs his hands together, as if trying to get a fire started.

'I've read about it on Wikipedia.'

The Monster's chest heaves up and down, taking frustrated breaths. He disappears into the bathroom and she hears the sound of gushing water again.

'My dad is sort of slightly compulsive as well!' Elsa calls out behind him, adding quickly, 'But, God, not like you. You're properly barmy!'

Only afterwards does she realise it sounded like an insult. That was not at all how she meant it. She just didn't mean to compare Dad's amateurish compulsive behaviour with The Monster's obviously professional obsessions.

The Monster returns to see the wurse nibbling at her backpack, where it clearly believes there are some Daim bars. The Monster looks as if he's trying to go to a happier place inside his head. And there they stand, all three of them: a wurse, a child and a monster with a need for cleanliness and order that clearly is not at all well suited to the company of wurses and children.

On the other side of the door, the police and Animal Control have just broken into a flat where there's a lethal hound, only to discover the telling absence of the said hound.

Elsa looks at the wurse. Looks at The Monster.

'Why do you have the key to . . . that . . . flat?' she asks The Monster.

The Monster seems to start breathing more heavily.

'You left it in letter. From Granny. In envelope,' he replies at long last, deep-throated.

Elsa tilts her head the other way.

'Did Granny write that you should take care of it?'

The Monster nods reluctantly.

'Wrote "protect the castle".'

Elsa nods. Their eyes meet fleetingly. The Monster looks a great deal as one does when wishing that people would just go home and filthify their own halls. Elsa looks at the wurse.

'Why does it howl so much at night?'

The wurse doesn't look as if it greatly appreciates being spoken of in the third person singular. That is, if it counts as a third person; the wurse seems unsure about the grammatical rules of the case. The Monster is getting tired of all the questions.

'Has grief,' he says in a low voice towards the wurse, rubbing his hands together although there is nothing left to rub in.

'Grief about what?' asks Elsa.

The Monster's gaze is fixed on his palms.

'Grief about your grandmother.'

Elsa looks at the wurse. The wurse looks at her with black, sad eyes. Later, when she thinks about it, Elsa assumes this is when she really, really starts liking it a lot. She looks at The Monster again.

'Why did my granny send you a letter?'

He rubs his hands harder.

'Old friend,' he mutters from behind his mountain of black hair.

'What did it say?'

'Just said "sorry". Just "sorry" . . .' he says, disappearing even deeper into his hair and beard.

'Why is my granny saying sorry to you?'

She is starting to feel very much excluded from this story, and Elsa hates feeling excluded from stories.

'Not matter for you,' says The Monster quietly.

'She was MY granny!' Elsa insists.

'Was my "sorry".'

Elsa clenches her fists.

'Touché,' she admits at last.

The Monster doesn't look up. Just turns around and goes back into the bathroom. More running of water. More Alcogel. More rubbing. The wurse has picked up Elsa's backpack now with its teeth and has its whole snout inserted into it. It growls with great disappointment when it finds there is a palpable absence of chocolate-related materials in it.

Elsa squints at The Monster, her tone stricter and more interrogative:

'When I gave you the letter you spoke our secret language!

You said "stupid girl"! Was it Granny who taught you our secret language?'

And then The Monster looks up properly for the first time. His eyes open wide, in surprise. And Elsa stares at him, her mouth agape.

'Not she who taught me. I . . . taught her,' says The Monster in a low voice, in the secret language.

Now Elsa sounds out of breath.

'You are . . . you are . . .'

And just at that moment as she hears the police closing up the remains of the door to the wurse's flat and walking out, while Britt-Marie protests wildly, Elsa looks directly into The Monster's eyes.

'You are . . . the Werewolf Boy.'

And, a breath later, she whispers in the secret language: 'You're Wolfheart.'

And The Monster nods sadly.

PROTEIN BARS

Granny's fairy tales from Miamas were fairly dramatic, as a rule. Wars and storms and pursuits and intrigues and stuff, because these were the sorts of action stories that Granny liked. They were hardly ever about everyday life in the Land-of-Almost-Awake. So Elsa knows very little about how monsters and wurses get along, when they don't have armies to lead and shadows to fight.

It turns out they don't really get along.

It starts with the wurse totally losing its patience with The Monster when The Monster tries to wash the floor under the wurse while the wurse is still lying on it, and then, because The Monster is extremely reluctant to touch the wurse, he accidentally spatters some Alcogel in its eye. Elsa has to intervene to stop a full-blown fight and later when The Monster with extreme frustration insists that Elsa must put one of those blue plastic bags on each of the wurse's paws, the wurse thinks it's gone far enough. In the end, once twilight is falling outside and she's certain that the police are not still hanging about on the stairs, Elsa forces them both outside into the snow, to give herself a bit of peace and quiet to think over the situation and decide what to do next.

She would have worried about being seen by Britt-Marie from the balcony, except that it's six o'clock sharp and Britt-Marie and Kent have their dinner at exactly six o'clock because 'only barbarians' eat their dinner at any other time. Elsa nestles her chin into her Gryffindor scarf and tries to think clearly. The wurse, still looking quite offended by the blue plastic bags, backs into a bush until only its nose is sticking out of the branches. It stays there, its eyes focused on Elsa with a very dissatisfied expression. It takes almost a minute before The Monster sighs and makes a pointed gesture.

'Crapping,' mumbles The Monster, and looks the other way.

'Sorry,' says Elsa guiltily to the wurse and turns away. They are using normal language again, because something in Elsa's stomach turns into a dark lump when she talks in the secret language to anyone but Granny. Either way, The Monster doesn't seem too keen on any language. Meanwhile, the wurse looks like you or I might if someone came barging in while you were attending to nature's needs, and it took a while before they understood how inappropriate it was to stand there gawking. Only then does Elsa realise that it actually can't have had a chance to relieve itself for several days, unless it did so inside its flat. Which she rules out because she can't see how it could have manoeuvred itself by using a toilet, and it certainly wouldn't have crapped on the floor, because this is not the sort of thing a wurse would demean itself by doing. So she assumes that one of the wurse's superpowers is clenching.

She turns to The Monster. He rubs his hands together and looks down at the tracks in the snow as if he'd like to smooth out the snow with an iron.

'Are you a soldier?' asks Elsa, pointing at his trousers.

He shakes his head. Elsa continues pointing at his trousers, because she has seen this type of trousers on the news.

'Those are soldier trousers.'

The Monster nods.

'Why are you wearing soldier's trousers if you're not a soldier, then?' she interrogates.

'Old trousers,' The Monster replies tersely.

'How did you get that scar?' asks Elsa, pointing at his face.

'Accident,' The Monster replies even more tersely.

'No shit, Sherlock – I wasn't implying you did it on purpose.'

('No shit, Sherlock' is one of her favourite expressions in English. Her father always says one should not use English expressions if there are perfectly good substitutes in one's own language, but Elsa actually doesn't think there is a substitute in this case.)

'Sorry, I didn't mean to sound rude. I just wanted to know what sort of accident.'

'Normal accident,' he growls, as if that settles matters. The Monster disappears under the huge hood of his jacket. 'Late now. Should sleep.'

She understands that he is alluding to her, not to himself. She points at the wurse.

'That one has to sleep with you tonight.'

The Monster looks at her as if she just asked him to get naked, roll in saliva and then run through a postage stamp factory with the lights off. Or maybe not exactly like that. But more or less. He shakes his head, so that his hood sways like a sail.

'Not sleep there. Can't. Not sleep there. Can't. Can't. Can't.'

Elsa puts her hands on her stomach and glares at him.

'Where's it going to sleep then?'

The Monster retracts deeper into his hood. Points at Elsa.

Elsa snorts.

'Mum didn't even let me get myself an owl! Do you get how she'd react if I came home with that t-h-i-n-g?'

The wurse comes out of the bushes, making a lot of noise and looking offended. Elsa clears her throat and apologises.

'Sorry. I didn't mean "that thing" in a bad sense.'

The wurse looks a bit as if it's close to muttering, 'Sure you didn't.' The Monster rubs his hands in circles faster and faster, and starts to look as if he's panicking, and hisses down at the ground:

'Shit on fur. Has shit on fur. Shit on fur.'

Elsa rolls her eyes, realising that if she presses the point he'll probably have a heart attack. The Monster turns away and looks as if he is trying to insert an invisible eraser into his brain to banish that image from his memory.

'What did Granny write in the letter?' she asks him.

The Monster breathes grimly under his hood.

'Wrote "sorry",' he says without turning round.

'But what else? It was a really long letter!'

The Monster sighs and shakes his head and nods towards the entrance of the house.

'Late now. Sleep,' he growls.

'Not until you tell me about the letter!'

The Monster looks like a very tired person being kept awake by someone thumping him at regular intervals, as hard as he can, with a pillowcase filled with yoghurt. Or more or less, anyway. He looks up and frowns and evaluates Elsa, as if trying to work out how far he could fling her.

'Wrote "protect castle",' he repeats.

Elsa steps closer to show that she's not afraid of him. Or to show herself.

'And what *else*?'

He hunches up inside his hood and starts walking off through the snow.

'Protect you. Protect Elsa.'

Then he disappears in the darkness and is gone. He disappears a lot, Elsa will learn in due course. He's surprisingly good at it for someone so large.

Elsa hears muted panting from the other side of the yard and turns round. George comes jogging towards the house. She knows it's George because he's wearing shorts over his joggers and the greenest jacket in the world. He doesn't see her and the wurse, because he's too busy bouncing up and down from a bench. George trains a lot at running and jumping up and down from things. Elsa sometimes thinks he's in a permanent audition to be in the next Super Mario game.

'Come!' whispers Elsa quickly to the wurse to get it inside before George catches sight of it. And to her surprise the mighty animal obeys her.

The wurse brushes past her legs so its coat tickles her all the way up to her forehead, and she's almost knocked down by the force of it.

She laughs. It looks at her and seems to be laughing as well.

Apart from Granny the wurse is the first friend Elsa has ever had.

She makes sure Britt-Marie is not prowling about on the stairs and that George still hasn't seen them, and then she leads the wurse down into the cellar. The storage units are each assigned to a flat, and Granny's unit is unlocked and empty.

'You have to stay here tonight,' she whispers. 'Tomorrow we'll find you a better hiding place.'

The wurse doesn't look hugely impressed, but it lies down and rolls onto its side and peers nonchalantly into the parts of the cellar that still lie steeped in darkness. Elsa checks where it's looking, then focuses on the wurse.

'Granny always said there were ghosts down here,' she says firmly. 'You mustn't scare them, d'you hear?'

The wurse lies unconcerned on its side on the floor, its mattock-sized incisors glinting through the darkness.

'I'll bring more chocolate tomorrow if you're nice,' she promises.

The wurse looks as if it is taking this concession into consideration. Elsa leans forward and kisses it on the nose. Then she darts up the stairs and closes the cellar door carefully behind her. She sneaks up without turning on the lights, to minimise the risk of anyone seeing her, but when she comes to Britt-Marie and Kent's flat she crouches and goes up the last flight in big leaps. She's almost sure that Britt-Marie is standing inside, peering out of the spyhole.

The next morning both The Monster's flat and the cellar storage unit are dark and empty. George drives Elsa to school. Mum has already gone to the hospital because, as usual, there's some emergency going on there and it's Mum's job to sort out emergencies.

George talks about his protein bars the whole way. He bought a whole box of them, he says, and now he can't find them anywhere. George likes talking about protein bars. And various functional items. Functional clothes and functional jogging shoes, for example. George loves functions. Elsa hopes no one ever invents protein bars with functions, because then George's head will probably explode. Not that Elsa would find that such a bad thing, but she imagines Mum would be upset about it, and there'd be an awful lot of cleaning. George drops her off in the parking area after asking her one more time if she's seen his missing protein bars. She groans with boredom and jumps out.

The other children keep their distance, watching her guardedly. Rumours of The Monster's intervention outside the park have spread, but Elsa knows it will only last a short while. It happened too far from school. Things that happen outside school may as well be happening in outer space, because she is protected in here anyway. She may have a respite of a couple of hours, but those who are chasing her will keep testing the boundaries, and once they drum up the courage to have another pop at her they'll hit her harder than ever.

And she knows that The Monster will never get anywhere near the fence for her sake, because schools are full of children and children are full of bacteria, and there's not enough Alcogel in the whole world for The Monster after that.

But she enjoys her freedom that morning in spite of all. It's the second to last day before the Christmas holidays and after tomorrow she can have a couple of weeks of rest from running. A couple of weeks without notes in her locker about how ugly she is and how they're going to kill her.

In the first break she allows herself a walk along the fence. She tightens her backpack straps from time to time, to make sure it isn't hanging too loose. She knows they won't be chasing her now, but it's a difficult habit to break. You run slower if your backpack's loose.

Eventually she lets herself drift off in her own thoughts. That is probably why she doesn't see it. She's thinking about Granny and Miamas, she wonders what plan Granny had in mind when she sent her out on this treasure hunt; that is, if she had any plan at all. Granny always sort of made her plans as she went along, and now she's no longer there Elsa is having problems recognising what the next step of the treasure hunt is supposed to be. Above all she wonders what Granny meant when she said she was worried that Elsa would hate her when she found out more about her. Up until now Elsa has only found out that Granny had some pretty dodgy friends, which was hardly a shock, you might say.

And Elsa obviously understands that Granny's statement about 'who you were before you became a granny' must have something to do with Elsa's mum, but she'd rather not ask Mum unless she has to. Everything Elsa says to Mum these days seems to end in an argument. And Elsa hates it. She hates that one can't be allowed to know things unless one starts arguing.

And she hates being as alone as one can only be without Granny.

So it must be for that reason that she doesn't notice it. Because she's probably no more than two or three metres away when she finally sees it, which is an insane distance not to see a wurse from. It's sitting by the gate, just outside the fence. She laughs, surprised. The wurse seems to be laughing as well, but internally.

'I looked for you this morning,' she says and goes into the street, even though this is not allowed during breaks. 'Were you nice to the ghosts?' asks Elsa.

The wurse doesn't look as if it was, but she throws hers arms round its neck all the same, buries her hands deep in its thick black fur and exclaims: 'Wait, I've got something for you!' The wurse greedily sticks its nose into her backpack, but looks remarkably disappointed when it pulls it back out again.

'They're protein bars,' says Elsa apologetically. 'We don't have any sweets at home because Mum doesn't want me to eat them, but George says these are mega-tasty!'

The wurse doesn't like them at all. It only has about nine of them. When the bell goes, Elsa hugs it hard, hard, hard one more time and whispers, 'Thanks for coming!'

She knows that the other children in the playground see her do it. The teachers may be able to avoid noticing the biggest, blackest wurse appearing out of nowhere in the morning break, but no child in the entire universe could.

No one leaves any notes in Elsa's locker that day.

12

MINT

Elsa stands alone on the balcony of Granny's flat. They used to stand here often. It was here that Granny first pointed at the cloud animals and talked about the Land-of-Almost-Awake, just after Mum and Dad had got divorced. That night Elsa got to see Miamas for the first time. She stares out blindly into the darkness and misses her more than ever. She has been lying on Granny's bed, looking up at the photos on the ceiling and trying to figure out what Granny was talking about at the hospital when she said Elsa mustn't hate her. And also, 'it's a grandmother's privilege never to have to show her grandchild who she was before she became a grandmother.' Elsa has spent hours trying to work out what this treasure hunt is for, or where the next clue can be found. If there even is one.

The wurse sleeps in the storage unit in the cellar. In the midst of all this it's good to know that the wurse is close at hand. It makes Elsa feel a little bit less lonely.

She peers over the balcony railing. Has a sense of something moving down there on the ground, in the darkness. She can't see anything, obviously, but she knows The Monster is there. Granny has planned the fairy tale in this way. The Monster is guarding the castle. Guarding Elsa.

She's just angry with Granny for never explaining what he's guarding it from.

A voice further off saws through the silence.

'. . . Yeah, yeah, I've got all the booze for the party, I'm only just getting back home now!' the voice declares irritably as it draws closer.

It's the woman in the black skirt, talking into the white lead. She's heaving four heavy plastic bags along, and they knock into each other and then against her shins at every step. The woman swears and fumbles with her keys by the door.

'Oh there'll be at least twenty of us – and you know how well the guys in the office hold their drink. Not that they had any time to help, mind . . . Yeah, isn't it? I know! As if I didn't have a full-time job as well?' is the last thing Elsa hears before the woman marches into the house.

Elsa doesn't know much at all about the woman in the black skirt, except that everything smells of mint and she always has very well-ironed clothes and always seems to be stressed out. Granny used to say it was 'because of her boys'. Elsa doesn't know what that's supposed to mean.

Inside, Mum is sitting on a high stool in the kitchen, talking on the telephone and fiddling restlessly with one of Granny's tea-towels. She never seems to have to listen very much to what the person at the other end of the line is saying. No one ever disagrees with Mum. Not that she raises her voice or interrupts; she's just not the sort of person anyone wants to get on the wrong side of. Mum likes to keep it like this, because conflict is bad for efficiency and efficiency is very important to her. George sometimes jokes that Mum will give birth to Halfie in her lunch break, to avoid any negative effect on the hospital's general efficiency. Elsa hates George for making all those stupid jokes. Hates him because he thinks he knows Mum well enough to make jokes about her.

Of course, Granny thought efficiency was rubbish, and she couldn't give a crap about the negative effect of conflict. Elsa heard one of the doctors at Mum's hospital saying that Granny 'could start a fight in an empty room', but when Elsa told Granny she just looked miffed and said, 'What if it was the room that started it?' And then she told the fairy tale about the girl who

107

said no. Even though Elsa had already heard it at least an eternity of times.

'The Girl Who Said No' was one of the first stories Elsa ever heard from the Land-of-Almost-Awake. It was about the Queen of Miaudacas, one of the six kingdoms. In the beginning the Queen had been a courageous and fair-minded princess very much liked by all, but unfortunately she grew up and became a frightened adult, as adults tend to be. She started loving efficiency and avoiding conflict. As adults do.

And then the Queen simply forbade all conflict in Miaudacas. Everyone had to get along the whole time. And because nearly all conflicts start with someone saying 'no', the Queen also made this word illegal. Anyone breaking this law was immediately cast into a huge 'Naysayers' Prison', and hundreds of soldiers in black armour who were known as 'Yea-Sayers' patrolled the streets to make sure there were no disagreements anywhere. Dissatisfied with this, the Queen had soon outlawed not only the 'no' word but also other words including 'not' and 'maybe' and 'perhaps.' Any of these were enough to get you sent straight to prison, where you'd never again see the light of day.

After a couple of years, words like 'possibly' and 'if' and 'wait and see' had also been made illegal. In the end no one dared say anything at all. And then the Queen felt that she might as well make all talking illegal, because almost every conflict tended to start with someone saying something. And after that there was silence in the kingdom for several years.

Until one day a little girl came riding in, singing as she went. And everyone stared at her, because singing was an extremely serious crime in Miaudacas, because there was a risk of one person liking the song and another disliking it. The Yea-Sayers sprang into action to stop the girl, but they couldn't catch her because she was very good at running. So the Yea-Sayers rang all the bells and called for reinforcements. Upon which the Queen's very own elite force, known as the Paragraph Riders – because they rode a very special kind of animal that was a cross between a giraffe and a rule book – came out to stop the girl. But not even the Paragraph Riders could lay their hands on her, and in the end the Queen in person came rushing out of her castle and roared at the girl to stop singing.

But then the girl turned to the Queen, stared her right in the eye and said, 'No.' And as soon as she had said it, a piece of masonry fell off the wall round the prison. And when the girl said 'no' one more time, another piece of masonry fell. And before long, not only the girl but all the other people in the kingdom, even the Yea-Sayers and the Paragraph Riders, were shouting 'No! No! No!' and then the prison crumbled. And that was how the people of Miaudacas learned that a queen only stays in power for as long as her subjects are afraid of conflict.

Or at least Elsa thinks that was the moral of the story. She knows this partly because she checked out 'moral' on Wikipedia and partly because the very first word Elsa learned to say was 'no'. Which led to a *lot* of arguing between Mum and Granny.

They fought about a lot of other things as well, of course. Once Granny said to Elsa's mum that she only became a manager as a way of expressing teenage rebellion – because the very worst rebellion Elsa's mum could dream up was to 'become an economist'. Elsa never really understood what was meant by that. But later that night, when they thought Elsa was sleeping, Elsa heard Mum rebuff Granny by saying, 'What do you know about my teenage years? You were never here!' That was the only time Elsa ever heard Mum saying anything to Granny while holding back the tears. And then Granny went very quiet and never repeated the comment about teenage rebellion to Elsa.

Mum finishes her call and stands in the middle of the kitchen floor with the tea-towel in her hand, looking as if she's forgotten something. She looks at Elsa. Elsa looks back dubiously. Mum smiles sadly.

'Do you want to help me pack some of your granny's things into boxes?'

Elsa nods. Even though she doesn't want to. Mum insists on packing boxes every night despite being told by both the doctor and George that she should be taking it easy. Mum isn't very good at either – taking it easy or being told.

'Your dad is coming to pick you up from school tomorrow afternoon,' says Mum in passing as she ticks things off on her Excel packing spreadsheet.

'Because you're working late?' asks Elsa, as if she means nothing in particular by the question.

'I'll be . . . staying on for a while at the hospital,' says Mum, because she doesn't like lying to Elsa.

'Can't George pick me up, then?'

'George is coming with me to the hospital.'

Elsa packs things haphazardly into the box, deliberately ignoring the spreadsheet.

'Is Halfie sick?'

Mum tries to smile again. It doesn't go so very well.

'Don't worry, darling.'

'That's the quickest way for me to know that I should be mega-worrying,' answers Elsa.

'It's complicated,' Mum sighs.

'Everything is complicated if no one explains it to you.'

'It's just a routine check-up.'

'No it isn't, no one has so many routine check-ups in a pregnancy. I'm not that stupid.'

Mum massages her temples and looks away.

'Please, Elsa, don't you start making trouble about this as well.'

'What do you mean, "as well"? What ELSE have I been making trouble with you about?' Elsa hisses, as one does when one is almost eight and feels slightly put upon.

'Don't shout,' says Mum in a composed voice.

'I'M NOT SHOUTING!' shouts Elsa.

And then they both look down at the floor for a long time. Looking for their own ways of saying sorry. Neither of them knows where to begin. Elsa thumps down the lid of the removal crate, stomps off into Granny's bedroom and slams the door.

You could hear a pin drop in the flat for about thirty minutes after that. Because that is how angry Elsa is, so angry

110

that she has to start measuring time in minutes rather than eternities. She lies on Granny's bed and stares at the black-and-white photos on the ceiling. The Werewolf Boy seems to be waving at her and laughing. Deep inside, she wonders how anyone who laughs like that can grow up into something as incredibly doleful as The Monster.

She hears the doorbell go and then a second ring following incredibly fast, much faster than would be feasible for a normal person when ringing a doorbell. So it can only be Britt-Marie.

'I'm coming,' Mum answers politely. Elsa can tell by her voice that she's been crying.

The words come flowing out of Britt-Marie, as if she's fitted with a wind-up mechanism and someone has cranked it up using a key on her back.

'I rang your door! No one opened!'

Mum sighs.

'No. We're not home. We're here.'

'Your mother's car is parked in the garage! And that hound is still loose on the property!' She's talking so quickly it's clear she can't prioritise her various upsets.

Elsa sits up in Granny's bed, but it takes almost a minute before she manages to take in what Britt-Marie just said. Then she bounces out of bed and has to muster all her self-control to stop herself dashing off down the hall, because she doesn't want to make the old busybody suspicious.

Britt-Marie stands on the landing with one hand very firmly inserted into the other, smiling at Mum in a well-meaning way, nattering on about how in this leaseholders' association they can't have rabid dogs running around.

'A sanitary nuisance, a sanitary nuisance is what it is!'

'The dog is probably far away by now, Britt-Marie. I wouldn't worry about it . . .'

Britt-Marie turns to Mum and smiles well-meaningly.

'No, no, of course you wouldn't, Ulrika. Of course you wouldn't. You're not the type to worry yourself about other people's safety, even your own child's, are you? It's something you've inherited, I see. Putting the career before the children. That is how it's always been in your family.'

Mum's face is utterly relaxed. Her arms hang down, apparently relaxed. The only thing that gives her away is that she's slowly, slowly clenching her fists. Elsa has never seen her do that before.

Britt-Marie also notices. Again she switches the position of her hands on her stomach. Looks as if she's sweating. Her smile stiffens.

'Not that there's anything wrong with that, Ulrika, obviously. Obviously not. You make your own choices and prioritisations, obviously!'

'Was there anything else on your mind?' says Mum slowly, but something in her eyes has changed hue, which makes Britt-Marie take a small, small step back.

'No, no, nothing else. Nothing else at all!'

Elsa sticks out her head before she has time to turn round and leave.

'What was that you said about Granny's car?'

'It's in the garage,' she says curtly, avoiding Mum's eye. 'It's parked in *my* space. And if it isn't moved *at once* I'll call the police!'

'How did it get there?'

'How am I supposed to know?!' Then she turns to Elsa's mum again, with renewed courage. 'The car has to be moved at once, otherwise I'm calling the *police*, Ulrika!'

'I don't know where the car keys are, Britt-Marie. And if you don't mind, I need to sit down – I seem to be getting a headache.'

'Maybe if you didn't drink so much coffee you wouldn't get headaches so often, Ulrika!' She turns round and stomps down the stairs so quickly no one has time to answer her.

Mum closes the door in a slightly less self-controlled and composed way than usual, and heads into the kitchen.

'What did she mean by that?' asks Elsa.

'She doesn't think I should drink coffee when I'm pregnant,' Mum replies. Her phone starts ringing.

'That's not what I meant,' says Elsa. She hates it when Mum pretends to be stupid.

Mum picks up her telephone from the kitchen counter.

'I have to answer this, sweetheart.'

'What did Britt-Marie mean when she said in our family we "put the career before the children"? She meant Granny, didn't she?'

The telephone continues ringing.

'It's from the hospital, I have to answer.'

'No you don't!'

They stand in silence looking at each other while the telephone rings two more times. Now it's Elsa's turn to clench her fists.

Mum's fingers steal across the display.

'I have to take this, Elsa.'

'No you *don't*!'

Mum closes her eyes and answers the telephone. By the time she starts talking into it, Elsa has already slammed the door to Granny's bedroom behind her.

When Mum gently opens the door half an hour later, Elsa pretends to be asleep. Mum sneaks up and tucks her in. Kisses her cheek. Turns off the lamp.

By the time Elsa gets up an hour after that, Mum is sleeping on the sofa in the living room. Elsa sneaks up and tucks her and Halfie in. Kisses Mum on the cheek. Turns out the lamp. Mum is still holding Granny's tea-towel in her hand.

Elsa fetches a torch from one of the boxes in the hall and puts on her shoes.

Because now she knows where to find the next clue in Granny's treasure hunt.

13

WINE

It's a bit tricky to explain, but some things in Granny's fairy tales are like that. You have to understand, first of all, that no creature in the Land-of-Almost-Awake is sadder than the sea-angel, and it's actually only once Elsa remembers this whole story that Granny's treasure hunt begins to make sense.

Elsa's birthday was always extremely important to Granny. Maybe because Elsa's birthday is two days after Christmas and Christmas is very important to everyone else, and as a result no child with a birthday two days after Christmas ever gets quite the same amount of attention as a child born in August or April. So Granny had a tendency to overcompensate. Mum had banned her from planning surprise parties, after that time Granny let off fireworks inside a hamburger restaurant and accidentally set fire to a seventeen-year-old girl who was dressed up as a clown and apparently supposed to be providing 'entertainment for the children'. She really was entertaining, Elsa should say in her defence. That day, Elsa learned some of her very best swear words.

The thing is, in Miamas you don't get presents on your birthday. You *give* presents. Preferably something you have at home and are very fond of, which you then give to someone you like even more. That's why everyone in Miamas looks forward to other people's birthdays, and that's the origin of the expression 'What do you get from someone who has everything?' When the enphants took this fairy tale into the real world someone here managed to get the wrong end of the stick, of course, making it 'What do you GIVE to someone who has everything?' But what else would you expect? These are the same muppets who managed to misinterpret the word 'interpret', which means something completely different in Miamas. In Miamas an 'interpreter' is a creature most easily described as a combination between a goat and a chocolate biscuit. Interpreters are extremely gifted linguistically, as well as excellent to grill on the barbecue. At least they were until Elsa became a vegetarian, after which Granny was not allowed to mention them any more.

Anyway: so Elsa was born two days after Christmas almost eight years ago, the same day that the scientists registered the gamma radiation from that magnetar. The other thing that happened that day was a tsunami in the Indian Ocean. Elsa knows that this is a sickeningly big wave caused by an earthquake. Except sort of at sea. So more like an ocean-quake, really, if you want to be pernickety about it. And Elsa is quite pernickety.

Two hundred thousand people died at the same time as Elsa started to live. Sometimes when Elsa's mum thinks Elsa can't hear, she tells George she still feels guilty – it cuts her to the quick to think that this was the happiest day of her life.

Elsa was five and about to turn six when she read about it online for the first time. On her sixth birthday, Granny told her the story of the sea-angel. To teach her that not all monsters are monsters in the beginning, and not all monsters look like monsters. Some carry their monstrosity inside.

The very last thing the shadows did before the ending of the War-Without-End was to destroy all of Mibatalos, the kingdom where all the warriors had been brought up. But then came Wolfheart and the wurses, and everything turned, and when the shadows fled the Land-of-Almost-Awake they charged out over the sea with terrible force from all the coastlines of the six kingdoms. And their imprint on the surface of the water stirred up hideous waves, which, one by one, smashed into each other until they had formed a single wave as high as the eternity of ten thousand fairy tales. And to stop anyone pursuing the shadows, the wave turned and threw itself back in towards land.

It could have crushed the whole Land-of-Almost-Awake. It could have broken over the land and decimated the castle and the houses and all those who lived in them far more terribly than all the armies of the shadows could have managed through all eternity.

That was when a hundred snow-angels saved the remaining five kingdoms. Because, while everyone else was running from the wave, the snow-angels rushed right into it. With their wings open and the power of all their epic stories in their hearts, they formed a magical wall against the water and stopped it coming in. Not even a wave created by shadows could get past a hundred snow-angels prepared to die so that a whole world of fairy tales could live.

Only one of them turned back from the massive body of water.

And even if Granny always said that those snow-angels were arrogant sods who sniffed at wine and made a right carry-on, she never tried to take away from them the heroism they showed on that day. For the day when the War-Without-End came to an end was the happiest day ever for everyone in the Land-of-Almost-Awake, apart from the hundredth snow-angel.

Since then, the angel had drifted up and down the coast, weighed down by a curse that prevented it from leaving the place that had taken away all those it loved. It did this for so long that the people in the villages along the coast forgot who it used to be and started calling it 'the sea-angel' instead. And as the years went by, the angel was buried deeper and deeper in an avalanche of sorrow, until its heart split in two and then its whole body split, like a shattered mirror. When the children from the villages sneaked down to the coast to catch a glimpse of it, one moment they might see a face of such beauty it took their breath away; but in the next, they would see something so terrible and deformed and wild looking back at them that they would run screaming all the way home.

Because not all monsters were monsters in the beginning. Some are monsters born of sorrow.

According to one of the most often-told stories in the Land-of-Almost-Awake, it was a small child from Miamas who managed to break the curse on the sea-angel, releasing it from the demons of memory that held it captive.

When Granny told Elsa that story for the first time on her sixth birthday, Elsa realised she was no longer a child. So she gave Granny her cuddly-toy lion as a present. Because Elsa didn't need it any more, she realised, and wanted it to protect her granny instead. And that night Granny whispered into Elsa's ear that if they were ever parted, if Granny ever got lost, she would send the lion to go and tell Elsa where she was.

It had taken Elsa a few days to work it out. Only tonight, when Britt-Marie mentioned that Renault had suddenly been parked in the garage without anyone knowing how it got there, did Elsa remember where Granny had put the lion on guard.

The glove compartment in Renault. That was where Granny kept her cigarettes. And nothing in Granny's life needed a lion guarding it more than that.

So Elsa sits in the passenger seat in Renault and inhales deeply. As usual, Renault's doors weren't locked, because Granny never locked anything, and he still smells of smoke. Elsa knows it's bad, but because it's Granny's smoke she takes deep breaths of it anyway.

'I miss you,' she whispers into the upholstery of the backrest.

Then she opens the glove compartment. Moves the lion aside and takes out the letter. On it is written: 'For Miamas's Bravest Knight, to be delivered to:' And then – scrawled in Granny's awful, awful handwriting – a name and an address.

Later that night Elsa sits on the top step outside Granny's flat until the ceiling lights switch themselves off. Runs her finger over Granny's writing on the envelope again and again, but doesn't open it. Just puts it in her backpack and stretches out on the cold floor and mostly keeps her eyes closed. Tries one more time to get off to Miamas. She lies there for hours without succeeding. Stays there until she hears the main door at the bottom of the house opening and closing again. She lies on the floor and mostly keeps her eyes closed until she feels the night embracing the windows of the house and hears the drunk start rattling around with something a few floors further down.

Elsa's mum doesn't like it when she calls the drunk the drunk. 'What do I call her then?' Elsa used to ask and then Mum used to look very unsure and sound a bit smarmy, while managing to suggest something like: 'It's . . . I mean, it's someone who's . . . tired.' And then Granny used to chip in, 'Tired? Hell yeah, of course you get tired when you're up boozing all night!' And then Mum used to yell 'Mum!' and then Granny used to throw out her hands and ask, 'Oh good God, what did I say wrong n-o-w, then?' and then it was time for Elsa to put on her headphones.

'Turn off the water, I said! No bathing at night!!!' the drunk stammers from below at no one in particular, whacking her shoehorn against the banister.

That's what the drunk always does. Roars and screams and bashes things with that shoehorn. Then sings that same old song of hers. Of course no one ever comes out and quietens her down, not even Britt-Marie, for in this house drunks are like monsters. People think if they ignore them they'll cease to exist.

Elsa sits up into a squatting position and peers down through the gap between the stairs. She can only make out a glimpse of the drunk's socks as she shambles past, swinging the shoehorn as if scything tall grass. Elsa can't quite explain to herself why she does it, but she heaves herself up on her tiptoes and sneaks down the first flight of stairs. Out of pure curiosity, perhaps. Or perhaps more likely because she is bored and frustrated about no longer being able to get to Miamas.

The door of the drunk's flat is open. There's a faint light cast by an overturned floor lamp. Photos on all the walls. Elsa has never seen so many photos – she thought Granny had a lot of them on her ceiling, but these must be in their thousands. Each of them is framed in a small white wooden frame and all are of two teenage boys and a man who must be their father. In one of the photos, the man and the boys are standing on a beach with a sparkling green sea behind them. The boys are both wearing wetsuits. They smile. They are bronzed. They look happy.

Under the frame is one of those cheap congratulatory cards, the kind you buy in a petrol station when you've forgotten to get a proper card. 'To Mum, from your boys,' it says on the front.

Beside the card hangs a mirror. Shattered.

The words reverberating over the landing are so sudden and so filled with fury that Elsa loses her balance and slips down the bottom four or five steps, right into the wall.

'WHATAREYOUDOINGHERE?'

Elsa peers up through the railings at the deranged person wielding the shoehorn at her, looking simultaneously incandescent and terrified. Her eyes flicker. That black skirt is full of creases now. She smells of wine, Elsa can feel it all the way from the floor below. Her hair looks like a bundle of string in which two birds have got themselves tangled up during a fight. She has purple bags under her eyes.

The woman sways. She probably means to yell, but it comes out as a wheeze:

'You're not allowed to bathe at night. The water . . . turn off the water. Everyone will drown . . .'

The white cable she always talks into sits in her ear, but the other end just dangles against her hip, disconnected. Elsa realises there has probably never been anyone there, and that's not an easy thing for an almost-eight-year-old to understand. Granny told many fairy tales about many things, but never about women in black skirts pretending to have telephone conversations while they went up the stairs, so their neighbours wouldn't think they'd bought all that wine for themselves.

The woman looks confused. As if she has suddenly forgotten where she is. She disappears and, in the next moment, Elsa feels her mum gently plucking her from the stairs. Feels her warm breath against her neck and her 'ssshhh' in her ear, as if they were standing in front of a roe deer and had got a bit too close.

Elsa opens her mouth but Mum puts her finger over her lips.

'Shush,' whispers Mum again and keeps her arms tight round her.

Elsa curls up in her arms in the dark, and they see the woman in the black skirt drifting back and forth down there like a flag that's torn itself free in the wind. Plastic bags lie scattered on the floor of her flat. One of the wine boxes has toppled over. A few last drops of red are dripping onto the parquet floor. Mum makes a gentle movement against Elsa's hand. They stand up quietly and go back up the stairs.

And that night Elsa's mum tells Elsa what everyone except Elsa's parents were talking about on the day Elsa was born. About a wave that broke over a beach ten thousand kilometres away and crushed everything in its path. About two boys who swam out after their father and never came back.

Elsa hears how the drunk starts singing her song. Because not all monsters look like monsters. There are some that carry their monstrosity inside.

14

TYRES

So many hearts broke the day Elsa was born. Shattered with such force by the wave that the shards of glass were dispersed all round the world. Improbable catastrophes produce improbable things in people, improbable sorrow and improbable heroism. More death than human senses can comprehend. Two boys carrying their mother to safety and then turning back for their father. Because a family does not leave anyone behind. And yet, in the end, that is precisely what they did, her boys. Left her alone.

Elsa's granny lived in another rhythm from other people. She operated in a different way. In the real world, in relation to everything that functioned, she was chaotic. But when the real world crumbles, when everything turns into chaos, then people like Elsa's granny can sometimes be the only ones who stay functional. That was another of her superpowers. When Granny was headed for some far-off place you could only be sure of one thing: that it was a place everyone else was trying to get away from. And if anyone asked her why she was doing it, she'd answer, 'I'm a doctor, for God's sake, and ever since I became one I've not allowed myself the luxury of choosing whose life I should be saving.'

She wasn't big on efficiency and economics, Granny, but everyone listened to her when there was chaos. The other doctors wouldn't be seen dead with her on a good day, but when the world collapsed into pieces they followed her like an army. Because improbable tragedies create improbable superheroes.

121

Once, late one night when they were on their way to Miamas, Elsa had asked Granny about it, about how it felt to be somewhere when the world crumbles. And how it was being in the Land-of-Almost-Awake during the War-Without-End and what it was like when they saw that wave breaking over the ninety-nine snow-angels. And Granny had answered: 'It's like the very worst thing you could dream up, worked out by the most evil thing you could imagine and multiplied by a figure you can't even imagine.' Elsa had been very afraid that night, and she had asked Granny what they would do if one day their world crumbled around them.

And then Granny had squeezed her forefingers hard and replied, 'Then we do what everyone does, we do everything we can.' Elsa had crept up into her lap and asked: 'But what can we do?' And then Granny had kissed her hair and held her hard, hard, hard and whispered: 'We pick up as many children as we can carry, and we run as fast as we can.'

'I'm good at running,' Elsa had whispered.

'Me too,' Granny had whispered back.

The day Elsa was born, Granny was far away. In a war. She had been there for months, but was on her way to an aircraft. On her way home. That was when she heard about the wave in another place even further away, from which everyone was in desperate flight. So she went, because they needed her. She had time to help many children escape death, but not the boys of the woman with the black skirt. So she brought home the woman with the black skirt instead.

'That was your grandmother's last journey,' says Mum. 'She came home after that.'

Elsa and Mum sit in Kia. It's morning and there's a traffic jam. Snowflakes as big as pillowcases are falling on the windscreen.

Elsa can't remember the last time she heard Mum tell such a long story. Mum hardly ever tells stories, but this one was so long that Mum fell asleep in the middle of it last night and had to pick it up in the car on the way to school.

'Why was it her last journey?' asks Elsa.

122

Mum smiles with an emotional combination of melancholy and joy that only she in the entire world has fully mastered.

'She got a new job.'

And then she looks as if she is remembering something unexpected. As if the memory just fell out of a cracked vase.

'You were born prematurely. They were concerned about your heart so we had to stay at the hospital for several weeks with you. Granny came back with her on the same day we came home . . .'

Elsa realises that she means the woman in the black skirt. Mum clutches Kia's steering wheel hard.

'I've never spoken much to her. I don't think anyone in the house wanted to ask too many questions. We let your grandmother handle it. And then . . .'

She sighs, and regret floods her gaze.

'. . . then the years just went by. And we were busy. And now she's just someone who lives in our house. To be quite honest with you I'd forgotten that was how she first moved in. You two moved in on the same day . . .'

Mum turns to Elsa. Tries unsuccessfully to smile.

'Does it make me a terrible person that I've forgotten?'

Elsa shakes her head. She was going to say something about The Monster and the wurse, but she doesn't because she's worried Mum won't let her see them anymore if she knows. Mums can have a lot of strange principles when it comes to social interaction between their children and monsters and wurses. Elsa understands that everyone is scared of them, and that it will take a long time to make them all understand that The Monster and the wurse – like the drunk – are not what they seem.

'How often did Granny go away?' she asks instead.

A silver-coloured car behind them sounds its horn when she allows a space to develop between her and the car in front. Mum releases the brake and Kia slowly rolls forward.

'It varied. It depended on where she was needed, and for how long.'

'Was that what you meant that time Granny said you became an economist just to spite her?'

The car behind them sounds its horn again.

'What?'

Elsa fiddles with the rubber seal in the door.

'I heard you. Like a mega-long time ago. When Granny said you became an economist because you were in teenage rebellion. And you said, "How do you know? You were never here?" That was what you meant, wasn't it?'

'I was angry, Elsa. Sometimes it's hard to control what you say, when you're angry.'

'Not you. You never lose control.'

Mum tries to smile again.

'With your grandmother it was . . . more difficult.'

'How old were you when Grandfather died?'

'Twelve.'

'And Granny left you?'

'Your grandmother went where she was needed, darling.'

'Didn't you need her though?'

'Others needed her more.'

'Is that why you were always arguing?'

Mum sighs deeply as only a parent who has just realised that she has strayed considerably further into a story than she was intending is capable of sighing.

'Yes. Yes, sometimes it was probably for that reason we were arguing. But sometimes it was about other things. Your grandmother and I were very . . . different.'

'No. You were just different in different ways.'

'Maybe.'

'What else did you argue about?'

The car behind the Kia beeps its horn again. Mum closes her eyes and holds her breath. And only when she finally releases the handbrake and lets Kia roll forward does she release the word from her lips, as if it had to force its way through.

'You. We always argued about you, darling.'

'Why?'

'Because when you love someone very much it's difficult to learn to share her with someone else.'

'Like Jean Grey,' Elsa observes, as if it were absolutely obvious.

'Who?'

'A superhero. From *X-Men*. Wolverine and Cyclops both loved her. So they argued so much about her, it was totally insane.'

'I thought those X-Men were mutants, not superheroes. Isn't that what you said last time we spoke about them?'

'It's complicated,' says Elsa, even though it isn't really, if one has read enough quality literature.

'So what kind of superpower does this Jean Grey have, then?'

'Telepathy.'

'Good superpower.'

'Insane.' Elsa nods in agreement.

She decides not to point out that Jean Grey can also do telekinetics, because she doesn't want to make things more complicated than necessary for Mum right now. She is pregnant, after all.

So, instead, Elsa pulls the rubber seal on the door. Peers down into the gap. She is incredibly tired, as tired as an almost-eight-year-old gets after staying up all night feeling angry. Elsa's mum never had a mum of her own, because Granny was always somewhere else, to help someone else. Elsa has never thought of Granny in that way.

'Are you angry with me because Granny was so much with me and never with you?' she asks carefully.

Mum shakes her head so quickly and vehemently that Elsa immediately understands whatever she's about to say will be a lie.

'No, my darling, darling girl. Never. Never!'

Elsa nods and looks down again into the gap in the door.

'I'm angry with her. For not telling the truth.'

'Everyone has secrets, darling.'

'Are you angry with me because Granny and I had secrets?' She thinks about the secret language, which they always spoke so Mum wouldn't understand. She thinks about the Land-of-Almost-Awake, and wonders if Granny ever took Mum there.

'Never angry . . .' whispers Mum, and reaches across the seat before she adds, in a whisper: 'Jealous.'

The feeling of guilt hits Elsa like cold water when you're least expecting it.

'So that's what Granny meant,' she states.

'What did she say?' Mum asks.

Elsa snorts.

'She said I'd hate her if I found out who she was before I was born. That's what she meant. That I'd find out that she was a crappy mum who left her own child—'

Mum turns to her with eyes so shiny that Elsa can see her own reflection in them.

'She didn't leave me. You mustn't hate your granny, darling.'

And when Elsa doesn't answer, Mum puts her hand against Elsa's cheek and whispers, 'All daughters are angry with their mothers about something. But she was a good grandmother, Elsa. She was the most fantastic grandmother anyone could imagine.'

Elsa defiantly pulls at the rubber seal.

'But she left you by yourself. All those times she went off, she left you on your own, didn't she?'

'I had your grandfather when I was small.'

'Yeah, until he died!'

'When he died I had the neighbours.'

'What neighbours?' Elsa wants to know.

The car behind beeps its horn. Mum makes an apologetic gesture at the back window and Kia rolls forward.

'Britt-Marie,' says Mum at last.

Elsa stops fiddling with the rubber seal in the door.

'What do you mean, Britt-Marie?'

'She took care of me.'

Elsa's eyebrows sink into a scowling V-shape.

'So why is she such a nightmare to you now, then?'

'Don't say that, Elsa.'

'But she is!'

Mum sighs through her nose.

'Britt-Marie wasn't always like that. She's just . . . lonely.'

'She's got Kent!'

Mum blinks so slowly that her eyes are closed.

'There are many ways of being alone, darling.'

Elsa goes back to fiddling with the rubber seal on the door.

'She's still an idiot.'

'People can turn into idiots if they're alone for long enough,' nods Mum.

The car behind them beeps its horn again.

'Is that why Granny isn't in any of the old photos at home?' asks Elsa.

'What?'

'Granny isn't in any of the photos from before I was born. When I was small I thought it was because she was a vampire, because they can't be seen in photos, and they can smoke like as much as they want without getting a sore throat. But she wasn't a vampire, was she? She was just never at home.'

'It's complicated.'

'Yes, until someone explains it to you! But when I asked Granny about it she always changed the subject. And when I ask Dad he says, "Eh . . . eh . . . what do you want? You want an ice cream? You can have an ice cream."!'

Mum suddenly laughs explosively. Elsa does a mean impersonation of her dad.

'Your dad doesn't exactly like conflict,' Mum giggles.

'Was Granny a vampire or not?'

'Your granny travelled round the world saving children's lives, darling. She was a . . .'

Mum looks as if she's looking for the right word. And once she does, she brightens and smiles radiantly.

'A superhero! Your granny was a superhero!'

Elsa stares down into the cavity in the door.

'Superheroes don't leave their own children.'

Mum is silent.

'All superheroes have to make sacrifices, darling,' she tries at last.

But both she and Elsa know she doesn't mean it.

The car behind them beeps its horn again. Mum's hand shoots up apologetically towards the back window, and Kia rolls forward a few metres. Elsa realises that she's sitting there hoping Mum will start yelling. Or crying. Or anything. She just wants to see her feel something.

Elsa can't understand how anyone can be in such a hurry to move five metres in a traffic jam. She looks in the back mirror at the man in the car behind them. He seems to think the traffic jam is being caused by Elsa's mum. Elsa wishes with every fibre of her being that Mum would do what she did when she was pregnant with Elsa, and get out of the car and roar at the guy and tell him enough's bloody enough.

Elsa's father told that story. He almost never tells stories, but one Midsummer's evening – at the time when Mum was looking sadder and sadder and going to bed earlier and earlier and Dad sat on his own in the kitchen at night and reorganised the icons on Mum's computer screen and cried – they were at a party together, all three of them. And then Dad drank three beers and told a story about how Mum, while heavily pregnant with Elsa, got out of the car and went up to a man in a silver-coloured car and threatened to 'give birth here and now on his sodding bonnet if he beeped her again!' Everyone laughed a lot at that story. Not Dad, of course, because he's not a big fan of laughing. But Elsa saw that even he found it funny. He danced with Mum that Midsummer. That was the last time Elsa saw them dancing together. Dad was spectacularly bad at dancing, he looked like a very large bear that had just got up and realised its foot had gone to sleep. Elsa misses it.

And she misses someone who gets out and shouts at men in silver-coloured cars.

The man in the silver-coloured car behind them beeps again. Elsa picks up her backpack from the floor, gets out the heaviest book she can find, throws the door open and jumps out onto the motorway. She hears Mum shouting for her to come back, but without turning round she runs towards the silver-coloured car and slams the book as hard as she can into its bonnet. It leaves a big dent. Elsa's hands are shaking.

The man in the silver-coloured car stares at her as if he can't quite believe what just happened.

'ENOUGH, you muppet!'

When he doesn't answer right away, she slams the book down again three more times, and points at him menacingly.

'Do you get that my mum is PREGNANT?'

At first, the man looks as if he's going to open the door. But then he seems to change his mind, and watches in amazement as she pummels the bonnet with her book.

Elsa hears the click of the doors locking.

'One more peep and my mum will come out and give birth to Halfie on YOUR BLOODY BONNET!' roars Elsa.

She stays where she is on the motorway between the silver-coloured car and Kia, hyperventilating, until she gets a headache. She hears Mum yelling, and Elsa is actually on her way back into Kia, she really is. It's not as if she planned all this. But then she feels a hand on her shoulder and a voice, asking:

'Do you need help?'

And when she turns round there's a policeman standing over her.

'Can we help you?' he says again in a friendly tone of voice.

He looks very young. As if he's only working as a policeman as a summer job. Even though it's winter.

'He keeps beeping his horn at us!' Elsa says defensively.

The summer intern policeman looks at the man in the silver-coloured car. The man inside the car is now terrifically busy not looking back. Elsa turns towards Kia, and she really doesn't mean to say it, it's almost as if the words accidentally fall out of her mouth.

'My mum's about to give birth and we're sort of having a hard day here—'

'Your mother's in labour?' he asks, visibly tightening.

'I mean, it's not . . .' Elsa begins.

But of course it's too late.

The policeman runs up to Kia. Mum has started getting out with great effort, and is on her way towards them with her hand against Halfie.

'Are you able to drive? Or . . . ?' shouts the policeman so loudly that Elsa irately shoves her fingers in her ears and moves demonstratively to the other side of Kia.

Mum looks slightly as if she's been caught on the back foot. 'What? Or what? Of course I can drive. Or what? Is there something wro—'

'I'll go on ahead!' yells the policeman without listening to the end of the sentence, shoving Mum back into Kia and running back to his patrol car.

Mum thumps back into the seat. Looks at Elsa. Elsa searches the glove compartment for a reason not to have to look back at her.

The patrol car thunders past with its sirens turned on. The summer intern policeman waves frantically at them to follow behind.

'I think he wants you to follow him,' mumbles Elsa without looking up.

'What's going on?' whispers Mum while Kia carefully potters along behind the patrol car.

'I guess he's escorting us to the hospital, because he thinks you're about to, y'know, give birth,' mumbles Elsa into the glove compartment.

'Why did you tell him I was about to give birth?'

'I didn't! But no one ever listens to me!'

'Right! And what should I do now, do you think?' hisses Mum back and sounds possibly a bit less self-controlled now.

'Well, we've been driving behind him for ages now, so he'll probably get quite pissed if he finds out you're not actually going to give birth for real,' Elsa states pedagogically.

'OH REALLY, YOU THINK SO!?' Mum roars in a way that is neither pedagogical nor especially self-controlled.

Elsa chooses not to enter into a discussion on whether Mum is being sarcastic or ironic there.

They stop outside the hospital's accident and emergency entrance and Mum attempts to get out of the car and confess everything to the summer intern policeman. But he pushes her back into the car and yells that he's going to fetch help. Mum looks mortified. This is her hospital. She's the boss here.

'This is going to be a nightmare to explain to the staff,' she mumbles and rests her forehead in despair against the steering wheel.

'Maybe you could say it was some sort of exercise?' Elsa suggests.

Mum doesn't answer. Elsa clears her throat again.

'Granny would have thought this was fun.'

Mum smiles faintly and turns her head so her ear is on the steering wheel. They look at each other for a long time.

'She would have found it bloody funny,' nods Mum.

'Don't swear,' says Elsa.

'You're always swearing!'

'I'm not a mum!'

Mum smiles again.

'Touché.'

Elsa opens and closes the glove compartment a few times. Looks up at the hospital façade. Behind one of those windows, she slept in the same bed as Granny the night Granny went off to Miamas for the last time. It feels like forever ago. Feels like forever since Elsa managed to get to Miamas on her own.

'What job was it?' she asks, mainly so she doesn't have to think about it.

'What?' Mum exclaims.

'You said that thing with the tsunami was Granny's last journey because she had found a new job. What job was it?'

Mum's fingertips brush against Elsa's when she whispers the answer.

'As a grandmother. She got a job as a grandmother. She never went away again.'

Elsa nods slowly. Mum caresses her arm. Elsa opens and closes the glove compartment. Then she looks up as if she's just thought of something, but mostly because she'd like to change the subject, because she doesn't want to think about how angry she is with Granny right now.

'Did you and Dad get divorced because you ran out of love?' she asks so quickly that the question actually surprises her.

Mum leans back. Pulls her fingers through her hair and shakes her head.

'Why are you asking?'

Elsa shrugs.

'We have to talk about something while we're waiting for the policeman to come back with the people you're the boss of and everything gets mega-embarrassing for you . . .'

Mum looks unhappy again. Elsa fiddles with the rubber seal. Realises that it was obviously too early to start making jokes about it.

'Don't people get married because they're full of love and then divorced when they run out of it?' she says in a low voice.

'Did you learn that one in school?'

'It's my own theory.'

Mum laughs very loudly, without any early warning. Elsa grins.

'Did Granddad and Granny run low on love as well?' she asks, when Mum has finished laughing.

Mum dabs her eyes.

'They were never married, darling.'

'Why not?'

'Your granny was special, Elsa. She was difficult to live with.'

'How do you mean?'

Mum massages her eyelids.

'It's difficult to explain. But in those days it can't have been so common for women to be like her. I mean . . . it can't have been so common for anyone to be like her. It wasn't common for women to become doctors in those days, for example. As for surgeons, forget it. The academic world would have been quite different . . . so . . .'

Mum goes quiet. Elsa raises her eyebrows as a way of telling her to get to the point.

'I think if your granny had been a man of her generation rather than a woman, she would have been called a "playboy".'

Elsa is silent for a long while. Then she nods, soberly.

'Did she have many boyfriends?'

'Yes,' says Mum cautiously.

'There's someone in my school who has many boyfriends,' states Elsa.

'Oh, well I wouldn't want to suggest that the girl in your school is a . . .' says Mum, feverishly backtracking.

'He's a boy,' Elsa corrects.

Mum looks confused.

Elsa shrugs. 'It's complicated,' she says.

Even though it really isn't. But Mum doesn't look massively less confused.

'Your granddad loved your granny very much. But they were never a . . . couple. Do you understand?'

'I get it,' says Elsa, because she has the internet.

Then she reaches out and takes Mum's index fingers and squeezes them in her hands.

'I'm sorry that Granny was a crappy mum, Mum!'

'She was a fantastic grandmother, Elsa. You were all her second chances,' says Mum and caresses Elsa's hair as she goes on. 'I think your grandmother functioned so well in chaotic places because she was herself chaotic. She was always amazing in the midst of a catastrophe. It was just all this, everyday life and normality, that she didn't quite know how to handle.

'And it was just . . . I mean . . . the reason there aren't any old photos of Granny is partly because she wasn't home very often. And slightly because I tore up all the ones there were.'

'Why?'

'I was a teenager. And angry. The two belong together. There was always chaos at home. Bills that didn't get paid and food that went off in the fridge when we actually had food, and sometimes no food at all, and . . . God. It's hard to explain, darling. I was just angry.'

Elsa crosses her arms and leans back in her seat and glares out of the window.

'People shouldn't have children if they don't want to take care of them.'

Mum reaches out, touches her shoulder with her fingertips.

'Your granny was old when she had me. Or, what I mean is, she was as old as I was when I had you. But that was old in Granny's times. And she didn't think she could have children. She'd had herself tested.'

Elsa presses her chin down over her wishbone.

'So you were a mistake?'

'An accident.'

'In that case I'm an accident as well.'

Mum's lips fold in on themselves.

'No one has ever wanted something as much as your father and I wanted you, darling. You're about as far from an accident as anyone can get.'

Elsa looks up at Kia's ceiling and blinks the haziness out of her eyes.

'Is that why order is your superpower? Because you don't want to be like Granny?'

Mum shrugs. 'I taught myself to fix things on my own, that's all. Because I didn't trust your grandmother. In the end things were even worse when she was actually here. I was angry at her when she was away, and even angrier when she was home.'

'I'm angry too . . . I'm angry because she lied about being sick and no one told me and now I know and I still miss her and THAT makes me angry!!!'

Mum shuts her eyelids tight and puts her forehead against Elsa's forehead.

Elsa's jaw is trembling.

'I'm angry with her for dying. I'm angry with her for dying and disappearing from me,' she whispers.

'Me too,' whispers Mum.

And that is when the summer intern policeman comes charging out of the emergency doors. He has two nurses with a stretcher running behind him.

Elsa turns a few centimetres towards Mum. Mum turns a few centimetres towards Elsa.

'What do you think your granny would have done now?' asks Mum calmly.

'She would have cleared out,' says Elsa, still with her forehead against Mum's forehead.

The summer intern policeman and the nurses with the stretcher are only a few metres from the car when Mum slowly nods. Then she puts Kia into gear and, with the tyres spinning in the snow, skids out into the road and drives off. It's the most irresponsible thing Elsa has ever seen her mother do.

She'll always love her for it.

15

WOOD SHAVINGS

Perhaps the most curious of all the curious creatures in the Land-of-Almost-Awake, even by Granny's yardstick, are the regretters. They are wild animals living in herds, whose grazing areas are just outside Miamas, where they forage widely, and really nobody knows how they survive, considering the circumstances. At first sight, regretters look more or less like white horses, although they are far more ambivalent and suffer from the biological defect of never being able to make up their minds. This obviously causes certain practical problems, because regretters are flock animals, and one regret therefore almost always crashes into another when heading off in one direction and then changing its mind. For this reason regretters always have enormous, oblong swellings on their foreheads, which, in various fairy tales from Miamas that have ended up in the real world, has made people consistently get them confused with unicorns. But in Miamas the storytellers learned the hard way not to cut costs by hiring a regretter to do the job of a unicorn, because, whenever they did, the fairy tales had a tendency never to get to the point. And also no one, really no one at all, feels good after standing behind a regretter in the queue for the lunch buffet.

'So there's no point changing your mind, all you get is a headache!' Granny used to say, smacking herself on her forehead. Elsa thinks about that now, sitting in Kia outside school and looking at Mum.

She wonders if Granny ever regretted all the times she left Mum. She wonders if Granny's head was full of bumps. She hopes so.

Mum is massaging her temples and swearing repeatedly through gritted teeth. She is obviously regretting speeding away from the hospital like that, since the first thing she has to do after dropping Elsa off at the school is drive straight back to the hospital so she can go to work. Elsa pats her on the shoulder.

'Maybe you can blame it on your baby brain?'

Mum shuts her eyes in resignation. She's had rather too much baby brain lately. So much so that she could not even find Elsa's Gryffindor scarf when they looked for it this morning, and so much so that she keeps putting her telephone in strange places. In the refrigerator and in the rubbish bin and the laundry basket and on one occasion in George's jogging shoes. This morning Elsa had to call Mum's telephone three times, which is not entirely uncomplicated as the display on Elsa's telephone is quite fuzzy after its encounter with the toaster. But in the end they found Mum's telephone ringing inside Elsa's backpack. The Gryffindor scarf was also there.

'You see!' Mum tried to say, 'Nothing is really gone until your mum can't find it!' But Elsa rolled her eyes and then Mum looked ashamed of herself and mumbled, 'It's my baby brain, I'm afraid.'

She looks ashamed of herself now as well. And full of regret.

'Darling, I don't think they'll let me be the head of a hospital if I tell them I had a police escort to Accident and Emergency.'

Elsa reaches out and pats Mum on the cheek.

'It'll get better, Mum. It'll be fine.'

Granny used to say that, Elsa realises as soon as she says it. Mum puts her hand on Halfie and nods with fake self-assurance in order to change the subject.

'Your dad will pick you up this afternoon, don't forget. And George will take you to school on Monday. I have a conference then and—'

Elsa patiently gives Mum's head a scratch.

'I'm not going to school on Monday, Mum. It's the Christmas holidays.'

Mum puts her hand on Elsa's hand and inhales deeply from the point where they are touching, as if trying to fill her lungs with Elsa. As mums do with daughters who grow up too fast.

'Sorry, darling. I . . . forgot.'

'It doesn't matter,' says Elsa.

Even though it does a little.

They hug each other hard before Elsa hops out of the car. She waits until Kia has disappeared before she opens her backpack and gets out Mum's mobile, then scrolls to Dad's name in the address book and sends him an SMS: **Actually, there is no need for you to pick up Elsa this afternoon. I can manage it!** Elsa knows this is how they talk about her. She is something that needs to be 'picked up' or 'sorted'. Like doing the laundry. She knows they mean no harm by it, but come on! No seven-year-old who has seen films about the Italian Mafia wants to be 'sorted' by her family.

Mum's mobile vibrates in Elsa's hand. She sees Dad's name on the display. And underneath, **I understand.** Elsa deletes it. And deletes the SMS she sent to Dad from the outgoing messages. Then stands on the pavement, counting down from twenty. When she's got to seven, Kia screeches back into the parking area and Mum, slightly out of breath, winds down the window. Elsa gives her the mobile. Mum mumbles, 'It's my baby brain'. Elsa kisses her on the cheek.

Mum touches her throat and asks if Elsa has seen her scarf.

'In your right-hand coat pocket,' says Elsa.

Mum pulls the scarf out. Takes Elsa's head in her hands and pulls her closer and kisses her forehead very hard. Elsa closes her eyes.

'Nothing is really gone until your daughter can't find it,' she whispers into Mum's ear.

'You're going to be a fantastic big sister,' Mum whispers back.

Elsa doesn't answer. She just stands there waving as Kia drives off. She couldn't answer because she doesn't want Mum to know that she doesn't want to be a big sister. Doesn't want anyone to know that she is this horrible person who hates her own half-sibling, just because Halfie is going to be more loved by them than Elsa. Doesn't want anyone to know she's afraid they'll abandon her.

She turns round and looks into the playground. No one has seen her yet. She reaches into her backpack and gets out the letter she found in Renault. She doesn't recognise the address, and Granny was always terrible at giving directions. Elsa isn't even sure this address exists in real life, because quite often when Granny was explaining where things were, she used landmarks that were no longer there. 'It's right by where those morons with the budgerigars lived, past the old tennis club down where the old rubber factory or whatever it was used to be,' she'd ramble on, and when people didn't get exactly what she was talking about, Granny got so frustrated that she had to smoke two cigarettes one after the other, lighting the second by the embers of the first. And then when someone said she couldn't do that indoors, she got so angry that it was utterly impossible after that to get any decent directions out of her, impossible in fact to get anything except her expletive middle finger.

Really what Elsa wanted to do was rip the letter into ten thousand pieces and let the wind blow it all away. That was what she had decided last night. Because she was angry at Granny. But now, after Mum has told her the whole story and Elsa has seen all that brokenness in Mum's eyes, she's made the decision not to do that. Elsa is going to deliver the letter, this and all the other letters Granny has left for her. This is going to be a grand adventure and a monstrous fairy tale, just as Granny planned it. But Elsa isn't doing it for Granny's sake.

First of all she's going to need a computer.

She looks at the playground again. And at the precise moment when the bell goes and everyone turns away from the street, she runs past the fence towards the bus stop. Gets off one stop later, runs into the shop and goes straight to the ice cream counter, then back to the house, where she sneaks into the cellar storage unit and buries her face in the wurse's fur. It's her new favourite place on earth.

'I've got ice cream in the bag,' she says at last when she lifts her head.

The wurse points its nose with interest.

'It's Ben & Jerry's New York Super Fudge Chunk – my favourite,' Elsa elaborates.

The wurse has eaten more than half the ice cream before she reaches the end of that sentence. She caresses its ears.

'I just have to get hold of a computer. Stay here and . . . you know . . . try to stay out of sight!'

The wurse looks at her like a very big wurse that has just been told to behave like a considerably smaller wurse.

Elsa promises to find it a much better hiding place. Soon.

She runs up the stairs. Checks carefully that Britt-Marie is not lurking anywhere, and once she's sure she's not, rings The Monster's doorbell. He doesn't open. She rings the bell again. Everything is silent. She groans and opens his letter box and peers inside. All of the lights are out, but that doesn't dissuade her.

'I know you're there!' she calls out.

No one answers. Elsa takes a deep breath.

'If you don't open I'll sneeze right inside! And I've got a mega-col—' she starts to say threateningly, before a hiss interrupts her from behind, like someone trying to make a cat jump down from a table.

She spins round. The Monster steps out of the shadows on the stairs. She can't understand how such a huge person can make himself invisible all the time. He's rubbing his hands together, turning the skin around his knuckles red.

'Don't sneeze, don't sneeze,' he implores, anxiously.

'I need to borrow your computer, because I think George could be at home and I can't surf on my mobile because the display is screwed because Granny had a Fanta and toaster-related incident with it . . .'

The hood over The Monster's head moves slowly from side to side.

'No computer.'

140

'Just let me borrow it so I can check the address!' Elsa whines, waving Granny's letter in the air.

The Monster shakes his head again.

'Fine, just give me your Wi-Fi password, then, so I can connect my iPad!' she manages to say, rolling her eyes until it feels as if her pupils are out of position when she stops. 'I don't have 3G on the iPad, because Dad bought the iPad and Mum got pissed because she didn't want me to have such expensive stuff, and she doesn't like Apple, so it was a compromise! It's complicated, OK? I only need to borrow your Wi-Fi, that's all! Good God!'

'No computer,' repeats The Monster.

'No . . . computer?' Elsa repeats with extreme disbelief.

The Monster shakes his head.

'You don't have a computer?'

The hood moves from side to side. Elsa peers at him as if he's having her on, is clinically insane, or both.

'How can you not have a COMPUTER?'

The Monster produces a small sealed plastic bag from one of his jacket pockets, and inside it is a small bottle of Alcogel. Carefully he squeezes out some of its contents and starts rubbing it into his palms and skin.

'Don't need computer,' he growls.

Elsa takes a deep, irritated breath and takes a look around the stairs. George may still be at home so she can't go inside, because then he'll ask why she's not at school. And she can't go to Maud and Lennart, because they're too kind to lie, so if Mum asks if they've seen Elsa they'll tell her the truth. The boy with a syndrome and his mum aren't here in the daytime. And forget Britt-Marie.

Which doesn't exactly leave a wealth of possibilities. Elsa collects herself and tries to think about how a knight of Miamas is never afraid of a treasure hunt, even if it's difficult. And then she goes up the stairs.

Alf opens the door after the seventh ring. His flat smells of wood shavings. He's wearing a sorry excuse for a dressing gown, and the remaining hairs on his head look like the last tottering bits of buildings after a hurricane. He's holding a large white cup on which it says 'Juventus' and there's a smell of coffee, strong like Granny always drank it. 'After Alf has made coffee you have to drive standing up all morning,' she used to say, and Elsa didn't quite know what she meant, although she understood what she was saying.

'Yes?' he grunts.

'You know where this is?' says Elsa and holds out the envelope with Granny's handwriting on it.

'Are you waking me up to ask about a bloody address?' answers Alf in every way inhospitably before taking a big gulp of coffee.

'Were you still sleeping?'

Alf takes another mouthful and nods at his wristwatch.

'I drive the late shift. This is night-time for me. Do I come to your flat in the middle of the night to ask you random questions?'

Elsa looks at the cup. Looks at Alf.

'If you're asleep why are you drinking coffee?'

Alf looks at the cup. Looks at Elsa. Looks totally puzzled. Elsa shrugs.

'Do you know where this is or not?' she asks and points at the envelope.

Alf looks a little as if he's repeating her question to himself inside his head, in a very exaggerated and contemptuous tone. Has another sip of coffee.

'I've been a taxi driver for more than thirty years.'

'And?' wonders Elsa.

'And so of course I bloody know where that is. It's by the old waterworks,' he says, then drains his cup.

'What?'

Alf looks resigned.

'Young people and their lack of history, I tell you. Where the rubber factory was until they moved it again. And the brickyard.'

Elsa's expression gives away the possibility that she doesn't have a clue what he's talking about.

Alf claws at the remains of his hair and disappears into the flat. Comes back with a topped-up cup of coffee and a map. Puts down the coffee cup with a slam on a shelf in the hall and marks the map with a thick ring using a biro.

'Oh theeere! That's where the shopping centre is. Why didn't you just say?'

Alf says something that Elsa can't quite make out and closes the door in her face.

'I'll keep the map!' Elsa hollers cheerfully into his letter box.

He doesn't answer.

'It's the Christmas holidays, if you're wondering! That's why I'm not at school!' she calls out.

He doesn't answer that either.

The wurse is lying on its side with two legs comfortably stretched up into the air when Elsa walks into the storage unit, as if it has very gravely misunderstood a Pilates exercise. The Monster is standing in the passage outside, rubbing his hands. He looks very uncomfortable.

Elsa holds up the envelope to him.

'Are you coming?'

The Monster nods. The hood glides away a few inches from his face, and the big scar gleams momentarily in the fluorescent light. He doesn't even ask where they're going. It's difficult not to feel a pang of affection for him.

Elsa looks first at him and then at the wurse. She knows that Mum is going to be angry with her for skiving and going off without permission, but when Elsa asks her why she's always so worried about her, Mum always says, 'Because I'm so bloody afraid something may happen to you.' But Elsa is having a pretty hard time thinking that anything can happen to you when you have a Monster and a wurse tagging along. So she feels it should be OK, given the circumstances.

The wurse tries to lick The Monster when it walks out of the storage unit. The Monster jumps in terror and snatches back his hand and grabs a broom leaning up against another storage unit. The wurse, as if it's teasing and having a bit of a laugh, sweeps its tongue back and forth in long, mischievous movements.

'Drop it!' Elsa tells it.

The Monster holds out the broom like a lance and tries to force the wurse back by pushing the bristles into its nose.

'I said drop it!' Elsa snaps at both of them.

The wurse closes its jaws round the broom and crunches it to smithereens.

'Drop i—' Elsa begins but doesn't have time to finish the last 'it' before The Monster has thrown both broom and wurse across the cellar with all his might, sending the heavy animal crashing hard into the wall several metres away.

The wurse rolls up and flexes its body in one movement, and is in the middle of a terrifying spring before it has even landed. Its jaws are open, and rows of kitchen-knife-sized teeth exposed. The Monster faces it with a broad chest and the blood pumping in his fists.

'CUT IT OUT I SAID!' Elsa roars, throwing her little body right between the two furious creatures, unprotected between claws as sharp as spears and fists probably big enough to separate her head from her shoulders. She stands her ground, armed with nothing but the indifference of an almost-eight-year-old to her own physical shortcomings. Which goes a long way.

The wurse stops itself mid-leap and lands softly beside her. The Monster takes a few steps back. Slowly, muscles relax and lungs release air. Neither of them meet her gaze.

'The idea here is that you're supposed to protect *me*,' Elsa says in a quieter voice, trying not to cry, which doesn't go so terrifically well. 'I've never had any friends and now you two try to kill the only two I've ever had, just after I've found you!'

The wurse lowers its nose. The Monster rubs his hands, disappears into his hood and makes a rocking motion towards the wurse.

'Started it,' The Monster manages to say.

The wurse growls back.

'Stop it!' She tries to sound angry but realises she mainly just sounds as if she's crying.

The Monster, concerned, moves the palm of his hand up and down along her side, as close as possible without actually touching her.

'Sor . . . ry,' he mumbles. The wurse buffets her shoulder. She rests her forehead against its nose.

'We have an important mission here, so you can't keep messing about. We have to deliver this letter because I think Granny wants to say sorry to someone else. And there are more letters. This is our fairy tale: to deliver every single one of Granny's sorries.'

With her face in the wurse's fur, she inhales deeply and closes her eyes.

'We have to do it for my mum's sake. Because I'm hoping that the last sorry will be to her.'

16

DUST

It turns into an epic adventure. A monstrous fairy tale.

Elsa decides they should begin by taking the bus, like normal knights on normal quests in more or less normal fairy tales when there aren't any horses or cloud animals available. But when all the other people at the bus stop start eyeing The Monster and the wurse and nervously shuffling as far away from them as it's possible to be without ending up at the next bus stop, she realises it's not going to be quite so straightforward.

On boarding the bus it becomes immediately clear that wurses are not all that partial to travelling by public transport. After it has snuffled about and stepped on people's toes and overturned bags with its tail and accidentally dribbled a bit on a seat a little too close to The Monster for The Monster to feel entirely comfortable, Elsa decides to forget the whole thing, and then all three of them get off. Exactly one stop later.

Elsa pulls the Gryffindor scarf tighter round her face, pushes her hands into her pockets and leads them through the snow. The wurse is so delighted about escaping the bus that it skips in circles around Elsa and The Monster like an overexcited puppy. The Monster looks disgusted. He doesn't seem used to being outdoors by daylight, Elsa notices. Maybe it's because Wolfheart is used to living in the dark forests outside Miamas where the daylight doesn't dare penetrate. At least that is where he lives in Granny's fairy tales, so if there is any sort of order to this story, this must surely be the logical explanation.

People who see them on the pavement react as people generally do when they catch sight of a girl, a wurse and a monster strolling along side by side: they cross the street. Some of them try to pretend that it has nothing to do with the fact that they are scared of monsters and wurses and girls, by demonstratively pretending to be having loud telephone conversations with someone who suddenly gives them different directions and tells them to go the opposite way. That is also what Elsa's dad does sometimes when he's gone the wrong way and he doesn't want strangers to realise he's one of those types who go the wrong way. Elsa's mum never has that problem, because if she goes the wrong way she just keeps going until whoever she was supposed to be meeting has to follow her. Granny used to solve the problem by shouting at the road signs. It varies, how people deal with it.

But others who run into the adventuring trio are not as discreet, and they watch Elsa from the other side of the road as if she's being abducted. Elsa feels that The Monster would probably be good at many things, but a kidnapper who can be put out of action by sneezing at him would probably not be a particularly effective kidnapper. It's a curious sort of Achilles heel for a superhero, she feels. Snot.

The walk takes more than two hours. Elsa wishes it was Halloween, because then they could take the bus without scaring normal people, everyone would just assume they were dressed up. That's why Elsa likes Halloween: on Halloween it's normal to be different.

It's almost lunchtime by the time they find the right address. Elsa's feet hurt and she's hungry and in a bad mood. She knows that a knight of Miamas would never whine or be afraid of a grand adventure when sent out on a treasure hunt, but whoever said a knight can't be hungry or ill-tempered?

There's a high-rise at the address, but also a hamburger restaurant across the street. Elsa tells the wurse and The Monster to wait, and she goes across even though she has firm moral objections to hamburger chains, as every almost-eight-year-old should.

But even almost-eight-year-olds can't eat their principles, so she grudgingly buys ice cream for the wurse, a hamburger for The Monster and a vegeburger for herself. And as she sneaks out she gets out her red felt-tip pen and crosses out the dash between 'Lunch' and 'menu'.

Despite the below-zero temperature clawing at their faces, they sit on a bench opposite the high-rise building. Or rather Elsa and the wurse sit, because The Monster looks at the bench as if it's also about to lick him. He refuses to even touch the greaseproof paper round his hamburger, so the wurse eats that as well. At one point the wurse drops a bit of his ice cream on the bench and licks it up without concern, and The Monster looks close to asphyxiation. After the wurse takes a bite of Elsa's burger and she carries on eating it regardless, she has to help him breathe from a paper bag.

When they're finally done, Elsa leans her head back and looks up the façade of the building. It must be fifteen floors high. She takes the envelope from her pocket, slides off the bench and marches inside. The Monster and the wurse follow her in silence, surrounded by a strong smell of Alcogel. Elsa quickly scans the board of residents on the wall and finds the name as written on the envelope, though preceded by the words 'Reg. Psychotherapist'. Elsa doesn't know what that means, but she's heard a good deal about terropists letting off bombs and causing all sorts of trouble, so a psycho-terropist must be even worsè.

She heads over to the lift at the other end of the corridor. The wurse stops when they get there, and refuses to take another step. Elsa shrugs and goes in. The Monster follows her, after a certain amount of hesitation, though he is careful not to touch any of the walls.

Elsa evaluates The Monster as they're going up. His beard sticks out of the hood like a large, curious squirrel, which makes him seem less and less dangerous the longer she knows him. The Monster clearly takes note of her examination of him, and he twists his hands uncomfortably. To her own surprise, Elsa realises that his attitude hurts her feelings.

'If it bothers you so much you could just stay on guard downstairs with the wurse, you know. It's not like something's going to happen to me while I'm handing over a letter to the terropist.'

She talks in normal language, because she refuses to speak in the secret language with him. Her jealousy about Granny's language not even being Granny's from the very beginning hasn't gone away.

'Anyway, you don't have to be right beside me the whole time to be able to guard me,' she says, sounding more resentful than she means to. She'd started thinking of The Monster as a friend, but remembers now that he's only here because Granny told him. The Monster just stands there in silence.

When the elevator doors glide open Elsa marches out ahead of him. They pass rows of doors until they find the terropist's door. Elsa knocks so hard she actually hurts her knuckles. The Monster backs off towards the wall on the other side of the narrow corridor, as if he realises that the person on the other side of the door may peer through the spyhole. He seems to be trying to make himself as small and unfrightening as possible. It's hard not to find this endearing, thinks Elsa – even if unfrightening is not a proper word.

Elsa knocks on the door again. Puts her ear against the lock. Another knock. Another silence.

'Empty,' says The Monster slowly.

'No shit, Sherlock.'

She really doesn't mean to be angry with him, because it's Granny she's angry with. She's just tired. So very, very tired. She looks around and catches sight of two wooden chairs.

'They must be out for lunch, we'll have to wait,' she says glumly and drops despondently into one of the chairs.

As far as Elsa is concerned, the silence goes from pleasant to hard work to unbearable in about one and a half eternities. And when she has occupied herself with everything she has been able to come up with: drumming her fingers against the tabletop, poking out all the stuffing from the chair cushion through a little hole in the fabric and carving her name into the soft wood of the armrest with the nail of her index finger, she shatters the silence with one of those questions that sound much more accusing than she means it to be.

'Why do you wear soldier's trousers if you're not a soldier?'

The Monster breathes slowly under his hood.

'Old trousers.'

'Have you been a soldier?'

The hood moves up and down.

'War is wrong and soldiers are wrong. Soldiers kill people!'

'Not that sort of soldier,' The Monster intones.

'There's only one sort of soldier!'

The Monster doesn't answer. Elsa carves a swear word into the wood of the armrest, using her nail. In actual fact she doesn't want to ask the question that's burning inside of her, because she doesn't want The Monster to know how wounded she is. But she can't stop herself. It's one of Elsa's big problems, they say at school. That she can never control herself.

'Was it you who showed my granny Miamas, or was it Granny who showed you?'

She spits out the words. The hood doesn't move, but she can see him breathing. She's just about to repeat the question when she hears, from the inside of it:

'Your granny. Showed. As a child.'

He says it the way he says everything in the normal language. As if the words come bickering out of his mouth.

'You were about my age,' Elsa says, thinking of the photos of the Werewolf Boy.

The hood moves up and down.

'Did she tell you fairy tales?' she asks quietly, and wishes he'd say no, even though she knows better.

The hood moves up and down.

'Did you meet during a war? Is that why she called you Wolfheart?' She really doesn't want to ask any more, because she can feel her jealousy growing. But the hood continues to nod.

'Camp. Camp for the one who flees.'

'A refugee camp. Did Granny bring you here with her? Was she the one who arranged it so you could live in the flat?'

There's a long exhalation from the hood.

'Lived in many places. Many homes.'

'Foster homes?' He nods. 'Why didn't you stay there?'

The hood moves from side to side, very slowly.

'Bad homes. Dangerous. Your granny came to get me.'

'Why did you become a soldier? Was it so you could go to the same places as Granny?' He nods. 'Did you also want to help people? Like she does?' Slowly, the hood moves up and down. 'Why didn't you become a doctor like Granny, then?' The Monster rubs his hands together.

'Blood. Don't like . . . blood.'

'Smart idea to become a soldier. Are you an orphan?'

The hood is still. The Monster is silent. But she notices that the beard withdraws even deeper into the darkness. Suddenly Elsa nods exuberantly to herself.

'Like the X-Men!' she exclaims with more enthusiasm than she's really willing to give away. Then she clears her throat, composes herself. 'X-Men are . . . mutants. And many X-Men are sort of orphans. It's quite cool.'

The hood doesn't move. Elsa pulls out some more stuffing from the chair cushion and feels stupid. She was about to add that Harry Potter was also an orphan, and to be like Harry Potter in any way at all is actually the coolest thing there is, but she's starting to realise that The Monster probably doesn't read as much quality literature as one might hope.

'Is Miamas a word in the secret language?' she asks instead. 'I mean, is it a word in your language? It doesn't sound like other words in the secret language – I mean, your language.'

The hood doesn't move. But the words come more softly now. Not like all the other words from The Monster, which all seem to be on their guard. These sound almost dreamy.

'Mama's language. "Miamas." My . . . mama's language.'

Elsa looks up and gazes intently into the darkness inside the hood.

151

'Did you not have the same language?'

The hood moves from side to side.

'Where did your mother come from?' asks Elsa.

'Other place. Other war.'

'What does Miamas mean, then?'

The words come out like a sigh.

'"I love."'

'So it was your kingdom. That was why it was called Miamas. It wasn't at all because I called pyjamas "mjamas".'

Elsa pulls out the last bit of stuffing and rolls it into a ball to distract herself from her churning jealousy. 'Typical bloody Granny thing, making up Miamas for you so you'd know your mother loved you,' she mumbles, abruptly silencing herself when she realises she is saying it aloud.

The Monster shifts his weight from foot to foot. Breathing more slowly. Rubbing his hands.

'Miamas. Not made up. Not pretend. Not for . . . a little one. Miamas. For real for . . . children.'

And then, while Elsa closes her eyes to avoid showing her agreement, he goes on tentatively:

'In letter. Grandmother's apology. Was apology to mother,' he whispers from under his hood.

Elsa's eyes open and she frowns.

'What?'

The Monster's chest heaves up and down.

'You asked. About Granny's letter. What Granny wrote. Wrote apology to my mother. We never found . . . my mother.'

Their eyes meet halfway, on different terms. A tiny but mutual respect is created between them, there and then, as Miamasians. Elsa realises that he is telling her what was in the letter because he understands what it's like when people have secrets from you just because you're a child. So she sounds considerably less angry when she asks:

'Did you look for your mother?'

The hood moves up and down.

'For how long?'

152

'Always. Since . . . the camp.'

Elsa's chin drops slightly.

'So that's why Granny was always going off on all these trips? Because you were looking for your mother?'

The speed of The Monster's hand-rubbing increases. His chest heaves. His hood moves down a fraction, then up again, infinitely slowly. And then everything is silent.

Elsa nods and looks down at her lap and, once again, her anger wells up unreasonably inside her.

'My granny was also someone's mother! Did you ever think about that?'

The Monster doesn't answer.

'You don't have to guard me!' Elsa snaps and starts scratching more swear words into the wooden armrest.

'Not guard,' The Monster finally growls from behind her. His black eyes emerge from under the hood. 'Not guard. Friend.'

He disappears back in under the hood. Elsa burrows her gaze into the floor and scrapes her heels against the wall-to-wall carpet, stirring up more dust.

'Thanks,' she whispers grumpily. But she says it in the secret language now. The Monster doesn't say anything, but when he rubs his hands together it's no longer as hard and frenetic.

'You don't like talking so much, do you?'

'No . . . but you do. All the time.'

And that's the first time Elsa believes he's smiling. Or almost, anyway.

'Touché.' Elsa grins.

Elsa doesn't know how long they wait, but they keep waiting long after Elsa has really decided to give up. They wait until the lift door opens with a little 'pling' and the woman in the black skirt walks into the corridor. She approaches the office with big strides but freezes mid-air as she sees the enormous, bearded man and the small girl who looks as if she'd fit into the palm of one of his hands. The girl stares at her. The woman in the black skirt is holding a small, plastic box of salad. It's trembling.

She looks as if she's considering turning round and running away, or maybe, like a child, believes that if she closes her eyes she'll no longer be visible. Instead, she stands frozen to the spot a few metres away from them, her hands grasping the edge of the box as if it was the edge of a cliff.

Elsa rises from her chair. Wolfheart backs away from them both. If Elsa had been looking at him, she would have noticed, as he moved away, an expression on his face that she had never seen in him before. A sort of fear that no one in the Land-of-Almost-Awake would have believed Wolfheart capable of. But Elsa doesn't look at him as she rises from the chair; she is only looking at the woman in the black skirt.

'I think I have a letter for you,' Elsa eventually manages to say.

The woman stands still with her knuckles whitening round the plastic box. Elsa insistently reaches towards her with the envelope.

'It's from my granny. I think she's saying sorry about something.'

The woman takes it. Elsa puts her hands in her pockets, because she doesn't quite know what to do with them. It's unclear what the woman in the black skirt is doing here, but Elsa is certain that Granny had some reason for making her bring the letter. Because there's no coincidence in Miamas, or in fairy tales. Everything that's there is meant to be there.

'It's not your name on the envelope, I know that, but it has to be for you.'

The woman smells of mint today, not wine. Carefully she opens the letter. Her lips tighten, the letter trembles in her hands.

'I . . . used to have this name, a long time ago. I changed back to my maiden name when I moved into your house, but this was my name when . . . when I met your grandmother.'

'After the wave,' ventures Elsa.

The woman's lips pinch inwards until they disappear.

'I . . . I planned to change the name on the office door as well. But . . . well, I don't know. It never . . . never happened.'

The letter starts trembling even more violently.

'What does it say?' asks Elsa, regretting that she didn't have a quick peek before handing it over. The woman in the black skirt makes all the right movements to start crying, but seems to be out of tears.

'Your grandmother writes "sorry",' she says slowly.

'For what?' Elsa asks at once.

'Because she sent you here.'

Elsa is just about to correct her and point at Wolfheart and say, 'Sent *us* here!' But when she looks up he's already gone. She didn't hear the elevator or the ground-floor door closing. He's just disappeared. 'Like a fart through an open window,' as Granny used to say when things weren't where they were supposed to be.

The woman with the black skirt moves towards the door, emblazoned with the words 'Reg. Psychotherapist', followed by the name she once had. She puts the key in the lock and gestures quickly for Elsa to come in, although it's quite obviously not what she wants at all.

When she notices that Elsa's eyes are still searching for her large-hewn friend, the woman with the black skirt whispers morosely: 'I had another office when your granny last came to see me with him. That's why he didn't know you were coming to me. He would never have come if he had known you were coming here. He is . . . is frightened of me.'

17

CINNAMON BUN

In one fairy tale from the Land-of-Almost-Awake, a girl from Miamas broke the curse and released the sea-angel. But Granny never explained how it happened.

Elsa sits by the desk of the woman with the black skirt in a chair that Elsa assumes must be for visitors. Judging by the cloud of dust that enveloped Elsa when she sat down, as if she'd accidentally stumbled into a smoke machine at a magic show, she decides the woman can't have very many visitors. Ill at ease, the woman sits on the other side of the desk, reading and rereading the letter from Granny, though Elsa is quite sure by now that she's only pretending to read it so she doesn't have to start talking to Elsa. The woman looked as if she regretted it as soon as she invited Elsa in. A bit like when people in TV series invite vampires in and then, as soon as they've crossed the threshold, think 'Oh shit!' to themselves just before they get bitten. At least this is what Elsa imagines one would be thinking in that type of situation. And that's also how the woman looks. The walls of the office are covered in bookshelves. Elsa has never seen so many books outside a library. She wonders if the woman in the black skirt has ever heard of an iPad.

And then, once again, her thoughts drift off to Granny and the Land-of-Almost-Awake. For if this woman is the sea-angel, basically, she's the third creature from that world, along with Wolfheart and the wurse, that lives in Elsa's building. Elsa doesn't know if this means that Granny took all her stories from the real world and placed them in Miamas, or if the stories from Miamas became so real that the creatures came across to the real world. But the Land-of-Almost-Awake and her house are obviously merging.

Elsa remembers how Granny said that 'the best stories are never completely realistic and never entirely made up.' That was what Granny meant when she called certain things 'reality-challenged'. To Granny, there was nothing that was entirely one thing or another. Stories were completely for real and at the same time not.

Elsa just wishes Granny had said more about the curse of the sea-angel, and how to break it. Because she supposes this is why she sent Elsa here, and if Elsa doesn't figure out what to do she'll probably never find the next letter. And then she'll never find the apology for Mum.

She looks up at the woman on the other side of the desk and clears her throat demonstratively. The woman's eyelids flicker, but she keeps staring down at the letter.

'Did you ever hear about the woman who read herself to death?' asks Elsa.

The woman's gaze glides up from the paper, brushes against her and then flees back into the letter.

'I don't know what . . . it means,' says the woman almost fearfully.

Elsa sighs.

'I've never seen so many books, it's almost insane. Haven't you heard of an iPad?'

The woman's gaze suddenly moves up again. Lingers for a longer time on Elsa.

'I like books.'

'You think I don't like books? You can keep your books on the iPad. You don't need a million books in your office.'

The woman's pupils dither back and forth over the desk. She gets out a mint tab from a little box and puts it on her tongue, with awkward movements as if her hand and tongue belonged to two different people.

'I like physical books.'

'You can have all sorts of books on an iPad.'

The woman's fingers tremble slightly. She peers at Elsa, a little as one peers at a person one meets outside a toilet, where one has spent just a tad too long.

'That's not what I mean by "a book". I mean a "book" in the sense of the dust jacket, the cover, the pages . . .'

'A book is the text. And you can read the text on an iPad!'

The woman's eyes open and close like large fans.

'I like holding the book when I'm reading.'

'You can hold an iPad.'

'I mean I like being able to turn the pages,' the woman tries to explain.

'You can turn the pages on an iPad.'

The woman nods, with the slowest nod Elsa has seen in all her life. Elsa throws her arms out.

'But, you know, do what you like! Have a million books! I was only, like, asking. It's still a book if you're reading it on an iPad. Soup is soup whatever bowl it's in.'

The woman's mouth moves spasmodically at the corners, spreading cracks in the surrounding skin.

'I've never heard that proverb.'

'It's from Miamas,' says Elsa.

The woman looks down at her lap. Doesn't answer.

She really doesn't look like an angel, thinks Elsa. But on the other hand she doesn't look like a drunk either. So maybe it evens itself out. Maybe this is how halfway creatures look.

'Why did Granny bring Wolfheart here?' asks Elsa.

'Sorry – who?'

'You said Granny brought him here. And that's why he's afraid of you.'

'I didn't know you called him Wolfheart.'

'That's his name. Why is he afraid of you if you don't even know who he is?'

The woman puts her hands in her lap and studies them as if she just caught sight of them for the first time and wonders what in the name of God they're doing there.

'Your grandmother brought him here to talk about the war. She thought I'd be able to help him, but he got scared of me. He got scared of all my questions and scared of . . . of his memories, I think,' she says at last. 'He has seen many, many wars. He has lived almost his whole life at war, in one way or another. It does . . . does unbearable things to a human.'

'Why does he carry on like that with his hands?'

'Sorry?'

'He washes his hands all the time. Like he's trying to wash off a smell of poo, sort of thing.'

'Sometimes the brain does strange things to one after a tragedy. I think maybe he's trying to wash away . . .'

She becomes silent. Looks down.

'What?' Elsa demands to know.

'. . . the blood,' the woman concludes, emptily.

'Has he killed someone?'

'I don't know.'

'Is he sick in the head?'

'Excuse me?'

'You're a terropist, aren't you?'

'Yes.'

'Can't they be fixed, people who are sick in the head? Maybe it's sort of rude to call them sick. Is it? Is he all broken up in the head?'

'All people who have seen war are broken.'

Elsa shrugs. 'He shouldn't have become a soldier, then. It's because of soldiers that we have wars.'

'I don't think he was that sort of soldier. He was a peace soldier.'

'There's only one sort of soldier.' Elsa snorts.

And she knows she's a hypocrite for saying it. Because she hates soldiers and she hates war, but she knows that if Wolfheart had not fought the shadows in the War-Without-End, the entire Land-of-Almost-Awake would have been swallowed up by grey death. And she thinks a lot about that. Times you're allowed to fight, and times when you're not. Elsa thinks about how Granny used to say, 'You have standards and I have double standards, and so I win.' But it doesn't make Elsa feel like a winner.

'Maybe so,' says the woman, in a low voice that skims over Elsa's thoughts.

'You don't have very many patients here, do you?' says Elsa with a pointed nod across the room.

The woman doesn't answer. Her hands fidget with Granny's letter. Elsa sighs impatiently.

'What else does Granny write? Does she say sorry for not being able to save your family?'

The woman's eyes waver.

'Yes. Among . . . among other things.'

Elsa nods.

'And for sending me here?'

'Yes.'

'Why?'

'Because she knew you'd ask a lot of questions. As a psychologist, I suppose I'm used to being the one that asks the questions.'

'What does "Reg. Psychoterropist" mean?'

'Registered psychotherapist.'

'Oh, I thought it had something to do with bombs.'

The woman doesn't quite know how to respond to that one. Elsa throws out her arm defensively, and snorts, 'Well, maybe it sounds stupid now, but it seemed more logical at the time! Everything seems obvious in hindsight!'

The woman does something with the corner of her mouth that Elsa thinks might be a smile of some kind. But it's more like a stiff twitching, as if the muscles round her mouth are new to this game. Elsa looks around the office again. There are no photos here, as there were in the woman's flat. Only books.

'You got any good ones, then?' she asks, scanning the shelves.

'I don't know what you think is good,' the woman answers carefully.

'Do you have any Harry Potters?'

'No.'

'Not even one?' Elsa asks, incredulous.

'No.'

'You have *all these books* and not a *single* Harry Potter? And they let you fix people whose heads are broken?'

The woman doesn't answer. Elsa leans back and tips the chair in that exact way her mum really hates. The woman takes another mint from the tin on the desk. She makes a movement towards Elsa to offer her one, but Elsa shakes her head.

'Do you smoke?' asks Elsa.

The woman looks surprised. Elsa shrugs.

'Granny also used to have a lot of sweets when she couldn't smoke, and she usually wasn't allowed to indoors.'

'I've stopped,' says the woman.

'Stopped or taking a break? It's not the same thing,' Elsa informs her.

The woman nods, setting a new record for slowness.

'That would be more of a philosophical question. So it's difficult to answer.'

Elsa shrugs again.

'Where did you meet Granny? Was it after the wave? Or is that also difficult to answer?'

'It's a long story.'

'I like long stories.'

The woman's hands take cover in her lap.

'I was on holiday. Or . . . we . . . me and my family. We were on holiday. And it happened . . . an accident happened.'

'The tsunami,' says Elsa gently.

The woman's gaze flies round the room and then she says, in passing, as if it only just occurred to her:

'Your grandmother found . . . found me . . .'

The woman sucks so hard on the mint in her mouth that her cheeks look like Granny's that time she was going to 'borrow' petrol from Elsa's dad's Audi by sucking it out of a plastic tube.

'After my husband and my . . . my boys . . .' the woman begins to say. The last words stumble and fall into the chasm between the others as they pass. As if the woman had suddenly forgotten that she was in the middle of a sentence.

'Drowned?' Elsa fills in, and then feels ashamed of herself when she realises that it's probably very unpleasant to speak that word to someone whose family did.

But the woman just nods, without looking angry. And then Elsa switches to the secret language and asks briskly:

'Do you also know our secret language?'

'Excuse me?'

'Ah, nothing,' Elsa mumbles in the usual language and looks down at her shoes.

It was a test. And Elsa is surprised that the sea-angel doesn't know the secret language, because everyone in the Land-of-Almost-Awake knows the secret language. But maybe that's a part of the curse, she thinks.

The woman looks at her watch.

'Shouldn't you be at school?'

Elsa shrugs.

'It's Christmas holidays.'

The woman nods. Probably more or less at a normal speed, now.

'Have you been to Miamas?' asks Elsa.

'Is this some kind of joke?'

'If I'd been joking I would have said, a blind guy walks into a bar. And a table. And a couple of chairs.'

The woman doesn't answer. Elsa throws out her arms.

'You get it? That a b-l-i-n-d guy walks into a bar and a tab—'

The woman looks into her eyes. Smiles faintly.

'I got it. Thanks.'

Elsa shrugs sourly.

'If you get it, laugh.'

The woman takes such a deep breath that if you threw a coin into it you'd never hear it hit the bottom.

'Did you think of that one yourself?' she asks after that.

'Which one?' Elsa counters.

'About the blind guy.'

'No. Granny told me.'

'My boys used to . . . they used to tell jokes like that. Asking something strange and then you had to answer and then they said something and laughed.' As she says the world 'laughed' she stands up, her legs as fragile as the wings of paper planes.

And then everything changes quickly. Her whole manner. Her way of talking. Even her way of breathing.

'I think you should leave now,' she says, standing by the window with her back towards Elsa. Her voice is weak, but almost hostile.

'Why?'

'I want you to leave,' the woman repeats, in a hard voice.

'But why? I've walked halfway across the city to give you Granny's letter and you've hardly had time to tell me anything and now you want me to leave? Do you get how cold it is out there?'

'You . . . shouldn't have come here.'

'I came here because you were Granny's friend.'

'I don't need charity! I can manage on my own,' says the woman grimly.

'Sure, you're really managing bloody well. Really. But I'm not here out of charity,' Elsa manages to reply.

'Well get out then, you little brat! Get the hell out!' hisses the woman, still without turning round.

Elsa starts breathing hard, frightened by the sudden aggression, and insulted by the woman not even looking at her. She hops off the chair with clenched fists.

'Right, then! So my mum was wrong when she said you were just tired! And Granny was right! You're just a bloody—'

And then it goes as with all anger attacks. They don't just consist of one anger, but many. A long series of angers, flung into a volcano in one's breast until it erupts. Elsa is angry at the woman in the black skirt because she doesn't say anything to make anything more understandable in this idiotic fairy tale. And she's angry at Wolfheart for abandoning her because he's afraid of this idiotic psychoterropist. And most of all she's angry

163

at Granny. And this idiotic fairy tale. And all those angers together get too much for her. She knows long before the word leaves her lips how wrong it is to yell it out:

'DRUNK! YOU'RE NOTHING BUT A DRUNK!!!'

She regrets it terribly in the same instant. But it's too late. The woman in the black skirt turns round. Her face is contorted into a thousand broken pieces of a mirror.

'Out!'

'I didn't m . . .', Elsa begins to say, reeling backwards across the office floor, holding out her hands, wanting to apologise.

'Sorr—'

'OOOUUUT!' screams the woman, hysterically clawing at the air as if looking for something to throw at her.

And Elsa runs.

She hurtles along the corridor and down the stairs and through a door to the entrance, sobbing so violently that she loses her footing, tumbles blindly and falls headlong. She feels her backpack whack against the back of her head and waits for the pain when her cheekbone meets the floor. But instead she feels soft, black fur. And then everything bursts for her. She hugs the enormous animal so hard that she can feel it gasping for air.

'Elsa.' Alf's voice can be heard from the front porch. Absolutely cut-and-dried. Not like a question. 'Come on, for Christ's sake,' he grunts. 'Let's go home. You can't lie there bloody sobbing your heart out.'

Elsa wants to yell out the whole story to Alf. Everything about the sea-angel and how Granny sends her out on idiotic adventures and she doesn't even know what she's expected to do, and how Wolfheart abandoned her when she needed him most and everything about Mum and the 'sorry' Elsa had hoped to find here, and everything about Halfie who will come and change everything. How Elsa is drowning in loneliness. She wants to shout it all out to Alf. But she knows he wouldn't understand anyway. Because no one does when you're almost eight.

'What are you doing here?' she sobs.

'You gave me the damned address,' he mutters, 'Someone had to bloody pick you up. I've been driving a taxicab for thirty years, so I know you just don't leave little girls anywhere, any-old-how.' He's quiet for a few breaths before adding, into the floor: 'And your grandmother would have bloody beaten the life out of me if I hadn't picked you up.'

Elsa nods and wipes her face on the wurse's pelt.

'Is that thing coming as well?' Alf asks grouchily. The wurse looks back at him even more grumpily. Elsa nods and tries not to start crying again.

'It'll have to go in the boot, then,' says Alf firmly.

But obviously that is not how things end up. Elsa keeps her face buried in its fur all the way home. It's one of the very, very best things about wurses: they're waterproof.

There's opera coming from the car stereo. At least Elsa thinks it must be opera. She hasn't really heard very much opera, but she's heard it mentioned and she supposes this is what it sounds like. When they're about halfway home, Alf peers with concern at her in the back mirror.

'Is there anything you want?'

'Like what?'

'I don't know. Coffee?'

Elsa raises her head and glares at him.

'I'm seven!'

'What the hell's that got to do with it?'

'Do you know any seven-year-olds who drink coffee?'

'I don't know very many seven-year-olds.'

'I can tell.'

'Well, bloody forget it, then,' he grunts.

Elsa lowers her face into the wurse's pelt. Alf swears a bit in the front, and then after a while he passes her a paper bag. It has the same writing on it as the bakery where Granny always went.

'There's a cinnamon bun in there,' he says, adding, 'But don't bloody cry all over it or it won't taste good.'

Elsa cries on it. It's good anyway.

When they get to the house she runs from the garage up to the flat without even thanking Alf or saying goodbye to the wurse, and without thinking about how Alf has seen the wurse now and might even call the police. Without saying a word to him, she walks right past the dinner that George has put on the kitchen table. When Mum comes home she pretends to be asleep.

And when the drunk starts yelling on the stairs that night, and the singing starts again, Elsa, for the first time, does what all the others in the house do.

She pretends she doesn't hear.

18

SMOKE

Every fairy tale has a dragon. Thanks to Granny, that is . . .

Elsa is having terrible nightmares tonight. She's always dreaded closing her eyes and no longer being able to get to the Land-of-Almost-Awake. The worst thing would be a dreamless sleep. But this is the night she learns of something even worse. Because she can't get to the Land-of-Almost-Awake, and yet she dreams about it. She can see it clearly from above, as if she's lying on her stomach on top of a huge glass dome, peering down at it. Without being able to feel any smells or hear any laughter or feel the rush of wind over her face when the cloud animals take off. It's the most terrifying dream of all the eternities.

Miamas is burning.

She sees all the princes and princesses and the wurses and the dream hunters and the sea-angel and the innocent people of the Land-of-Almost-Awake running for their lives. Behind them the shadows are closing in, banishing imagination and leaving nothing but death as they pass. Elsa tries to find Wolfheart in the inferno, but he's gone. Cloud animals, mercilessly butchered, lie in the ashes. All of Granny's tales are burning.

One figure wanders among the shadows. A slim man enveloped in a cloud of cigarette smoke. That's the only scent Elsa can smell up there on top of the dome, the smell of Granny's tobacco. Suddenly the figure looks up and two clear blue eyes penetrate the haze. A shroud of mist seeps between his thin lips. Then he points directly at Elsa, his forefinger deformed into a grey claw, and he shouts something, and in the next moment hundreds of shadows launch themselves from the ground and engulf her.

Elsa wakes up when she throws herself out of the bed and lands face down against the floor. She cowers there, her chest heaving, her hands covering her throat. It feels as if millions of eternities have passed before she can trust that she's back in the real world. She's not had a single nightmare since Granny and the cloud animals first brought her to the Land-of-Almost-Awake. She had forgotten how nightmares feel. She stands up, sweaty and exhausted, checks to see she's not been bitten by one of the shadows, and tries to get her thoughts into order.

She hears someone talking in the hall and has to muster all her powers of concentration to scatter the mists of sleep and be able to hear what's happening.

'I see! But surely you understand, Ulrika, that it's a bit odd for them to be calling you. Why don't they call Kent? Kent is actually the chairman of this residents' association and I am in charge of information and it's common practice for the accountant to call the chairman with these types of errands. Not just any old person!'

Elsa understands that 'any old person' is an insult. Mum's sigh as she answers is so deep that it feels as if Elsa's bedlinen is ruffled by the draught:

'I don't know why they called me, Britt-Marie. But the accountant said he would come here today to explain everything.'

Elsa opens the bedroom door and stands in her pyjamas in the doorway. Not only Britt-Marie is standing there in the hall; Lennart and Maud and Alf are also there. Samantha is sleeping on the landing. Mum is only wearing her dressing gown, hurriedly tied across her belly. Maud catches sight of Elsa and smiles mildly, with a biscuit tin in her arms. Lennart gulps from a coffee Thermos.

For once Alf doesn't look entirely in a bad mood, which means he only looks irritated in an everyday way. He nods curtly at Elsa, as if she has forced him into a secret. Only then does

Elsa remember that she left him and the wurse in the garage yesterday when she ran up to the flat. Panic wells up inside of her, but Alf glares at her and makes a quick 'stay calm' gesture, so that's what she tries to do. She looks at Britt-Marie and tries to figure out if she's worked up today because she has found the wurse, or if it's a quite normal fuss about the usual Britt-Marie stuff. It seems to be the latter, thank God, but directed at Mum.

'So the landlords have suddenly had the notion that they might be willing to sell the flats to us? After all the years that Kent has been writing them letters! Now they have *suddenly* decided! Just like that, easy-peasy? And then they contact you instead of Kent? That's curious, don't you find that curious, Ulrika?'

Mum tightens her dressing gown sash. 'Maybe they couldn't get hold of Kent. And maybe since I've lived here so long they thought— We've actually lived here the longest, Ulrika. Kent and I have lived here longer than anyone else!'

'Alf has lived in the house the longest,' Mum corrects her.

'Granny has lived here the longest,' Elsa mumbles, but no one seems to hear her. Especially not Britt-Marie.

'Isn't Kent away on a business trip?' asks Mum.

Britt-Marie pauses at this and nods imperceptibly.

'Maybe that's why they didn't get hold of him. That's why I called you as soon as I hung up after speaking to the acc—'

'But surely it's *common practice* to contact the chair-person of the leaseholders' association!' says Britt-Marie with consternation.

'It isn't a leaseholders' association yet,' Mum sighs.

'But it will be!'

'And that is what the landlord's accountant wants to come and talk about today – he says they're finally willing to convert our rental contracts into leaseholds. That's what I've been trying to tell you. As soon as I'd hung up the phone after talking to him I contacted you. And then you woke up the whole house and now here we are. What more do you want me to do, Britt-Marie?'

'What sort of nonsense is that, coming here on a Saturday? Surely one doesn't have meetings like this on a Saturday, surely one doesn't, Ulrika? Do you think one does? Probably you do, Ulrika!'

Mum massages her temples. Britt-Marie inhales and exhales fairly demonstratively and turns to Lennart and Maud and Alf for support. Maud tries to smile encouragingly. Lennart offers Britt-Marie a shot of coffee while they are waiting. Alf looks as if he's now approaching his usual level of ill-humour.

'Well we can't have the meeting without Kent,' Britt-Marie splutters.

'No, of course, only if Kent can make it back,' Mum agrees exhaustedly. 'Why don't you try calling him again?'

'His plane hasn't landed yet! He's actually on a *business trip*, Ulrika!'

Alf grunts something behind them. Britt-Marie spins round. Alf pushes his hands into his jacket pockets and grunts something again.

'Sorry?' say Mum and Britt-Marie at the same time, but in diametrically opposed tones of voice.

'I'm just bloody saying that I sent Kent a text twenty minutes ago when you started making a bloody racket about this, and he got back to tell me he's on his bloody way,' says Alf, and then adds, 'The idiot wouldn't miss this for all the tea in China.'

Britt-Marie seems not to hear the last bit. She brushes invisible dust from her skirt and folds her hands and gives Alf a superior glance, because she knows quite clearly that it's impossible for Kent to be on his way here, because, in fact, his plane hasn't landed yet and, in fact, he's on a business trip. But then there comes the sound of the door slamming on the ground floor and Kent's footsteps. You can tell they're Kent's because someone is screaming German into a telephone, the way Nazis speak in American films.

'Ja, Klaus! JA! We will dizcuzz thiz in Frankfurt!'

Britt-Marie immediately sets off down the stairs to meet him and tell him about the impudence that's been impudent enough to take place here in his absence.

George comes out of the kitchen behind Mum, wearing leggings shorts, a very green jumper and an even greener apron. He gives them an amused look, while holding a smoking frying pan.

'Anyone want some breakfast? I've made eggs.' He looks as if he's going to add that there are also some newly bought protein bars on offer, but seems to change his mind when he realises they may run out.

'I've brought some biscuits,' says Maud expansively, giving Elsa the whole tin and patting her tenderly on the cheek. 'You have that, I can get some more,' she whispers and walks into their flat.

'Is there coffee?' asks Lennart nervously, having another shot of stand-by coffee as he follows her.

Kent strides up the stairs and appears in the doorway. He is wearing jeans and an expensive jacket. Elsa knows that because Kent usually tells her how much his clothes cost, as if he's awarding points in the final of the Eurovision Song Contest. Britt-Marie hurries along behind him, mumbling repeatedly, 'The rudeness, the sheer *rudeness* of not calling you, of just calling any old person. Isn't that just so rude? Things can't be allowed to go on like this, Kent.'

Kent doesn't really acknowledge his wife's raving, but points dramatically at Elsa's mum.

'I want to know *exactly* what the accountant said when he called.'

But before Mum has time to say anything, Britt-Marie brushes off some invisible dust from Kent's arm, and whispers to him in a radically changed tone of voice.

'Maybe you should go down first and change your shirt, Kent?'

'Please, Britt-Marie, we're doing business here,' Kent says dismissively, more or less like Elsa when Mum wants her to wear something green.

She looks crestfallen.

'I can throw it in the machine, come along Kent. There are freshly ironed shirts in your wardrobe. You really can't be wearing a wrinkly shirt when the accountant comes, Kent, what will the accountant think of us then? Will he think we can't iron our shirts?' She laughs nervously.

Mum opens her mouth to try to say something again, but Kent catches sight of George.

'Ah! You've got eggs?' Kent bursts out enthusiastically.

George nods with satisfaction. Kent immediately darts past Mum into the hall. Britt-Marie hurries after him with a frown. When she passes Mum, Britt-Marie looks bothered as she lets slip, 'Oh well, when one is busy with a career like you are, Ulrika, there's no time to clean, of course not.' Even though every millimetre of the flat is in perfect order.

Mum ties the sash of her dressing gown round her a little tighter, and says, with a deeply controlled sigh, 'Just come on in, all of you. Make yourselves at home.'

Elsa dives into her room and changes out of her pyjamas into jeans as quick as she can, so she can run down and check on the wurse in the cellar while everyone is busy up here. Kent interrogates Mum in the kitchen about the accountant and Britt-Marie echoes him with an 'mmm' after every other word.

The only one who stays in the hall is Alf. Elsa sticks her thumbs in her jean pockets and pokes her toes against the edge of the threshold, trying to avoid looking him in the eye.

'Thanks for not saying anything about the . . .' she starts to say, but she stops herself before she has to say 'wurse'.

Alf shakes his head grumpily.

'You shouldn't have rushed off like that. If you've taken that animal on you have to bloody shoulder your responsibility for it, even if you're a kid.'

'I'm not a bloody kid!' snaps Elsa.

'So quit behaving like one, then.'

'Touché,' Elsa whispers at the threshold.

'The animal is in the storage unit. I've put up some sheets of plywood so people can't see inside. Told it to keep its mouth shut. I think it got the point. But you have to find a better hiding place. People will find it sooner or later,' says Alf.

Elsa understands that when he says 'people' he means 'Britt-Marie'. And she knows he's right. She has a terribly bad conscience about abandoning the wurse yesterday. Alf could have called the police and they would have shot it. Elsa abandoned it like Granny abandoned Mum, and this scares her more than any nightmares.

'What are they talking about?' she asks Alf, with a nod towards the kitchen, to shake off the thought.

Alf snorts.

'The bloody leaseholds.'

'What does it mean?'

'Jesus, I can't stand here explaining everything,' he groans. 'The difference between a rental contract and a leasehold in a bloo—'

'I know what a bloody leasehold is, I'm not bloody thick,' says Elsa.

'Why are you asking, then?' says Alf defensively.

'I'm asking what it *means*; why are they all talking about it!' Elsa clarifies, in the way one clarifies things without being very clear at all.

'Kent has been going on about these sodding leaseholds ever since he moved back in, he won't be satisfied until he can wipe his arse with the money he's shat out first,' explains Alf, in the manner of one who doesn't know very many seven-year-olds. At first Elsa is going to ask what Alf meant when he said that Kent 'moved back in,' but she decides to take one thing at a time.

'Won't we all make money? You and Mum and George and all of us?'

'If we sell the flats and move, yeah,' grunts Alf.

Elsa ponders. Alf creaks his leather jacket.

'And that's what Kent wants, the bastard. He's always wanted to move out of here.'

That is why she's having all these nightmares, she realises. Because if the creatures from the Land-of-Almost-Awake turn up in the house now, then maybe the house will start to become a part of the Land-of-Almost-Awake, and if they all want to sell their flats, then . . .

'Then we won't be escaping Miamas. We'll be leaving of our own free will,' says Elsa out loud to herself.

'What?'

'Nothing,' mumbles Elsa.

The door slamming at the bottom of the house echoes through the stairwell. Then discreet footsteps, heading up. It's the accountant.

Britt-Marie drowns out Kent's voice in the kitchen. She doesn't get any response from Kent in so far as the shirt change goes, so she compensates with a lot of indignation about other things. There is a rich supply of such topics. It's difficult for her to decide which is most upsetting, of course, but she has time to run through several matters, including her threat to call the police if Elsa's mum doesn't *immediately* move Granny's car from Britt-Marie's space in the garage, and also that Britt-Marie will make the police break the lock of the pram that's still chained up by the entrance, and that she won't hesitate to put pressure on the landlord to put up cameras on the stairs, so they can stop the vile malpractice of people coming and going as they please and putting up notices without first informing the head of information. She's interrupted by the very short man with the very friendly face now standing in the doorway, knocking tentatively against the door frame.

'I'm the accountant,' he says amicably.

And when he catches sight of Elsa he winks at her. As if they share a secret. Or at least Elsa thinks that's what he means.

Kent steps authoritatively out of the kitchen with his hands on his hips over his overcoat and looks the accountant up and down.

'Well, well? What about these leaseholds, then?' he demands at once. 'What price per square metre are you offering?'

Britt-Marie storms out of the kitchen from behind and points at the accountant accusingly.

'How did you get in?'

'The door was open,' says the accountant amicably.

Kent breaks in impatiently. 'So about the leaseholds: what's your price?'

The accountant points amicably at his briefcase and makes an amicable gesture towards the kitchen.

'Should we sit down, perhaps?'

'There's coffee,' Lennart says expansively.

'And biscuits,' Maud says, with a nod.

'And eggs!' George hollers from the kitchen.

'Please excuse the mess, they're all so preoccupied with their careers in this family,' says Britt-Marie well-meaningly. Mum does her absolute best to pretend she didn't hear that. As they all head into the kitchen, Britt-Marie stops, turns to Elsa and clasps her hands together.

'You do understand, dear, I would obviously never ever think you and your grandmother's friends had anything to do with "junkies". Obviously I'm not to know if the gentleman who was looking for you yesterday took drugs or not. That's not at all what I mean to say.'

Elsa gawks at her, puzzled.

'What? What friends? Who was asking for me yesterday?'

She almost asks 'Was it Wolfheart?' and then stops herself, because she can't imagine how Britt-Marie could possibly know that Wolfheart is her friend.

'Your friend who was here looking for you yesterday. The one I jettisoned from the premises. There's a smoking ban on the stairs, you can tell him that. That is not how we behave in this leaseholders' association. I understand that you and your granny have very curious acquaintances but rules apply to everyone, they really do!' She straightens an invisible wrinkle in her skirt and clasps her hands on her stomach before continuing: 'You know who I mean. He was very slim and stood here smoking on the stairs. He was looking for a child, a family friend, he said, and then he described you. He looked exceedingly unpleasant, actually, so I told him that in this leaseholders' association we do not allow smoking indoors.'

Elsa's heart shrinks. Consumes all the oxygen in her body. She has to hold on to the door frame to stop herself collapsing. No one sees her, not even Alf. But she understands what's about to happen in this adventure now.

Because every fairy tale has a dragon.

19

SPONGE CAKE MIX

Fairy tales from Miamas tell of an infinite number of ways to defeat a dragon. But if this dragon is a shadow, the most evil kind of being one can possibly imagine, and yet it looks like a human, then what? Elsa doubts that even Wolfheart could defeat something like that, even while he was the most renowned warrior in the Land-of-Almost-Awake. And now? When he's afraid of snot and can't wash away the thought of blood from his own fingers?

Elsa doesn't know anything about the shadow. Only that she has seen it twice, the first time at the undertaker's and then from the bus that day on her way to school. And that she's dreamed of it, and now it's come to the house looking for her. And there's no coincidence in Miamas. In fairy tales everything is always exactly as it's meant to be.

So this must have been what Granny meant by 'protect your castle, protect your friends.' Elsa only wishes that Granny had given her an army to do it with.

She waits until late at night, when it's dark enough for a child and a wurse to pass unseen under Britt-Marie's balcony, before she goes down to the cellar. George is out jogging, Mum is still out preparing everything for tomorrow. Since the meeting with the accountant this morning she's been talking endlessly on the telephone with the whale-woman from the undertaker's and the florist and the vicar and then with the hospital and the vicar again. Elsa has been sitting in her room reading

Spider-Man, doing her best not to think of tomorrow. It hasn't gone very well.

She brings the wurse some biscuits she got from Maud and, once the contents have been mopped up, has to snatch back the tin so quickly that she almost gets an incisor manicure. Granny always said that wurse saliva was bloody hard to wash off, and Elsa is planning to give the tin back to Maud. But the wurse, who in all ways is a typical wurse, rummages round quite ravenously in her backpack, apparently having considerable difficulty understanding how she could have come down with just one paltry tin for it.

'I'll try and get you some more biscuits, but for now you're going to have to eat this.' She opens a Thermos. 'This is sponge cake mix. I don't know how to mix it properly though,' she mumbles apologetically. 'I found it in the cupboard in the kitchen and it said "ready sponge cake mix" on the packet but it was only powder. So I added water. It's more like gunk than proper mix.'

The wurse looks sceptical but its towel-sized tongue immediately licks all the gunk out of the Thermos anyway. Just to be on the safe side. An insanely flexible tongue is one of the most prominent superpowers of wurses.

'There's been a man here looking for me,' whispers Elsa into its ear, trying to sound brave. 'I think he's one of the shadows. We have to be on our guard.'

The wurse buffets its nose against her throat. She throws her arms round it, and feels the taut muscles under its fur. It tries to seem playful, but she understands that it's doing what wurses do best: preparing for battle. She loves it for that.

'I don't know where it comes from, Granny never told me about those kinds of dragons.'

The wurse buffets her throat again and looks at her with large, empathic eyes. It seems to be wishing it could tell her everything. Elsa wishes Wolfheart was here. She rang his door just now but there was no answer. She didn't want to call out, in case Britt-Marie smelled a rat, but she made a loud sniffing

178

sound through the letter box to clearly signal she was about to sneeze the kind of sticky sneeze that instantly covers everything in camouflage paint. It had no effect.

'Wolfheart has disappeared,' she finally admits to the wurse.

Elsa tries to be brave. It goes quite well while they are walking through the cellar. And it's quite OK while they go up the cellar stairs. But when they're standing in the vestibule inside the main door she feels the smell of tobacco smoke, the same kind of tobacco that Granny used to smoke, and a lingering fear from her nightmare paralyses her. Her shoes weigh a thousand tonnes. Her head thumps as if something has worked itself loose and is rattling around in there.

It's strange how quickly the significance of a certain smell can change, depending on what path it decides to take through the brain. It's strange how close love and fear live to each other.

She tells herself she's just imagining it, but it doesn't help. The wurse stands patiently next to her, but her shoes won't budge.

A newspaper blows past outside the window. It's the kind of newspaper you get through the letter box even if you have a 'No junk mail, please!' sticker on the door. It reminds Elsa of Granny. She stands there, still frozen, and the newspaper makes her angry, because it's Granny who put her in this situation. It's all Granny's fault.

Elsa remembers the time Granny called the newspaper office and gave them a roasting for putting it in her letter box even though she had a 'No junk mail, ever. Thanks!' message in surprisingly clear letters on the door. Elsa had thought a lot about why it said 'Thanks!' because Elsa's mum always said that if one can't say thanks as if one means it, one may as well not bother. And it didn't sound like the note on Granny's door meant it at all.

But the people answering the telephone at the office of the newspaper told Granny their newspaper wasn't in the business of advertising but in fact 'social information', which can be put in people's letter boxes irrespective of whether people thank them not to do so. Granny had demanded to know who owned the company that produced the newspaper, and after that she demanded a word with him. The people at the other end of the telephone line said that surely Granny could understand that the owner did not have time for this sort of nonsense.

Of course, they shouldn't have said that, because there were actually an awful lot of things that Granny didn't 'surely understand' at all. Also, unlike the man who owned the company that produced the free newspaper, she had a lot of spare time. 'Never mess with someone who has more spare time than you do,' Granny used to say. Elsa used to translate that as, 'Never mess with someone who's perky for her age.'

In the following days Granny had picked up Elsa as usual from school, and then they'd patrolled the block with yellow IKEA carrier bags, ringing all the doorbells. People seemed to find it a bit weird, especially as everyone knows you're actually not allowed to take those yellow IKEA bags from the store. If anyone started asking too many questions, Granny just said they were from an environmental organisation collecting recyclable paper. And then people didn't dare make any more fuss. 'People are afraid of environmental organisations, they think we'll storm the flat and accuse them of not handling their waste properly. They watch too many films,' Granny had explained as she and Elsa loaded the stuffed carrier bags into Renault. Elsa never quite understood what kinds of films Granny had seen, and where that sort of thing would ever happen. She did know that Granny hated environmental organisations, which she called 'panda fascists'.

Whatever the case, you're actually not supposed to take those yellow carrier bags out of the store. Of course, Granny had just shrugged it off. 'I never stole the bags, I just haven't given them back yet,' she muttered and gave Elsa a thick felt-tip pen to write with. And then Elsa said she wanted at least four tubs of Ben & Jerry's New York Super Fudge Chunk for this. And then Granny said 'One!' and then Elsa said 'Three!' and then Granny said 'Two!' and then Elsa said, 'Three, or I'm telling Mum!' and then Granny yelled, 'I'm not negotiating with terrorists!' And then Elsa pointed out that if one looked up 'terrorist' on Wikipedia there were quite a lot of things in the definition of the word that applied to Granny but not a single one that applied to Elsa. 'The goal of terrorists is to create chaos and Mum says that's exactly what you're busy doing all day long,' said Elsa. And then Granny had agreed to give Elsa four tubs if she just took the felt-tip pen and promised to keep her mouth shut. And so that's what Elsa did. Late into the night she'd sat in the dark in Renault on the other side of town, on guard duty, while Granny ran in and out of houses' entrances with her yellow IKEA carrier bags. The next morning the man who owned the company that produced the free newspaper was woken by the neighbours ringing his doorbell, very upset because someone had apparently filled the lift with hundreds of copies of the free newspaper. Every letter box was stuffed full of them, and every square centimetre of the large glass entrance door had been covered in taped-up copies and, outside every flat, great tottering piles had been left that collapsed and fell down the stairs when the doors were opened. On every copy of the newspaper, the man's name had been written in large, neat felt-tip letters, and just below, 'Complimentary social information, for yor reading plesure!!!'

On the way back home, Granny and Elsa had stopped at a petrol station to buy ice cream. A few days later Granny called the newspaper once again, and after that she never received a single free copy.

'Coming in or going?'

Alf's voice cuts through the gloom of the stairwell like laughter. Elsa turns round and instinctively wants to throw herself into his arms, but she stops herself because she realises he would probably dislike that almost as much as Wolfheart would. He shoves his hands in his pockets with a creak of his leather jacket and nods sharply at the door.

'In or out? There are others apart from you who fancy a bloody walk, you know.'

Elsa and the wurse give him blank looks. He mutters something and goes past them and opens the door. Immediately they fall into step just behind him, though he never asked for their company. When they've gone round the corner of the house, out of sight from Britt-Marie's balcony, the wurse backs into a bush and growls at them as politely as can be expected of a wurse in need of a bit of concentration. They turn away; Alf looks unamused in every possible way by his uninvited company. Elsa clears her throat and tries to think of something to make small-talk about, to keep him there.

'The car's going well, is it?' she bursts out, because that's what she's heard her dad say when he's at a loss.

Alf nods. Nothing more. Elsa breathes loudly.

'What did the accountant say at the meeting?' she asks instead, in the hope that this might make Alf as upset and talkative as he gets at the residents' meetings. It's easier to get people talking about things they dislike than things they like, Elsa has noticed. And it's easier not to get frightened of shadows in the dark when someone is talking, whatever they're talking about.

'That accountant bastard said the owners had decided to sell the bloody flats to the residents' association bastards, if everyone in the house agrees.'

Elsa observes the corners of his mouth. He almost seems to be smiling.

'Is that funny?'

'Are you living in the same house as me? They'll solve the Israel–Palestine conflict before people in this house agree about anything.'

'Will anyone want to sell their flat if the house is converted to leaseholds?' she asks.

The corners of Alf's mouth flatten into a more Alf-like shape.

'I don't know about wanting, most will bloody well have to.'

'Why?'

'Good area. Expensive bloody flats. Most people in the house won't be able to afford that kind of bastard bank loan.'

'Will you have to move?'

'Probably.'

'Mum and George and me, then?'

'I don't bloody know, do I?'

Elsa thinks.

'What about Maud and Lennart?'

'You've got a bloody lot of questions.'

'Well what are you doing out here if you don't want to talk?'

Alf's jacket creaks towards the wurse in the bush.

'I was only going for a bloody walk. No one bloody invited you and that thing.'

'It's just insane how much you swear, did anyone ever tell you that? My dad says it's a sign of a bad vocabulary.'

Alf glares at her and shoves his hands in his pockets.

'Maud and Lennart will have to move. And the girl and her kid on the first bloody floor as well, most likely. The psychologist bastard you went to yesterday, I don't know, she probably has a hell of a lot of money . . .'

He stops himself. Summons some kind of self-restraint.

'That . . . lady. She probably has a . . . heck of a lot of money, that . . . woman,' he self-corrects.

'What did my granny think about it?'

There's another brief twitch at the corners of Alf's mouth.

'Usually the diametric opposite of what Britt-Marie thought.'

Elsa draws miniature snow-angels with her shoe.

'Maybe it'll be good? If there are leaseholds then maybe everyone can move somewhere . . . good?' she says tentatively.

'It's good here. We're doing fine here. This is our bloody home.'

Elsa doesn't protest. This is her home too.

Another free newspaper tumbles past in the wind. It gets caught on her foot for a moment, before it tears itself free and keeps rolling like an angry little star fish. It makes Elsa furious again. Gets her thinking about how much Granny was willing to fight to get them to stop putting newspapers in her letter box. It makes Elsa furious because it was a typical Granny thing to do, because Granny was only doing it for Elsa's sake. Granny things were always like that. For Elsa's sake.

Because Granny actually liked those newspapers, she used to stuff them into her shoes when it had been raining. But one day when Elsa read on the internet how many trees it took to make just one edition of a newspaper, she put up 'No junk mail ever, thanks!' notices on both Mum and Granny's doors, because Elsa is a big fan of the environment. The newspapers kept coming, and when Elsa called the company they just laughed at her. And they shouldn't have done that. Because no one laughs at Granny's grandchild.

Granny hated the environment, but she was the kind of person you brought along when you were going to war. So she became a terrorist for Elsa's sake. Elsa is furious at Granny for that, in fact, because Elsa wants to be furious at Granny. For everything else. For the lies and for abandoning Mum and for dying. But it's impossible to stay angry at someone who's prepared to turn terrorist for the sake of her grandchild. And it makes Elsa furious that she can't be furious.

She can't even be angry at Granny in a normal way. Not even that is normal about Granny.

She stands in silence next to Alf and blinks until her head hurts. Alf tries to look unconcerned but Elsa notices that he's scanning the darkness, as if looking for someone. He watches their surroundings much like Wolfheart and the wurse. As if he's also on guard duty. She squints and tries to fit him into Granny's life, like a piece of a puzzle. She can't recall Granny ever talking very much about him, except that he never knew how to lift his feet, which was why the soles of his shoes were always so worn down.

'How well did you know Granny?' she asks.

The leather jacket creaks.

'What do you mean, "knew"? We were bloody neighbours, that's all,' Alf answers evasively.

'So what did you mean when you picked me up in the taxi, when you said Granny "would never have forgiven" you if you'd left me there?'

More creaking.

'I didn't mean anything, not a blo— nothing. I just happened to be in the area. Bloody . . .'

He sounds frustrated. Elsa nods, pretending to understand in a way that Alf clearly doesn't appreciate at all.

'Why are you here, then?' she asks teasingly.

'What?'

'Why did you follow me outside? Shouldn't you be driving your taxi now or something?'

'You don't have a blo— you don't have exclusive rights to taking walks, you know.'

'Sure, sure.'

'I can't let you and the mutt run loose here at night on your own. Your granny would have blo—'

He interrupts himself. Grunts. Sighs.

'Your granny would never have forgiven me if something happened to you.'

He looks as if he already regrets saying that.

'Did you and Granny have an affair?' Elsa asks, after waiting for what seems a more than adequate length of time. Alf looks like she just threw a yellow snowball in his face.

'Aren't you a bit young to know what that means?'

'There are loads of things I'm too young to know about, but I know about them anyway.' She clears her throat and carries on: 'Once when I was small, Mum was going to explain what her work was, because I'd asked Dad and he didn't really seem to know. And then Mum said she worked as an economist. And then I said, "What?" and then she said, "I work out how much money the hospital has, so we know what we can buy." And then I said, "What, like in a shop?" And then she said that, yeah, sort of like in a shop, and it wasn't hard to get it at all and so really Dad was being a bit thick about it.

Alf checks his watch.

'But then, anyway, I saw a TV series where two people had a shop. They were also having an affair, or at least I think they did. So now I get what it means, sort of thing. And I thought that was kind of how you and Granny knew each other! So . . . did you or didn't you?'

'Is that mutt done now or what? Some of us have jobs to go to,' Alf mutters, which isn't much of an answer. He turns towards the bushes.

Elsa scrutinises him thoughtfully.

'I just thought you could be Granny's type. Because you're a bit younger than she is. And she always flirted with policemen who were about your age. They were sort of too old to be policemen but they were still policemen. Not that you're a policeman, I mean. But you're also old without being . . . really old. Get what I mean?'

Alf doesn't look like he really gets it. And he looks like he's got a bit of a migraine.

The wurse finishes, and the three of them head back inside, Elsa in the middle. It's not a big army, but it's an army, thinks Elsa and feels a little less afraid of the dark. When they part ways in the cellar between the door to the garage and the door to the storage units, Elsa scrapes her shoe against the floor and asks Alf. 'What was that music you were listening to in the car when you came to pick me up? Was it opera?'

'Holy Christ, enough questions!'

'I was only asking!'

'Blo . . . yeah. It was a bastard opera.'

'What language was it in?'

'Italian.'

'Can you talk Italian?'

'Yeah.'

'For real?'

'What other bloody way is there to know Italian?'

'But, like, fluently?'

'You have to find another hiding place for that thing, I told you,' he says gesturing at the wurse, clearly trying to change the subject. 'People will find it sooner or later.'

'Do you know Italian or not?'

'I know enough to understand an opera. You got any other bast— questions?'

'What was that opera about in the car, then?' she persists.

Alf pulls open the garage door.

'Love. They're all about love, the whole lot.'

He pronounces the world 'love' a little as one would say words like 'white goods' or 'two-inch screw'.

'WERE YOU IN LOVE WITH MY GRANNY THEN?' Elsa yells after him, but he's already slammed the door.

She stays there, grinning. The wurse does too, she's almost sure about that. And it's much more difficult being afraid of shadows and the dark while grinning.

'I think Alf is our friend now,' she whispers.

The wurse looks like it agrees.

'We're going to need all the friends we can get. Because Granny didn't tell me what happens in this fairy tale.'

The wurse snuggles up against her.

'I miss Wolfheart,' Elsa whispers into its fur.

Reluctantly, the wurse seems to agree with that too.

20

CLOTHES SHOP

Today's the day. And it starts with the most terrible night.

Elsa wakes with her mouth wide open but her scream fills her head rather than the room. She roars silently and reaches out with her hand to toss aside the bedclothes, but they're already on the floor. She walks into the flat – it smells of eggs. George smiles carefully at her from the kitchen. She doesn't smile back. He looks upset. She doesn't care.

She has a shower so hot her skin feels as if it's about to come away from her flesh like clementine peel. Walks out into the flat. Mum left home hours ago. She's gone to fix everything, because that is what Mum does.

George calls out something behind Elsa, but she neither listens nor answers. She puts on the clothes that Mum has put out for her and crosses the landing, locking the front door behind her. Granny's flat smells wrong. It smells clean. The towers of removal boxes throw shadows across the hall, like monuments to everything that is now absent.

She stands inside the door, incapable of going any further inside. She was here last night, but it's more difficult by daylight. It's harder work remembering things when the sun is forcing its way in through the blinds. Cloud animals soar past in the sky. It's a beautiful morning but a terrible day.

Elsa's skin is still burning after her shower. It makes her think of Granny, because Granny's shower hadn't worked in over a year, and instead of calling the landlord and asking him to sort out the problem, she just used Mum and George's shower. And sometimes she forgot to do up her dressing gown when she went back through the flat. And sometimes she forgot her dressing gown altogether. Once, Mum shouted at her for what must have been fifteen minutes because she didn't show any respect about George also living in Mum and Elsa's flat. But that was soon after Elsa had starting reading the collected works of Charles Dickens. Granny was not much use at reading books, so Elsa used to read them to her while they were driving Renault, because Elsa wanted to have someone she could discuss them with afterwards. Especially *A Christmas Carol*, which Elsa had read several times, because Granny liked Christmas stories.

So when Mum said that thing about how Granny shouldn't run about naked in the flat, out of respect to George, then Granny, still naked, turned to George and said, 'What's all this respect rubbish? You're cohabiting with my daughter, for goodness sake.' And then Granny bowed very deeply and very nakedly and added ceremoniously: 'I am the spirit of future Christmases, George!'

Mum was very angry at Granny about that, but she tried not to show it, for Elsa's sake. So, for Mum's sake, Elsa tried not to show how proud she was of Granny for being able to quote Charles Dickens.

Elsa goes into the flat without taking off her shoes. She's wearing the kind of shoes that scratch the parquet flooring, so Mum has told her she can't wear them inside, but it doesn't matter in Granny's place, because the floor already looks as if someone went skating on it. Partly because it's old, and partly because Granny actually once went skating on it.

Elsa opens the door of the big wardrobe. The wurse licks her face. It smells of protein bars and sponge cake mix. Elsa had just gone to bed last night when she realised that Mum would most likely send George down to the cellar storage unit today to get the spare chairs, because everyone is coming here afterwards for coffee. Because today is the day, and everyone drinks coffee somewhere after days like this.

Mum and George's cellar unit is next to Granny's unit, and it's the only storage unit you can see the wurse from now that Alf has put up the plywood sheets. So Elsa sneaked down in the night, unable to decide whether she was more afraid of shadows or ghosts or Britt-Marie, and brought the wurse upstairs.

'There would be more space to hide you in here if Granny wasn't dead,' says Elsa apologetically, because then the wardrobe wouldn't have stopped growing. 'Then again, if Granny hadn't died you wouldn't need to hide in the first place.'

The wurse licks her face again and squeezes its head through the opening and looks for her backpack. Elsa runs to fetch it from the hall and pulls out three tins of dreams and a litre of milk.

'Maud left them with Mum last night,' Elsa explains, but when the wurse immediately starts snuffling her hands as if about to eat the biscuits with the tin still round them, she raises an admonishing forefinger.

'You can only have two tins! One is for ammunition!'

The wurse barks at her a bit about that, but in the end recognises its poor bargaining position and only polishes off two of the tins and half of the third. It is a wurse, after all. And these are biscuits.

Elsa takes the milk and goes looking for her moo-gun. She's a bit slow on the uptake today. Because she hasn't had any nightmares in years, she's only realising now that she may need it. The first time the shadow came to her in the nightmare, she tried to shake it all off the next morning. As you do. Tried to persuade herself that 'it was only a nightmare.' But she should have known better. Because everyone who has ever been in the Land-Of-Almost-Awake knows better.

So last night when she had the same dream, she realised where she had to go to fight the nightmares. To reclaim her nights from them.

'Mirevas!' she calls out firmly to the wurse, when it comes out of one of Granny's smaller wardrobes followed by an unnameable jumble of things that Mum has not yet had time to put into boxes.

'We have to go to Mirevas!' announces Elsa to the wurse, waving her moo-gun.

Mirevas, one of the kingdoms adjoining Miamas, is the smallest principality in the Land-of-Almost-Awake and for that reason almost forgotten. When children in the Land-of-Almost-Awake are learning geography and have to reel off the names of the six kingdoms, Mirevas is the one they always forget. Even those who live there. Because the Mirevasians are incredibly humble, kindly and cautious creatures, who go to great lengths to avoid taking up unnecessary space or causing the slightest inconvenience. Yet they have a very important task, actually one of the most important tasks in a kingdom where imagination is the most important thing you can have: for it is in Mirevas that the nightmare hunters are trained.

Only smart-arses in the real world who don't know any better would say something as idiotic as 'it was only a nightmare.' There are no 'only' nightmares – they're living creatures, dark little clouds of insecurity and anguish that come sneaking between the houses when everyone is asleep, trying all the doors and windows to find some place to slip inside and start causing a commotion. And that is why there are nightmare hunters. And anyone who knows anything about anything knows one has to have a moo-gun to chase a nightmare. Someone who doesn't know better might mistake a moo-gun for a quite ordinary paintball gun customised by someone's granny with a milk carton at the side and a catapult glued to the top. Elsa, though, knows what she's got in her hands. She loads the carton with milk and puts a biscuit in the firing chamber in front of the rubber band on the biscuit gun.

You can't kill a nightmare, but you can scare it. And there's nothing so feared by nightmares as milk and biscuits.

Just as she's starting to feel more confident, though, she's startled by the doorbell, and to the infinite chagrin of the wurse she accidentally fires loads of milk at it but no biscuit, and it scurries off in a huff. For a moment she wonders how a nightmare can be ringing the doorbell, but it's only George. He looks upset. She doesn't care.

191

'I'm going down to pick up the spare chairs in the cellar storage,' he says and tries to smile at her like stepdads do on days when they have an extra-strong sense of being sidelined.

Elsa shrugs and slams the door in his face. The wurse has reappeared, so she climbs onto its back and peers out of the spyhole to see George lingering there for what must be a minute, looking upset. Elsa hates him for that. Mum always tells Elsa that George just wants her to like him because he cares. As if Elsa doesn't get that. She knows he cares, and that's why she can't like him. Not because she wouldn't like him if she tried, but rather because she knows she definitely would. Because everyone likes George. It's his superpower.

And she knows that in this case she'll only be disappointed when Halfie is born and George forgets she exists. It's better not to like him from the start.

If you don't like people they can't hurt you. Almost-eight-year-olds who are often described as 'different' learn that very quickly.

She jumps down from the wurse's back. The wurse closes its jaws round the moo-gun and gently but firmly takes it away from her, then shambles off and puts it on a stool out of reach of her trigger finger. But it avoids eating the biscuit, which, as anyone who understands just how much wurses love biscuits, is a significant sign of respect for Elsa.

There's another ring at the door. Elsa throws it open and is just about to snap impatiently at George when she realises just in time that it's not George.

There's a silence lasting for probably half a dozen eternities.

'Hello, Elsa,' says the woman in the black skirt, sounding a bit lost. She's wearing jeans, not a black skirt, today, admittedly. And she smells of mint and looks scared. She breathes so slowly that Elsa fears she's about to expire from a shortage of oxygen.

'I'm . . . I'm very sorry I shouted at you in my office,' she begins.

They scrutinise each other's shoes.

'It's cool,' Elsa manages to say at last.

The corners of the woman's mouth vibrate gently.

'I was a bit caught off guard when you came to the office. I don't get many people visiting me there. I'm . . . I'm not so good at visits.'

Elsa nods guiltily without looking up from the woman's shoes.

'It doesn't matter. Sorry for saying that about . . .' she whispers, unable to get out the last few words.

The woman waves her hand dismissively.

'It was my fault. It's difficult for me to talk about my family. Your grandmother tried to make me do it, but it only made me . . . well . . . angry.'

Elsa pokes at the floor with the tip of her toe.

'People drink wine to forget things that are hard, right?'

'Or to have the strength to remember. I think.'

Elsa snuffles.

'You're also broken, right? Like Wolfheart?'

'Broken in . . . in another way. Maybe.'

'Couldn't you mend yourself, then?'

'You mean because I'm a psychologist?'

Elsa nods. 'Doesn't that work?'

'I don't think surgeons can operate on themselves. It's probably more or less the same thing.'

Elsa nods again. For an instant the woman in the jeans looks as if she's about to reach out towards her, but she stops herself and absent-mindedly scratches the palm of her hand instead.

'Your granny wrote in the letter that she wanted me to look after you,' she whispers.

Elsa nods.

'That's what she writes in all the letters, apparently.'

'You sound angry.'

'She didn't write any letters to me.'

The woman reaches into a bag on the floor and gets something out.

'I . . . I bought these Harry Potter books yesterday. I haven't had time to get very far yet, but, you know.'

'What made you change your mind?'

'I . . . I understand Harry Potter is important to you.'

'Harry Potter is important for everyone!'

The skin around the woman's mouth cracks again. She takes another long, deep breath, looks into Elsa's eyes and says:

'I like him a lot too, that's what I wanted to say. It's been a long time since I had such an amazing reading experience. You almost never do, once you grow up, things are at their peak when you're a child and then it's all downhill from there . . . well . . . because of the cynicism, I suppose. I just wanted to thank you for reminding me of how things used to be.'

Those are more words than Elsa has ever heard the woman say without stuttering. The woman offers her what's in the bag. Elsa takes it. It's also a book. A fairy tale. *The Brothers Lionheart*, by Astrid Lindgren. Elsa knows that, because it's one of her favourite stories that doesn't come from the Land-of-Almost-Awake. She read it aloud to Granny many times while they were driving around in Renault. It's about Karl and Jonatan, who die and come to Nangijala, where they have to fight the tyrant Tengil and the dragon Katla.

The woman's gaze loses its footing again.

'I used to read it to my boys when their granny died. I don't know if you've read it. You probably have.'

Elsa shakes her head and holds the book tightly.

'No,' she lies. Because she's polite enough to know that if someone gives you a book you owe that person the pretence that you haven't read it.

The woman in jeans looks relieved. Then she takes such a deep breath that Elsa fears her wishbone is about to snap.

'You know . . . you asked if we met at the hospital. Your granny and I. After the tsunami I . . . they . . . they had laid out all the dead bodies in a little square. So families and friends could look for their . . . after . . . I . . . I mean, she found me there. In the square. I had been sitting there for . . . I don't know. Several weeks. I think. She flew me home and she said I could live here until I knew where I was . . . was going.'

Her lips open and close, in turn, as if they're electric.

'I just stayed here. I just . . . stayed.'

Elsa looks down at her own shoes this time.

'Are you coming today?' she asks.

In the corner of her eye she can see the woman shaking her head. As if she wants to run away again.

'I don't think I . . . I think your grandmother was very disappointed in me.'

'Maybe she was disappointed in you because you're so disappointed in yourself.'

There's a choking sound in the woman's throat. It takes a while before Elsa understands it's probably laughter. As if that part of her throat had been in disuse and has just found the key to itself and flicked some old electrical switch.

'You're really a very different little child,' says the woman.

'I'm not a little child. I'm almost eight!'

'Yes, sorry. You were a newborn. When I moved in here. Newborn.'

'There's nothing wrong with being different. Granny said that only different people change the world.'

'Yes. Sorry. I . . . I have to go. I just wanted to say . . . sorry.'

'It's OK. Thanks for the book.'

The woman's eyes hesitate, but she looks straight at Elsa again.

'Has your friend come back? Wolf – what was it you called him?'

Elsa shakes her head. There's something in the woman's eyes that actually looks like genuine concern.

'He does that sometimes. Disappears. You shouldn't worry. He . . . gets scared of people. Disappears for a while. But he always comes back. He just needs time.'

'I think he needs help.'

'It's hard to help those who don't want to help themselves.'

'Someone who wants to help himself is possibly not the one who's most in need of other people's help,' Elsa objects.

The woman nods, without answering.

'I have to go,' she repeats.

Elsa wants to stop her but she's already halfway down the stairs. She has almost disappeared on the floor below when Elsa leans over the railing, gathers her strength and calls out:

'Did you find them? Did you find your boys in the square?'

The woman stops. Holds the banister very hard.

'Yes.'

Elsa bites her lip.

'Do you believe in life after death?'

The woman looks up at her.

'That's a difficult question.'

'I mean, you know, do you believe in God?' asks Elsa.

'Sometimes it's hard to believe in God,' answers the woman.

'Because you wonder why God didn't stop the tsunami?'

'Because I wonder why there are tsunamis at all.'

Elsa nods.

'I saw someone in a film once say, "faith can move mountains",' Elsa goes on, without knowing why, maybe mainly because she doesn't want to lose sight of the woman before she has time to ask the question she really wants to ask.

'So I hear,' says the woman.

Elsa shakes her head.

'But you know that's actually true! Because it comes from Miamas, from a giant called Faith. She was so strong it was insane. And she could literally move mountains!'

The woman looks as if she's trying to find a reason to disappear down the stairs. Elsa takes a quick breath.

'Everyone says I may miss Granny now but it'll pass. I'm not so sure.'

The woman looks up at her again. With her empathic eyes.

'Why not?'

'It hasn't passed for you.'

The woman half-closes her eyes.

'Maybe it's different.'

'How?'

'Your granny was old.'

'Not to me. I only knew her for seven years. Almost eight.'

The woman doesn't answer. Elsa rubs her hands together like Wolfheart does.

'You should come today!' Elsa calls out after her but the woman has already disappeared.

Elsa hears the door of her flat closing and then everything is silent until she hears Dad's voice from the door at the bottom.

She collects herself and wipes her tears and forces the wurse to hide in the wardrobe again with half of the moo-gun ammunition as a bribe. Then she closes the door of Granny's flat without locking it and runs down the stairs, and a few moments later she's lying in Audi with the seat reclined as far as it'll go, staring out of the glass ceiling.

The cloud animals are soaring lower now. Dad is wearing a suit and is also silent. It feels strange, because Dad hardly ever wears a suit. But today is the day.

'Do you believe in God, Dad?' asks Elsa, in the way that always catches him unaware like water balloons thrown from a balcony. Elsa knows that because Granny loved water balloons and Dad learned never to walk right beneath her balcony.

'I don't know,' he answers.

Elsa hates him for not having an answer but she loves him a bit for not lying. Audi stops outside a black steel gate. They sit for a while, waiting.

'Am I like Granny?' says Elsa without taking her eyes off the sky.

'You mean in physical appearance?' asks Dad, hesitantly.

'No, like, as a *person*,' sighs Elsa.

Dad looks as if he's fighting his hesitation for a moment, like you do when you have daughters aged about eight. It's almost as if Elsa has just asked him to explain where babies come from. Again.

'You must stop saying "like" and "sort of" all the time. Only people with a bad vocabulary—' he begins to say instead, because he can't stop himself. Because that's the way he is. One of those who find it very important to say 'one of those' and not 'one of them'.

'So bloody leave it then!' Elsa snaps, much more vehemently than she means to, because she's not in the mood for his corrections today.

Usually it's their thing, correcting one another. Their only thing. Dad has a word jar, where Elsa puts difficult words she has learned, like 'concise' and 'pretentious', or complex phrases like 'My fridge is a taco sauce graveyard.' And every time the jar is full she gets a gift voucher for a book to download on the iPad. The word jar has financed the entire Harry Potter series for her, although she knows Dad is ridiculously dubious about Harry Potter because Dad can't get his head round a story unless it's based on reality.

'Sorry,' mumbles Elsa.

Dad sinks into his seat. They compete at seeing who can feel most ashamed. Then he says, slightly less tentatively:

'Yes. You're very much like her. You've got all your best qualities from her and your mother.'

Elsa doesn't answer, because she doesn't know if that was the answer she wanted. Dad doesn't say anything either, because he's unsure whether that was what he should have said. Elsa wants to tell him she wants to stay with him more. Every other weekend is not enough. She wants to yell at him that once Halfie comes along and is quite normal, George and Mum won't want to have Elsa at home any more, because parents want normal children, not different children. And Halfie will stand next to Elsa and remind them of all the differences between them. She wants to yell that Granny was wrong, that different is not always good, because different is a mutation and almost no one in *X-Men* has a family.

She wants to yell out the whole thing. But she doesn't. Because she knows he'd never understand. And she knows he wouldn't want her to live with him and Lisette because Lisette has her own children. Undifferent children.

Dad sits in silence like you do when you don't feel like wearing a suit. But just as Elsa opens Audi's door to jump out, he turns to her hesitantly and says in a low voice:

'. . . but there are moments when I sincerely hope that not ALL your best traits come from Granny and Mum, Elsa.'

And then Elsa squeezes her eyes together tightly and puts her forehead against his shoulder and her fingers into her jacket pocket and spins the lid of the red felt-tip pen that he gave her when she was small, so she could add her own punctuation marks, and which is still the best present he's ever given her. Or anyone.

'You gave me your words,' she whispers.

He tries to blink his pride out of his eyes. She sees that. And she wants to tell him that she lied to him last Friday. That she was the one who sent the SMS from Mum's phone about how he didn't have to pick her up from school. But she doesn't want to disappoint him, so she stays quiet. Because you hardly ever disappoint anybody if you just stay quiet. All almost-eight-year-olds know that.

Dad kisses her hair. She raises her head and pretends to say in passing, 'Will you and Lisette have children?'

'I don't think so,' Dad replies sadly, as if it's quite self-evident.

'Why not?'

'We have all the children we need.'

And it sounds as if he stops himself from saying 'more than we need'. Or at least that's how it feels.

'Is it because of me you don't want more children?' she asks and hopes he'll say 'no'.

'Yes,' he says.

'Because I turned out different?' she whispers.

He doesn't answer. And she doesn't wait. But just as she's about to slam the door of Audi from the outside, Dad reaches across the seat and catches her fingertips and when she meets his eyes he looks back tentatively, like he always does. But then he whispers:

'Because you turned out to be perfect.'

She's never heard him so non-tentative. And if she'd said that aloud, he would have told her that there's no such word. And she loves him for that.

* * *

199

George stands by the gate looking sad. He's also wearing a suit. Elsa runs past him and Mum catches hold of her, her mascara running, and Elsa presses her face against Halfie. Mum's dress smells of boutique. The cloud animals are flying low.

And that's the day they bury Elsa's granny.

21

CANDLE GREASE

There are storytellers in the Land-of-Almost-Awake who say we all have an inner voice, whispering to us what we must do, and all we must do is listen. Elsa has never really believed it, because she doesn't like the thought of someone else having a voice inside her, and Granny always said that only psychologists and murderers have 'inner voices'. Granny never liked proper psychology. Though she really did try with the woman in the black skirt.

But, in spite of all, in a moment Elsa will hear a voice in her head as clear as a bell. It won't be whispering, it will be yelling. It will be yelling 'Run!' And Elsa will run for her life. With the shadow behind her.

Of course, she doesn't know that when she goes into the church. The quiet murmuring of hundreds of strangers rises towards the ceiling, like the hissing of a broken car stereo. The legions of smart-arses point at her and whisper. Their eyes are oppressive.

She doesn't know who they are and it makes her feel tricked. She doesn't want to share Granny with others. She doesn't want to be reminded of how Granny was her only friend, while Granny herself had hundreds of others.

She concentrates hard on walking straight-backed through the crush, doesn't want them to see that she feels as if she's going to collapse any moment and doesn't even have the strength to be upset any more. The church floor sucks at her feet, the coffin up there stings her eyes.

'The mightiest power of death is not that it can make people die, but that it can make the people left behind want to stop living,' she thinks, without remembering where she heard that. On second thought she decides it probably comes from the Land-of-Almost-Awake, although this seems unlikely when one considers what Granny thought about death. Death was Granny's nemesis. That's why she never wanted to talk about it. And that was also why she became a surgeon, to cause death as much aggravation as she could.

But it might also come from Miploris, realises Elsa. Granny never wanted to ride to Miploris when they were in the Land-of-Almost-Awake, but sometimes she did it anyway because of Elsa's nagging. And sometimes Elsa rode there on her own when Granny was at some inn in Miamas playing poker with a troll or arguing about wine with a snow-angel.

Miploris is the most beautiful of all the kingdoms of the Land-of-Almost-Awake. The trees sing there, the grass massages the soles of your feet and there's always a smell of fresh-baked bread. The houses are so beautiful that, to be on the safe side, you have to be sitting down when you look at them. But no one lives there, they are only used for storage. For Miploris is where all fairy creatures bring their sorrow, and where all leftover sorrow is stored. For an eternity of all fairy tales.

People in the real world always say, when something terrible happens, that the sadness and loss and aching pain of the heart will 'lessen as time passes', but it isn't true. Sorrow and loss are constant, but if we all had to go through our whole lives carrying them the whole time, we wouldn't be able to stand it. The sadness would paralyse us. So in the end we just pack it into bags and find somewhere to leave it.

That is what Miploris is: a kingdom where lone storytelling travellers come slowly wandering from all directions, dragging unwieldy luggage full of sorrow. A place where they can put it down and go back to life. And when the travellers turn back, they do so with lighter steps, because Miploris is constructed in such a way that irrespective of what direction you leave it, you always have the sun up ahead and the wind at your back.

The Miplorisians gather up all the suitcases and sacks and bags of sorrow and carefully make a note of them in little pads. They scrupulously catalogue every kind of sadness and pining. Things are kept in very good order in Miploris; they have an extensive system of rules and impeccably clear areas of responsibility for all kinds of sorrows. 'Bureaucratic bastards' was what Granny called the Miplorisians, because of all the forms that have to be filled out nowadays by whoever is dropping off some sorrow or other. But you can't put up with disorder when it comes to sorrow, say the Miplorisians.

Miploris used to be the smallest kingdom in the Land-of-Almost-Awake, but after the War-Without-End it became the biggest. That was why Granny didn't like riding there, because so many of the stores had her name on signs outside. And in Miploris people talk of inner voices, Elsa remembers now. Miplorisians believe that the inner voices are those of the dead, coming back to help their loved ones.

Elsa is pulled back into the real world by Dad's gentle hand on her shoulder. She hears his voice whispering, 'You've arranged everything very nicely, Ulrika,' to Mum. In the corner of her eye she sees how Mum smiles and nods at the programmes lying on the church pews and then replies: 'Thanks for doing the programmes. Lovely font.'

Elsa sits at the far end of the wooden pew at the front of the chapel, staring down into the floor until the mumbling dies down. The church is so packed that people are standing all along the walls. Many of them have insanely weird clothes, as if they've been playing outfit roulette with someone who can't read washing instruction tags.

Elsa will put 'outfit roulette' in the word jar, she thinks. She tries to focus on that thought. But she hears languages she can't understand, and she hears her name being squeezed into strange pronunciations, and this takes her back to reality. She sees strangers pointing at her, with varying degrees of discretion.

She understands that they all know who she is, and it makes her mad, so that when she glimpses a familiar face along one of the walls she has trouble placing him at first. Like when you see a celebrity in a café and instinctively burst out, 'Oh, hi there!' before you realise that your brain has had time to tell you, 'Hey, that's probably someone you know, say hi!' but not, 'No wait, it's just that guy from the TV!' Because your brain likes to make you look an idiot.

His face disappears behind a shoulder for a few moments, but when he reappears he's looking right at Elsa. It's the accountant who came to speak about the leasehold conversion yesterday. But he's dressed as a priest now. He winks at her.

Another priest starts talking about Granny, then about God, but Elsa doesn't listen. She wonders if this is what Granny would have wanted. She's not sure that Granny liked church so very much. Granny and Elsa hardly ever talked about God, because Granny associated God with death.

And this is all fake. Plastic and make-up. As if everything's going to be fine just because they're having a funeral. Everything is not going to be fine for Elsa, she knows that. She breaks into a cold sweat. A couple of the strangers in the weird clothes come up to the microphone and talk. Some of them do so in other languages and have a little lady who translates into another microphone. But no one says 'dead'. Everyone just says that Granny has 'passed away' or that they've 'lost her'. As if she's a sock that's been lost in the tumble-drier. A few of them are crying, but she doesn't think they have the right. Because she wasn't their granny, and they have no right to make Elsa feel as if Granny had other countries and kingdoms to which she never brought Elsa.

So when a fat lady who looks like she's combed her hair with a toaster starts reading poems, Elsa thinks it's just about enough and she pushes her way out between the pews. She hears Mum whispering something behind her, but she just shuffles along the shiny stone floor and squeezes out of the church doors before anyone has time to come after her.

* * *

The winter air bites at Elsa; it feels like she's being yanked out of a boiling hot bath by her hair. The cloud animals are hovering low and ominous. Elsa walks slowly and takes such deep breaths of the December air that her eyes start to black out. She thinks about Storm. Storm has always been one of Elsa's favourite superheroes, because Storm's superpower is that she can change the weather. Even Granny used to admit that as superpowers went, that one was pretty cool.

Elsa hopes that Storm will come and blow away this whole bloody church. The whole bloody churchyard. Bloody everything.

The faces from inside spiral round inside her head. Did she really see the accountant? Was Alf standing in there? She thinks so. She saw another face she recognised, the policewoman with the green eyes. She walks faster, away from the church because she doesn't want any of them to come after her and ask if she's OK. Because she's not OK. None of this will ever be OK. She doesn't want to listen to their mumbling or have to admit that they are talking about her. Over her. Around her. Granny never talked around her.

She's gone about fifty metres between the headstones when she picks up a smell of smoke. At first there's something familiar about it, something almost liberating. Something that Elsa wants to turn round to and embrace and bury her nose in, like a freshly laundered pillowcase on a Sunday morning. But then there's something else.

And her inner voice comes to her.

She knows where the man between the headstones is before she has even turned round. He's only a few metres away from her. Casually holding his cigarette between his fingertips. It's too far from the church for anyone to hear Elsa scream, and with calm, cold movements he blocks her way back.

Elsa glances over her shoulder towards the gate. Twenty metres away. When she looks back he's taken a long stride towards her.

And the inner voice comes to Elsa. And it's Granny's voice. But it isn't whispering. It's yelling.

Run.

Elsa feels his rough hand grasping her arm, but she slips out of his grip. She runs until the wind scrapes her eyes like nails against a frosty windscreen. She doesn't know for how long. Eternities. And when the memory of his eyes and his cigarette crystallises in her brain, when every breath punches into her lungs, she realises that he was limping; that's why she got away. Another second of hesitation and he would have grabbed her by her dress, but Elsa is too used to running. Too good at it. She runs until she's no longer sure whether it's the wind or her grief that is making her eyes run. Runs until she realises she's almost at her school.

She slows down. Looks round. Hesitates. Then she charges right into the black park on the other side of the street, with her dress tossing around her. Even the trees look like enemies in there. The sun seems too exhausted to go down. She hears scattered voices, the wind screaming through the branches, the rumbling of traffic further and further away. Out of breath and furious, she stumbles towards the interior of the park. Hears voices. Hears that some of them are calling out after her. 'Hey! Little girl!' they call out.

She stops, exhausted. Collapses on a bench. Hears the 'little-girl' voice coming closer. She understands that it means her harm. The park seems to be creeping under a blanket. She hears another voice beside the first, slurring and stumbling over its words as if it's put on its shoes the wrong way round. Both of the voices seem to be picking up speed as they come towards her. Realising the danger, she's on her feet and running in a fluid movement. They follow. It dawns on her with sudden despair that the winter gloom is making everything look the same in the park, and she doesn't know the way out. Good God, she's a seven-year-old girl who watches television a hell of a lot, how could she be so stupid? This is how people end up on the sides of milk cartons, or however they advertise missing children these days.

But it's too late. She runs between two dense, black hedges that form a narrow corridor, and she feels her beating heart in her throat. She doesn't know why she charged into the park – the junkies will get her, just as everyone at school said they would. Maybe that's just it, she thinks to herself. Maybe she wants someone to catch her and kill her.

Death's greatest power is not that it can make people die, but that it can make people want to stop living.

She never hears the snapping of branches in the bush. Never hears the ice being crushed under his feet. But in an instant the slurring voices behind her are gone. Her eardrums grate until she wants to scream. And then everything goes back to silence. Slowly she's lifted off the ground. Closes her eyes. Doesn't open them until she's been carried out of the park.

Wolfheart stares down at her. She stares back, lying in his arms. Her consciousness seems to float off. If it wasn't for the realisation, in some part of her inner self, that there aren't enough paper bags in the whole world to breathe into if she dribbles on Wolfheart in her sleep, she would probably have gone to sleep there and then. So she struggles to stay awake and, after all, it would be a bit impolite to go to sleep now that he's saved her. Again.

'Not run alone. Never run alone,' growls Wolfheart.

She's still not quite sure if she wanted to be saved, although she's happy to see him. Happier than she expected to be, actually. She thought she'd be angrier at him.

'Dangerous place,' growls Wolfheart towards the park and starts putting her back down on the ground.

'I know,' she mumbles.

'Never again!' he orders, and she can hear that he's afraid.

She puts her arms round his neck and whispers 'thanks' in the secret language before he can straighten up his enormous body. Then she sees how uncomfortable it makes him and she lets go at once.

'I washed my hands really carefully, I had a mega-long shower this morning!' she whispers.

Wolfheart doesn't answer, but she can see in his eyes that he'll be, like, bathing in Alcogel when he gets home.

Elsa looks around. Wolfheart rubs his hands together and shakes his head when he notices.

'Gone now,' he says gently.

Elsa nods.

'How did you know I was here?'

Wolfheart's gaze drops into the asphalt.

'Guard you. Your granny said . . . guard you.'

Elsa nods.

'Even if I don't always know you're close by?'

Wolfheart's hood moves up and down. She feels that her legs are about to give way beneath her.

'Why did you disappear?' she whispers accusingly, 'Why did you leave me with that terropist?' Wolfheart's face disappears under his hood.

'Psychologists want to talk. Always talk. About war. Always. I . . . don't want to.'

'Maybe you'd feel better if you talked?'

Wolfheart rubs his hands together in silence. He watches the street as if waiting to catch sight of something.

Elsa wraps her arms round her body and realises that she left both her jacket and her Gryffindor scarf in the church. It's the only time she's ever forgotten her Gryffindor scarf.

Who the hell would forget a Gryffindor scarf?

She also looks up and down the street, searching for she doesn't know what. Then she feels something being swept over her shoulders, and when she turns round she realises that Wolfheart has put his coat round her. It drags along the ground by her feet. Smells of detergent. It's the first time she's seen Wolfheart without the upturned hood. Oddly enough he looks even bigger without it. His long hair and black beard billow in the wind.

'You said "Miamas" means "I love" in your mother's language, right?' asks Elsa and tries not to look directly at his scar, because she can see he rubs his hands even harder when she does.

He nods. Scans the street.

'What does "Miploris" mean?' asks Elsa.

When he doesn't answer at first she assumes it's because he doesn't understand the question, so she clarifies:

'One of the six kingdoms in the Land-of-Almost-Awake is called "Miploris". That's where all the sorrow is stored. Granny never wanted t—'

Wolfheart interrupts her, but gently.

'I mourn.'

Elsa nods.

'And Mirevas?'

'I dream.'

'And Miaudacas?'

'I dare.'

'And Mimovas?'

'Dance. I dance.'

Elsa lets the words touch down inside her before she asks about the last kingdom. She thinks about what Granny always said about Wolfheart, that he was the invincible warrior who defeated the shadows and that only he could have done it, because he had the heart of a warrior and the soul of a storyteller. Because he was born in Miamas, but he grew up in Mibatalos.

'What does Mibatalos mean?' she asks.

He looks right at her when she asks that. With those big dark eyes wide open with everything that is kept in Miploris.

'Mibatalos. "I fight." Mibatalos . . . gone now. No Mibatalos any more.'

'I know! The shadows destroyed it in the War-Without-End and all the Mibatalosians died except you, for you are the last of your people and—' Elsa starts saying, but Wolfheart rubs his hands together so hard that she stops herself.

Wolfheart's hair falls into his face. He backs away a step.

'Mibatalos not exist. I don't fight. Never more fight.'

And Elsa understands, the way you always understand such things when you see them in the eyes of those saying them, that he did not hide in the forests at the far reaches of the Land-of-Almost-Awake because he was afraid of the shadows, but because he was afraid of himself. Afraid of what they made him into in Mibatalos.

His eyes flit past her and she hears Alf's voice. When she spins round, Taxi is parked with its engine running by the edge of the pavement. Alf's shoes shuffle through the snow. The policewoman stays by Taxi, her eyes making rapid hawk-like sweeps over the park. When Alf picks up Elsa, still rolled up in Wolfheart's sleeping bag-sized coat, he says calmly: 'Let's get you home now, shall we, you can't bloody stay here getting frozen!' But Elsa hears in his voice that he's afraid, afraid as one can only be if one knows what was chasing Elsa in the church-yard, and she can tell by the watchful gaze in the policewoman's green eyes that she also knows. They all know more than they are letting on.

Elsa doesn't look round as Alf carries her back towards Taxi. She knows that Wolfheart has already gone. And when she throws herself into Mum's arms back at the church she also knows that Mum knows more than she's letting on. And she's always known more than she lets on.

Elsa thinks about the story of the Lionheart brothers. About the dragon, Katla, who could not be defeated by any human. And about the terrible constrictor snake, Karm, the only one that could destroy Katla in the end. Because sometimes in the tales, the only thing that can destroy a terrible dragon is something even more terrible than the dragon.

A monster.

22

O'BOY

Elsa has been chased hundreds of times before, but never like in that churchyard. And the fear she feels now is something else. Because she had time to see his eyes just before she ran, and they looked so determined, so cold, like he was ready to kill her. That's a lot for an almost-eight-year-old to handle.

Elsa tried never to be afraid while Granny was alive. Or at least she tried never to show it. Because Granny hated fears. Fears are small, fiery creatures from the Land-of-Almost-Awake, with rough pelts that coincidentally look quite a lot like blue tumble-drier fluff, and if you give them the slightest opportunity they jump up and nibble your skin and try to scratch your eyes. Fears are like cigarettes, said Granny: the hard thing isn't stopping, it's not starting.

It was the Noween who brought the fears to the Land-of-Almost-Awake, in another of Granny's tales, more eternities ago than anyone could really count. So long ago that at the time there were only five kingdoms, not six.

The Noween is a prehistoric monster that wants everything to happen immediately. Every time a child says 'in a minute' or 'later' or 'I'm just going to . . .' the Noween bellows with furious force: 'Nooo! IT HAS TO BE DONE NOOOW!' The Noween hates children, because children refuse to accept the Noween's lie that time is linear. Children know that time is just an emotion, so 'now' is a meaningless word to them, just as it was for Granny. George used to say that Granny wasn't a time-optimist,

211

she was a time-atheist, and the only religion she believed in was Do-it-later-Buddhism.

The Noween brought the fears to the Land-of-Almost-Awake to catch children, because when a Noween gets hold of a child it engulfs the child's future, leaving the victim helpless where it is, facing an entire life of eating now and sleeping now and tidying up right away. Never again can the child postpone something boring till later and do something fun in the meantime. All that's left is now. A fate far worse than death, Granny always said, so the tale of the Noween started by clarifying that it hated fairy tales. Because nothing is better at making a child postpone something than a fairy tale. So one night the Noween slithered up Telling Mountain, the highest mountain peak in the Land-of-Almost-Awake, where it caused a massive landslide, which demolished the entire peak. Then it lay in wait in a dark cave. For Telling Mountain is the mountain the enphants have to climb in order to be able to release the tales so they can glide over into the real world, and if the tales can't leave Telling Mountain the whole kingdom of Miamas will suffocate, and then the whole Land-of-Almost-Awake will suffocate. For no stories can live without children listening to them.

When dawn came, all the bravest fighters from Mibatalos tried to climb the mountain and defeat the Noween, but no one managed it. Because the Noween was breeding fears in the caves. Fears need to be handled carefully, because threats just make them grow bigger. So every time a parent somewhere threatened a child it worked as fertiliser. 'Soon,' a child said somewhere, and then a parent yelled, 'No, nooow! Or I'll—' And bang, another fear was hatched in one of the Noween's caves.

When the warriors from Mibatalos came up the mountain the Noween released the fears, and they immediately transformed themselves into each individual soldier's worst nightmare. For all beings have a mortal fear, even the warriors from Mibatalos, and the air in the Land-of-Almost-Awake slowly grew thinner. Storytellers found it increasingly difficult to breathe.

(Elsa obviously interrupted Granny at this point because her whole thing about fears transforming themselves into what you are most afraid of was actually nicked from Harry Potter, because that's how a boggart works. And then Granny had snorted and answered, 'Maybe it's that Harry muppet who nicked it from me?' And then Elsa had sneered, 'Harry Potter doesn't steal!' And then they had argued for quite a long time about that, and in the end Granny gave up and mumbled, 'Fine, then! Forget the whole bloody thing! Fears don't transform themselves, they just bite and try to scratch your eyes, are you SATISFIED now or what?' And then Elsa had left it there and they went on with the story.)

That's when the two golden knights showed up. Everyone tried to warn them about riding up the mountain, but they didn't listen, of course. Knights can be so damned obstinate. But when they came up the mountain and all the fears welled out of the caves, the golden knights didn't fight. They didn't yell and swear as other warriors would have done. Instead the knights did the only thing you can do with fears: they laughed at them. Loud, defiant laughter. And then all the fears were turned to stone, one by one.

Granny was fond of rounding off fairy tales with things being turned to stone because she wasn't very good at endings. Elsa never complained, though. The Noween was obviously put in prison for an indeterminate length of time, which made it insanely angry. And the ruling council of the Land-of-Almost-Awake decided to appoint a small group of inhabitants from each of the kingdoms, warriors from Mibatalos and dream hunters from Mirevas and sorrow-keepers from Miploris and musicians from Mimovas and storytellers from Miamas, to keep guard over Telling Mountain. The stones of the fears were used to rebuild the peak higher than ever, and at the foot of the mountain the sixth kingdom was built: Miaudacas. And in the fields of Miaudacas, courage was cultivated, so that no one would ever again have to be afraid of the fears.

(Or, well. That is what they did until, as Granny once told Elsa, after the harvest they took all the courage plants and made a special drink of them, and if you had some of it you became incredibly brave. And then Elsa did a bit of Googling and then she pointed out to Granny that it wasn't a very responsible analogy to divulge to a child. And then Granny groaned, 'Oh right, OK, let's say they don't drink it, it's just THERE, OK!?' So that's the whole story of the two golden knights who defeated the fears. Granny told it every time Elsa was afraid of anything, and even though Elsa was often quite right about her criticism of Granny's storytelling technique, it actually worked every time. She wasn't at all as afraid afterwards.

The only thing the story never worked on was Granny's fear of death. And now it wasn't working on Elsa either. Because not even fairy tales defeat shadows.

'Are you scared?' asks Mum.

'Yes,' admits Elsa.

Mum doesn't tell Elsa not to be afraid, and she doesn't try to trick her into believing that she shouldn't be. Elsa loves her for that.

They are in the garage and have pushed the backrest down in Renault. The wurse floats out over everything between them, and Mum unconcernedly scratches its pelt. She wasn't even angry when Elsa confessed that she'd been keeping it hidden in the storage unit. And she wasn't scared when Elsa introduced her. She just started stroking it behind its ear as if it was a kitten.

Elsa reaches out and feels Mum's belly and Halfie contentedly kicking in there. Halfie is not afraid either. Because she-he is completely Mum and George, whereas Elsa is half her dad and Elsa's dad is afraid of everything. So Elsa gets afraid of about half of everything.

Shadows more than anything.

'Do you know who he was? The man who was chasing me?' she asks.

The wurse buffets its head against hers. Mum gently caresses her cheek.

'Yes. We know who he is.'

'Who's we?'

Mum takes a deep breath.

'Lennart and Maud. And Alf. And me.' It sounds as if she's going to reel off more names, but she stops herself.

'Lennart and Maud?' Elsa bursts out.

Mum nods. 'I'm afraid they know him best of all.'

'So why did you never tell me about him, then?' Elsa demands.

'I didn't want to scare you.'

'That hardly worked, did it?'

Mum sighs. Scratches the wurse's pelt. The wurse, in turn, licks Elsa's face. It still smells of sponge cake mix. Unfortunately it's quite difficult to be angry when someone smelling of sponge cake mix is licking your face.

'It's a shadow,' whispers Elsa.

'I know,' whispers Mum.

'Do you?'

'Your grandmother tried to tell me the stories, darling. About the Land-of-Almost-Awake and the shadows.'

'And Miamas?' asks Elsa.

Mum shakes her head.

'No. I know you had things there that she never showed me. And it was long ago. I was about as old as you are now. The Land-of-Almost-Awake was very small then. The kingdoms didn't have names yet.'

Elsa interrupts impatiently:

'I know! They got their names when Granny met Wolfheart, she named them after things in his mother's language. And she took his own language and made it into the secret language so he'd teach her and she could talk to him. But why didn't she bring you with her, in that case? Why didn't Granny show you the Land-of-Almost-Awake?'

Gently, Mum bites her lip.

'She wanted to bring me, darling. Many times. But I didn't want to go.'

'Why not?'

'I was getting older. I was an angry teenager, and I didn't want my mother telling me fairy tales on the phone any more, I wanted to have her here. I wanted her in reality.'

Elsa hardly ever hears her say, 'My mother.' She almost always says, 'Your grandmother.'

'I wasn't an easy child, darling. I argued a lot. I said no to everything. Your grandmother always called me "the girl who said no".'

Elsa's eyes open wide. Mum sighs and smiles at the same time, as if one emotional expression is trying to swallow the other.

'Well, I was probably many things in your grandmother's stories. Both the girl and the queen, I think. In the end I didn't know where the fantasy ended and reality began. Sometimes I don't even think your grandmother knew, herself.'

Elsa lies in silence staring up at the ceiling, with the wurse breathing softly in her ear. She thinks about Wolfheart and the sea-angel, living next door for so many years without anyone knowing the first thing about them. If holes were drilled in the walls and floors of the house, all the neighbours could reach out and touch one another, that was how close their lives were, and yet in the end they knew almost nothing about the others. And so the years just went by.

'Have you found the keys?' asks Elsa, pointing at Renault's dashboard.

Mum shakes her head.

'I think your grandmother hid them. Presumably just to tease Britt-Marie. That must be why it's parked in Britt-Marie's space . . .'

'Does Britt-Marie even have her own car?' asks Elsa, because from where she's lying she can clearly see BMW, Kent's ridiculously oversized car.

'No. But she had a car many years ago. A white one. And it's still her parking spot. I think it's about the principle. It's usually about the principle with Britt-Marie,' says Mum with a smirk.

Elsa doesn't quite know what that means. She doesn't know if it makes any difference either.

'How did Renault get here, then? If no one has the key for it?' she thinks aloud, although she knows Mum won't be able to answer because she doesn't know either. So she asks Mum to tell her about the shadow. Mum brushes her hand over her cheek again and stands up laboriously from the seat, with one hand over Halfie.

'I think Maud and Lennart will have to tell you about him, darling.'

Elsa wants to protest but Mum has already climbed out of Renault, so Elsa doesn't have much choice but to follow her. That is Mum's superpower, after all. Mum brings Wolfheart's coat. She says she's going to wash it so he can have it when he comes home. Elsa likes thinking about that. How he's coming home.

They put blankets over the wurse in the back seat and Mum calmly cautions it to stay still if it hears anyone coming. And it agrees. Elsa promises it several times that she'll find a better hiding place, although it can't seem to see the point of this. On the other hand it looks very pleased about her going off to find more biscuits.

Alf is standing guard at the bottom of the cellar stairs.

'I made coffee,' he mutters.

Mum gratefully accepts a cup. Alf hands Elsa the other cup.

'I told you I don't drink coffee,' says Elsa tiredly.

'It's not bloody coffee, it's one of those O'boy drinking-chocolate bastards,' Alf answers indignantly.

Elsa peers into the cup, surprised.

'Where'd you get this from?' she asks. Mum never lets her have O'boy at home because there's too much sugar in it.

'From home,' mutters Alf.

'You have O'boy at home?' Elsa asks sceptically.

'I can bloody go to the shop, can't I?' says Alf sourly.

Elsa grins at him. She's thinking of calling Alf the Knight of Invective because she's read about invective on Wikipedia and she feels all in all there are too few knights of it. Then she takes a deep gulp and comes close to spitting it all out over Alf's leather jacket.

'How many spoonfuls of O'boy did you put in this?'

'I don't know. Fourteen or fifteen, maybe?' Alf mutters defensively.

'You're supposed to put in, like, three!'

Alf looks indignant. Or at least Elsa thinks so. She put 'indignant' in Dad's word jar one time, and she imagines that's what it looks like.

'It's should bloody taste of something, shouldn't it?'

Elsa eats the rest with a spoon.

'So you also know who was chasing me in the churchyard, don't you?' she asks Alf, with half of the cup's contents in the corners of her mouth and on the tip of her nose.

'It's not you he's after.'

'Err, hello? He was *chasing* me.'

Alf just slowly shakes his head.

'Yes. But you're not the one he's hunting.'

23

DISHCLOTH

Elsa has a thousand questions about what Alf just said, but doesn't ask any of them because Mum is so tired once they've gone up into the flat that she and Halfie have to go straight to bed. Mum gets like that these days, tired as if someone pulled the plug. It's Halfie's fault, apparently. George says that to compensate for Halfie keeping them awake for the next eighteen years, Halfie is making Mum fall asleep all the time for the first nine months. Elsa sits on the edge of the bed stroking her hair; Mum kisses her hands, whispering, 'It will get better, darling. It will be fine.' Like Granny used to say. And Elsa wants so, so much to believe that. Mum smiles sleepily.

'Is Britt-Marie still here?' she says, with a nod towards the door.

Britt-Marie's nagging voice emanates from the kitchen, so the question immediately becomes rhetorical. She's demanding 'a decision' from George on Renault, which is still parked in Britt-Marie's slot in the garage. ('We can't live without rules, George! Even Ulrika has to understand that!'). George answers cheerfully that he can understand that well enough, because George can understand everyone's point of view. It's one of the annoying things about him, and, sure enough, seems to be getting Britt-Marie into a huff. And then George offers her some eggs, which she ignores, insisting instead that all tenants 'submit to a full investigation' regarding the pram, which is still locked up at the bottom of the stairs.

'Don't worry, darling, we'll find a better hiding place for your friend tomorrow,' Mum mumbles half in her sleep, and then adds with a smile: 'Maybe we can hide it in the pram?'

Elsa laughs. But only a little. And she thinks that the mystery of the locked pram is like the opening of an insanely awful Agatha Christie novel. Elsa knows that because almost all of Agatha Christie's novels can be read on the iPad, and Agatha Christie has never had such a stereotypical villain as Britt-Marie. More likely she'd be a victim, because Elsa can imagine a murder mystery in which someone has bludgeoned Britt-Marie to death with a candlestick in the library, and then everyone who knew her would be a suspect because everyone would have a motive: 'The hag was a nightmare!' And then Elsa feels a bit ashamed for thinking along these lines. But only a little.

'Britt-Marie doesn't mean any harm, she just needs to feel important,' Mum tries to explain.

'She's still just a nagging old busybody,' Elsa mutters.

Mum smiles.

And then she gets comfortable on the pillows and Elsa helps her push one of them under her back, and Mum strokes her cheek and whispers:

'I want to hear the stories now, if that's all right. I want to hear the fairy tales from Miamas.'

And then Elsa whispers calmly that Mum has to close her eyes but only halfway, and then Mum does as she says, and Elsa has a thousand questions but does not ask any of them. Instead she talks about the cloud animals and the enphants and the regretters and lions and trolls and knights and the Noween and Wolfheart and the snow-angels and the sea-angel and the dream hunters and she starts talking about the princess of Miploris and the two princelings who fought for her love, and the witch who stole the princess's treasure, but by then Mum and Halfie are asleep.

And Elsa still has a thousand questions but does not ask any of them. She just covers Mum and Halfie with the blanket and kisses Mum on the cheek and forces herself to be brave. Because she has to do what Granny made her promise to do: protect the castle, protect her family, protect her friends.

Mum's hand fumbles for her as she's standing up, and just as Elsa is about to go, Mum whispers in a half-asleep state:

'All the photos on the ceiling in your grandmother's bedroom, darling. All the children in the photos. They were the ones who came to the funeral today. They're grown-up now. They were allowed to grow up because your granny saved their lives . . .'

And then Mum is asleep again. Elsa is not entirely sure that she even woke up.

'No shit, Sherlock,' whispers Elsa as she switches off the lamp. Because it wasn't so hard working out who the strangers were. It was forgiving them that was hard.

Mum sleeps with a smile on her lips. Elsa carefully shuts the door.

The flat smells of dishcloth, and George is collecting used coffee cups. The strangers were all here today drinking coffee after the funeral. They smiled empathically at Elsa and Elsa hates them for it. Hates that they knew Granny before she did. She goes into Granny's flat and lies on Granny's bed. The streetlight outside plays against the photos on the ceiling, and, as she watches, Elsa still doesn't know if she can forgive Granny for leaving Mum on her own so she could save other children. She doesn't know if Mum can forgive it either. Even if she seems to be trying.

She goes out of the door, onto the stairwell, thinking to herself that she'll go back to the wurse in the garage. But instead, she sinks listlessly onto the floor. Sits there for ever. Tries to think but only finds emptiness and silence where usually there are thoughts.

She can hear the footsteps coming from several floors down – soft, padding gently, as if they're lost. Not at all the self-assured, energetic pacing the woman in the black skirt used to have when she was still smelling of mint and talking into a white cable. She wears jeans now. And no white cable. She stops about ten steps below Elsa.

'Hi,' says the woman.

She looks small. Sounds tired, but it's a different kind of tiredness than usual. A better tiredness, this time. And she smells of neither mint nor wine. Just shampoo.

'Hello,' says Elsa.

'I went to the churchyard today,' says the woman slowly.

'You were at the funeral?'

The woman shakes her head apologetically. 'I wasn't there. Sorry. I . . . I couldn't. But I . . .' She swallows the words. Looks down at her hands. 'I went to my . . . my boys' graves. I haven't been there in a very long time.'

'Did it help?' asks Elsa.

The woman's lips disappear.

'I don't know.'

Elsa nods. The lights in the stairwell go out. She waits for her eyes to grow accustomed to the darkness. Finally the woman seems to gather all her strength into a smile, and the skin round her mouth doesn't crack quite as much any more.

'How was the funeral?' she asks.

Elsa shrugs.

'Like a normal funeral. Far too many people.'

'Sometimes it's hard to share one's sorrow with people one doesn't know. But I think . . . there were many people who were very fond of your grandmother.'

Elsa lets her hair fall over her face. The woman scratches her neck.

'It's . . . I understand it's hard. To know that your granny left home to help strangers somewhere else . . . Me, for instance.'

Elsa looks slightly suspicious. It's as if the woman read her thoughts.

'It's known as "the trolley problem". In ethics. I mean, for students. At university. It's . . . It's the discussion of whether it's morally right to sacrifice one person in order to save many others. You can probably read about it on Wikipedia.'

Elsa doesn't respond. The woman seems to become ill at ease.

'You look angry.'

Elsa shrugs and tries to decide what she's most angry about. There's a fairly long list.

'I'm not angry at you. I'm just angry at stupid Britt-Marie,' she decides to say in the end.

The woman looks slightly confused and glances down at what she's holding in her hands. Her fingers drum against it.

'Don't fight with monsters, for you can become one. If you look into the abyss for long enough, the abyss looks into you.'

'What are you talking about?' Elsa bursts out, secretly pleased that the woman speaks to her as if Elsa was not a child.

'Sorry, that's . . . that was Nietzsche. He was a German philosopher. It's . . . ah, I'm probably misquoting him. But I think it could mean that if you hate the one who hates, you could risk becoming like the one you hate.'

Elsa's shoulders shoot up to her ears.

'Granny always said: "Don't kick the shit, it'll go all over the place!"'

And that's the first time Elsa hears the woman in the black skirt, who now wears jeans, really burst out laughing.

'Yes, yes, that's probably a better way of putting it.'

She's beautiful when she laughs. It suits her. And then she takes two steps towards Elsa and reaches out as far as she can to give her the envelope that she's holding, without having to move too close.

'This was on my boys' . . . on their . . . it was on their headstone. I don't . . . don't know who put it there. But your granny – maybe she figured out that I'd come . . .'

Elsa takes the envelope. The woman in jeans has disappeared down the stairs before she has time to look up from the envelope. On it, it says, 'To Elsa! Give this to Lennart and Maud!'

And that is how Elsa gets hold of Granny's third letter.

Lennart is holding a coffee cup in his hand when he opens the door. Maud and Samantha are behind him, both looking very sweet. They smell of biscuits.

'I have a letter for you,' Elsa declares.

Lennart takes it and is just about to say something, but Elsa goes on:

'It's from my granny! She's probably sending her regards and saying sorry, because that's what she's doing in all the letters.'

Lennart nods meekly. Maud nods even more meekly.

'We're so terribly sad about this whole thing with your grandmother, dear Elsa. But it was such a wonderfully beautiful funeral, we thought. We're so glad that we were invited. Come in and have a dream – and Alf brought over some of that chocolate drink as well.' Maud beams.

Samantha barks. Even her bark sounds friendly. Elsa takes a dream from the proffered tin, filled to the top. She smiles cooperatively at Maud.

'I have a friend who likes dreams very much. And he's been on his own all day. Do you think it would be all right to bring him up?'

Maud and Lennart nod as if it goes without saying.

24

DREAMS

Maud doesn't look quite as convinced once the wurse is sitting on her kitchen rug a few moments later. Especially as it's literally sitting on the entire kitchen rug.

'I told you it likes dreams, didn't I?' says Elsa cheerfully.

Maud nods mutely. Lennart sits on the other side of the table, with an immeasurably terrified-looking Samantha on his lap. The wurse eats dreams, a dozen at a time.

'What breed is that?' says Lennart very quietly to Elsa, as if he's afraid the wurse may take offence.

'A wurse!' says Elsa with satisfaction.

Lennart nods like you do when you don't have a clue what something means. Maud opens a new tin of dreams and carefully pushes it across the floor with the tips of her toes. The wurse empties it in three slavering bites, then lifts its head and peers at Maud with eyes as big as hubcaps. Maud takes down another two tins and tries not to look flattered. It doesn't go so very well.

Elsa looks at the letter from Granny. It's lying unfolded and open on the table. Lennart and Maud must have read it while she was in the cellar getting the wurse. Lennart notices her looking, and he puts his hand on her shoulder.

'You're right, Elsa. Your grandmother says sorry.'

'For what?'

Maud gives the wurse some cinnamon buns and half a length of sweet cake.

225

'Well, it was quite a list. Your grandmother was certainly—'

'Different,' Elsa interjects.

Maud laughs warmly and pats the wurse on the head.

Lennart nods at the letter.

'First of all she apologises for telling us off so often. And for being angry so often. And for arguing and causing problems. It's really nothing to apologise about, all people do that from time to time!' he says, as if apologising for Granny apologising.

'You don't,' thinks Elsa and likes them for it. Maud starts giggling.

'And then she apologised about that time she happened to shoot Lennart from her balcony with one of those, what are they called, paint-bomb guns!'

Suddenly she looks embarrassed.

'Is that what it's called? Paint-bomb?'

Elsa nods. Even though it isn't. Maud looks proud.

'Once your grandmother even got Britt-Marie – there was a big pink stain on her floral-print jacket, and that's Britt-Marie's favourite jacket and the stain wouldn't even go away with Vanish! Can you imagine?'

Maud titters. And then she looks very guilty.

'What else does Granny apologise about?' Elsa asks, hoping for more stories about someone shooting that paintball gun at Britt-Marie. But Lennart's chin drops towards his chest. He looks at Maud and she nods and Lennart turns to Elsa and says:

'Your granny wrote that she was sorry for asking us to tell you the whole story. Everything you have to know.'

'What story?' Elsa's about to ask, but she suddenly becomes aware of someone standing behind her. She twists round in her chair, and the boy with a syndrome is standing in the bedroom doorway with a cuddly lion in his arms.

He looks at Elsa, but when she looks back at him he lets his hair fall over his brow, like Elsa sometimes does. He's about a year younger, but almost exactly as tall, and they have the same hairstyle and almost the same colour too. The only thing that sets them apart is that Elsa is different and the boy has a syndrome, which is a very special kind of difference.

The boy doesn't say anything, because he never does. Maud kisses his forehead and whispers, 'Nightmare?' and the boy nods. Maud gets a big glass of milk and a whole tin of dreams, takes his hand and leads him back into the bedroom, while robustly saying: 'Come on, let's chase them away at once!'

Lennart turns to Elsa.

'I think your grandmother wanted me to start at the beginning.'

And that was the day Elsa heard the story of the boy with a syndrome. A fairy tale she'd never heard before. A tale so terrible it makes you want to hug yourself as hard as you can. Lennart tells her about the boy's father, who has more hatred in him than anyone could think would be possible to fit into one person. The father used narcotics. Lennart stops himself, and seems worried about frightening Elsa, but she straightens her back and buries her hands in the wurse's fur and says it doesn't matter. Lennart asks if she knows what narcotics are, and she says she's read about them on Wikipedia.

Lennart describes how the father became a different creature when he used drugs. How he became dark in his soul. How he hit the boy's mother while she was pregnant, because he didn't want to become anyone's father. Lennart's eyes start blinking more and more slowly, and he says that maybe it was because the father feared the child would be as he was. Filled with hatred and violence. So when the boy was born, and the doctors said he had a syndrome, the father was beside himself with rage. He couldn't tolerate that the child was different. Maybe it was because he hated everything that was different. Maybe because, when he looked at the boy, he saw everything that was different in himself.

So he drank alcohol, took more of that stuff on Wikipedia, and disappeared for entire nights and sometimes for weeks on end, without anyone knowing where he was. Sometimes he came home utterly calm and withdrawn. Sometimes he cried, explaining that he'd had to keep out of the way until he'd wrung his own anger out of himself. As if there was something dark living in him that was trying to transform him, and he was struggling against. He could remain calm for weeks after that. Or months.

Then one night the dark took possession of him. He hit and hit and hit them until neither of them were moving any more. And then he ran.

Maud's voice moves gently through the silence that Lennart leaves behind him in the kitchen. In the bedroom the boy with a syndrome snores, which is one of the first sounds Elsa has ever heard him make. Maud's fingertips scramble about among the empty biscuit tins on the kitchen top.

'We found them. We'd been trying, for such a long time, to make her take the boy and leave, but she was so afraid. We were all so afraid. He was a terribly dangerous man,' she whispers.

Elsa grips the wurse tighter.

'Then what did you do?'

Maud crumples up by the kitchen table. She has an envelope in her hand, the same as the one Elsa arrived with.

'We knew your grandmother. From the hospital. We ran a café back then, you see, for the doctors, and your grandmother came there every day. A dozen dreams and a dozen cinnamon buns, every single day! I don't know how it started, really. But your grandmother was the sort of person one told things to, if you see what I mean? I didn't know what to do about Sam. I didn't know who to turn to. We were so terribly frightened, all of us, but I called her. She arrived in her rusty old car in the middle of the night—'

'Renault!' Elsa exclaims, because for some reason she has a sense that he deserves his name in the fairy tale if he's the one who came to their rescue. Lennart clears his throat with a sad smile.

'Her Renault, yes. We took the boy and his mother with us and your grandmother drove here. Gave us the keys to the flats. I can't think how she got her hands on them, but she said she'd clear it with the owners of the building. We've been living here ever since.'

'And the father? What happened when he realised everyone was gone?' Elsa wants to know, although she actually doesn't want to know.

Lennart's hand seeks Maud's fingers.

'We don't know. But your grandmother came here with Alf, and said this is Alf and he's going to fetch all the boy's things. And she went back there with Alf and the boy's father turned up and he was . . . nothing but darkness then. Darkness from deep inside. He hit Alf something terrible—'

Lennart stops himself the way one does when suddenly reminding oneself that one is talking to a child. Fast-forwards through the story.

'Well, of course, he was already gone by the time the police came. And Alf, gosh, I don't know. He was patched up at the hospital and drove home by himself and never said a word about it again. And two days later he was driving his cab again. He's made of steel, that man.'

'And the father?' Elsa persists.

'He disappeared. Disappeared for years. We thought he'd never give up trying to find us, but he was gone for so long that we hoped—' says Lennart, interrupting himself as if the words are too heavy for his tongue.

'But now he's found us,' Maud fills in.

'How?' asks Elsa.

Lennart's eyes creep along the tabletop.

'Alf thinks he found your grandmother's death notice, you see. And using that he found the undertaker's. And there he found—' he starts to say, then looks as if he's reminding himself of something once again.

'Me?' Elsa gulps.

Lennart nods and Maud lets go of his hand and runs round the table and embraces Elsa.

'Dear, dear Elsa! You have to understand, he hasn't seen the boy in many years. And you're about the same size and you have the same hair. He thinks you're our grandchild.'

Elsa closes her eyes. Her temples are burning, and for the first time in her life she uses pure and furious willpower to go to the Land-of-Almost-Awake without even being close to sleeping. With all the most powerful force of imagination she can muster she calls up the cloud animals and flies to Miaudacas. Gathers up all the courage she can carry. Then she prises her eyes open and looks at Lennart and Maud and says:

'So you're his mother's parents?'

Lennart's tears fall onto the tablecloth like rain against a windowsill.

'No. We're his father's parents.'

Elsa squints.

'You're the father's parents?'

Maud's chest rises and sinks and she pats the wurse on the head and goes to fetch a chocolate cake. Samantha looks cautiously at the wurse. Lennart goes to get more coffee. His cup trembles so much that it spills onto the bench.

'I know it sounds terrible, Elsa, taking a child from his father. To do that to your own son. But when you become grandparents, then you are grandparents first and foremost . . .' he whispers sadly.

'You're a grandmother and grandfather above all things! Always! *Always!*' Maud adds with unshakeable defiance, and her eyes burn in a way that Elsa wouldn't have believed was possible in Maud.

Then she gives Elsa the envelope she got from the bedroom.

It has Granny's handwriting on it. Elsa doesn't recognise the name, but she understands it's for the boy's mother.

'She changed her name when we moved here,' Maud explains and, in the softest voice possible, adds: 'Your grandmother left this letter with us months ago. She said you had to come for it. She knew you'd come.'

Lennart inhales unhappily. His and Maud's eyes meet again, then he explains:

'But I'm afraid that first of all we have to tell you about our son, Elsa. We have to tell you about Sam. And that's one of

230

the things your grandmother apologises for in her letter. She writes that she's sorry she saved Sam's life . . .'

Maud's voice cracks until her words are like little whistles:

'And then she wrote that she was sorry for writing to say she was sorry about it, sorry for regretting that she had saved our son's life. Sorry because she no longer knew if he deserved to live. Even though she was a doctor . . .'

Night comes to the streets outside the window. The kitchen smells of coffee and chocolate cake. And Elsa listens to the story of Sam.

The son of the world's kindest couple, yet who became more evil than anyone could understand. Who became the father of the boy with a syndrome, who, in turn, had less evil in him than anyone could have believed, as if his father took it all on his shoulders and passed none of it on. She heard the story of how Sam was once a little boy himself, and how Maud and Lennart, who had waited for a child for so long and who had loved him, as parents love their children. And like all parents, even the very, very worst possible, must at some point have loved their children. That is how Maud puts it. 'Because otherwise one can't be a human being, I just can't imagine one could be a human otherwise,' she whispers. And she insists that it has to be her fault, because she can't imagine that any child is born evil. It has to be the mother's fault if a boy who was once so small and helpless grows up into something so terrible, she's quite sure of that. In spite of Elsa saying that Granny always said some people are actually just shits and that it's no one else's fault than the shit.

'But Sam was always so angry, I don't know where all that anger came from. There must have been a darkness in me that I passed over to him and I don't know where it came from,' Maud whispers, quite crushed.

And then she talks about a boy who grew up and always fought, always tormented other children at school, always chased those who were different. And about how when he was an adult he became a soldier and went to far-off lands because he thirsted for war, and how he met a friend there. His first real friend. About how everyone who saw it said that it had changed him, brought out something good in him. His friend was also a soldier, but another sort of soldier, without that thirst. They became inseparable. Sam said his friend was the bravest warrior he had ever seen.

They went home together and his friend introduced Sam to a girl he knew and she saw something in Sam and for a brief moment Lennart and Maud also got to see a glimpse of someone else. A Sam beyond the darkness.

'We thought she'd save him, we all hoped so much that she'd save him, because it would have been like a fairy tale, and when one has lived in the dark for so long it's so very difficult not to believe in fairy tales,' Maud admits, while Lennart clasps her hand.

'But then those little circumstances of life came up,' Lennart sighs, 'like in so many fairy tales. And maybe it wasn't Sam's fault. Or maybe it was entirely Sam's fault. Maybe it's for people much wiser than I to decide whether every person is completely responsible for their actions or not. But Sam went back to the wars. And he came home even darker.'

'He used to be an idealist,' Maud interjects gloomily. 'Despite all that hatred and anger he was an idealist. That's why he wanted to be a soldier.'

And then Elsa asks if she can borrow Maud and Lennart's computer.

'If you have a computer, I mean!' she adds apologetically, because she thinks about the palaver she had with Wolfheart when she asked him the same thing.

'Of course we have a computer,' says Lennart, puzzled. 'Who doesn't these days?'

Quite right, thinks Elsa, and decides to bring it up with Wolfheart next time he turns up. If there is another time.

Lennart leads her past the bedroom. In the little study at the far end of the flat, he explains that their computer is very old, of course, so she has to have a bit of patience. And on a table in there is the most unwieldy computer Elsa has ever seen, and at the back of the actual computer is a gigantic box, and on the floor is another box.

'What's that?' says Elsa, pointing at the box on the floor.

'That's the actual computer,' says Lennart.

'And what about that?' asks Elsa and points at the other box.

'That's the monitor,' says Lennart and presses a big button on the box on the floor, then adds: 'It'll take a minute or so before it starts, so we'll have to wait a bit.'

'A MINUTE!' Elsa bursts out, and mumbles: 'Wow. It really is old.'

But when the old computer has eventually got started and Lennart after many ifs and buts has got her on to the internet and she has found what she is looking for, she goes back into the kitchen and sits opposite Maud.

'So it means a dreamer. An idealist, I mean. It means a dreamer.'

'Yes, yes, you could probably say that,' says Maud with a friendly smile.

'It's not that you could say it. It's what it actually means,' Elsa corrects.

And then Maud nods, even friendlier. And then she tells the story of the idealist who turned into a cynic, and Elsa knows what it means because a teacher at Elsa's preschool once called Elsa that. There was an uproar when Elsa's mum found out about it, but the teacher stood his ground. Elsa can't remember the exact details, but she thinks it was that time she told the other preschool pupils how sausages were made.

She wonders if she's thinking about these things as a kind of defence mechanism. For this tale really has too much reality in it. It often happens, when you're almost eight, that there's just too much reality.

Maud describes how Sam went off to a new war. He had his friend with him, and for several weeks they had been protecting a village from attack by people who, for some reason unknown to Maud, wanted to kill all who lived there. In the end they received an order to abandon the place, but Sam's friend refused. He convinced Sam and the rest of the soldiers to stay until the village was safe, and took as many injured children as they could fit into their cars to the nearest hospital, many miles away, because Sam's friend knew a woman who worked as a doctor there, and everyone said she was the most skilful surgeon in the whole world.

They were on their way through the desert when they hit the mine. The explosion was merciless. There was a rain of fire and blood.

'Did anyone die?' asks Elsa, without really wanting to know the answer.

'All of them,' says Lennart, without wanting to speak the words out loud. Except Sam's friend and Sam himself. Sam was unconscious, but his friend dragged him out of the fire, Sam was the only one he had time to save. The friend had shrapnel in his face and terrible burns, but when he heard the shots and realised they'd been ambushed, he grabbed his rifle and ran into the desert and didn't stop firing until only he and Sam lay there in the desert, panting and bleeding.

The people who had been shooting at him were boys. Children, just like the children the soldiers had just tried to save. Sam's friend could see that, as he stood over their dead bodies, with their blood on his hands. And he was never the same again.

Somehow he managed to carry Sam through the desert and didn't stop until he came to the hospital and Elsa's grandmother came running towards them. She saved Sam's life. He would always have a slight limp in one leg, but he would survive, and it was at that hospital that Sam started smoking Granny's brand of cigarettes. Granny also apologises about that in the letter.

Maud carefully places the photo album in front of Elsa, as if it was a small creature with feelings. Points at a photo of the boy with a syndrome's mother. She's standing between Lennart and Maud and wearing a bridal gown and they are laughing, all three of them.

'I think Sam's friend was in love with her. But he introduced her to Sam and they fell in love instead. I don't think Sam's friend ever said anything. They were like brothers, those two, can you imagine? I think his friend was just too kind to mention his own feelings, do you understand?'

Elsa understands. Maud smiles.

'He was always such a soft boy, Sam's friend. I always thought he had the soul of a poet. They were so different, him and Sam. It's so terribly difficult to imagine he would do all that he did to save Sam's life. That the place they were in could have made him such a fearsome . . .'

She is silent for a long time, overcome with sorrow.

'Warrior,' she whispers, turning the pages of the photo album.

Elsa doesn't need to see the photo to know who it's of.

It's Sam. He is standing somewhere in a desert, wearing a uniform and supporting himself on crutches. Next to him stands Elsa's granny with a stethoscope round her neck. And between them stands Sam's best friend. Wolfheart.

25

It was the cloud animals that saved the Chosen One when the shadows came in secret to the kingdom of Mimovas to kidnap him. For while Miamas is made of fantasy, Mimovas is made of love. Without love there is no music, and without music there is no Mimovas, and the Chosen One was the most beloved in the whole kingdom. So if the shadows had taken him, it would eventually have led to the downfall of the Land-of-Almost-Awake. If Mimovas falls then Mirevas falls, and if Mirevas falls then Miamas falls, and if Miamas falls then Miaudacas falls, and if Miaudacas falls then Miploris falls. Because without music there can't be any dreams, and without dreams there can't be any fairy tales, and without fairy tales there can't be any courage, and without courage no one would be able to bear any sorrows, and without music and dreams and fairy tales and courage and sorrow there would only be one kingdom left in the Land-of-Almost-Awake: Mibatalos. But Mibatalos can't live alone, because the warriors there would be worthless without the other kingdoms, because they'd no longer have anything to fight for.

Granny also stole that from Harry Potter, that bit about having something to fight for. But Elsa forgave her because it was quite good. You're allowed to nick stuff if it's good.

And it was the cloud animals that saw the shadows stealing along between the houses in Mimovas, and they did what cloud animals do: they swept down like arrows and up again like mighty ships, they transformed themselves into dromedaries and apples and old fishermen with cigars, and the shadows threw themselves into the trap. Because soon they didn't know who or what they were chasing. Then all at once the cloud animals disappeared, and one of them bore away the Chosen One. All the way to Miamas.

And that was how the War-Without-End began. And if it hadn't been for the cloud animals it would have ended there, that day, and the shadows would have won.

Elsa is in the Land-of-Almost-Awake all night. She can get there whenever she wants now, as if it had never been a problem. She doesn't know why, but assumes it's because she has nothing to lose any more. The shadow is in the real world now, Elsa knows who he is, and she knows who Granny was and who Wolfheart is and how it all hangs together. She's not frightened any more. She knows that the war will come, that it's inevitable, and the mere fact of knowing it makes her strangely calm.

The Land-of-Almost-Awake is not burning as it was in the dream. Wherever she rides, it's as beautiful and tranquil as ever. Only when she wakes up does she realise that she has avoided venturing into Miamas. She rides to all five other kingdoms, even the ruins where Mibatalos used to be before the War-Without-End. But never to Miamas. Because she doesn't want to know if Granny is there. Doesn't want to know if Granny *isn't* there.

Dad is standing in the doorway of her bedroom. At once she's wide awake, as if someone just squirted menthol up her nose. (Which, just as an aside, works insanely well if you want to wake someone up. You'd know that if you have the kind of granny Elsa had.)

'What's the matter? Is Mum ill? Is it Halfie?'

Dad looks dubious. And slightly nonplussed. Elsa blinks away her sleep and remembers that Mum is at a meeting at the hospital, because she tried to wake Elsa up before she left, but she pretended to be asleep. And George is in the kitchen, because he came in a bit earlier to ask if she wanted any eggs, but she pretended to be asleep. So she looks at her father with confusion.

'It's not your day for you to be with me, is it?'

Dad clears his throat. Looks like dads do when it suddenly dawns on them that something they used to do because it was important to their daughters has now become one of those things their daughters do because it's important to their dads. It's a very thin line to cross. Neither dads nor their daughters ever forget when they do cross it.

Elsa counts the days in her head, instantly remembers and instantly apologises. She was right, it isn't Dad's day. But she was wrong, because today's the day before Christmas, which is a terrible thing to forget. Because the day before Christmas is her and Dad's day. Christmas-tree day.

As the name subtly suggests, this is the day that Elsa and Dad buy their Christmas tree. A plastic one, obviously, because Elsa refuses to buy a real tree. But because Dad enjoys the annual tradition so much, Elsa insists on buying a new plastic tree every year. Some people find it a bit of an odd tradition, but Granny used to say that 'every child of divorce has the right to get a bit bloody eccentric now and then.'

Mum, of course, was very angry at Granny about the whole plastic tree thing, because she likes the smell of a real spruce tree and always said that the plastic tree was something Granny had duped Elsa about. Because it was Granny who had told Elsa about the Christmas tree dance in Miamas, and no one who's heard that story wants to have a spruce tree that someone has amputated and sold into slavery. In Miamas, spruce trees are living, thinking creatures with – considering that they're coniferous trees – an unaccountably strong interest in home design.

They don't live in the forest but in the southern districts of Miamas, which have become quite trendy in recent years, and they often work in the advertising industry and wear scarves indoors. And once every year, soon after the first snow has fallen, all the spruce trees gather in the big square below the castle and compete for the right to stay in someone's house over Christmas. The spruce trees choose the houses, not the other way round, and the choice is decided by a dance competition. In the olden days they used to have duels about it, but spruce trees are generally such bad shots that it used to take for ever. So now they do spruce-dancing, which looks a bit unusual, because spruce trees don't have feet. And if a non-spruce-tree wants to imitate a dancing spruce tree, they just jump up and down. It's quite handy, particularly on a crowded dancefloor.

Elsa knows that because when Dad drinks a glass and a half of champagne on New Year's Eve he sometimes does the spruce dance in the kitchen with Lisette. But for Dad it's just known as 'dancing'.

'Sorry, Dad, I do know what day it is!' Elsa yells, hopping into her jeans, getting into her jumper and jacket and running into the hall. 'I just have to do one thing first!'

Elsa hid the wurse in Renault last night. She brought it down a bucket of cinnamon buns from Maud and told it to hide under the blankets in the back seat if anyone came down into the garage. 'You have to pretend you're a pile of clothes or a TV or something!' suggested Elsa, though the wurse didn't look entirely convinced. So Elsa had to go and get a sack of dreams from Maud, after which the wurse gave in and crept under the blankets. It didn't look much like a TV, though.

Elsa said goodnight, sneaked back up the stairs and stood in the dark outside the flat where the mother and the boy with a syndrome lived. She was going to ring the doorbell, but she couldn't quite make herself do it. Didn't want to hear any more stories. Didn't want to know about shadows and darkness. So she just put the letter in the slot in the door and ran away.

Their door is locked and shut today. All the other doors too. Anyone who's awake has left the house; everyone else is still asleep. So Elsa hears Kent's voice several floors up, even though he's whispering, because that's how the acoustics of stairwells work. Elsa knows that because 'acoustics' is a word for the word jar. She hears Kent whispering, 'Yes, I promise I'll be back tonight.' But when she comes down the last flight of stairs, past the wurse and Wolfheart's flats and the boy and the mother's flat, Kent suddenly starts talking in a loud voice and calling out, 'Yes, Klaus! In Frankfurt! Yez, yez, yez!' And then he turns round and pretends that he's only just noticed Elsa standing behind him.

'What are you doing?' asks Elsa suspiciously.

Kent asks Klaus to hold the line, as you do when there is actually no Klaus at all on the line. He is wearing a rugby shirt with numbers and a little man on a horse on his chest. Kent has told Elsa that this sort of shirt costs more than a thousand crowns, and Granny always used to say that those sorts of shirts were a good thing, because the horse functioned as a sort of manufacturer's warning that the shirt was highly likely to be transporting a muppet.

'What do you want?' sneers Kent.

Elsa stares at him. Then at the small red bowls of meat that he's distributing down the stairwell.

'What are those?'

Kent throws out his hands so quickly that he almost throws Klaus into the wall.

'That hound is still running around here, it reduces the value of the leasehold conversion!'

Elsa backs away watchfully, without taking her eyes off the bowls of meat. Kent seems to realise that he has expressed himself a little clumsily, so he makes another attempt, in the sort of voice that men of Kent's age think one must put on when talking to girls of Elsa's age, so they'll understand:

'Britt-Marie found dog hairs on the stairs, you understand, darling? We can't have wild animals roving round the building – it reduces the value of the leasehold conversion, you see?' He smiles condescendingly; she can see that he's glancing insecurely at his telephone. 'It's not like we're going to kill it! It'll just go to sleep for a bit, OK? Now why don't you be a good girl and go home to your mummy?'

Elsa doesn't feel so very good. And she doesn't like the way Kent makes quotation marks in the air when he says 'go to sleep'. 'Who are you talking to on the phone?'

'Klaus, a business contact from Germany,' answers Kent as one does when doing no such thing.

'Sure,' says Elsa.

Kent's eyebrows sink.

'Are you giving me attitude?'

Elsa shrugs.

'I think you should run home to your mummy now,' Kent repeats, a touch more menacingly.

Elsa points at the bowls. 'Is there poison in them?'

'Listen, girlie, stray dogs are *vermin*. We can't have vermin running about here, and rust-heaps down in the garage and all kinds of crap. It'll lower the value, don't you understand? It's better for everyone this way.'

But Elsa hears something ominous in his voice when he says 'rust-heaps', so she pushes past him and charges down the cellar stairs. Throws open the door to the garage and stands there with her hands shaking and her heartbeat thumping through her body. She knocks her knees against every step on the way back up.

'WHERE'S RENAULT! WHAT THE HELL HAVE YOU DONE WITH RENAULT!?' she yells at Kent. She waves her fists at him, but only manages to grab hold of Klaus, so she throws Klaus down the cellar stairs so the glass display and plastic cover are smashed and tumble down in a miniature electronic avalanche towards the storage units.

'Are you out of your fu— bloody . . . out of your bloody *mind*, you stupid kid? You know what that telephone *cost*?' yells Kent, and then he tells her it bloody cost eight thousand crowns.

Elsa informs him that she couldn't give a damn what it cost. And then Kent informs her with a sadistic gleam in his eye exactly what he did with Renault.

She runs up the stairs to fetch Dad, but stops abruptly on the penultimate floor. Britt-Marie is standing in her doorway. She's

241

clasping her hands over her stomach, and Elsa can see that she's sweating. The kitchen behind her smells of Christmas food, and she's wearing her flower-print jacket with her large brooch. The pink paintball stain is hardly visible at all.

'You mustn't let Kent kill it,' pleads Elsa, wide-eyed. 'Please, Britt-Marie, it's my friend . . .'

Britt-Marie meets her eyes, and for a single fleeting second there's some humanity in them. Elsa can see that. But then Kent's voice can be heard, calling to Britt-Marie from the stairwell that she has to bring more poison, and then the normal Britt-Marie is back.

'Kent's children are coming here tomorrow. They're afraid of dogs,' she explains firmly.

She straightens out a wrinkle that isn't there on her skirt, and brushes something invisible off her floral-print jacket.

'We're having a traditional Christmas dinner here tomorrow. With some normal Christmas food. Like a civilised family. We're not barbarians, you know.'

Then she slams the door. Elsa stays where she is and realises that Dad is not going to be able to solve this, because tentativeness is not a very useful superpower in this type of emergency situation. She needs reinforcements.

She has been banging on the door for more than a minute before she hears Alf's dragging footsteps. He opens it with a cup of coffee in his hand that smells so strong that she's sure a spoon would get stuck in it.

'I'm sleeping,' he grunts.

'He's killing Renault!' sobs Elsa.

'Killing? Nothing's going to be killed round here. It's only a bloody car,' says Alf, swallows a mouthful of coffee and yawns.

'It's not just a car! It's RENAULT!'

'Who the hell has told you he's going to kill Renault?'

'Kent!'

Elsa hasn't even had time to explain what's in Renault's back seat before Alf has put down the coffee cup, stepped into his shoes and set off down the stairs. She hears Alf and Kent roaring at each other so terribly that she has to cover her ears. She can't hear what they're saying, except that it's a lot of swear words and Kent shouts something about leaseholds and how one can't have 'rust-heaps' parked in the garage because then people will think the house is full of 'socialists'. Which is Kent's way of saying 'bloody idiot', Elsa understands. And then Alf shouts 'bloody idiot', which is his way of saying exactly that, because Alf is not big on complicating things.

And then Alf comes stamping up the stairs again, wild eyed, and muttering:

'The bastard got someone to tow the car away. Is your dad here?'

Elsa nods. Alf storms up the stairs without a word and a few moments later Elsa and Dad are sitting in Taxi, even though Dad doesn't want to at all.

'I'm not sure I want to do this,' says Dad.

'Someone has to bloody drive the damned Renault home,' grunts Alf.

'How do we find out where Kent sent it, then?' asks Elsa, at the same time as Dad does his best not to look completely tentative.

'I've been driving a damned taxi for thirty years,' says Alf.

'And?' hisses Elsa.

'And so I bloody know how to find a Renault that's been towed away!'

Twenty minutes later they're standing in a scrapyard outside the city, and Elsa is hugging the bonnet of Renault in the exact same way you hug a cloud animal: with your whole body. She can see that the TV in the back seat is shuffling about, fairly displeased about not being the first to be hugged, but if you're almost eight and forget to hug a wurse in a Renault, it's because you're less worried about the wurse than the poor scrapyard worker who happens to find it.

Alf and the fairly fat foreman argue for a short while about what it's going to cost to take Renault away. And then Alf and Elsa argue for a fairly long time about why she never mentioned that she didn't have a key to Renault. And then the fat man walks around mumbling that he was sure he left his moped here earlier and where the hell was it now? And then Alf and the fat man negotiate about what it'll cost to tow Renault back to the house. And then Dad has to pay for it all.

It's the best present he's ever given Elsa. Even better than the red felt-tip pen.

Alf ensures that Renault is parked in Granny's slot in the garage, not in Britt-Marie's. When Elsa introduces them to each other, Dad stares at the wurse with the expression of someone preparing for a root filling. The wurse glares back, a bit cocky. Too cocky, thinks Elsa, so she hauls it over the coals about whether it ate the scrapyard foreman's moped. Whereupon the wurse stops looking cocky and goes to lie down under the blankets and looks a bit as if it's thinking that if people don't want it to eat mopeds then people should be more generous with the cinnamon buns.

She tells Dad, to his immense relief, that he can go and wait in Audi. Then Elsa and Alf gather all the red food bowls from the stairwell and put them in a big black bin-bag. Kent catches them and fumes that the poison bloody cost him six hundred crowns. Britt-Marie just stands there.

And then Elsa goes with Dad to buy a plastic tree. Because Britt-Marie is wrong, Elsa's family are no barbarians. Anyway the proper term is 'baa-baa-rians' because in Miamas that is what the spruce trees call those dumb sheep in the real world who chop down living trees, then carry them off and sell them into slavery.

'I'll give you three hundred,' says Elsa to the man in the shop.

'My dear, there's no bargaining in this shop,' says the man in the shop in exactly the sort of tone one might expect of men in shops. 'It costs four hundred and ninety-five.'

'I'll give you two fifty,'

The man smiles mockingly.

'Now I'll only give you two hundred,' Elsa informs him.

The man looks at Elsa's dad. Dad looks at his shoes. Elsa looks at the man and shakes her head seriously.

'My dad is not going to help you. I'll give you two hundred.'

The man arranges his face into something that's probably supposed to look like an expression of how you look at children when they're cute but stupid.

'This is not how it works, my dear.'

Elsa shrugs. 'What time do you close today?'

'In five minutes,' sighs the man.

'And do you have a big warehouse space here?'

'What's that got to do with it?'

'I was just wondering.'

'No. We don't have any warehouse space at all.'

'And are you open on Christmas Eve?'

He pauses. 'No.'

Elsa pouts her lips with pretend surprise.

'So you have a tree here. And no warehouse. And what day is it tomorrow, again?'

Elsa gets the tree for two hundred. She gets a box of balcony lights and an insanely big Christmas elk thrown in for the same price.

'You MUSTN'T go back in and give him any money!' Elsa warns Dad while he's loading it all into Audi. Dad sighs.

'I only did it once, Elsa. On one occasion. And that time you were actually exceptionally unpleasant to the salesman.'

'You have to negotiate!'

Granny taught Elsa to do that. Dad also used to hate going to the shops with her.

Audi stops outside the house. As usual, Dad has turned down the volume of the stereo so Elsa doesn't have to listen to his music. Alf comes out to help Dad carry up the box, but Dad insists on carrying it himself. Because it's a tradition that he brings the tree home for his daughter. Before he leaves, Elsa wants to tell him that she'd like to stay with him more after Halfie's been born. But she doesn't want to upset him, so in the end she says nothing. She just whispers, 'Thanks for the tree, Dad,' and he's happy and then he goes home to Lisette and her children. And Elsa stands there watching as he leaves.

Because no one gets upset if you don't say anything. All almost-eight-year-olds know that.

26

PIZZA

In Miamas you celebrate Christmas the evening before, because
that's when the Christmas tales are told. All tales are regarded
as treasures in Miamas, but the Christmas tales are something
truly special. A normal story can either be funny or sad or
exciting or scary or dramatic or sentimental, but a Christmas
tale has to be all those things. 'A Christmas tale has to be written
with every pen you own,' Granny used to say. And they have to
have happy endings, which is something that Elsa has decided
completely on her own.

Because Elsa's no fool. She knows if there was a dragon at the
beginning of the story, the dragon will turn up again before
the story is done. She knows everything has to become darker
and more horrible before everything works out just fine at the
end. Because that is how all the best stories go.

She knows she's going to have to fight, even though she's tired
of fighting. So it has to end happily, this fairy tale.

It has to.

She misses the smell of pizza when she goes down the stairs.
Granny said there was a law in Miamas about having to eat
pizza at Christmas. Granny was full of nonsense, of course, but
Elsa went along with it, because she likes pizza and Christmas
food kind of sucks if you're a vegetarian.

The pizza also had the added bonus of making a cooking
smell in the stairwell that drove Britt-Marie into a fury. Because
Britt-Marie hangs Christmas decorations on her and Kent's front

door, because Kent's children always come for Christmas and Britt-Marie wants to 'make the stairs look nice for everyone!' And then the Christmas decorations smell of pizza all year, which provokes Britt-Marie and makes her condemn Granny as 'uncivilised'.

'As if THAT old bat can talk about being uncivilised?! No one is more damned civilised than I am!' Granny would snort every year while she sneaked about, as was the tradition, hanging little pieces of calzone all over Britt-Marie's Christmas decorations. And when Britt-Marie appeared at Mum and George's flat on Christmas morning in such a foul mood, in that way of hers, that she said everything twice, Granny defended herself by saying that they were 'Pizza Christmas decorations' and that Granny actually just wanted to 'make things look nice for everyone!' On one occasion she actually dropped the whole calzone through Britt-Marie and Kent's letter box, and then Britt-Marie got so angry on Christmas morning that she forgot to put on her floral-print jacket.

No one was ever able to explain how one can drop a whole calzone through someone's letter box.

Elsa takes a couple of deep, controlled breaths on the stairs, because that's what Mum has told her to do when she gets angry. Mum really does everything that Granny never did. Such as asking Elsa to invite Britt-Marie and Kent for Christmas dinner with all the other neighbours, for example. Granny would never have done that. 'Over my dead body!' Granny would have roared if Mum had suggested it. Which she couldn't have done now that her body was actually dead, Elsa realises, but still. It's about the principle. That's what Granny would have said if she'd been here.

But Elsa can't say no to Mum right now, because Mum, after a lot of nagging, has agreed to let the wurse hide in Granny's flat over Christmas. It's quite difficult saying no to a mum who lets you bring a wurse home, even if Mum still sighs about Elsa 'exaggerating' when Elsa says Kent is trying to kill it.

On the other hand Elsa is happy that the wurse took an instant dislike to George. Not that Elsa feels anyone should hate George, but really no one ever has, so it's nice just for a change.

The boy with a syndrome and his mum are about to move into Granny's flat. Elsa knows that because she played hide-the-key with the boy all afternoon while Mum, George, Alf, Lennart, Maud and the boy's mother sat in the kitchen talking about secrets. They deny it, of course, but Elsa knows how secretive voices sound. You know that when you're almost eight. She hates that Mum has secrets from her. When you know someone is keeping secrets from you it makes you feel like an idiot, and no one likes feeling like an idiot. Mum of all people should know that.

Elsa knows they're talking about Granny's flat being easier to defend if Sam comes here. She knows that Sam will come sooner or later, and that Mum is going to assemble Granny's army on the top floor. Elsa was in Lennart and Maud's flat with the wurse when Mum told Maud to just 'pack the essentials' and tried to sound as if it wasn't at all serious. And then Maud and the wurse packed all the biscuit tins they could find into big bags, and when Mum saw that she sighed and said: 'Please, Maud, I said just the essentials!' And then Maud looked at Mum in a puzzled way and replied: 'Biscuits are the essentials.'

The wurse growled happily at that statement, then looked at Mum as if it was more disappointed than angry and pointedly pushed an extra jar of chocolate and peanut biscuits into the bag. Then they carried it all upstairs to Granny's flat and George invited everyone for mulled wine. The wurse drank the most mulled wine of them all. And now all the grown-ups are sitting in Mum and George's kitchen, having secrets together.

Although Britt-Marie and Kent's door is full of Christmas decorations, no one answers when Elsa rings the doorbell. She finds Britt-Marie in the corridor downstairs, just inside the entrance. She stands with her hands clasped together on her stomach, staring disconsolately at the pram, which is still locked to the banister. She's wearing the floral-print jacket and the brooch. And there's a new notice on the wall.

The first sign was the one that said it was forbidden to leave prams there. And then someone took that sign down. And now someone has put up a new sign. And the pram is still there. And it's actually not a sign, Elsa notices when she goes closer. It's a crossword.

Britt-Marie is startled when she catches sight of her.

'I suppose you find this funny,' she starts. 'You and your family. Making the rest of us look foolish in this house. But I'll get to the bottom of it and find those who are responsible for this, you can be quite sure about that. It's actually a fire risk to have prams in the stairwell and to keep taping up notices on the walls! The paper can actually start burning!'

She rubs an invisible stain from her brooch.

'I'm actually not an idiot, I'm actually not. I know you talk behind my back in this leaseholders' association, I know you do!'

Elsa doesn't quite know what happens inside her at that point, but it must be the combination of the words 'not an idiot' and 'behind my back', perhaps. Something very unpleasant and acidic and foul-smelling rises in Elsa's throat and it takes a long time before, with disgust, she has to admit to herself that it's sympathy.

No one likes feeling like an idiot.

So Elsa says nothing about how maybe Britt-Marie could try to stop being such a bloody busybody the whole time, if she wants people to talk to her a bit more. She doesn't even mention that this is not actually a leaseholders' association. She just swallows all the pride she's feasting on and mumbles:

'Mum and George want to invite you and Kent for Christmas dinner tomorrow. Everyone in the house is going to be there.'

Britt-Marie's gaze wavers for just an instant. Elsa briefly recalls the look she gave earlier today, the human look, but then she seems to snap out of it.

'Well, well, I can't respond to invitations just like that, because Kent is actually at the office right now, and certain people in this house have *jobs* to take care of. You can give your mother that message. Not all people have *time off* all Christmas. And Kent's children are coming tomorrow and they actually don't like running about, going to other people's parties, they like being home with me and Kent. And we're eating some ordinary Christmas food, like a civilised family. We are. You can give your mother that message!'

Britt-Marie storms off; Elsa stays where she is, shaking her head and mumbling, 'Muppet, muppet, muppet.' She looks at the crossword above the pram; she doesn't know who put it there, but now she wishes she'd thought of it herself, because it's obviously driving Britt-Marie barmy.

Elsa goes back up the stairs and knocks on the door of the woman with the black skirt.

'We're having Christmas dinner at ours tomorrow. You're welcome, if you like,' says Elsa, and adds: 'It could actually be quite nice, because Britt-Marie and Kent aren't coming!'

The woman freezes.

'I . . . I'm not so good at meeting people.'

'I know. But you don't seem so good at being on your own either.'

The woman looks at her for a long time, drags her hand slowly through her hair. Elsa stares back determinedly.

'I . . . maybe I can come. A . . . short while.'

'We can buy pizza! If you don't, you know, like Christmas food,' says Elsa hopefully.

The woman smiles. Elsa smiles back.

Alf comes out of Granny's flat just as the woman's climbing the stairs. The boy with a syndrome is circling him happily, doing a little dance, and Alf has an enormous toolbox in one hand, which he tries to hide when he catches sight of Elsa.

'What are you doing?' asks Elsa.

'Nothing,' Alf says evasively.

The boy jumps into Mum and George's flat and heads towards a large bowl of chocolate Santas. Alf tries to get past Elsa on the stairs but Elsa stands in his way.

'What's that?' she asks, pointing at the toolbox.

'Nothing!' Alf repeats and tries to hide it behind his back.

He smells strongly of wood shavings, Elsa notices.

'Sure it's nothing!' she says, grumpily.

She tries to stop feeling like an idiot. It doesn't go so very well.

She looks into the flat at the boy. He looks happy in the way that only an almost-seven-year-old can look happy when standing in front of a whole big bowl of chocolate Santas. Elsa wonders if he's waiting for the real Santa, who isn't made of chocolate. Obviously, Elsa doesn't believe in Santa, but she has a lot of faith in people that do believe in him. She used to write letters to Santa every Christmas, not just wish lists but whole letters. They weren't very much about Christmas, mainly about politics. Because Elsa mostly felt that Santa wasn't involving himself enough in social questions, and believed he needed to be informed about that, in the midst of the floods of greedy letters that she knew he must be receiving from all the other children every year. Someone had to take a bit of responsibility. One year she'd seen the Coca-Cola advert, and that time her letter was quite a lot about how Santa was a 'soulless sell-out'. Another year she'd seen a TV documentary about child labour and, immediately after that, quite a few American Christmas comedies, and because she was unsure whether Santa's definition of 'elf' should be classified as the same as the elves that exist in Old Norse mythology or the ones that live in forests in Tolkien's world, or just in the general sense of a 'short person, sort of thing', she demanded that Santa immediately get back to her with a precise definition.

Santa never did, so Elsa sent another letter that was very long and angry. The year after, Elsa had learned how to use Google, so then she knew the reason for Santa never answering was that he didn't exist. So she didn't write any more letters. She mentioned to Mum and Granny the next day that Santa didn't exist, and Mum got so upset that she choked on her mulled wine, and when Granny saw this she immediately turned dramatically to Elsa and pretended to be even more upset, and burst out: 'DON'T you talk like that, Elsa! If you do, you're just reality-challenged!'

Mum didn't laugh at all about that, which didn't bother Granny, but on the other hand Elsa did laugh a good deal, and that pleased Granny immeasurably. And the day before Christmas, Elsa had a letter from Santa in which he gave her a right ticking-off because she'd 'got herself an attitude', and then there followed a long haranguing passage that started with 'you ungrateful bloody brat' and went on to say that because Elsa had stopped believing in Santa, the elves hadn't been able to reach a proper collective agreement on salaries that year.

'I know you wrote this,' Elsa had hissed at Granny.

'How?' Granny asked with exaggerated outrage

'Because not even Santa is so dumb that he spells "collective" with a double "t"!'

And then Granny had looked a little less outraged and apologised. And then she tried to get Elsa to run to the shop to buy a cigarette lighter, in exchange for Granny 'timing her'. But Elsa didn't fall for that one.

And then Granny had grumpily got out her newly purchased Santa suit, and they went to the children's hospital where Granny's friend worked. Granny went round all day telling fairy tales to children with terrible diseases and Elsa followed behind her, distributing toys. That was Elsa's best ever Christmas. They would make a tradition of it, Granny promised, but it was a really crappy tradition because they only had time to do it one year before she went and died.

Elsa looks at the boy, then at Alf, and locks eyes with him. When the boy catches sight of a bowl of chocolate rabbits and disappears into the flat, Elsa slips into the hall, opens the chest in there and pulls out the Santa suit. She goes back onto the landing and presses it into Alf's arms.

Alf looks at it, as if it just tried to tickle him.

'What's that?'

'What does it look like?' asks Elsa.

'Forget it!' says Alf dismissively, pushing the costume back towards Elsa.

'Forget that you can forget about it!' says Elsa, and pushes the costume back even more.

'Your grandmother said you don't even believe in bloody Santa,' mutters Alf.

Elsa rolls her eyes.

'No, but not everything in the world is about me, right?'

She points into the flat. The boy is sitting on the floor in front of the TV. Alf looks at him and grunts.

'Why can't Lennart be Santa?'

'Because Lennart couldn't keep a secret from Maud,' Elsa answers impatiently.

'What's the bloody relevance of that?'

'The relevance is that Maud can't keep a secret from anyone!'

Alf squints at Elsa. Then he reluctantly mutters that that's true enough. Because Maud really couldn't keep a secret even if was glued to the insides of her hands. While George was playing hide-the-key with Elsa and the boy with a syndrome earlier that evening, Maud had walked behind them and repeatedly whispered, 'Maybe you should look in the flowerpot in the bookshelf,' and when Elsa's mum explained to Maud that the whole point of the game was sort of to find out where the key was hidden, Maud looked disconsolate and said, 'The children look so sad while they're searching, I don't want them to be sad.'

'So you have to be Santa,' Elsa says conclusively.

'What about George?' Alf tries.

'He's too tall. And anyway it'll be too obvious, because he'll wear his jogging shorts on the outside of the Santa suit.'

Alf doesn't look as if that would make much of a difference to him. He takes a couple of dissatisfied steps across the landing and into the hall, where he peers over the edge of the chest as if hoping to find a better option. But the only thing he sees there is bedlinen and then Elsa's Spider-Man suit.

'What's that?' asks Alf, and pokes at it, as if it might poke him back.

'My Spider-Man suit,' grunts Elsa, trying to close the lid.

'When do you get to wear that?' wonders Alf, apparently expecting to know the exact date of the annual Spider-Man day.

'I was supposed to be wearing it when school starts again. We've got a class project.' She closes the chest with a slam. Alf stands there with the Santa suit in his hand and doesn't seem interested. At all, actually. Elsa groans.

'If you h-a-v-e to know I'm not going to be Spider-Man, because apparently girls aren't allowed to be Spider-Man! But I don't care because I haven't got the energy to fight with everyone all the bloody time!'

Alf has already started walking back to the stairs. Elsa swallows her tears, so he doesn't hear them. Maybe he hears them all the same, though. Because he stops by the corner of the railing. Crumples up the Santa suit in his fist. Sighs. Says something that Elsa doesn't hear.

'What?' Elsa says irritably.

Alf sighs again, harder.

'I said I think your grandmother would have wanted you to dress up as any bloody thing you like,' he repeats brusquely, without turning round.

Elsa pushes her hands in her pockets and glares down at the floor.

'The others at school say girls can't be Spider-Man . . .'

Alf takes two dragging steps down the stairs. Stops. Looks at her.

'Don't you think a lot of bastards said that to your grandmother?'

Elsa peers at him.

'Did she dress up as Spider-Man?'

'No.'

'What are you talking about, then?'

'She dressed up as a doctor.'

'Did they tell her she couldn't be a doctor? Because she was a girl?'

Alf shifts something in the toolbox and then stuffs in the Santa suit.

'Most likely they told her a whole lot of damned things she wasn't allowed to do, for a range of different reasons. But she damned well did them all the same. A few years after she was born they were still telling girls they couldn't vote in the bleeding elections but now, the girls do it all the same. That's damned well how you stand up to bastards who tell you what you can and can't do. You bloody do those things all the bloody same.'

Elsa watches her shoes. Alf watches his toolbox. Then Elsa goes into the hall, takes two chocolate Santas, eats one of them and throws the other to Alf, who catches it in his spare hand. He shrugs slightly.

'I think your grandmother would have wanted you to dress up as any old damned thing you wanted.'

With that he slopes off, his Italian opera music seeping out as he opens his door and closes it behind him. Elsa goes into the hall and fetches the whole bowl of chocolate Santas. Then she takes the boy's hand and calls the wurse. All three of them go across the landing to Granny's flat, where they crawl into the magic wardrobe that stopped growing when Granny died. It smells of wood shavings in there. And, in fact, it has magically grown to the exact dimensions needed to accommodate two children and a wurse.

The boy with a syndrome mainly keeps his eyes shut, and Elsa brings him to the Land-of-Almost-Awake. They fly over all six kingdoms, and when they turn towards Mimovas the boy

256

recognises where he is. He jumps off the cloud animal and starts running. When he gets to the city gates, where the music of Mimovas comes pouring out, he starts dancing. He dances beautifully. And Elsa dances with him.

27

MULLED WINE

The wurse wakes Elsa up later that night because it needs a pee. She mumbles sleepily that maybe the wurse shouldn't have drunk so much mulled wine and tries to go back to sleep. But unfortunately the wurse begins to look sort of like wurses do when they're planning to pee on a Gryffindor scarf, whereupon Elsa snatches the scarf away and reluctantly agrees to take it out.

When they get out of the wardrobe, Elsa's mum and the boy with a syndrome's mum are still up making up the beds.

'It needs a pee,' Elsa explains wearily. Mum nods reluctantly but says she has to take Alf with her.

Elsa nods. The boy with a syndrome's mum smiles at her.

'I understand from Maud that it might have been you that left your grandmother's letter in our letter box yesterday.'

Elsa fixes her gaze on her socks.

'I was going to ring the doorbell, but I didn't want to, you know. Disturb. Sort of thing.'

The boy's mum smiles again.

'She wrote sorry. Your grandmother, I mean. Sorry for not being able to protect us any more. And she wrote that I should trust you. Always. And then she asked me to try and get you to trust me.'

'Can I ask you something that could be sort of impolite?' ventures Elsa, poking at the palm of her hand.

'Absolutely.'

258

'How can you stand being alive and being afraid all the time? I mean, when you know there's someone like Sam out there hunting you?'

'Darling, Elsa . . .' whispers Elsa's mum and smiles apologetically at the boy's mother, who just waves her hand dismissively to show that it doesn't matter at all.

'Your grandmother used to say that sometimes we have to do things that are dangerous, because otherwise we aren't really human.'

'She nicked that from *The Brothers Lionheart*,' says Elsa.

The boy's mother turns to Elsa's mum and looks as if she'd like to change the subject. Maybe more for Elsa's sake than her own. 'Do you know if it's a boy or a girl?'

Mum grins almost guiltily and shakes her head.

'We want to wait until the birth.'

'It's going to be a she-he,' Elsa informs her. Her mum looks embarrassed.

'I didn't want to know either until he was born,' says the boy's mother warmly, 'but then I wanted to know everything about him immediately!'

'Yes, exactly, that's how I feel. It doesn't matter what it is, as long as it's healthy!'

Guilt wells up in Mum's face as soon as the last word has escaped her lips. She glances past Elsa towards the wardrobe, where the boy lies sleeping.

'Sorry. I didn't mean to . . .' she manages to say, but the boy's mum interrupts her at once.

'Oh don't say sorry. It's fine. I know what people say. But he is healthy. He's just a bit of extra everything, you could say.'

'I like extra everything!' Elsa exclaims happily, but then she also looks ashamed and mumbles: 'Except Quornburgers. I always get rid of the tomato.'

And then both the mothers laugh so hard that the sound of their voices echoes off the walls. And that's what they both seem to be most in need of. So even though it wasn't her intention, Elsa decides to take the credit for that.

* * *

Alf is waiting for her and the wurse on the stairs. She doesn't know how he knew they were coming. The darkness outside the house is so compact that if you threw a snowball you'd lose sight of it before it left your glove. They sneak under Britt-Marie's balcony so they don't give the wurse away. The wurse backs into a bush and looks as though it would have appreciated having a newspaper or something.

Elsa and Alf turn away respectfully. Elsa clears her throat.

'Thanks for helping me with Renault.'

Alf grunts. Elsa shoves her hands in her jacket pockets.

'Kent's an arsewipe. Someone should poison *him*!'

Alf's head turns slowly.

'Don't say that.'

'What?'

'Don't bloody talk like that.'

'What? He is an arsewipe, isn't he?'

'Maybe so. But you don't damn well call him that in front of me!'

'You call him a "bloody idiot", like, all the time!'

'Yes. I'm allowed to. You're not.'

'Why not?'

Alf's leather jacket creaks.

'Because I'm allowed to get shitty about my little brother. You're not.'

It takes many different kinds of eternities for Elsa to digest that piece of information.

'I didn't know that,' she manages to say at last. 'Why are you so horrible to each other if you're brothers?'

'You don't get to choose your siblings,' mutters Alf.

Elsa doesn't really know how to answer that. She thinks about Halfie. She'd rather not, so she changes the subject:

'Why don't you have a girlfriend?'

'Never you bloody mind.'

'Have you ever been in love?'

'I'm a damned grown-up. It's bloody obvious I've been in love. Everyone's been in bloody love some time.'

'How old were you?'

'The first time?'

'Yes.'

'Ten.'

'And the second time?'

Alf's leather jacket creaks. He checks his watch and starts heading back to the house.

'There was no second time.'

Elsa is about to ask something else. But that's when they hear it. Or rather it's the wurse that hears it. The scream. The wurse leaps out of the bush and hurtles into the darkness like a black spear. Then Elsa hears its bark for the first time. She thought she'd heard it barking before, but she was wrong. All she's heard before are yelps and whines compared to this. This bark makes the foundations of the house quake. It's a battle-cry.

Elsa gets there first. She's better at running than Alf.

Britt-Marie is standing, white-faced, a few metres from the door. There's a carrier bag of food dropped on the snow. Lollipops and cartoon magazines have spilled out of it. A stone's throw away stands Sam.

With a knife in his hand.

The wurse stands resolutely between them, its front paws planted like concrete pillars in the snow, its teeth bared. Sam isn't moving, but Elsa can see that he's hesitating. He slowly turns round and sees her, and his gaze pulverises her spine. Her knees want to give way and sink into the snow and disappear. The knife glitters in the glow of the streetlights. Sam's hand hovers in the air, his body rigid with animosity. His eyes eat their way into her, cold and warlike. But the knife isn't directed at her, she can see that.

Elsa can hear Britt-Marie sobbing. She doesn't know where the instinct comes from, or the courage, or maybe it's just pure stupidity – Granny always used to say that she and Elsa were the sort of people who, deep down, were a bit soft in the head, and it would get them in trouble sooner or later – but Elsa runs. Runs right at Sam. She can see him bring the knife down confidently by a few inches, and that the other hand is raised like a claw to catch her as she leaps.

But she doesn't have time to get there. She collides with something dry and black. Feels the smell of dry leather. Hears the creaking of Alf's jacket.

And then Alf is standing in front of Sam, with the same ominous body language. Elsa sees the hammer sliding into his palm from the coat-arm. Alf swings it calmly from side to side. Sam's knife doesn't move. They do not take their eyes off each other.

Elsa doesn't know how long they stand there. For how many eternities of fairy tales. It feels like all of them. It feels as if she has time to die. As if the terror is cracking her heart.

'The police are on their way,' Alf finally utters in a low voice. He sounds as if he thinks it's a pity. That they can't just finish this here and now.

Sam's eyes wander calmly from Alf to the wurse. The wurse's hackles are raised. It growls like rolling thunder from its lungs. A faint smile steals across Sam's lips for an unbearable length of time. Then he takes a single step back and the darkness engulfs him.

The police car skids into the street, but Sam is long gone by then. Elsa collapses into the snow as if her clothes have been emptied of whatever was in there. She feels Alf catching her and hears him hissing at the wurse to run up their stairs before the police catch sight of it. She hears Britt-Marie panting and the police crunching through the snow. But her consciousness is already fading, far away. She's ashamed of it, ashamed of being so afraid that she just closes her eyes and escapes into her mind. No knight of Miamas was ever so paralysed with fear. A real knight would have stayed in position, straight-backed, not taken refuge in sleep. But she can't help it. It's too much reality for an almost eight-year-old.

She wakes up on the bed in Granny's bedroom. It's warm. She feels the wurse's nose against her shoulder and pats its head.

'You're so brave,' she whispers.

The wurse looks as if maybe it deserves a biscuit. Elsa slips out of the sweaty sheets, onto the floor. Through the doorway she sees Mum standing in the hall, her face grey. She's shouting furiously at Alf, so angry she's crying. Alf stands there in silence, taking it. Elsa runs through into Mum's arms.

'It wasn't their fault, they were only trying to protect me!' Elsa sobs.

Britt-Marie's voice interrupts her.

'No, it was obviously my fault! My fault, it was. Everything was obviously my fault, Ulrika.'

Elsa turns to Britt-Marie, realising as she does so that Maud and Lennart and the boy with a syndrome's mum are also in the hall. Everyone looks at Britt-Marie. She clasps her hands together over her stomach.

'He was standing outside the door, hiding, but I caught the smell of those cigarettes. So I told him that in this lease-holders' association we don't smoke! And then he got out that . . .'

Britt-Marie can't bring herself to say 'knife' without her voice breaking again. She looks offended, as you do when you're the last to learn a secret.

'You all know who he is, of course! But obviously none of you thought to warn me about it, oh no. Even though I'm the information officer in this residents' association!'

She straightens out a wrinkle in her skirt. A real wrinkle, this time. The bag of lollipops and comics is by her feet. Maud tries to put a tender hand on Britt-Marie's arm, but Britt-Marie removes it. Maud smiles wistfully.

'Where is Kent?' she asks softly.

'He's at a business meeting!' Britt-Marie snaps.

Alf looks at her, then at the bag from the supermarket, and then at her again.

'What were you doing out so late?'

'Kent's children get lollipops and comics when they come for Christmas! Always! I was in the shop!'

'Sorry, Britt-Marie. We just didn't know what to say. Look, why don't you just stay here tonight, at least? It may be safer if we're all together?'

Britt-Marie surveys them over the tip of her nose.

'I'm sleeping at home. Kent is coming home tonight. I'm always home when Kent arrives.'

The policewoman with the green eyes comes up the stairs behind her. Britt-Marie spins round. The green eyes stay on her, watchfully.

'It's about time you turned up!' Britt-Marie says. The green-eyed officer doesn't say anything. Another officer is standing behind her, and Elsa can see that he's flummoxed by just having caught sight of Elsa and Mum. He seems to remember escorting them to the hospital only to be given the slip once they got there.

Lennart tries to invite them both in for coffee, and the summer intern policeman looks like this would be preferable to searching the area with dogs, but after a stern glance from his superior he shakes his head at the floor. The green-eyed policewoman talks with the sort of voice that effortlessly fills a room.

'We're going to find him,' she says, her gaze still riveted to Britt-Marie. 'Also, the dog that Kent called about yesterday, Britt-Marie? He said you'd found dog hairs on the stairs. Did you see it tonight?'

Elsa stops breathing. So much that she forgets to wonder about why Green-eyes is referring to Kent and Britt-Marie by their first names. Britt-Marie peers around the room, at Elsa and Mum and Maud and Lennart and the boy with a syndrome's mum. Last of all at Alf. His face is devoid of expression. The green eyes sweep over the hall. There's sweat all over Elsa's palms when she opens and closes her hands to make them stop shaking. She knows that the wurse is sleeping just a few metres behind her, in Granny's bedroom. She knows that everything is lost, and she doesn't know what to do to stop it. She'll never be able to escape with the wurse through all the police she can hear at the bottom of the stairs, not even a wurse could pull that off. They'll shoot it. Kill it. She wonders if that was what the shadow had been planning all along. Because it didn't dare fight the wurse. Without the wurse, and without Wolfheart, the castle is defenceless.

Britt-Marie purses her lips when she sees Elsa staring at her. Changes her hands round on her stomach and snorts, with a sudden, newly acquired self-confidence, at Green-eyes.

'Maybe we misjudged it, Kent and I. Maybe they weren't dog hairs, it may have been some other nuisance. It wouldn't be so strange, with so many odd people running about on these stairs these days,' she says, half-apologetically and half-accusingly and adjusts the brooch of the floral-print jacket.

The green eyes glance quickly at Elsa. Then the policewoman nods briskly, as if the matter is over and done with, and assures them they'll keep the house under surveillance for the night. Before anyone has time to say anything else, the two officers are already on their way down the stairs. Elsa's mum is breathing heavily. She holds out her hand to Britt-Marie, but Britt-Marie moves away.

'Obviously you find it amusing to have secrets from me. It's amusing to make me look like an idiot, that's what you think!'

'Please, Britt-Marie,' Maud tries to say, but Britt-Marie shakes her head, picks up her bag and stamps out of the door. Well-meaningly.

But Elsa sees the way Alf looks at her when she leaves. The wurse is standing in the bedroom doorway with the same expression. And now Elsa knows who Britt-Marie is.

Mum also goes down the stairs, Elsa doesn't know why. Lennart puts on some coffee. George gets out some eggs and makes more mulled wine. Maud distributes biscuits. The boy with a syndrome's mother crawls into the wardrobe to find her son, and Elsa hears him laughing. That's one good superpower he's got there.

Alf goes onto the balcony and Elsa goes after him. Stands hesitantly behind him for a long time before joining him and peering over the railing. Green-eyes is standing in the snow, talking to Elsa's mum. She smiles the way she smiled at Granny that time in the police station.

'Do they know each other?' Elsa asks, surprised. Alf nods.

'Knew, at least. They were best friends when they were your age.'

Elsa looks at Mum, and she can see that she's still angry. Then she peers at the hammer that Alf has put away in a corner of the balcony floor.

'Were you going to kill Sam?'

Alf's eyes are apologetic but honest.

'No.'

'Why was Mum so angry at you, then?'

Alf's leather jacket heaves slightly.

'She was angry because she wasn't there holding the hammer.'

Elsa's shoulders sink; she wraps her arms round herself against the cold. Alf hangs his leather jacket over her. Elsa hunches up inside it.

'Sometimes I think I'd like someone to kill Sam.'

Alf doesn't answer. Elsa looks at the hammer.

'I mean . . . sort of kill, anyway. I know one shouldn't think people deserve to die. But sometimes I'm not sure people like him deserve to live . . .'

Alf leans against the balcony railing.

'It's human.'

'Is it human to want people to die?'

Alf shakes his head calmly.

'It's human not to be sure.'

Elsa hunches up even more inside the jacket. Tries to feel brave.

'I'm scared,' she whispers.

'Me too,' says Alf.

And they don't say anything else about it.

They sneak out with the wurse when everyone has gone to sleep, but Elsa knows that her mum sees them go. She's certain that Green-eyes also sees them. That she's also keeping a watch over them, somewhere in the dark, like Wolfheart would have done, if he were there. And Elsa tries not to feel reproachful to Wolfheart, for not being there, for letting her down after he promised to always protect her. It doesn't go very well.

266

She doesn't talk to Alf. He doesn't say anything either. It's the night before Christmas but everything just feels odd.

As they're making their way back up the stairs Alf stops briefly outside Britt-Marie's front door. Elsa sees the way he looks at it. Looks at it, as one does when there was once a first time, but never a second, and never anything more. Elsa looks at the Christmas decorations, which, for the first time ever, don't smell of pizza.

'How old are Kent's children?' she asks.

'They're grown-ups,' says Alf bitterly.

'So why did Britt-Marie say they want comics and lollipops, then?'

'Britt-Marie invites them over for dinner every Christmas. They never come. The last time they came they were still children. They liked lollipops and comics then,' Alf answers emptily.

When he moves off up the stairs with his dragging footsteps and Elsa follows on behind, the wurse stays where it is. Considering how smart she is, it takes Elsa an unaccountably long time before she realises why.

The Princess of Miploris was so beloved of the two princes that they fought for her love, until they hated one another. The Princess of Miploris once had a treasure stolen by a witch, and now she lives in the kingdom of sorrow.

And the wurse is guarding the gates of her castle. Because that's what wurses do.

28

POTATOES

Elsa wasn't eavesdropping. She's not the sort of person who eavesdrops. Especially on Christmas morning.

She just happened to be standing there on the stairs early the next morning, and that's when she heard Britt-Marie and Kent talking. It wasn't on purpose – she was looking for the wurse and her Gryffindor scarf. And the door of Kent and Britt-Marie's flat was open. After she'd stood there for a while listening she realised that if she walked past their door now they'd spot her, and it would look as if maybe she'd been standing on the stairs eavesdropping *deliberately*. So she just stayed put.

'*Britt-Marie!*' hollered Kent from inside – judging by the echo he was in the bathroom, and judging by the volume of his shouting she was very far away.

'Yes?' answered Britt-Marie, sounding as if she was standing quite close to him.

'Where is my damn electric razor?' yelled Kent without apologising for yelling. Elsa disliked him a lot for that. Because it's 'damned', not 'damn'.

'Second drawer,' answered Britt-Marie.

'Why did you put it there? It's always in the first drawer!'

'It's always been in the second drawer.'

A second drawer was opened, then came the sound of an electric razor. But not the slightest little sound of Kent saying

'Thanks.' Britt-Marie went into the hall and leaned out of the front door with Kent's suit in her hand. Gently brushed invisible fluff from one arm. She didn't see Elsa, or at least Elsa didn't think she did. And because Elsa wasn't quite sure, she realised that now she had to stay where she was and look as if she was supposed to be there. As if she was just out inspecting the quality of the railings, or something like that. Not at all as if she was eavesdropping. It got very complicated, the whole thing.

Britt-Marie disappeared back into the flat.

'Did you talk to David and Pernilla?' she asked pleasantly.

'Yes, yes.'

'So when are they coming?'

'Damned if I know.'

'But I have to plan the cooking, Kent . . .'

'Let's just eat when they come – six, or seven maybe,' Kent said dismissively.

'Well which, Kent?' asked Britt-Marie, sounding worried. 'Six or seven?'

'Jesus Christ, Britt-Marie, it doesn't make any damn difference.'

'If it doesn't make any difference then maybe half-six is about right?'

'Fine, whatever.'

'Did you tell them we normally eat at six?'

'We *always* eat at six.'

'But you did you say that to David and Pernilla?'

'We've been having dinner at six since the beginning of time; they've probably worked that out by now,' said Kent with a sigh.

'I see. Is there something wrong with that now, all of a sudden?'

'No, no. Let's say six, then. If they're not here they're not here,' said Kent, as if he was anyway quite sure they wouldn't come. 'I have to go now, I have a meeting with Germany,' he added, walking out of the bathroom.

'I'm only trying to arrange a nice Christmas for the whole family, Kent,' said Britt-Marie despondently.

'Can't we just bloody heat up the food when they come?!'

'If I can just know when they are coming, I can make sure the food is hot when they arrive,' said Britt-Marie.

'Let's just eat when everyone is here, if it's so bloody important'.

'And when will everyone be here, then?'

'Damn, Britt-Marie! I don't know! You know what they're like – they could come at six or they could come at half past eight!'

Britt-Marie stood in silence for a few grim seconds. Then she took a deep breath and tried to stabilise her voice as you do when not wanting it to be obvious that you're yelling inside.

'We can't have Christmas dinner at half past eight, Kent.'

'I know that! So the kids will just have to eat when they damn well get here, won't they!'

'There's no need to get short,' said Britt-Marie, sounding a bit short.

'Where are my damn cufflinks?' asked Kent and started tottering around the flat with his half-knotted tie trailing behind him.

'In the second drawer in the chest,' Britt-Marie replied.

'Aren't they usually in the first?'

'They've always been in the second . . .'

Elsa just stands there. Not eavesdropping, obviously. But there's a big mirror hanging in the hall just inside the front door, and when Elsa stands on the stairs she can see Kent's reflection in it. Britt-Marie is neatly turning down his shirt collar over the tie and gently brushing the lapel of his suit jacket.

'When are you coming home?' she asks in a low voice.

'I don't bloody know, you know how the Germans are, don't wait up for me,' Kent answers evasively, extricating himself and heading for the door.

'Put the shirt directly in the washing machine when you come in, please,' says Britt-Marie and comes padding after him to brush something from his trouser-leg.

Kent looks at his watch the way men with very expensive watches do when they look at them. Elsa knows that because Kent told Elsa's mum that his watch cost more than Kia.

'In the washing machine, please, Kent! Directly, as soon as you come home!' Britt-Marie calls out.

Kent steps onto the landing without answering. He catches sight of Elsa. He doesn't seem to think she's been eavesdropping at all, but on the other hand he doesn't look very pleased to see her.

'Yo!' he says with a grin, in that way grown men say 'yo' to children because they think that's how children talk.

Elsa doesn't answer. Because she doesn't talk like that. Kent's telephone rings. It's a new telephone, Elsa notices. Kent looks as if he'd like to tell her what it cost.

'That's Germany calling!' he says to Elsa, and looks as if he's only just remembering that she was very much implicated in the cellar-stairs-related incident yesterday that resulted in his last phone being rendered out of action.

He looks as if he remembers the poison as well, and what it cost. Elsa shrugs, as if she's challenging him to a fight. Kent starts yelling, 'Yez Klaus!' into his new phone as he disappears down the stairs.

Elsa takes a few steps towards the stairs, but stops in the doorway. In the hall mirror she sees the bathroom. Britt-Marie is standing in there, carefully rolling up the lead of Kent's electric shaver before putting it in the third drawer.

She comes out into the hall. Catches sight of Elsa. Folds her hands over her stomach.

'Oh I see, I see . . .' she starts.

'I wasn't eavesdropping!' says Elsa at once.

Britt-Marie straightens the coats on the hangers in the hall and carefully brushes the back of her hand over all of Kent's overcoats and jackets. Elsa shoves the tips of her fingers into the pockets of her jeans and mumbles:

'Thanks.'

Britt-Marie turns round, surprised.

'Pardon me?'

Elsa groans like you do when you're almost eight and have to say thanks twice.

'I said thanks. For not saying anything to the police about—' she says, stopping herself before she says 'the wurse.'

Britt-Marie seems to understand.

'You should have informed me about that horrible creature, young lady.'

'It's not a horrible creature.'

'Not until it bites someone.'

'It never will bite anyone! And it saved you from Sam!' growls Elsa.

Britt-Marie looks as if she's about to say something. But she leaves it. Because she knows it's true. And Elsa is going to say something, but she also leaves it. Because she knows that Britt-Marie actually returned the favour.

She looks into the flat through the mirror.

'Why did you put the razor in the wrong drawer?' she asks.

Britt-Marie brushes, brushes, brushes her skirt. Folds her hands.

'I don't know what you're talking about,' she says, even though Elsa very well sees that she does.

'Kent said it was always in the first drawer. But you said it was always in the second drawer. And then after he'd gone you put it in the third drawer,' said Elsa.

And then Britt-Marie looks distracted for just a few moments. Then something else. Alone, perhaps. And then she mumbles:

'Yes, yes, maybe I did. Maybe I did.'

Elsa tilts her head.

'Why?'

And then there's a silence for an eternity of fairy tale silences. And then Britt-Marie whispers, as if she's forgotten that Elsa is standing there in front of her:

'Because I like it when he shouts my name.'

And then Britt-Marie closes the door.

And Elsa stands outside and tries to dislike her. It doesn't go all that well.

29

SWISS MERINGUES

You have to believe. Granny always said that. You have to believe in something in order to understand the tales. 'It's not important what exactly you believe in, but there's got to be something, or you may as well forget the whole damned thing.'

And maybe in the end that's what everything, all of this, is about.

Elsa finds her Gryffindor scarf in the snow outside the house, where she dropped it when she charged at Sam the night before. The green-eyed policewoman is standing a few metres away. The sun has hardly risen. The snow sounds like popcorn popping as she walks over it.

'Hello,' offers Elsa.

Green-eyes nods, silently.

'You're not much of a talker, are you?'

Green-eyes smiles. Elsa wraps the scarf round herself.

'Did you know my granny?'

The policewoman scans along the house wall and over the little street.

'Everyone knew your grandmother.'

'And my mum?' Green-eyes nods again. Elsa squints at her. 'Alf says you were best friends.' She nods again. Elsa wonders how that would feel. To have a best friend who's your own age. Then she stands in silence beside the policewoman and watches the sun come up. It's going to be a beautiful Christmas Eve, despite everything that's happened. She clears her throat and heads back to the front entrance, stopping with her hand on the door handle.

'Have you been on guard here all night?'

She nods again.

'Will you kill Sam if he comes back?'

'I hope not.'

'Why not?'

'Because it's not my job to kill.'

'What is your job, then?'

'To protect.'

'Him or us?' Elsa asks reproachfully.

'Both.'

'He's the one who's dangerous. Not us.'

Green-eyes smiles without looking happy.

'When I was small your grandmother used to say that if you become a police officer you can't choose who to protect. You have to try to protect everyone.'

'Did she know you wanted to become a policewoman?' asks Elsa.

'She's the one who made me want to become one.'

'Why?'

Green-eyes starts smiling. Genuinely, this time.

'Because I was afraid of everything when I was small. And she told me I should do what I was most afraid of. I should laugh at my fears.'

Elsa nods, as if this confirms what she already knew.

'It was you and Mum, wasn't it – the golden knights that saved the Telling Mountain from the Noween and the fears. And built Miaudacas. It was you and Mum.'

The policewoman raises her eyebrows imperceptibly.

'We were many things in your grandmother's fairy tales, I think.'

Elsa opens the door, puts her foot in the opening, and stops there.

'Did you know my mum first or my granny?'

'Your grandmother.'

'You're one of the children on her bedroom ceiling, aren't you?'

Green-eyes looks directly at her. She smiles again in the real way.

'You're smart. She always said you were the smartest girl she ever met.'

Elsa nods. The door closes behind her. And it ends up being a beautiful Christmas Eve. Despite everything.

She looks for the wurse in the cellar storage unit and in Renault, but they are both empty. She knows the wardrobe in Granny's flat is also empty, and the wurse is definitely not in Mum and George's flat because no healthy being can stand being there on a Christmas morning. Mum is even more efficient than usual at Christmas.

She normally starts her Christmas shopping in May each year. She says it's because she's 'organised', Granny used to disagree and say it was actually because she was 'anal', and then Elsa used to have to wear her headphones for quite a long time. But this year Mum decided to be a bit free-spirited and crazy, so she waited until the first of August before asking what Elsa wanted for Christmas. She was very angry when Elsa refused to tell her, even though Elsa expressly asked if she understood how much someone changes as a person in half a year when they're almost eight. So Mum did what Mum always does: she went and bought a present on her own initiative. And it went as it usually went: to hell. Elsa knew that because she knew where Mum hid her presents. What do you expect when you buy an almost-eight-year-old her present five months early?

So this year, Elsa is having three books that are about different themes in some way or other touched upon by various characters in the Harry Potter books. They're wrapped in a paper that Elsa likes very much. Elsa knows that because Mum's first present was utterly useless and when Elsa informed her of that in October they argued for about a month and then Elsa's mum gave up and gave Elsa money instead, so she could go and buy 'what she wanted, then!' And then she wrapped them in a paper she liked very much. And put the parcel in Mum's not-so-secret place and praised Mum for again being so considerate and sensitive that she knew exactly what Elsa wanted this year. And then Mum called Elsa a 'Grinch'.

Elsa had become very attached to this tradition.

She rings on Alf's door half a dozen times before he opens. He's got his dressing gown on, his irritated expression and his Juventus coffee cup.

'What's the matter?' he barks.

'Merry Christmas!' says Elsa without answering the question.

'I'm sleeping,' he grunts.

'It's Christmas morning,' Elsa informs him.

'I do know that,' he says.

'Why are you sleeping, then?'

'I was up late last night.'

'Doing what?'

Alf takes a sip of his coffee.

'What are you doing here?'

'I asked first,' Elsa insists.

'I'm not the one standing at your door in the middle of the night!'

'It's not the middle of the night. And it's *Christmas*!'

He drinks some more coffee. She kicks his doormat irritably.

'I can't find the wurse.'

'I know that as well,' nods Alf casually.

'How?'

'Because it's here.'

Elsa's eyebrows shoot up as if they just sat down in wet paint.

'The wurse is here?'

'Yes.'

'Why didn't you say so?'

'I just bloody did.'

'Why is it here?'

'Because Kent came home at five this morning, and it couldn't sit on the stairs. Kent would have bloody called the police if he'd found out it was still in the house.'

Elsa peers into Alf's flat. The wurse is sitting on the floor, lapping at something in a big metal bowl in front of it. It says 'Juventus' on it. The metal bowl, that is.

'How do you know what time Kent came home?'

'Because I was in the garage when he arrived in his BMW bastard,' says Alf impatiently.

'What were you doing in the garage?' asks Elsa patiently.

Alf looks as if that is an incredibly stupid question.

'I was waiting for him.'

'How long did you wait?'

'Until five o'clock, I bloody said,' he grunts.

Elsa thinks about giving him a hug, but leaves it. The wurse peers up from the metal bowl, looking enormously pleased. Something black is dripping from its nose. Elsa turns to Alf.

'Alf, did you give the wurse . . . coffee?'

'Yes,' says Alf, and looks as if he can't understand what could reasonably be wrong about that.

'It's an ANIMAL! Why did you give it COFFEE?'

Alf scratches his scalp, which, for him, is the same thing as scratching his hair. Then he adjusts his dressing gown. Elsa notices that he has a thick scar running across his chest. He sees her noticing and looks grumpy about it.

Alf goes into his bedroom and closes the door, and when he comes out again he is wearing his leather jacket with the taxi badge. Even though it's Christmas Eve. They have to let the wurse pee in the garage, because there are even more police outside the building now, and not even a wurse can hold out for very long after drinking a bowl of coffee.

Granny would have loved that one. Peeing in the garage. It will drive Britt-Marie to distraction.

When they come up, Mum and George's flat smells of Swiss meringues and pasta gratin with Béarnaise sauce, because Mum has decided that everyone in the house is having Christmas together this year. No one disagreed with her, partly because it was a good idea, and partly because no one ever disagrees with Mum. And then George suggested that everyone should make their own favourite dish for a Christmas buffet. He's good like that, George, which infuriates Elsa.

The boy with a syndrome's favourite food is Swiss meringue, so his mum made it for him. Well, his mum got out all the ingredients and Lennart picked all the meringues up off the floor and Maud made the actual Swiss meringue while the boy and his mother were dancing.

And then Maud and Lennart thought it was important that the woman in the black skirt also felt involved, because they're good like that, so they asked if she wanted to prepare anything in particular. She just sat glued to her chair at the far end of the flat and looked very embarrassed and mumbled that she hadn't cooked any food for several years. 'You don't cook very much when you live alone,' she explained. And then Maud looked very upset and apologised for being so insensitive. And then the woman in the black skirt felt so sorry for Maud that she made a pasta gratin with Béarnaise sauce. Because that was her boys' favourite dish. So they all have Swiss meringue and pasta gratin with Béarnaise sauce, because that's the sort of Christmas it is. In spite of it all.

The wurse gets two buckets of cinnamon buns from Maud, and George goes to the cellar to fetch up the bathing tub Elsa had when she was a baby and fills it with mulled wine. With this as an incentive, the wurse agrees to hide for an hour in the wardrobe in Granny's flat, and then Mum goes down and invites up the police outside the house. Green-eyes sits next to Mum. They laugh. The summer intern is there too; he eats the most Swiss meringue of them all and falls asleep on the sofa.

The woman in the black skirt sits in silence at the table, in the far corner. After they've eaten, while George is washing up and Maud wiping down the tables and Lennart sitting on a stool with a stand-by cup of coffee, waiting for the percolator and making sure it's not going to get up to any tricks, the boy with a syndrome goes through the flat and crosses the landing and goes into Granny's flat. When he comes back he has cinnamon bun crumbs all round his mouth and so many wurse hairs on his jumper that he looks like someone invited him to a fancy dress party and he decided to dress up as a carpet. He gets a blanket from Elsa's room and walks up to the woman in the black skirt, looks at her for a long time, then reaches up, standing on his tiptoes, and pinches her nose. Startled, she jumps, and the boy's mother makes the sort of scream that mothers make when their children pinch complete strangers' noses and rushes towards him. But Maud gently catches hold of her arm and stops her, and when the boy holds up his thumb, poking out between his index finger and his long finger, while looking at the woman in the black skirt, Maud explains pleasantly:

'It's a game. He's pretending he stole your nose.'

The woman stares at Maud. Stares at the boy. Stares at the nose. And then she steals his nose. And he laughs so loudly that the windows start rattling. He falls asleep in her lap, wrapped up in the blanket. When his mother, with an apologetic smile, tries to lift him off, observing as she does so that 'it's actually not at all like him to be so direct,' the woman in the black skirt touches her hand tremulously and whispers:

'If . . . if it's all right I . . . could I hold him a little longer . . . ?'

The boy's mother puts both her hands round the woman's hand and nods. The woman puts her forehead against the boy's hair and whispers:

'Thanks.'

George makes more mulled wine and everything feels almost normal and not at all frightening. After the police have thanked them for their hospitality and headed back down the stairs, Maud looks unhappily at Elsa and says she can understand it must have been frightening for a child to have police in the house on Christmas Eve. But Elsa takes her by the hand and says:

'Don't worry, Maud. This is a Christmas tale. They always have a happy ending.'

And it's clear that Maud believes it.

Because you have to believe.

30

PERFUME

Only one person collapses with a heart attack late on Christmas
Eve. But two hearts are broken. And the house is never quite
the same again.

It all starts with the boy waking up late in the afternoon
and feeling hungry. The wurse and Samantha come flopping
out of the wardrobe because the mulled wine is finished. Elsa
marches in circles round Alf and intimates that it's time to get
the Santa suit. Elsa and the wurse follow Alf down to the
garage. He gets into Taxi. When Elsa opens the passenger door
and sticks her head in and asks what he's doing, he turns the
ignition key and grunts:

'If I have to impersonate Santa for the rest of the day I'm
nipping out for a newspaper first.'

'I don't think my mum wants me to go anywhere.'

'No one invited you!'

Elsa and the wurse ignore him and jump in. When Alf starts
railing at her that you can't just jump into people's cars like
that, Elsa says that this is actually Taxi and that is precisely
what one does with Taxi. And when Alf grumpily taps the meter
and points out that taxi journeys cost money, Elsa says that
she'd like to have this taxi journey as her Christmas present.
And then Alf looks very grumpy for a long time, and then they
go off for Elsa's Christmas present.

Alf knows of a kiosk that's open even on Christmas Eve. He
buys a newspaper. Elsa buys two ice creams. The wurse eats all

of its own and half of hers. Which, if one knows how much wurses like ice cream, shows how immensely considerate it was being. It spills some of it in the back seat, but Alf only shouts at it for about ten minutes. Which, if one knows how much Alf dislikes wurses spilling ice cream in the back seat of Taxi, shows how immensely considerate he was being.

'Can I ask you something?' asks Elsa, even though she knows full well that this is also a question. 'Why didn't Britt-Marie spill the beans about the wurse to the police?'

'She can be a bit of a nag-bag sometimes. But she's not bloody evil,' Alf clarifies.

'But she hates dogs,' Elsa persists.

'Ah, she's just scared of them. Your granny used to bring back loads of strays to the house when she moved in. We were just little brats back then, Britt-Marie and Kent and me. One of the mutts bit Britt-Marie and her mum made a hell of a commotion about it,' Alf says, a shockingly lengthy description given that it was coming from Alf.

Taxi pulls into the street. Elsa thinks of Granny's stories about the Princess of Miploris.

'So you've been in love with Britt-Marie since you were ten years old?' she asks.

'Yes,' Alf replies as if it was absolutely self-evident. Bowled over by this, Elsa looks at him and waits, because she knows that only by waiting will she get him to tell the whole story. You know things like that when you're almost eight.

She waits for as long as she needs to.

Then after two red lights Alf sighs resignedly, like you do while preparing yourself to tell a story even though you don't like telling stories. And then he recounts the tale of Britt-Marie. And himself. Although the latter part may not be his intention. There are quite a lot of swear words in it, and Elsa has to exert herself quite a lot not to correct the grammar. But after a lot of ifs and buts and quite a few damneds, Alf has explained that he and Kent grew up with their mother in the flat where Alf now lives. When Alf was ten, another family moved into

283

the flat above theirs, with two daughters of the same age as Alf and Kent. The mother was a renowned singer and the father wore a suit and was always at work. The elder sister, Ingrid, apparently had an outstanding singing talent. She was going to be a star, her mother explained to Alf and Kent's mother. She never said anything about the other daughter, Britt-Marie. Alf and Kent caught sight of her anyway. It was impossible not to.

No one remembers exactly when the young female medical student first showed up in the house. One day she was just there in the enormous flat that took up the entire top floor of the house in those days, and when Alf and Kent's mother interrogated her about why she lived by herself in such a big flat, the young female medical student replied that she'd 'won it in a game of poker.' She wasn't at home a great deal, of course, and whenever she was, she was always accompanied by outlandish friends and, from time to time, stray dogs. One evening she brought home a large black cur that she'd apparently also won in a game of poker, Alf explains. Alf and Kent and the daughters of the neighbouring family only wanted to play with it; they didn't understand that it was sleeping. Alf was quite certain it never meant to bite Britt-Marie, it was just caught unawares. She was too.

The dog disappeared after that. But Britt-Marie's mother still hated the young medical student, and nothing anyone said could make her change her mind. And then came the car accident in the street just outside the house. Britt-Marie's mother never saw the lorry. The impact shook the whole building. The mother emerged from the front seat of the car with nothing worse than a few grazes, reeling and confused, but no one came out of the back seat. The mother screamed the most terrible of screams when she saw all the blood. The young medical student came running out in her nightie, her whole face full of cinnamon bun crumbs, and she saw the two girls in the back seat. She had no car of her own and she could only carry one girl. She wedged the door open and saw that one of them was breathing and the other wasn't. She picked up the girl who was still breathing and ran. Ran all the way to the hospital.

Alf goes silent. Elsa asks what happened to the sister. Alf is silent for three red lights. Then he says, in a voice heavy with bitterness:

'It's a terrible bloody thing when a parent loses a child. That family was never properly whole again. It wasn't the mother's fault. It was a bastard car accident, it was no one's fault. But she probably never got over it. And she damned well never forgave your grandmother.'

'For what?'

'Because she thought your grandmother saved the wrong daughter.'

Elsa's silence feels like a hundred red lights.

'Was Kent also in love with Britt-Marie?' she asks at last.

'We're brothers. Brothers compete.'

'And Kent won?'

A sound comes from Alf's throat; Elsa can't quite tell if it's a cough or a laugh.

'Like hell. I won.'

'What happened then?'

'Kent moved. Got married, too damned young, to a nasty piece of work. Had the twins, David and Pernilla. He loves those kids, but that woman made him bloody unhappy.'

'What about you and Britt-Marie?'

One red light. One more.

'We were young. People are bloody idiots when they're young. I went away. She stayed here.'

'Where did you go?'

'To a war.'

Elsa stares at him.

'Were you also a soldier?'

Alf pulls his hand through his lack of hair.

'I'm old, Elsa. I've been a hell of a lot of things.'

'What happened to Britt-Marie, then?'

'I was on my way home. She was going to come and give me a surprise. And she saw me with another woman.'

'You had an affair?'

'Yes.'

'Why?'

'Because people are bloody idiots when they're young.'

Red light.

'Then what did you do?' asks Elsa.

'Went away,' he answers.

'For how long?'

'Bloody long.'

'And Kent?'

'He got divorced. Moved back in with Mum. Britt-Marie was still there. Yeah, what the hell, he'd always loved her. So when her parents died they moved into their flat. Kent had got wind of the owners maybe selling the whole place as leasehold flats. So they stayed on and waited for the dough. They got married and Britt-Marie probably wanted children but Kent thought the ones he already had were bloody enough. And now things are the way they are.'

Elsa opens and closes Taxi's glove compartment.

'Why did you come home from the wars, then?'

'Some wars finish. And Mum got ill. Someone had to take care of her.'

'Didn't Kent do that?'

Alf's nails wander round his forehead like nails do when wandering among memories and opening doors that have long been closed.

'Kent took care of Mum while she was still alive. He's an idiot but he was always a good son, you can't take that away from the bastard. Mother never lacked for anything while she was alive. So I took care of her while she was dying.'

'And then?'

Alf scratches his head. Doesn't seem to know the exact answer himself.

'Then I just sort of . . . stayed on.'

Elsa looks at him with seriousness. Takes a deep, concluding breath and says:

'I like you very much, Alf. But you were a bit of a shit when you went away like that.'

Alf coughs or laughs again.

After the next red light he mutters:

'Britt-Marie took care of your mother when her father died. While your grandmother was still travelling a lot, you know. She wasn't always the nag-bag as she is now.'

'I know,' says Elsa.

'Did your grandmother tell you that?'

'In a way. She told me a story about a princess in a kingdom of sorrow, and two princes who loved her so much that they began to hate each other. And the wurses were driven into exile by the princess's parents, but then the princess fetched them back when the war came. And about a witch who stole a treasure from the princess.'

She goes silent. Crosses her arms. Turns to Alf.

'I was the treasure, right?'

Alf sighs.

'I'm not so big on fairy tales.'

'You could make an effort!'

'Britt-Marie has given her whole life to being there for a man who is never home, and trying to make someone else's children love her. When your grandfather died and she could be there for your mother it was perhaps the first time she felt . . .'

He seems to be looking for the right word. Elsa gives it to him.

'Needed.'

'Yes.'

'And then Mum grew up?'

'She moved away. Went to university. The house went bloody quiet, for a bloody long time. And then she came back with your father and was pregnant.'

'I was going to be all of Britt-Marie's second chances,' Elsa says in a low voice, nodding.

'And then your grandmother came home,' says Alf and stops by a stop sign.

They don't say a lot more about that. Like you don't when there's not a great deal more to be said. Alf briefly puts his hand on his chest, as if something is itching under his jacket.

Elsa looks at the zip.

'Did you get that scar in a war?'

Alf's gaze becomes somewhat defensive. She shrugs.

'You've got a massive scar on your chest. I saw it when you were wearing your dressing gown. You really should buy yourself a new dressing gown, by the way.'

'I was never in that sort of war. No one ever fired at me.'

'So that's why you're not broken?'

'Broken like who?'

'Sam. And Wolfheart.'

'Sam was broken before he became a soldier. And not all soldiers are like that. But if you see the shit those boys saw, you need some help when you get back. And this country's so bloody willing to put billions into weapons and fighter jets, but when those boys come home and they've seen the shit they've seen, no one can be bothered to listen to them even for five minutes.'

He looks gloomily at Elsa.

'People have to tell their stories, Elsa. Or they suffocate.'

'Where did you get the scar, then?'

'It's a pacemaker.'

'Oh!'

'You know what it is?' Alf asks, sceptically.

Elsa looks slightly offended.

'You really are a different damned kid.'

'It's good to be different.'

'I know.'

They drive up the motorway while Elsa tells Alf that Iron Man, who's a kind of superhero, has a type of pacemaker. But really it's more of an electromagnet, because Iron Man has shrapnel in his heart and without the magnet the shrapnel would cut holes in it and then he'd die. Alf doesn't look as though he entirely understands the finer points of the story, but he listens without interrupting.

'But they operate on him and remove the magnet at the end of the third film!' Elsa tells him excitedly, then she clears her throat and adds, slightly shamefaced: 'Spoiler alert. Sorry.'

Alf doesn't look as if this is concerning him very much. To be entirely honest he doesn't look as if he knows exactly what a 'spoiler' is, unless it's a part of a car.

It's snowing again, and Elsa decides that even if people she likes have been shits on earlier occasions, she has to learn to carry on liking them. You'd quickly run out of people if you had to disqualify all those who at some point have been shits. She thinks to herself that this will have to be the moral of this story. Christmas stories are supposed to have morals.

Alf's telephone rings from the compartment between the seats. He checks the display and sees it is Kent's number. He doesn't answer. It rings again.

'Aren't you going to answer?' wonders Elsa.

'It's Kent. I suppose he wants to mouth off about some crap to do with the accountant and those leasehold conversion bastards, that's all he ever thinks about. He can bloody go on about it tomorrow,' mutters Alf.

The telephone rings again; Alf doesn't answer. It rings a third time. Elsa picks it up, irritated, and answers even though Alf swears at her. There's a woman at the other end. She's crying. Elsa hands the phone to Alf. It trembles against his ear. His face becomes transparent.

It's Christmas Eve. The taxi makes a U-turn. They go to the hospital.

Alf doesn't stop for a single red light.

Elsa sits on a bench in a corridor talking to Mum on the telephone, while Alf is in a room talking to a doctor. The nurses think Elsa is a grandchild, so they tell her that he had a heart attack but he's going to be all right.

There's a young woman standing outside the room. She's crying and she's beautiful. Smells strongly of perfume. She smiles faintly at Elsa and Elsa smiles back. Alf steps out of the room and nods without smiling at the woman; the woman disappears out of the door without meeting his eyes.

Alf doesn't say a word, just marches back to the entrance and out into the car park, with Elsa behind him. And only then does Elsa see Britt-Marie. She's sitting absolutely still on the bench, wearing nothing but her floral-print jacket although it's below freezing. She's forgotten her brooch. The paintball stain is shining. Britt-Marie's cheeks are blue and she's spinning her wedding ring on her finger. She has one of Kent's shirts in her lap; it smells freshly laundered and has been perfectly ironed.

'Britt-Marie?' Alf's voice rasps out in the evening gloom, and he stops a metre from her.

She doesn't answer. Just lets her hand wander over the shirt collar in her lap. Gently brushes away something invisible from a fold. Carefully folds one cuff under the other. Straightens out a wrinkle that isn't there.

Then she lifts her chin. Looks old. Every word seems to leave a little track on her face.

'I've actually been absolutely brilliant at pretending, Alf,' she whispers firmly.

Alf doesn't answer. Britt-Marie looks down into the snow and spins her wedding ring.

'When David and Pernilla were small they always said I was so bad at coming up with stories. I always wanted to read the ones that were in books. They always said, "make one up!" but I don't understand why one should sit there and make things up just like that, when there are books where everything has been written down from the very start. I really don't.'

She had raised her voice now. As if someone needed convincing.

'Britt-Marie—' Alf says quietly, but she interrupts him coldly.

'Kent told the children I couldn't make up stories because I didn't have any imagination, but it isn't true. It's not. I have an absolutely excellent imagination. I am very good at pretending.' Alf runs his fingers across his head and blinks for a long time. Britt-Marie caresses the shirt in her lap as if it was a baby about to go to sleep. 'I always bring a newly washed shirt if I'm meeting him somewhere. Because I don't use perfume.'

Her voice grows muted. 'David and Pernilla never came for Christmas dinner. They were busy, they said. I can understand they're busy, they've been busy for years. So Kent called and said he was staying at the office for a few hours. Just a few hours, he was having another conference call with Germany. Even though it's actually Christmas in Germany as well. But he never came home. So I tried calling him. He didn't answer. I left a message. Eventually the telephone rang, but it wasn't Kent.'

Her lower lip trembles.

'I don't use perfume, but she does. So I always see to it that he has a fresh shirt. That's all I ask, that he should put his shirt directly in the washing machine when he comes home. Is that so much to ask?'

'Please, Britt-Marie . . .'

She swallows spasmodically and spins her wedding ring.

'It was a heart attack. I know that because she called and told me, Alf. She called me. Because she couldn't stand it, she couldn't. She said she couldn't sit there in the hospital and know that maybe Kent would die without my knowing. She simply couldn't stand it . . .' She puts one hand in the other, closes her eyes and adds in a quivering voice:

'I have an excellent imagination, actually. It is excellently good. Kent always said he was going for dinners with the Germans or that the plane was delayed by snow or that he was just passing by the office for a bit. And then I pretended I believed it. I pretended so brilliantly that I believed it myself.'

She rises from the bench, turns round and hangs the shirt elaborately on the edge of the bench. As if she could not allow herself even now to take out her feelings on something freshly ironed.

'I'm very good at pretending,' she whispers.

'I know that,' whispers Alf.

And then they leave the shirt on the bench and go home.

It has stopped snowing. They travel in silence. Mum comes to meet them at the front entrance. She hugs Elsa. Tries to hug Britt-Marie. Britt-Marie keeps her at a distance. Not vehemently, just with determination.

'I don't hate her, Ulrika,' she says.

'I know,' Mum says with a slow nod.

'I don't hate her and I don't hate the dog and I don't hate her car.'

Mum nods and takes her hand. Britt-Marie closes her eyes.

'I don't hate at all, Ulrika. I actually don't. I only wanted you to listen to me. Is that so much to ask? I just didn't want you to leave the car in my place. I actually just didn't want you to come and take my place.' She spins her wedding ring.

Mum leads her up the stairs, her hand firmly but lovingly round the floral-print jacket. Alf never shows up in the flat but Santa does. The boy with a syndrome's eyes light up as children's eyes do when someone tells them about ice cream and fireworks and climbing trees and splashing about in puddles.

Maud sets an extra place at the table and gets out more gratin. Lennart puts on more coffee. George washes up. After the presents have been handed round, the boy and the woman in the black skirt sit on the floor and watch *Cinderella* on the TV.

Britt-Marie sits slightly ill at ease next to Elsa on the sofa. They peer at one another. They don't say anything, but probably this is their cessation of hostilities. So when Elsa's mum tells her she has to stop eating chocolate Santas now or she'll get a stomachache, and Elsa keeps eating them, Britt-Marie doesn't say anything.

And when the evil stepmother turns up in *Cinderella*, and Britt-Marie discreetly gets up and straightens out a crease in her skirt and goes into the hall to cry, Elsa follows her.

And they sit on the chest together and eat chocolate Santas.

Because you can be upset while you're eating chocolate Santas. But it's much, much, much more difficult.

31

PEANUT CAKE

The fifth letter drops into Elsa's lap. Literally.

She wakes the next morning in Granny's magic wardrobe. The boy sleeps surrounded by his dreams, with the moo-gun in his arms. The wurse has dribbled a bit on Elsa's jumper and it's set like cement.

She lies in the darkness for a long time. Breathing in the smell of wood shavings. She thinks about the Harry Potter quotation that Granny nicked for one of her stories from the Land-of-Almost-Awake. It's from *Harry Potter and the Order of the Phoenix*, which is obviously ironic, and to understand this one would need to be fairly well informed about the differences between the Harry Potter books and Harry Potter films, as well as fairly well informed about the meaning of 'ironic'.

Because *Harry Potter and the Order of the Phoenix* is the Harry Potter film Elsa likes the least, in spite of it having one of the Harry Potter quotations Elsa likes best. The one where Harry says that he and his friends have one advantage in the approaching war with Voldemort, because they have one thing that Voldemort doesn't have: 'Something worth fighting for.'

It's ironic because that quotation isn't in the book, which Elsa likes a lot more than the film, though the book is not one of her favourite Harry Potter books. Now when she thinks of it, possibly it isn't ironic after all. She has to Wikipedia this properly, she thinks, sitting up. And that is when the letter drops into her lap. It's been taped to the wardrobe ceiling. She has no idea how long it's been there.

But this sort of thing is logical in fairy tales.

A minute later, Alf is standing in his doorway. He's drinking coffee and looks like he hasn't slept all night. He looks at the envelope. It just says 'ALF' on it, in unnecessarily large letters.

'I found it in the wardrobe. It's from Granny. I think she wants to say sorry about something,' Elsa informs him.

Alf makes a 'shush' sound and points to the radio behind him, which she really doesn't appreciate. There's the traffic news on the radio. 'There's been some damned accident up on the motorway. All city-bound traffic has been stuck for hours,' he says, as if this is something that will interest Elsa. It doesn't – she's too interested in the letter. Alf only reads it after a lot of nagging.

'What does it say, then?' Elsa demands the second he seems to have finished.

'It says sorry.'

'Yes, but sorry for *what*?'

Alf sighs in the way he's generally been sighing at Elsa lately. 'It's my damned letter, isn't it?'

'Does she write sorry for always saying that you didn't lift your feet when you walked and that's why you have such worn-out shoes?'

'What's wrong with my shoes?' says Alf, looking at his shoes. This doesn't seem to have been one of the themes of the letter.

'Nothing. There's nothing at all wrong with your shoes,' mumbles Elsa.

'I've had these shoes for more than five years!'

'They're very nice shoes,' Elsa lies.

Alf doesn't quite look as if he trusts her. Again, he looks down at the letter sceptically.

'Me and your grandmother had a bloody row before she died, all right? Just before she had to go to the hospital. She'd borrowed my electric screwdriver and never bloody bothered to give it

295

back, but she said she bloody had given it back even though I knew damned well she never bloody did.'

Elsa sighs in that way she's started generally sighing at Alf lately.

'Did you ever hear about the bloke who swore himself to death?'

'No,' says Alf, as if the question was seriously meant.

Elsa rolls her eyes.

'What does Granny write about the electric screwdriver, then?'

'She just writes sorry for losing it.'

He folds up the letter and puts it back in the envelope. Elsa stubbornly stays where she is.

'What else? I saw there was more than that in the letter. I'm not an idiot, you know!'

Alf puts the envelope on the hat shelf.

'It says sorry about loads of things.'

'Is it complicated?'

'There wasn't a crap in your grandmother's life that wasn't complicated.'

Elsa presses her hands further into her pockets. Peers down her chin at the Gryffindor emblem on her scarf. At the stitches, where Mum mended it after the girls at school had torn it. Mum still thinks it tore when Granny climbed the fence at the zoo.

'Do you believe in life after death?' she asks Alf, without looking at him.

'Haven't got a bloody clue,' says Alf, not unpleasantly and not all pleasantly, just in a very Alf-like way.

'I mean, like, do you believe in . . . paradise . . . sort of thing,' mumbles Elsa.

Alf drinks his coffee and thinks about it.

'It would be bloody complicated. Logistically, I mean. Paradise must be where there aren't so many damned people,' he mutters at last.

Elsa considers this. Realises the logic of it. Paradise for Elsa is, after all, a place where Granny is, but paradise for Britt-Marie must probably be a place totally dependent on Granny not being there.

'You're quite deep sometimes,' she says to Alf.

He drinks coffee and looks as if he finds that a bit of a bloody mouthful for an eight-year-old.

Elsa is intending to ask him something else about the letter, but she never has time. And when she looks back she will think that if she'd made some different choices, this day would not have worked out as terribly as it did in the end. But by then it's too late for that.

And Dad is standing on the stairs behind her. He's out of breath.

Which is not at all like Dad.

Elsa's eyes open wide when she sees him, and then she looks at Alf's flat. At the radio. Because there's no coincidence in fairy tales. And there's a Russian playwright who once said that if there's a pistol hanging on the wall in the first act it has to be fired before the last act is over. Elsa knows that. And those who can't understand by now how Elsa understands things like that just haven't been paying attention. So Elsa understands that the whole thing with the radio and the accident on the motorway must have something to do with the fairy tale they're in.

'Is it . . . Mum?' she manages to say.

Dad nods and throws a nervous glance at Alf. Elsa's face trembles.

'Is she at the hospital?'

'Yes, she was called in this morning to take part in a meeting. There was some kind of cri—' Dad starts, but Elsa interrupts him:

'She was in the car accident, wasn't she? The one on the motorway?'

Dad looks spectacularly puzzled.

'What accident?'

'The car accident!' Elsa repeats, quite beyond herself.

'No . . . no!' And then he smiles. 'You're someone's big sister now. Your mum was at the meeting when her waters broke!'

It doesn't quite go into Elsa's head, it really doesn't. It's quite obvious. Although she's very familiar with what happens when the waters break.

'But the car accident? What's it got to do with the car accident?' she mumbles.

Dad looks breathtakingly tentative.

'Nothing, I think. Or, I mean, what do you mean?'

Elsa looks at Alf. Looks at Dad. Thinks about it so hard that she feels the strain right inside her sinuses.

'Where's George?' she asks.

'At the hospital,' answers Dad.

'How did he get there? They said on the radio all traffic on the motorway is stuck!'

'He ran,' says Dad, with a small twinge of what dads experience when they have to say something positive about the new guy.

And that's when Elsa smiles. 'George is good in that way,' she whispers.

'Yes,' Dad admits.

And she decides that maybe the radio by now has in some way earned its place in this fairy tale, in spite of it all. Then she bursts out anxiously:

'But how are we going to get to the hospital if the motorway is blocked?'

'You take the old bloody road,' Alf says impatiently. Dad and Elsa look at him as if he just spoke to them in a make-believe language. Alf sighs. 'The old road, damn it. Past the old abattoir. Where that factory used to be where they made heat exchangers before the bastards moved everything to Asia. You can take that road to the hospital. Young people today, I tell you – they think the whole bloody world is a motorway.'

And there's the moment right there when Elsa is thinking that she and the wurse will go in Taxi. But then she changes her mind and decides they'll go in Audi instead, because she doesn't want Dad to be upset. And if she hadn't changed her mind it's possible that the day wouldn't have ended up as loathsome and terrible as it will soon become. Because when terrible things happen one always thinks, 'If I only hadn't . . .' And, afterwards, this will turn out to be one of those moments.

Maud and Lennart also decide they will come along to the hospital. Maud has brought biscuits and Lennart decides when he gets to the entrance to bring the coffee percolator, because he's worried they may not have one at the hospital. And even if they do, Lennart has the feeling it will probably be one of those modern coffee makers with a lot of buttons. Lennart's percolator only has one button. Lennart is very fond of that button.

The boy with a syndrome and his mother also come along. Also the woman in jeans. Because they're sort of a team now, which Elsa is very pleased about. Mum told her yesterday that now, when so many people are living in Granny's flat, the whole house feels like that house Elsa always goes on about where all the X-Men live. She rings on Britt-Marie's door as well. But no one opens it.

In retrospect, Elsa will recall that she paused briefly by the locked pram in the stairwell. The notice with the crossword was still on the wall above it. And someone had solved it. All the squares were filled. In pencil.

If Elsa had stopped and reflected a little on it, maybe things would have turned out differently. But she didn't. So they didn't. It's possible that the wurse hesitated for a moment outside Britt-Marie's door. Elsa would have understood if it had done that, just like she supposes that wurses hesitate sometimes when they're unsure about who in this fairy tale they've really been sent to protect. Wurses actually guard princesses in normal fairy tales, and even in the Land-of-Almost-Awake Elsa was never more than a knight. Yet if the wurse had any hesitation it didn't show it. It went with Elsa. Because that's the sort of friend it is.

If it hadn't gone with Elsa, maybe things would have worked out differently.

Alf convinces the police to make a pass round the block 'to make sure everything is safe'. Elsa never finds out exactly what he says to them, but Alf can be quite persuasive when he wants to be. Maybe he says that he's seen footprints in the snow. Or heard someone in the house on the other side of the street tell him something. Elsa doesn't know, but she sees the summer intern policeman get into the car, and Green-eyes do the same after lengthy deliberation. Elsa meets her gaze for a second, and if she had only told Green-eyes the truth about the wurse then maybe everything would have ended up differently. But she didn't. Because she wanted to protect the wurse. Because that's the sort of friend she is.

Alf goes back into the house and down into the garage to fetch Taxi.

When the police car swings round the corner at the top of the street, Elsa and the wurse and the boy with a syndrome scurry out of the front entrance and across the street and into Audi, which is parked there. The children jump in first.

The wurse stops mid-step. Its hackles rise.

Probably only a few seconds go by, but it feels like for ever. Afterwards Elsa will remember that it felt both as if she had time to think a billion thoughts and as if she didn't have time to think at all.

There's a smell inside Audi that makes her feel surprisingly peaceful. She doesn't quite know why. She looks at the wurse through the open window and before she has time to realise what is about to happen, she wonders if maybe it doesn't want to jump into the car because it's in pain. She knows it is feeling pain, pain the way Granny had pain everywhere in her body at the end.

Elsa starts getting out a biscuit from her pocket. Because no real friend of a wurse would leave home nowadays without at least one biscuit for emergencies. But she doesn't have time, of course, because she realises what is causing that smell in Audi.

Sam comes darting out from behind the back seat, Elsa feels the coldness against her lips when his hand closes over her mouth. His muscles tense round her throat, she feels the hairs on his skin scraping like gravel through the gaps in the Gryffindor scarf.

She has time to see the brief confusion in Sam's eyes when he sees the boy. It's the moment when he realises he's been hunting the wrong child. She has time to understand that the shadows in the fairy tale didn't want to kill the Chosen One. Only steal him. Make him their own. Kill whoever stood in their way.

And then the wurse's jaws close round Sam's other wrist, just as he's making a grab for the boy. Sam roars. Elsa has a split-second to react, when he lets go of her. She sees the knife in the rear mirror.

And everything after that is black.

Elsa can feel herself running, she feels the boy's hand in hers and she knows that they have to make it to the front entrance. They have to have time to scream so Dad and Alf can hear them.

Elsa sees her feet moving, but she's not guiding them herself. Her body is running by instinct. She thinks that she and the boy have had time to make half a dozen steps when she hears the wurse howling in horrendous pain and she doesn't know if it's the boy who lets go of her hand, or if she lets go of his. Her pulse is beating so hard that she can feel it in her eyes. The boy slips and falls to the ground. Elsa hears the back door of Audi opening and sees the knife in Sam's hand. Sees the blood on it. She does the only thing she can do: picks the boy up as best she can and runs as fast as possible.

She's good at running. But she knows it won't be enough. She can hear Sam straining behind her, feels the tug at her arm as the boy is torn from her grasp; her heart lurches, she closes her eyes and the next thing she remembers is the pain in her forehead. And Maud's scream. And Dad's hands. The hard floor in the stairwell. The world spins until it lands, swaying upside down in front of her, and she thinks that this must be how it is when you die. Like falling inwards, towards who-knows-what.

She hears banging without understanding where it comes from. Then the echo. 'Echo,' she has time to think, and realises she is indoors. She feels as if she's got gravel under her eyelids. She hears the light feet of the boy running up the stairs as a boy's feet can run only when they have known for many years that this could happen. She hears the terrified voice of the boy's mother, trying to keep herself calm and methodical as she runs after him, as only a mother can do and only when she has grown accustomed to fear as the natural state of things.

The door of Granny's house is closed and locked behind them. Elsa feels that Dad's hands aren't holding her up, they're holding her back. She doesn't know from what. Until she sees the shadow through the glass in the entrance door. Sees Sam on the other side. He's standing still. And something about his face is so deeply uncharacteristic of him that, at first, Elsa can't quite shake off the feeling that she is imagining the whole thing.

Sam is afraid.

In the blink of an eye another shadow descends over him, so enormous that Sam's shadow is engulfed in it. Wolfheart's heavy fists rain down with fury, with a violence and a darkness no fairy tale could describe. He doesn't hit Sam, he hammers him into the snow. Not to make him harmless. Not to protect. To destroy.

Elsa's dad picks her up and runs up the stairs. Presses her against his jacket so she can't see. She hears the door flung open from inside and she hears Maud and Lennart pleading with Wolfheart to stop hitting, stop hitting, stop hitting. But judging by the dull thumping sounds, like when you drop milk cartons on the floor, he isn't stopping. He doesn't even hear them. In the tales Wolfheart fled into the dark forests long before the War-Without-End, because he knew what he was capable of.

Elsa tears herself free of Dad and sprints down the stairs. Maud and Lennart stop screaming before she has reached the bottom. Wolfheart's mallet of a fist is raised so high above Sam that it brushes the stretched-out fingers of the cloud animals before it turns back and hurtles down.

But Wolfheart freezes in the middle of the movement. Between him and the blood-covered man stands a woman who looks so small and frail that the wind should be able to pass right through her. She has an insignificant ball of blue tumble-drier fluff in her hand, and a thin white line on her finger where her wedding ring used to be. Every ounce of her being seems to be yelling at her to run for her life. But she stays where she is, staring at Wolfheart with the resolute gaze of someone who has nothing left to lose.

She rolls up the tumble-drier fluff in the palm of one hand and puts that hand against her other hand and clasps them together on her stomach, then she looks with determination at Wolfheart and says, with authority:

'We don't beat people to death in this leaseholders' association.'

Wolfheart's fist is still vibrating in the air. His chest heaves up and down. But his arms slowly fall down at his sides.

She is still standing between Wolfheart and Sam, between the monster and the shadow, when the police car comes skidding into their street. The green-eyed policewoman jumps out, her weapon drawn, long before the car has stopped. Wolfheart has dropped on his knees in the snow.

Elsa shoves the door open and charges outside. The police roar at Wolfheart. They try to stop Elsa, but it's like holding water in cupped hands: she slips through their fingers. For reasons she won't understand for many years, Elsa has time to think about what her mother said to George once when she thought Elsa was sleeping. That this is how it is, being the mother of a daughter who is starting to grow up.

The wurse lies immobile on the ground halfway between Audi and the front entrance. The snow is red. It tried to get to her. Crawled out of Audi and crept along until it collapsed. Elsa wriggles out of her jacket and the Gryffindor scarf and spreads them over the animal's body, curling up in the snow next to it and hugging it hard, hard, feeling how its breath smells of peanut cake, and she whispers, 'Don't be afraid, don't be afraid,' over and over again into its ear. 'Don't be afraid, don't be afraid, Wolfheart has defeated the dragon and no fairy tales can end until the dragon has been defeated.'

When she feels Dad's soft hands picking her up off the ground, she calls out loudly, so the wurse will hear her even if it's already halfway to the Land-of-Almost-Awake:

'YOU CAN'T DIE! YOU HEAR!? YOU CAN'T DIE BECAUSE ALL CHRISTMAS TALES HAVE HAPPY ENDINGS!'

32

GLASS

It's hard to reason about death. Hard to let go of someone you love.

Granny and Elsa used to watch the evening news together. Now and then Elsa would ask Granny why grown-ups were always doing such idiotic things to each other. Granny usually answered that it was because grown-ups were generally people, and people are generally shits. Elsa countered that grown-ups were also responsible for a lot of good things in between all the idiocy – space exploration, the UN, vaccines and cheese slicers, for instance. Granny then said the real trick of life was that almost no one is entirely a shit and almost no one is entirely not a shit. The hard part of life is keeping as much on the 'not-a-shit' side as one can.

Once Elsa asked why so many not-shits had to die everywhere, and why so many shits didn't. And why anyone at all had to die, whether a shit or not. Granny tried to distract Elsa with ice cream and change the subject, because Granny preferred ice cream to death. But Elsa was capable of being a bewilderingly obstinate kid, so Granny gave up in the end and admitted that she supposed something always had to give up its own space so that something else could take its place.

'Like when we're on the bus and some old people get on?' asked Elsa. And then Granny asked Elsa if she'd agree to more ice cream and another topic of conversation if Granny answered 'Yes'. Elsa said she could go for that.

In the oldest fairy tales from Miamas they say a wurse can die only of a broken heart. Otherwise, they're immortal. This is why it became possible to kill them after they were sent into exile from the Land-of-Almost-Awake for biting the princess: because they were sent away by the very people they had protected and loved. 'And that was why they could be killed in the last battle of the War-Without-End,' Granny explained – for hundreds of wurses died in that last battle – 'because the hearts of all living creatures are broken in war.'

Elsa thinks about that while sitting in the waiting room at the veterinary surgery. It smells of birdseed. Britt-Marie sits next to her with her hands clasped together in her lap, watching a cockatoo sitting in its cage on the other side of the room. Britt-Marie doesn't seem so very keen on cockatoos. Elsa isn't wholly conversant with the exact emotional utterances of cockatoos, but she reckons the feeling is mutual.

'You don't have to wait here with me,' says Elsa, her voice clogged with sorrow and anger.

Britt-Marie brushes some invisible seeds from her jacket and answers, without taking her eyes off the cockatoo, 'It's no trouble, dear Elsa. You shouldn't feel like that. No trouble at all.'

Elsa understands that she doesn't mean it unpleasantly. The police are interviewing Dad and Alf about everything that has happened, and Britt-Marie was the first to be questioned, so she offered to sit with Elsa and wait for the veterinary surgeon to come out and say something about the wurse. So Elsa does understand that there's nothing unpleasant about it. It's just difficult for Britt-Marie to say anything at all without it sounding that way.

Elsa wraps her hands in her Gryffindor scarf. Inhales deeply.

'It was very brave of you to step between Wolfheart and Sam,' she offers in a low voice.

Britt-Marie brushes some invisible seeds and possibly some invisible crumbs from the table in front of her into the palm of her hand. Sits there with her hand closed round them, as if looking for an invisible waste paper bin to throw them in.

'As I said, we don't beat people to death in this leaseholders' association,' she replies quickly, so Elsa can't hear how her emotion is overwhelming her.

They are silent. As you are when you make peace for the second time in two days, but don't quite want to spell it out to the other person. Britt-Marie fluffs up a cushion at the edge of the waiting-room sofa.

'I didn't hate your grandmother,' she says without looking at Elsa.

'She didn't hate you either,' says Elsa, without looking back.

'And actually, I've never wanted the flats to be converted to leaseholds. Kent wants it, and I want Kent to be happy, but he wants to sell the flat and make money and move. I don't want to move.'

'Why not?'

'It's my home.'

It's hard not to like her for that.

'Why were you and Granny always fighting?' Elsa asks, although she already knows the answer.

'She thought I was a . . . a nagging busybody,' says Britt-Marie, not revealing the actual reason.

'Why are you like that, then?' asks Elsa, thinking about the princess and the witch and the treasure.

'Because you need to care about *something*, Elsa. As soon as anyone cared about anything in this world your granny always dismissed it as "nagging", but if you don't care about anything you're actually not alive at all. You're only existing . . .'

'You're quite deep, you know, Britt-Marie.'

'Thanks.' She clearly has to resist the impulse to start brushing something invisible from Elsa's coat-arm. She satisfies herself with fluffing up the sofa cushion again, even though it's been many years since there was last any stuffing in it to fluff up. Elsa threads the scarf round each of her fingers.

'There's this poem about an old man who says he can't be loved, so he doesn't mind, sort of, being disliked instead. As long as someone sees him,' says Elsa.

'*Doctor Glas,*' says Britt-Marie with a nod.

'Wikipedia,' Elsa corrects.

'No, it's a quote from *Doctor Glas*,' insists Britt-Marie.

'Is that a site?'

'It's a play.'

'Oh.'

'What's Wikipedia?'

'A site.'

Britt-Marie puts her hands together in her lap.

'In fact, *Doctor Glas* is a novel, as I understand. I haven't read it. But they put it on in the theatre,' she says hesitantly.

'Oh,' says Elsa.

'I like theatre.'

'Me too.'

They both nod.

'Doctor Glas would have been a good superhero name.'

She thinks it would actually have been a better name for a superhero nemesis, but Britt-Marie doesn't look like she reads quality literature on a regular basis, so Elsa doesn't want to make it too complicated for her.

'"We want to be loved,"' quotes Britt-Marie. '"Failing that, admired; failing that, feared; failing that, hated and despised. At all costs we want to stir up some sort of feeling in others. Our soul abhors a vacuum. At all costs it longs for contact."'

Elsa is not quite sure what this means, but she nods all the same. 'What do you want to be, then?'

'It's complicated being a grown-up sometimes, Elsa,' Britt-Marie says evasively.

'It's not, like, easy-peasy being a kid either,' Elsa replies belligerently.

The tips of Britt-Marie's fingers wander carefully over the white circle on the skin of her ring finger.

'I used to stand on the balcony early in the mornings. Before Kent woke up. Your grandmother knew this, that's why she made those snowmen. And that's why I got so angry. Because she knew my secret and it felt as if she and the snowmen were trying to taunt me for it.'

'What secret?'

Britt-Marie clasps her hands together firmly.

'I was never like your grandmother. I never travelled. I was just here. But sometimes I liked to stand on the balcony in the mornings, when it was windy. It's silly, of course, everyone obviously thinks it's silly, they do, of course.' She purses her mouth. 'But I like to feel the wind in my hair.'

Elsa thinks about how Britt-Marie may, despite everything, not be a total shit after all.

'You didn't answer the question – what do you want to be?' she says, winding her scarf through her fingers.

Britt-Marie's fingertips move hesitantly over her skirt, like a person moving across a dancefloor to ask someone to dance. And then, cautiously, she utters the words:

'I want someone to remember I existed. I want someone to know I was here.'

Unfortunately Elsa doesn't hear the last bit, because the veterinary surgeon comes out of the door with a look on his face that creates a surging noise inside Elsa's head. She has run past him before he has even had time to open his mouth. Elsa hears them shouting after her as she charges down the corridor and starts throwing doors open, one after the other. A nurse tries to grab her, but she just keeps running, throws more doors open, doesn't stop until she hears the wurse howling. As if it knows she's on her way and is calling for her. When she finally storms into the right room, she finds it lying on a cold table, a bandage round its stomach. There's blood everywhere. She buries her face deep, deep, deep in its coat.

Britt-Marie is still there in the waiting room. Alone. If she left right now, probably no one would remember that she'd been there. She looks as if she's thinking about that for a moment, then brushes something invisible from the edge of the table, straightens a crease in her skirt, stands up and leaves.

The wurse closes its eyes. It almost looks as if it's smiling. Elsa doesn't know if it can hear her. Doesn't know if it can feel her heavy tears dropping into its pelt. 'You can't die. You can't die, because I'm here now. And you're my friend. No real friend would just go and die like that, do you understand? Friends don't die on each other,' Elsa whispers, trying to convince herself more than the wurse.

It looks as if it knows. Tries to dry her cheeks with the warm air from its nose. Elsa lies next to it, curled up on the treatment table, as she lay in the hospital bed that night when Granny didn't come back with her from Miamas.

She lies there for ever. With her Gryffindor scarf buried in the wurse's pelt.

The policewoman's voice can be heard between the wurse's breaths as they grow slower and the thumping on the other side of the thick black fur gets more and more drawn out. Her green eyes watch the girl and the animal from the doorway.

'We have to take your friend to the police station, Elsa.' Elsa knows she's talking about Wolfheart.

'You can't put him in prison! He did it in self-defence!' Elsa roars.

'No, Elsa, he didn't. He wasn't defending himself.'

And then she backs away from the door. Checks her watch as if pretending to be disoriented, as if she has just realised there is something extremely important that she has to get on with in an entirely different place, and how crazy it would be if someone she was under very clear orders to bring to the police station would not be watched for a moment so that he could talk to a child who was about to lose a wurse. It would be crazy, really.

And then she's gone. And Wolfheart is standing in the doorway. Elsa flings herself off the table and throws her arms round him and couldn't give a crap about whether or not he has to bathe in Alcogel when he gets home.

'The wurse mustn't die! Tell him he mustn't die!' whispers Elsa.

Wolfheart breathes slowly. Stands with his hands held out awkwardly, as if someone has spilled something acidic on his jumper. Elsa realises she still has his coat at home in the flat.

'You can have your coat back, Mum has washed it really carefully and hung it up in the wardrobe inside a plastic cover,' she whispers apologetically and keeps hugging him.

He looks as if he'd really appreciate it if she didn't. Elsa doesn't care.

'But you're not allowed to fight again!' she orders, her face thrust into his jumper, before she lifts her head and wipes her eyes with her wrist. 'I'm not saying you can never fight, because I haven't quite decided where I stand on that question. I mean morally, sort of thing. But you can't fight when you're as good at fighting as you are!' she sobs.

And then Wolfheart does something very curious. He hugs her back.

'The wurse. Very old. Very old wurse, Elsa,' he growls in the secret language.

'I can't take everyone dying the whole time,' Elsa weeps.

Wolfheart holds her by both her hands. Gently squeezes her forefingers. He's trembling as if he's holding white-hot iron, but he doesn't let go, as one doesn't when one realises there are more important things in life than being afraid of children's bacteria.

'Very old wurse. Very tired now, Elsa.'

And when Elsa just shakes her head hysterically and yells at him that no one else can die on her now, he lets go of one of her hands and reaches into his trouser pocket, from which he takes a very crumpled piece of paper and puts it in her hand. It's a drawing. It's obvious that it's Granny who drew it, because she draws about as well as she spells.

'It's a map,' Elsa sobs as she unfolds it, the way one sobs when the tears have run out but not the crying.

Wolfheart gently rubs his hands together in circles. Elsa brushes her fingers over the ink.

'It's a map of the seventh kingdom,' she says, more to herself than to him.

She lies down again on the table with the wurse. So close that its pelt pricks her through her jumper. Feels its warm breathing from the cold nose. It's sleeping. She hopes it's sleeping. She kisses its nose, so her tears end up in its whiskers. Wolfheart gently clears his throat.

'Was in the letter. Grandmother's letter,' he says in the secret language and points at the letter.

'"Mipardonus". The seventh kingdom. Your grandmother and I . . . we were going to build it.'

Elsa studies the map more carefully. It's actually of the whole of the Land-of-Almost-Awake, but with completely the wrong proportions, because proportions were never really Granny's thing.

'This "Seventh Kingdom" is exactly where the ruins of Mibatalos lie,' she whispers.

Wolfheart rubs his hands together.

'Can only build Mipardonus on Mibatalos. Your grandmother's idea.'

'What does Mipardonus mean?' asks Elsa, with her cheek pressed to the wurse's.

'Means "I forgive."'

The tears from his cheeks are the size of swallows. His enormous hand descends softly on the wurse's head. The wurse opens its eyes, but only slightly, and looks at him.

'Very old, Elsa. Very, very tired,' whispers Wolfheart.

Then he tenderly puts his fingers over the wound that Sam's knife cut through the thick pelt.

It's hard to let go of someone you love. Especially when you are almost eight.

Elsa crawls close to the wurse and holds it hard, hard, hard. It manages to look at her one last time. She smiles and whispers, 'You're the best first friend I've ever had,' and it slowly licks her on the face and smells of sponge cake mix. And she laughs out loud, with her tears raining down.

When the cloud animals land in the Land-of-Almost-Awake, Elsa hugs it hard as she can, and whispers: 'You've completed your mission, you don't have to protect the castle any more. Protect Granny now. Protect all the fairy tales!' It licks her face one final time.

And then it runs off.

When Elsa turns to Wolfheart he squints at the sun as you do when you haven't been to the Land-of-Almost-Awake for an eternity of many fairy tales. Elsa points down at the ruins of Mibatalos.

'We can bring Alf here. He's good at building things. At least he's good at making wardrobes. And we'll also need wardrobes in the seventh kingdom, won't we? And Granny will be sitting on a bench in Miamas when we're ready. Just like the granddad in *The Brothers Lionheart*. There's a fairy tale with the name, I read it to Granny, so I know she'll wait on a bench because it's typical of her to nick something like that from other people's fairy tales. And she knows *The Brothers Lionheart* is one of my favourite fairy tales!'

She is still crying. Wolfheart as well. But they do what they can. They construct words of forgiveness from the ruins of fighting words.

The wurse dies on the same day that Elsa's brother is born. Elsa decides that she will tell her brother all about it when he's older. Tell him about her first best friend. Tell him that sometimes things have to clear a space so something else can take its place. Almost as if the wurse gave up its place on the bus for Halfie.

And she thinks about how she will be very particular about pointing out to Halfie that he mustn't feel sad or have a bad conscience about it.

Because wurses hate travelling by bus.

33

BABY

It's difficult ending a fairy tale. All tales have to end sometime, of course. Some can't finish soon enough. This one, for example, could feasibly have been rounded off and packed away long ago. The problem is this whole issue of heroes at the end of fairy tales, and how they are supposed to 'live happily to the end of their days'. This gets tricky, from a narrative perspective, because the people who reach the end of their days must leave others who have to live out their days without them.

It is very, very difficult to be the one that has to stay behind and live without them.

It's dark by the time they leave the vet's. They used to make snow-angels outside the house on the night before Elsa's birthday. That was the only night of the year Granny didn't say crappy things about the angels. It was one of Elsa's favourite traditions. She goes with Alf in Taxi. Not so much because she doesn't want to go with Dad, but because Dad told her Alf was furious with himself for being in the garage with Taxi when the whole thing with Sam happened. Angry because he wasn't there to protect Elsa.

Alf and Elsa don't talk very much in Taxi, of course; this is what happens when you don't have so much to say. And when Elsa at last says she has to do something at home on their way to the hospital, Alf doesn't ask why. He just drives. He's good in that way, Alf.

'Can you make snow-angels?' asks Elsa when Taxi stops outside the house.

'I'm bloody sixty-four years old,' grunts Alf.

'That's not an answer.'

Alf turns off Taxi's engine. 'I may be sixty-four years old, but I wasn't sixty-four when I was born! Course I can make bloody snow-angels!'

And then they make snow-angels. Ninety-nine of them. And they never talk much about it afterwards. Because certain kinds of friends can be friends without talking much.

The woman in jeans sees them from her balcony. She laughs. She's getting good at that.

Dad is waiting for them at the hospital entrance when they get there. A doctor goes past who, for a moment, Elsa thinks she might recognise. And then she sees George, and she runs across the entire waiting room and throws herself into his arms. He is wearing his shorts over his tights and he has a glass of ice-cold water for Mum in his hand.

'Thanks for running!' says Elsa, with her arms round him.

Dad looks at Elsa and you can see he's jealous but trying not to show it. He's good like that. George looks at her too, overwhelmed.

'I'm quite good at running,' he says quietly.

Elsa nods.

'I know. That's because you're different.'

And then she goes with Dad to see Mum. And George stays behind for so long with the glass of water that in the end it's back to room temperature.

There's a stern-looking nurse standing outside Mum's room who refuses to let Elsa inside, because apparently Mum has had a complicated delivery. That's how the nurse puts it, sounding very firm and emphatic when she pronounces the 'com' in 'complicated'. Elsa's dad clears his throat.

'Are you new here, by any chance?'

'What's that got to do with anything?' the nurse thunders. 'No visitors today!' she snaps with absolute certainty before spinning round and marching back into Mum's room.

Dad and Elsa stay where they are, patiently waiting and

nodding, because they suspect this will sort itself out. For Mum may be Mum, but she is also Granny's daughter. Remember the man in the silver car, just before Elsa was born? No one should mess with Mum when she's giving birth.

It takes maybe thirty seconds before the corridor reverberates until the pictures on the wall are practically rattling.

'BRING MY DAUGHTER IN HERE BEFORE I THROTTLE YOU WITH THE STETHOSCOPE AND LEVEL THE HOSPITAL TO THE GROUND, DO YOU UNDERSTAND?'

Thirty seconds was considerably longer than Elsa and Dad thought it would take. But in probably no more than another three or four seconds, Mum adds another roar:

'I COULDN'T GIVE A SHIT! I'LL FIND A STETHO-SCOPE SOMEWHERE IN THIS HOSPITAL AND THEN I'LL THROTTLE YOU WITH IT!'

The nurse steps out into the corridor again. She doesn't look quite as self-assured any more. The doctor that Elsa thought she recognised turns up behind her and says in a friendly voice that they can 'probably make an exception this time.' He smiles at Elsa. Elsa inhales determinedly and steps over the threshold.

Mum has tubes everywhere, all over her body. They hug as hard as Elsa dares without accidentally pulling one of them out. She imagines that one of them may be an electrical power cable, and that Mum will go out like a light if that happens. Mum repeatedly runs her hand through Elsa's hair.

'I am so very, very sorry about your friend the wurse,' she says gently.

Elsa sits in silence for so long on the edge of her bed that her cheeks dry and she has time to think about an entirely new way of measuring time. This whole thing with eternities and the eternities of fairy tales is becoming a bit unmanageable. There must be something less complicated – blinking, for example, or the beating of a hummingbird's wings. Someone must have thought about this. She's going to Wikipedia it when she gets home.

She looks at Mum, who looks happy. Elsa pats her hand. Mum grabs on to it.

'I know I'm not a perfect mum, darling.'

Elsa puts her forehead against Mum's forehead.

'Not everything has to be perfect, Mum.'

They sit so close that Mum's tears run down the tip of Elsa's nose.

'I work so much, darling. I used to be so angry at your grandmother for never being home, and now I'm just the same myself . . .'

Elsa wipes both their noses with her Gryffindor scarf.

'No superheroes are perfect, Mum. It's cool.'

Mum smiles. Elsa as well.

'Can I ask you something?'

'Of course you can,' says Mum.

'How am I like your father?'

Mum looks hesitant. As mums get when they are accustomed to being able to predict their daughter's questions, and then suddenly find they were wrong about that. Elsa shrugs.

'From Granny I have the thing about being different. And I'm a know-it-all like Dad, and I always end up rowing with everyone, which I have from Granny. So what do I have from your dad? Granny never told me any stories about him.'

Mum can't quite bring herself to answer. Elsa breathes tensely through her nose. Mum lays her hands on Elsa's cheeks and Elsa dries Mum's cheeks with the Gryffindor scarf.

'I think she talked about your grandfather without your noticing,' whispers Mum.

'How am I like him, then?'

'You have his laugh.'

Elsa retracts her hands into her jumper. And slowly swings the empty sleeves in front of her.

'Did he laugh a lot?'

'Always. Always, always, always. That was why he loved your grandmother. Because she got him to laugh with every bit of his body. Every bit of his soul.'

Elsa climbs up next to Mum in the hospital bed and lies there for probably a billion wingbeats of a hummingbird. 'Granny wasn't a complete shit. She just wasn't not a complete shit either,' she says.

'Elsa! Language!' And then Mum laughs out loud. Elsa as well. Grandfather's laugh.

And then they lie there talking about superheroes for quite a while. Mum says now that Elsa has become someone's big sister she has to bear in mind that big sisters are always idols to their younger siblings. And it's a great power to have. A great force.

'And with great power comes great responsibility,' whispers Mum.

Elsa sits up bolt upright in the bed.

'Have you been reading Spider-Man!?'

'I Googled him,' Mum says with a proud grin.

And then all the guilty feelings rush over her face. As they do with mothers who have realised that the time has come to reveal a great secret.

'Elsa . . . my darling . . . the first letter from Grandmother. It wasn't you who got it. There was another letter before yours. Grandmother gave it to me. The day before she died . . .'

Mum looks as if she's standing on the edge of a high diving board with everyone watching and has just decided she can't go through with it.

But Elsa just nods calmly, shrugs and pats Mum on the cheek, as you do with a small child who has done wrong because it doesn't know any better.

'I know, Mum. I know.'

Mum blinks awkwardly at her.

'What? You know? How do you know?'

Elsa sighs patiently.

'I mean, yeah, OK, it took me a bit of time to figure it out. But it wasn't exactly, like, quantum physics. First of all not even Granny would have been so irresponsible as to send me out on a treasure hunt without telling you first. And secondly only you and I can drive Renault, because he's a bit different but I drove him sometimes when Granny was eating kebab and

318

you drove him sometimes when Granny was drunk. So it must have been one of us that parked him in the garage in Britt-Marie's space. And it wasn't me. And I'm sort of not an idiot. I can count.'

Mum laughs so loudly and for so long about it that Elsa starts getting seriously worried about the hummingbird.

'You're the sharpest person I know, do you know that?'

And she thinks, well, that's nice and all that, but Mum really needs to get out there and meet a few more people.

'What did Granny write in your letter?' asks Elsa.

Mum's lips come together.

'She wrote sorry.'

'For being a bad mother?'

'Yes.'

'Have you forgiven her?'

Mum smiles and Elsa wipes her cheeks again with the Gryffindor scarf.

'I'm trying to forgive us both, I think. I'm like Renault. I have a long braking distance,' whispers Mum.

Elsa hugs her until the hummingbird gives up and just goes off to do something else.

'Your grandmother saved children because she was saved herself when she was small, darling. I never knew that, but she wrote it in the letter. She was an orphan,' whispers Mum.

'Like the X-Men.' Elsa nods.

'You know whereabouts the next letter is hidden, I take it?' says Mum with a smile.

'It's enough to say "where",' says Elsa, because she can't stop herself.

But she does know, of course she knows. She's known all along. She's not stupid. And this isn't exactly the most unpredictable of fairy tales.

Mum laughs again. Laughs until the evil nurse comes stamping in and says there's got to be an end to this now, or she'll have problems with the tubes.

Elsa stands up. Mum takes her hand and kisses it.

'We've decided what Halfie's going to be called. It's not going to be Elvir. It'll be another name. George and I decided as soon as we saw him. I think you're going to like it.'

She's right about that. Elsa likes it. She likes it a lot.

A few moments later she's standing in a little room, looking at him through a pane of glass. He's lying inside a little plastic box. Or a very big lunchbox. It's hard to tell which. He's got tubes everywhere and his lips are blue and his face looks as if he is running the whole time against an insanely strong wind, but all the nurses tell Elsa it's not dangerous. She doesn't like it. This is the most obvious way of figuring out that it actually is dangerous.

She cups her hands against the glass when she whispers, so he'll be able to hear on the other side. 'Don't be afraid, Halfie. You've got a sister now. And it's going to get better. Everything's going to be fine.'

And then she switches to the secret language:

'I'll try not to be jealous of you. I've been jealous of you for an insane length of time but I have a pal whose name is Alf and he and his little brother have been at loggerheads for like a hundred years. I don't want us to be at loggerheads for a hundred years. So I think we have to start working at liking each other right from the start, you get what I mean?'

Halfie looks like he gets it. Elsa puts her forehead against the glass.

'You have a granny as well. She's a superhero. I'll tell you all about her when we get home. Unfortunately I gave the moo-gun to the boy downstairs but I'll make you another one. And I'll bring you to the Land-of-Almost-Awake, and we'll eat dreams and dance and laugh and cry and be brave and forgive people, and we'll fly with the cloud animals and Granny will be sitting on a bench in Miamas, smoking and waiting for us. And one day my granddad will come wandering along as well. We'll hear him from far away because he laughs with his whole body. He laughs so much that I think we'll have to build an eighth kingdom for him. I'll ask Wolfheart what "I laugh" i in his mother's language. And the wurse is also there in the Land-of-Almost-Awake. You're going to like the wurse. There's no better friend than a wurse!'

Halfie looks at her from the plastic box. Elsa wipes the glass with the Gryffindor scarf.

'You've got a good name. The best name. I'll tell you all about the boy you got it from. You'll like him.'

She stays by the glass until she realises that the whole hummingbird thing was probably basically a bad idea, in spite of all. She'll stick to eternities and the eternities of fairy tales for a bit longer. Just for the sake of simplicity. And maybe because it reminds her of Granny.

Before she goes she whispers through cupped hands to Halfie, in the secret language:

'It's going to be the greatest adventure ever having you as a brother, Harry. The greatest, greatest adventure!'

Things are turning out as Granny said. Things are getting better. Everything is going to be fine. The doctor that Elsa felt she recognised is standing next to Mum's bed when she comes back into the room. He's waiting, without moving, as if he knows that it will take her a moment to remember where she saw him. And when the penny finally drops, he smiles as if there was never any other alternative.

'You're the accountant,' Elsa bursts out suspiciously, and then adds, 'And the vicar from the church. I saw you at Granny's funeral and you were dressed as a priest!'

'I am many things,' the doctor answers in a blithe tone of voice, with the sort of expression on his face that no one ever had when Granny was around.

'Also a doctor?' asks Elsa.

'A doctor first and foremost,' says the doctor and offers his hand as he introduces himself:

'Marcel. I was a good friend of your grandmother.'

'I'm Elsa.'

'So I understand,' smiles Marcel.

'You were Granny's lawyer,' says Elsa, as one does when remembering details of telephone calls from the beginning of fairy tales, say around the end of chapter two.

'I am many things,' Marcel repeats and gives her a paper.

It's a printout from a computer, and it's correctly spelled, so she knows it's Marcel and not Granny who wrote it. But some of Granny's handwriting can be seen on the bottom of it. Marcel folds his hands together on his stomach, not unlike the way Britt-Marie does it.

'Your grandmother owned the house you live in. Maybe you already worked that out. She says she won it in a game of poker, but I don't know for certain.'

Elsa reads the paper. Pouts her lips.

'And what? Now it's mine? The whole house?'

'Your mother will act as your guardian until you're eighteen. But your grandmother has ensured that you'll be able to do what you want with it. If you want to, you can sell the flats as lease-holds. And if you don't want to, you don't have to.'

'So why did you tell everyone in the house that it would be turned into leaseholds if everyone agreed?'

'If you don't agree then, technically, you're not all agreed. Your grandmother was convinced you would go with what the neighbours wanted if they were all agreed about it, but she was also certain you wouldn't do anything with the house that might bring anyone who lived in it to harm. That was why she had to make sure you'd got to know all your neighbours by the time you saw the testament.'

He puts his hand on her shoulder.

'It's a big responsibility, but your grandmother forbade me from giving it to anyone but you. She said you were "smarter than all those other lunatics put together." And she always said that a kingdom consists of the people that live in it. She said you'd understand that.'

Elsa's fingertips caress Granny's signature at the bottom of the paper.

'I understand.'

'I can run through the details with you but it's a very complicated contract,' says Marcel helpfully.

Elsa brushes her hair out of her face.

'Granny wasn't exactly an uncomplicated person.'

Marcel belly-laughs. You'd have to call it that. A belly-laugh.
It's far too noisy to be a laugh. Elsa likes it a great deal. It's
quite impossible not to.

'Did you and Granny have an affair?' she asks suddenly.

'ELSA!' Mum interrupts, so distressed that the tubes almost
come loose.

Offended, Elsa throws out her arms.

'What's wrong with ASKING?' She turns demandingly to
Marcel. 'Did you have an affair or not?'

Marcel puts his hands together. Nods with sadness, also happi-
ness. Like when one has eaten a very large ice cream and realises
it is now gone.

'She was the love of my life, Elsa. She was the love of many
men's lives. Women as well, actually.'

'Were you hers?'

Marcel pauses. He doesn't look angry. Or bitter. Just slightly
jealous.

'No,' he says. 'That was you. It was always you, dear Elsa.'

Tenderly he reaches out and pats Elsa's cheek, like you do
when you see someone you have loved in the eyes of their
grandchild.

Elsa and Mum and the letter share the silence for seconds and
eternities and hummingbird wingbeats. Then Mum touches Elsa's
hand and tries to make the question sound as if it's not so terribly
important, just something she just thought of spontaneously:

'What do you have from me?'

Elsa stands in silence. Mum looks despondent.

'I was just; well, you know. You said you had inherited certain
things from your grandmother and from your father, and I was
just thinking, you know . . .'

She goes silent. Ashamed of herself as mothers are when they
realise they have passed that point in life when they want more

from their daughters than their daughters want from them. And Elsa puts her hands over Mum's cheeks and says mildly:

'Just everything else, Mum. I just have everything else from you.'

Dad gives Elsa a lift back to the house. He turns off the stereo in Audi so Elsa doesn't have to listen to his music, and he stays the night in Granny's flat. They sleep in the wardrobe. It smells of wood shavings and it's just big enough for Dad to be able to stretch out and touch the walls on both sides with his fingertips and the tips of his toes. It's good in that way, the wardrobe.

When Dad has gone to sleep, Elsa sneaks down the stairs. Stands in front of the pram, which is still locked up inside the front entrance. She looks at the crossword on the wall. Someone has filled it in with a pencil. In every word is a letter which, in turn, meshes with four longer words. And in each of the four words is a letter written in a square that's bolder than the others.

E. L. S. A.

Elsa checks the padlock with which the pram is fixed to the stair railing. It's a combination lock, but the four rolls don't have numbers. They have letters.

She spells her name and unlocks it. Pushes the pram away. And that is where she finds Granny's letter to Britt-Marie.

34

GRANNY

You never say goodbye in the Land-of-Almost-Awake. You just say, 'See you later.' It's important to people in the Land-of-Almost-Awake that it should be this way, because they believe that nothing really ever completely dies. It just turns into a story, undergoes a little shift in grammar, changes tense from 'now' to 'then'.

A funeral can go on for weeks, because few events in life are a better opportunity to tell stories. Admittedly on the first day it's mainly stories about sorrow and loss, but gradually as the days and nights pass, they transform into the sorts of stories that you can't tell without bursting out laughing. Stories about how the deceased once read the instructions 'Apply to the face but not around the eyes' on the packaging of some skin cream, and then called the manufacturer with extreme annoyance to point out that this is precisely where the face is positioned. Or how she employed a dragon to caramelise the tops of all the crème brûlées before a big party in the castle, but forgot to check whether the dragon had a cold. Or how she stood on her balcony with her dressing gown hanging open, shooting at people with a paintball gun.

And the Miamasians laugh so loudly that the stories rise up like lanterns around the grave. Until all stories are one and the tenses are one and the same. They laugh until no one can forget that this is what we leave behind when we go: the laughs.

'Halfie turned out a boy-half. He's going to be called Harry!' Elsa explains proudly as she scrapes snow from the stone.

'Alf says it's lucky he turned out to be a boy, because the women in our family are "so bonkers they're a safety hazard",' she chuckles, making quotation marks in the air and grumpily dragging her feet through the snow, Alf-style. The cold is nipping at her cheeks. She nips it back. Dad digs away the snow and scrapes his spade along the top layer of earth. Elsa tightens her Gryffindor scarf round her neck. Scatters the wurse's ashes over Granny's grave and a thick layer of cinnamon bun crumbs over the ashes.

Then she hugs the gravestone tight, tight, tight, and whispers:

'See you later!'

She's going to tell all their stories. She's already telling him the first few as she wanders back to Audi with Dad. And Dad listens. He turns down the volume of the stereo before Elsa has time to jump in. Elsa scrutinises him.

'Were you upset yesterday when I hugged George at the hospital?' she asks.

'No.'

'I don't want you to be upset.'

'I don't get upset.'

'Not even a little?' says Elsa, offended.

'Am I allowed to be upset?' wonders Dad.

'You can be a *little* bit upset,' mutters Elsa.

'OK . . . I am a bit upset,' Dad tries, and actually does look upset.

'That looks a bit too upset.'

'Sorry,' says Dad, beginning to sound stressed.

'Don't look so upset that I feel guilty about it. Just upset enough so it doesn't feel like you're not bothered!' explains Elsa.

He tries again. 'Now you're not looking *at all* upset!'

'Maybe I'm upset on the inside?'

Elsa scrutinises him before conceding:

'Deal.' She says it in English.

Dad nods dubiously and manages to stop himself from pointing out that she should avoid using English words when there are perfectly good alternatives in her own language. Elsa opens and shuts the glove compartment as Audi glides up the motorway.

'He's quite OK. George, I mean.'

'Yes,' says Dad.

'I know you don't mean that,' Elsa protests.

'George is OK,' nods Dad as if he means it.

'So why don't we ever have Christmas together, then?' mutters Elsa with irritation.

'How do you mean?'

'I thought you and Lisette never came to us at Christmas because you don't like George.'

'I have nothing at all against George.'

'But?'

'But?'

'But there's a "but" coming here, isn't there? It feels like there's a "but" coming,' mumbles Elsa.

Dad sighs.

'But I suppose George and I are quite different in terms of our . . . personalities, perhaps. He's very . . .'

'Fun?'

Dad looks stressed again.

'I was going to say he seems very outgoing.'

'And you're very . . . in-going?'

Dad fingers the steering wheel nervously.

'Why can't it be your mother's fault? Perhaps we don't visit you at Christmas because Mum doesn't like Lisette.'

'Is that it?'

Dad looks uncomfortable. He's a rubbish liar. 'No. *Everyone* likes Lisette. I'm well aware of it.' He says it as people do when considering an extremely irritating character trait in the person they live with.

Elsa looks at him for a long time before she asks:

'Is that why Lisette loves you? Because you are very in-going?'

Dad smiles.

'I don't know why she loves me, if I'm to be quite honest.'

'Do you love her?'

'Incredibly,' he says without any hesitation.

But then he immediately looks quite hesitant again.

'Are you going to ask why Mum and I stopped loving each other?'

'I was going to ask why you started.'

'Was our marriage so terrible, in your view?'

Elsa shrugs.

'I mean, you're very different, that's all. She doesn't like Apple, that sort of thing. And you kind of don't like *Star Wars*.'

'There are plenty of people who don't like *Star Wars*.'

'Dad, there's NO ONE who doesn't like *Star Wars* except you!'

Dad seems unwilling to take issue with this.

'Lisette and I are also very different,' he points out.

'Does she like *Star Wars*?'

'I have to admit I've never asked.'

'How can you NOT have asked her that!?'

'We're different in other ways. I'm almost sure about that.'

'So why are you together, then?'

'Because we accept each other as we are, perhaps.'

'And you and Mum tried to change each other?'

He leans over and kisses her forehead.

'I worry about how wise you are sometimes, darling.'

Elsa blinks intensely. Takes a deep breath. Gathers her energy and whispers:

'Those texts from Mum you got on the last day of school before the Christmas holiday. About not having to pick me up? I wrote them. I lied, so I could deliver one of Granny's letters—'

'I knew,' he interrupts.

Elsa squints suspiciously at him. He smiles.

'The grammar was too perfect. I knew right away.'

It's still snowing. It's one of those magical winters when it never seems to end. After Audi has stopped outside Mum's house Elsa turns to him very seriously.

'I want to stay with you and Lisette more often than every other weekend. Even if you don't want that.'

'You . . . my darling . . . you can stay with us as often as you like!' Dad stammers, quite overwhelmed.

'No. Only every other weekend. And I get that it's because I'm different and it upsets your "family harmony". But Mum is having Halfie now. And actually Mum can't do everything all the time because no one's perfect all the time. Not even Mum!'

'Where . . . "family harmony" . . . where did you get that from?'

'I read things.'

'We didn't want to take you away from the house,' he whispers.

'Because you didn't want to take me away from Mum?'

'Because none of us wanted to take you away from your granny.'

The last words between them dissipate into the air and leave nothing behind. The snowflakes are falling so densely against Audi's windscreen that the world in front of them seems to have disappeared. Elsa holds Dad's hand. Dad holds hers even tighter.

'It's hard for a parent to accept that you can't protect your child from everything.'

'It's hard for a child to accept it too,' says Elsa and pats him on the cheek. He holds on to her fingers.

'I'm an ambivalent person. I know this makes me a bad father. I've always worried my life should be in better order before you start living with us for longer periods. I thought it was for your sake. That's what parents often do, I think, we persuade ourselves we're doing everything for the sake of the child. It's too painful to us to admit that our children won't wait to grow up because their parents are busy with other things . . .'

Elsa's forehead rests in the palm of his hand when she whispers: 'You don't need to be a perfect dad, Dad. But you have to be my dad. And you can't let Mum be more of a parent than you just because she happens to be a superhero.'

Dad buries his nose in her hair.

'We just didn't want you to become one of those children who have two homes but feel like a visitor in both,' he says.

'Where's that from?' Elsa snorts.

'We read things.'

'As smart people go, you and Mum are really insanely unsmart sometimes,' Elsa says, and then smiles. 'But don't worry about how it'll be when you're living with me, Dad. I promise we can make some things really boring!'

Dad nods and tries not to look puzzled when Elsa tells him they're going to celebrate her birthday at his and Lisette's house, because Mum and George and Halfie are still at the hospital. And Dad tries not to look stressed when Elsa says that she has already called Lisette and arranged everything. But he looks much calmer when Elsa tells him he can make the invitation cards. Because Dad immediately starts thinking about suitable fonts, and fonts have a very calming effect on Dad.

'They have to be ready this afternoon, though!' says Elsa, and Dad promises they will be.

They actually end up being ready in March. But that's another story.

Elsa is about to jump out of the car. But since Dad already seems more hesitant and stressed than usual, she turns his stereo on so he can listen to his crappy music for a while. But no music comes out, and it probably takes two or three pages before it really sinks in for Elsa.

'This is the last chapter of *Harry Potter and the Philosopher's Stone*,' she finally manages to say.

'It's an audiobook,' Dad admits with embarrassment.

Elsa stares at the stereo. Dad keeps his hands on the steering wheel, concentrating. Even though Audi has been stationary for a while now.

'When you were small we always read together. I always knew which chapter you were on in every book. But you read so quickly now, and keep up with all the things you like. Harry Potter seems to mean such a lot to you, and I want to understand the things that mean a lot to you,' he says, red-faced, as he looks down at the horn.

Elsa sits in silence. Dad clears his throat.

'It's actually a bit of a pity that you get on so well with Britt-Marie nowadays, because while I was listening to this book it

330

struck me I could have called her "She-Who-Must-Not-Be-Named" at some suitable opportunity. I had a feeling that would make you laugh . . .'

And it's actually a bit of a pity, thinks Elsa. Because it's the funniest thing Dad has ever said. It seems to set him off, as he suddenly becomes animated.

'There's a film about Harry Potter, did you know that?' he grins.

Elsa pats him indulgently on the cheek.

'Dad. I love you. I really do. But do you live under a stone or what?'

'You knew that already?' asks Dad, a little surprised.

'Everyone knows that, Dad.'

Dad nods. 'I don't really watch films. But maybe we could see this Harry Potter one some time, you and me? Is it very long?'

'There are seven books, Dad. And eight films,' says Elsa carefully.

And then Dad looks very, very stressed again.

Elsa hugs him and gets out of Audi. The sun is reflecting against the snow.

Alf is trudging about outside the entrance, trying not to slip in his worn-down shoes, with a snow shovel in his hands. Elsa thinks about the tradition in the Land-of-Almost-Awake of giving away presents on your birthday, and decides that next year she'll give Alf a pair of shoes. But not this year, because this year he's having an electric screwdriver.

Britt-Marie's door is open. She's wearing her floral-print jacket. Elsa can see in the hall mirror that she's making the bed in the bedroom. There are two suitcases inside the threshold. Britt-Marie straightens a last crease in the bedspread, sighs deeply, turns round and goes into the hall.

She looks at Elsa and Elsa looks at her and neither of them can quite bring themselves to say anything, until they both burst out at the same time:

'I have a letter for you!'

And then Elsa says 'What?' and Britt-Marie says 'Excuse me?' at the exact same moment. It's all rather disorienting.

'I have a letter for you, from Granny! It was taped to the floor under the pram by the stairs!'

'I see, I see. I also have a letter for you. It was in the tumble-drier filter in the laundry room,'

Elsa tilts her head. Looks at the suitcases.

'Are you going somewhere?'

Britt-Marie clasps her hands together slightly nervously over her stomach. Looks as if she'd like to brush something off the sleeve of Elsa's jacket.

'Yes.'

'Where?'

'I don't know,' admits Britt-Marie.

'What were you doing in the laundry?'

Britt-Marie purses her mouth.

'I was hardly going to leave without making the beds and cleaning the tumble-drier filter first, Elsa. Just imagine if something were to happen to me while I was away? I'm not going to let people think I was some sort of barbarian!'

Elsa grins. Britt-Marie doesn't grin, but Elsa has a feeling she may be grinning on the inside.

'It was you who taught the drunk to sing that song when she was on the stairs, yelling, wasn't it? And then the drunk grew completely calm and went to bed. And your mother was a singing teacher. And I don't think drunks can sing songs like that.'

Britt-Marie clasps her hands together even harder. Nervously rubs the white streak where her wedding ring used to be.

'David and Pernilla used to like it when I sang them that song, when they were small. Of course they don't remember that now, but they used to like it very much, they really did.'

'You're not a complete shit, Britt-Marie, are you?' says Elsa with a smile.

'Thanks,' says Britt-Marie hesitantly, as if she's been asked a trick question.

And then they exchange letters. On Elsa's envelope it says 'ELSA' and, on Britt-Marie's, 'THE BAT'. Britt-Marie reads hers out without Elsa even having to ask. She's good in that way, Britt-Marie. It's quite long, of course. Granny has quite a lot to apologise about, and most people haven't had anywhere near as many reasons over the years to be apologised to as Britt-Marie. There's an apology about that thing with the snowman. And an apology about the blanket fluff in the tumble-drier. And an apology about that time Granny happened to shoot at Britt-Marie with the paintball gun when she had just bought it and was 'testing it out a bit' from the balcony. Apparently, one time, she hit Britt-Marie on the bum when Britt-Marie was wearing her best skirt and you actually can't even hide stains with brooches if the stains are on your bum. Because it's not civilised to wear brooches on your bum. Granny writes that she can understand that now.

But the biggest apology comes at the end of the letter, and when Britt-Marie is reading it out the words get stuck at the back of her throat, so Elsa has to lean forward and read it herself.

'Sorry I never told you you desserve much bettre then Kent. Because you do. Even if you are an old bat!'

Britt-Marie carefully folds up the letter with the edges exactly together, and then she looks at Elsa and tries to smile like a normal human being.

Elsa pats her on the arm.

'Granny knew you'd solve the crossword on the stairs.'

Britt-Marie fidgets with Granny's letter, as if at a loss.

'How did you know it was me?'

'It was done in pencil. Granny always said you were one of those who had to make all the beds before you went on holiday and couldn't even solve a crossword in ink unless you'd had two glasses of wine first. And I've never seen you drink wine.'

And then she points at the envelope in Britt-Marie's hand. There's something else inside. Something that's jingling. Britt-Marie opens the seal and leans her head over the opening, peering inside as if she assumes Granny in person will shortly be jumping out and roaring 'WAAAAAAAAAAAAH!'

And then she sticks her hand inside and gets out Granny's car keys.

Elsa and Alf help her with the bags. Renault starts on the first try. Britt-Marie takes the deepest breath Elsa has ever seen any person take. Elsa sticks her head inside on the passenger side and yells over the din of the engine:

'I like lollipops and comics!'

Britt-Marie looks as if she's trying to answer but something is lodged in her throat. So Elsa grins and shrugs and adds:

'I'm just saying. In case you ever have any going spare.'

Britt-Marie seems to brush her damp eyes away with the sleeve of the floral-print jacket. Elsa closes the door. And then Britt-Marie drives off. She doesn't know where. But she's going to see the world and she's going to feel the wind in her hair. And she's going to solve all her crosswords in ink.

But that, as in all fairy tales, is a completely different story.

Alf stays in the garage and keeps looking long after she's out of sight. He shovels snow the whole evening and most of the next morning.

Elsa sits in Granny's wardrobe. It smells of Granny. The whole house smells of Granny. There's something quite special about a granny's house. Even if ten or twenty or thirty years go by, you never forget how it smells. And the envelope with her last letter smells just like the house. Smells of tobacco and monkey and coffee and lilies and cleaning agents and leather and rubber and soap and alcohol and protein bars and mint and wine and snuff and wood shavings and dust and cinnamon buns and smoke and sponge cake mix and candle grease and O'boy and dishcloth and dreams and spruce tree and pizza and mulled wine and potato and meringues and perfume and peanut cake and ice cream and baby. It smells of Granny. Smells like the best of someone who was mad in the best possible way.

Elsa's name is written in almost neat letters on the envelope and it's apparent that Granny really did her utmost to spell everything correctly. It didn't go so very well.

But the first five words are: "Sory I have to dye."

And that's the day Elsa forgives her granny about that.

EPILOGUE

To my knight Elsa.

    Sorry I have to dye. Sorry I dyed. Sorry I got old.

    Sorry I left you and sorry for this bloody cancer. Sorry I was a shit moor than a not-shit sometimes.

    I luv you more than 10000 eternities of fairytails. Tell Halfie the fairytails! And protect the castel! Protect your frends because they will protect you. The castel is yours now. No one is braver and wyser and stronger than you. You are the best of us all. Grow up and be diffrent and don't let anyone tell you not to be diffrent, because all superheros are diffrent. And if they mess with you then kick them in the fusebox! Live and larf and dream and bring new fairytails to Mjamas. I will wait there. Maybe grandad as well – buggered if I know. But it's going to be a grate adventure anyways.

    Sorry I was mad.

    I luv you.

    Damn, how I luv you.

Granny's spelling really was atrocious.

Epilogues in fairy tales are also difficult. Even more difficult than endings. Because although they aren't necessarily supposed to give you all the answers, it can be a bit unsatisfying if they stir up even more questions. Because life, once the story has ended, can be both very simple and very complicated.

Elsa celebrates her eighth birthday with Dad and Lisette. Dad drinks three glasses of mulled wine and dances the 'spruce dance'. Lisette and Elsa watch *Star Wars*. Lisette knows all the dialogue off by heart. The boy with a syndrome and his mum are there, and they laugh a lot, because that is how you overcome fears. Maud bakes biscuits and Alf is in a bad mood and Lennart gives Lisette and Dad a new coffee percolator. Lennart noticed that Lisette and Dad's coffee percolator has loads of buttons, and Lennart's is better because it only has one button. Dad seems to appreciate this observation.

And it's getting better. It's going to be fine.

Harry is christened in a little chapel in the churchyard where Granny and the wurse are buried. Mum insists on all the windows being kept open, even though it's snowing outside, so everyone can see.

'And what will the boy's name be?' asks the vicar, who's also an accountant and a doctor and, it's emerged, works a bit on the side as a librarian.

'Harry,' says Mum, smiling.

The vicar nods and winks at Elsa.

'And will the child have godparents?'

Elsa snorts loudly.

'He doesn't need any godparents! He has a big sister!'

And she knows that people in the real world don't understand that sort of thing. But in Miamas a newborn doesn't get a godparent, newborns get a Laugher instead. After the child's parents and Granny and a few other people that Elsa's granny, when she was telling Elsa the story, didn't seem to think were terribly important, the Laugher is the most important person in a child's life in Miamas. And the Laugher is not chosen by the parents, because Laughers are far too important to be chosen by parents. It's the child who does the choosing. So when a child is born in Miamas, all the family's friends come to the cot and tell stories and pull faces and dance and sing and make jokes, and the first one to make the child laugh

337

becomes the Laugher. They are personally responsible for making it happen as often and as loudly and in as many situations as possible, particularly those that cause embarrassment to the parents.

Of course, Elsa knows very well that everyone will tell her Harry is too small to understand the whole thing about having a big sister. But when she looks down at him in her arms, the two of them know damned well that it's the first time he's laughing.

They go back to the house, where the people continue to live their lives. Once every other week, Alf gets into Taxi and drives Maud and Lennart to a large building where they get to sit in a little room and wait for a very long time. And when Sam enters through a small door with two large security guards, Lennart gets out some coffee and Maud produces some biscuits. Because biscuits are the most important thing.

And probably a lot of people think Maud and Lennart shouldn't do that, and that types like Sam shouldn't even be allowed to live, let alone eat biscuits. And those people are probably right. And they're probably wrong too. But Maud says she's firstly a grandmother and secondly a mother-in-law and thirdly a mother, and this is what grandmothers and mothers-in-law and mothers do. They fight for the good. And Lennart drinks coffee and agrees. And Maud bakes biscuits, because when the darkness is too heavy to bear and too many things have been broken in too many ways to ever be fixed again, Maud doesn't know what weapon to use if one can't use dreams.

So that's what she does. One day at a time. One dream at a time. And one could say it's right and one could say it's wrong. And probably both would be right. Because life is both complicated and simple.

Which is why there are biscuits.

Wolfheart comes back to the house on New Year's Eve. The police have decided it was self-defence even though everyone knows it wasn't himself he was protecting. That could also be right or wrong, possibly.

He stays on in his flat. The woman in jeans stays on in hers. And they do what they can. Try to learn to live with themselves, try to live rather than just existing. They go to meetings. They tell their stories. No one knows if this is the way they are going to mend everything that's broken inside them, but at least it's a way towards something. It helps them breathe. They have dinner with Elsa and Harry and Mum and George every Sunday. Everyone in the house does. Sometimes Green-eyes also comes. She's surprisingly good at telling stories. And the boy with a syndrome still doesn't talk, but he teaches them all how to dance beautifully.

Alf wakes up one morning because he's thirsty. He gets up and has some coffee and is just on his way back to bed when there's a knock on the door. He opens it, taking a deep slug of coffee. Looks at his brother for a long time. Kent is supporting himself on a crutch and looking back at him.

'I've been a bloody idiot,' mutters Kent.

'Yes,' mutters Alf.

Kent's fingers grip the crutch even harder.

'The company went bankrupt six months ago.'

They stand there in craggy silence, with a whole life of conflict between them. As brothers do.

'You want some coffee, or what?' grunts Alf.

'If you have some ready,' grunts Kent.

And then they drink coffee. As brothers do. Sit in Alf's kitchen and compare postcards from Britt-Marie. Because she writes to them both every week. As women like Britt-Marie do.

They all still have a residents' meeting once every month in the room on the bottom floor. They all argue, as ever. Because it's a normal house. By and large. And neither Granny nor Elsa would have wanted it any other way.

The Christmas holidays come to an end and Elsa goes back to school. She knots her gym shoes tightly and carefully tightens the straps of her backpack as children like Elsa do after the Christmas holidays. But Alex starts in her class that day and she is also different. They become best friends as immediately as you only can when you've just turned eight, and they never have to run away again. When they're called in to the headmaster's office the first time that term, Elsa has a black eye and Alex has scratch marks on her face. When the headmaster sighs and tells Alex's mum that she 'has to try to fit in,' Alex's mum tries to throw the globe at him. But Elsa's mum gets there first.

Elsa will always love her for that.

A few days go by. Maybe a few weeks. But after that, one by one, other different children start tagging along with Alex and Elsa in the playground and corridors. Until there are so many of them that no one dares to chase them any more. Until they're an army in themselves. Because if a sufficient number of people are different, no one has to be normal.

In the autumn, the boy with a syndrome starts in the first year. When there's a fancy dress party he comes dressed up as a princess. A group of older boys laugh and make fun of him, until he starts crying. Elsa and Alex notice this and take him outside into the parking area and Elsa calls her dad. He arrives with a bag of new clothes.

When they go back in, Elsa and Alex are also dressed up as princesses. Spider-Man princesses.

And after that, they're the boy's superheroes.

Because all seven-year-olds deserve superheroes.

And whoever disagrees with that needs their head examined.

/

AUTHOR'S THANKS

Neda. Everything is still to make you laugh. Never forget that. (Sorry about the wet towels on the bathroom floor.) Asheghetam.

My maternal grandmother, who is not the least bit crazy, but has always baked some of the best biscuits a seven-year-old could ever ask for.

My paternal grandmother. Who has always believed in me most of all.

My sister. Who is stronger than a lion.

My mother. Who taught me to read.

Astrid Lindgren. Who taught me to love it.

All the librarians of my childhood. Who saw that a boy was afraid of heights and lent him wings.

Thanks also to:

My Obi-Wan, Niklas Natt och Dag. My editor, John Häggblom.

My agent, Jonas Axelsson. The language attack force, Vanja Vinter. Fredrik Söderlund (for letting me borrow the Noween).

Johan Zillén (who got it before all others). Kersti Forsberg (for giving a kid a chance once). Nils Olsson (for two amazing covers). All who have been involved in both this book and *A Man Called Ove* at Forum, Månpocket, Bonnier Audio, Bonnier Agency, Tre Vänner and Partners in Stories. An extra thanks in advance to the linguistic 'besserwissers' who will no doubt locate the grammatical failings in the names of the seven kingdoms (tense high-five).

Most of all thanks to you who read. Without whose highly dubious judgement I would very likely have to go out and find myself a proper job.

MY GRANDMOTHER SENDS HER REGARDS & apologises

by FREDRIK BACKMAN

READING GROUP QUESTIONS

My Grandmother Sends Her Regards and Apologises begins with the pronouncement, "Every seven-year-old deserves a superhero." Do you agree? Why is it so important that children have heroes? Who were your heroes when you were a child?

Elsa's mother grew up in a non-traditional family environment. Do you think this influenced her parenting style with Elsa?

Were you surprised by the ways in which each of the apartment tenants were connected to the others? Which relationship surprised you the most, and why?

Whether seen as a mother, grandmother, doctor, neighbour or carer, Granny is a polarizing figure. Do you think the other characters' opinions of her are justified?

Discuss the role that books, especially the Harry Potter novels, play in Elsa's life. When you were growing up, were there books you particularly loved to escape to?

Next, think about the author's use of traditional (and less traditional) fairy tales. What lessons does Elsa take away from the tales her Granny tells her about life in the land of Miamas?

In this book, as in his previous novel *A Man Called Ove*, Fredrik Backman paints a vivid portrait of the relationship between an older person nearing the end of his or her life, and a young child. What can people at the opposite ends of life learn from one another? When you were very young, was there an elderly person who played a significant role in your life? What did you learn from them?

The novel blends moments of great humour with moments of intense sadness. Which do you think wins out?

If you had to leave a letter behind apologising to someone for something, who would you write to?

What do you think Elsa will be when she grows up?

Turn the page for the first chapter of
FREDRIK BACKMAN'S
next novel

Britt-Marie Was Here

For as long as anyone can remember, Britt-Marie has
been an acquired taste. It's not that she's judgemental,
or fussy, or difficult – she just expects things to be done
in a certain way. A cutlery drawer should be arranged in
the right order, for example (forks, knives, *then* spoons).
We're not animals, are we?

But behind the passive-aggressive, socially awkward,
absurdly pedantic busybody is a woman who has
more imagination, bigger dreams and a warmer
heart than anyone around her realizes.

So when Britt-Marie finds herself unemployed,
separated from her husband of 20 years, left to fend
for herself in the miserable provincial backwater that
is Borg – of which the kindest thing one can say is
that it has a road going through it – and somehow
tasked with running the local football team, she is a
little unprepared. But she will learn that life may have
more to offer her that she's ever realised, and love might
be found in the most unexpected of places.

The number 1 European bestseller by the author of
A Man Called Ove, Britt-Marie Was Here is a funny,
poignant and uplifting tale of love, community,
and second chances.

SCEPTRE

1

Forks. Knives. Spoons.

In that order.

Britt-Marie is certainly not the kind of person who judges other people. Far from it.

But surely no civilised person would even think of arranging a cutlery drawer in a different way from how cutlery drawers are supposed to be arranged?

We're not animals, are we?

It's a Monday in January. She's sitting at a desk in the unemployment office. Admittedly there's no cutlery in sight, but it's on her mind because it sums up everything that's gone wrong recently. Cutlery should be arranged as it always has been, because life should go on unchanged. Normal life is presentable. In normal life you clean up the kitchen and keep your balcony tidy and take care of your children. It's hard work – harder than one might think. In normal life you certainly don't find yourself sitting in the unemployment office.

The girl who works here has staggeringly short hair, Britt-Marie thinks, like a man's. Not that there's anything wrong with that, of course – it's modern, no doubt. The girl points at a piece of paper and smiles, evidently in a hurry.

'Just fill in your name, social security number, and address here, please.'

Britt-Marie has to be registered. As if she were a criminal. As if she has come to steal a job rather than find one.

'Milk and sugar?' the girl asks, pouring some coffee into a plastic mug.

Britt-Marie doesn't judge anyone. Far from it. But who would behave like that? A plastic mug! Are we at war? She'd like to say just that to the girl, but because Kent is always urging Britt-Marie to 'be more socially aware' she just smiles as diplomatically as she can and waits to be offered a coaster.

Kent is Britt-Marie's husband. He's an entrepreneur. Incredibly, incredibly successful. Has business dealings with Germany and is extremely, extremely socially aware.

The girl offers her two tiny disposable cartons of the sort of milk that doesn't have to be kept in the fridge. Then she holds out a plastic mug with plastic teaspoons protruding from it. Britt-Marie could not have looked more startled if she'd been offered roadkill.

'No milk and sugar after all?' asks the girl.

Britt-Marie shakes her head and brushes her hand over the table as if it was covered in invisible crumbs. There are papers everywhere, in any old order. The girl clearly doesn't have time to tidy them up, Britt-Marie realises – she's probably far too busy with her career.

'OK,' says the girl pleasantly, turning back to the form, 'Just write your address here.'

Britt-Marie fixes her gaze on her lap. She misses being at home with her cutlery drawer. She misses Kent, because Kent is the one who fills in all the forms.

When the girl looks about to open her mouth again, Britt-Marie interrupts her.

'You forgot to give me a coaster,' says Britt-Marie, smiling, with all the social awareness she can muster. 'I don't want to make marks on your table. Could I trouble you to give me something to put my . . . coffee cup on?'

She uses that distinctive tone, which Britt-Marie relies on whenever she has to summon all her inner goodness, to refer to it as a 'cup' even though it is a plastic mug.

'Oh don't worry, just put it anywhere.'

As if life was as simple as that. As if using a coaster or organising the cutlery drawer in the right order didn't matter. The girl – who clearly doesn't appreciate the value of coasters, or proper cups, or even mirrors, judging by her hairstyle – taps her pen against the paper, by the 'address' box.

'But surely we can't just put our cups on the table? That causes marks on a table, surely you see that.'

The girl glances at the surface of the desk, which looks as if toddlers have been trying to eat potatoes off it. With pitchforks. In the dark.

'It really doesn't matter, it's so old and scratched up already!' she says with a smile.

Britt-Marie is screaming inside.

'I don't suppose you've considered that it's because you don't use coasters,' she mutters, not at all in a 'passive-aggressive' way, which is how Kent's children once described her when they thought she wasn't listening. Britt-Marie is not actually passive-aggressive. She's considerate. After she heard Kent's children saying she was passive-aggressive she was extra-considerate for several weeks.

The unemployment office girl looks a little strained. 'OK . . . what did you say your name was? Britt, right?'

'Britt-Marie. Only my sister calls me Britt.'

'OK, Britt-Marie, if you could just fill in the form. Please.'

Britt-Marie peers at the paper, which requires her to give assurances about where she lives and who she is. An unreasonable amount of paperwork is required these days just to be a human being. A preposterous amount of administration for society to let one take part. In the end she reluctantly fills in her name, social security number and her mobile telephone number. The address box is left empty.

'What's your educational background, Britt-Marie?'

Britt-Marie squeezes her handbag.

'I'll have you know that my education is excellent.'

'But no formal education?'

'For your information, I solve an enormous number of

3

crosswords. Which is not the sort of thing one can do without an education.'

She takes a very small gulp of the coffee. It doesn't taste like Kent's coffee at all. Kent makes very good coffee, everyone says so. Britt-Marie takes care of the coasters and Kent takes care of the coffee.

'OK . . . What sort of life experience do you have?'

'My latest employment was as a waitress. I had outstanding references.'

The girl looks hopeful 'And when was that?'

'1978.'

'Ah . . . and you haven't worked since then?'

'I have worked *every day* since then. I've helped my husband with his company.'

Again the girl looks hopeful. 'And what sorts of tasks did you perform in the company?'

'I took care of the children and saw to it that our home was presentable.'

The girl smiles to hide her disappointment, as people do when they don't have the ability to distinguish between 'a place to live' and 'a home.' It's actually thoughtfulness that makes the difference. Because of thoughtfulness there are coasters and proper coffee cups and beds that are made so tightly in the mornings that Kent jokes with his acquaintances about how, if you stumble on the threshold on the way into the bedroom, there's 'a smaller risk of breaking your leg if you land on the floor than the bedspread.' Britt-Marie loathes it when he talks that way. Surely civilised people lift their feet when they walk across bedroom thresholds?

Whenever Britt-Marie and Kent go away, Britt-Marie sprinkles the mattress with bicarbonate of soda for twenty minutes before she makes the bed. The bicarbonate of soda absorbs dirt and humidity, leaving the mattress much fresher. Bicarbonate of soda helps almost everything, in Britt-Marie's experience. Kent usually complains about being late; Britt-Marie clasps her hands together over her stomach and says: 'I absolutely must be allowed to make the bed before we leave, Kent. Just imagine if we die!'

4

This is the actual reason why Britt-Marie hates travelling. Death. Not even bicarbonate of soda has any effect on death. Kent says she exaggerates, but people do actually drop dead all the time when they're away, and what would the landlord think if they had to break down the door only to find an unclean mattress? Surely they'd conclude that Kent and Britt-Marie lived in their own dirt?

The girl checks her watch.

'O . . . K,' she says.

Britt-Marie feels her tone has a note of criticism in it.

'The children are twins and we have a balcony. It's more work than you think, having a balcony.'

The girl nods tentatively.

'How old are your children?'

'Kent's children. They're thirty.'

'So they've left home?'

'Obviously.'

'And you're sixty-three years old?'

'Yes,' says Britt-Marie dismissively, as if this was highly irrelevant.

The girl clears her throat as if, actually, it's very relevant indeed.

'Well, Britt-Marie, quite honestly, because of the financial crisis and all that, I mean, there's a scarcity of jobs for people in your . . . situation.'

The girl sounds a bit as if 'situation' was not her first choice as a way of concluding the sentence. Britt-Marie smiles patiently.

'Kent says that the financial crisis is over. He's an entrepreneur, you must understand. So he understands these kind of things, which are possibly a little outside your field of competence.'

The girl blinks for an unnecessary amount of time. Checks her watch. She seems uncomfortable, which stresses Britt-Marie. She quickly decides to give the girl a compliment, just to show her goodwill. She looks around the room for something to compliment her about, and finally manages to say, with as generous a smile as she can muster:

5

'You have a very modern hairstyle.'

'What? Oh. Thanks,' she replies, her fingertips moving self-consciously towards her scalp.

'It's very courageous of you to wear your hair so short when you have such a large forehead.'

Why does the girl look offended, Britt-Marie wonders? Clearly that's how it goes when you try to be sociable towards young people these days. The girl rises from her chair.

'Thanks for coming, Britt-Marie. You are registered on our database. We'll be in touch!'

She holds out her hand to say goodbye. Britt-Marie stands up and places the plastic mug of coffee in her hand.

'When?'

'Well, it's difficult to say.'

'I suppose I'm supposed to just sit and wait,' counters Britt-Marie with a diplomatic smile, 'As if I didn't have anything better to do?'

The girl swallows.

'Well, my colleague will be in touch with you about a jobseekers' training course, an—'

'I don't want a course. I want a job.'

'Absolutely, but it's difficult to say when something will turn up . . .'

Britt-Marie gets out a notebook from her pocket.

'Shall we say tomorrow, then?'

'What?'

'Could something turn up tomorrow?'

The girl clears her throat.

'Well, it could, or I'd rather s . . .'

Britt-Marie gets out a pencil from her bag, eyes the pencil with some disapproval and then looks at the girl.

'Might I trouble you for a pencil sharpener?' she asks.

'A pencil sharpener?' asks the girl, as if she had been asked for a thousand-year-old magical artefact.

'I need to put our meeting on the list.'

Some people don't understand the value of lists, but

6

Britt-Marie is not one of those people. She has so many lists that she has to keep a separate list to list all the lists. Otherwise anything could happen. She could die. Or forget to buy bicarbonate of soda.

The girl offers her a biro and says something to the effect of, 'Actually I don't have time tomorrow,' but Britt-Marie is too busy peering at the biro to hear what she's saying.

'Surely we can't write lists in *ink*?' she bursts out.

'That's all I've got.' The girl says this with some finality. 'Is there anything else I can help you with today, Britt-Marie?'

'Ha,' Britt-Marie responds after a moment.

Britt-Marie often says that. 'Ha.' Not as in 'ha-ha' but as in 'Aha,' spoken in a particularly disappointed tone. Like when you find a wet towel thrown on the bathroom floor.

'Ha.' Immediately after saying this, Britt-Marie always firmly closes her mouth, to emphasise this is the last thing she intends to say on the subject. Although it rarely is the last thing.

The girl hesitates. Britt-Marie grasps the biro as if it's sticky. Looks at the list marked 'Tuesday' in her notebook, and, at the top, above 'Cleaning' and 'Shopping,' she writes 'Unemployment office to contact me.'

She hands back the pen.

'It was very nice to meet you,' says the girl robotically. 'We'll be in touch!'

'Ha,' says Britt-Marie with a nod.

Britt-Marie leaves the unemployment office. The girl is obviously under the impression that this is the last time they'll meet, because she's unaware of how scrupulously Britt-Marie sticks to her lists. Clearly the girl has never seen Britt-Marie's balcony.

It's an astonishingly, astonishingly presentable balcony.

It's January outside, a winter chill in the air but no snow on the ground – below zero without any evidence of it. The very worst time of year for balcony plants.

After leaving the unemployment office, Britt-Marie goes to a supermarket that is not her usual supermarket, where she buys everything on her list. She doesn't like shopping on her own, because she doesn't like pushing the shopping trolley. Kent always pushes the shopping trolley, while Britt-Marie walks at his side and holds on to a corner of it. Not because she's trying to steer, only that she likes holding on to things while he is also holding on to them. For the sake of the feeling of going somewhere at the same time.

She eats her dinner cold at exactly six o'clock. She's used to sitting up all night waiting for Kent, so she tries to put his portion in the fridge. But the only fridge here is full of very small bottles of alcohol. She lowers herself on to a bed that isn't hers, while rubbing her ring finger, a habit she falls into when she's nervous.

A few days ago she was sitting on her own bed, spinning her wedding ring, after cleaning the mattress extra-carefully with bicarbonate of soda. Now she's rubbing the white mark on her skin where the ring used to be.

The building has an address, but it's certainly neither a place to live nor a home. On the floor are two rectangular plastic boxes for balcony flowers, but the hostel room doesn't have a balcony. Britt-Marie has no one to sit up all night waiting for.

But she sits upanyway.

The *New York Times* bestseller

A man called OVE

At first sight, Ove is almost certainly the grumpiest man you will ever meet. He thinks himself surrounded by idiots - neighbours who can't reverse a trailer properly, joggers, shop assistants who talk in code, and the perpetrators of the vicious *coup d'etat* that ousted him as Chairman of the Residents' Association. He will persist in making his daily inspection rounds of the local streets.

But isn't it rare, these days, to find such old-fashioned clarity of belief and deed? Such unswerving conviction about what the world should be, and a lifelong dedication to making it just so?

the end, you will see, there is something about Ove that is quite irresistible...

'It's warm, funny, with the laughs based on a solid grasp of character; and ultimately **almost unbearably moving.**' *Daily Mail*

'Delightful... there's a bit of Ove in all of us - which makes it **the perfect holiday read.**' *Evening Standard*

SCEPTRE

Join a literary community of
like-minded readers who seek out
the best in contemporary writing.

From the thousands of submissions Sceptre
receives each year, our editors select the books
we consider to be outstanding.

We look for distinctive voices, thought-provoking
themes, original ideas, absorbing narratives and
writing of prize-winning quality.

If you want to be the first to hear about our
new discoveries, and would like the chance to
receive advance reading copies of our books
before they are published, visit

www.sceptrebooks.co.uk

Follow @sceptrebooks

'Like' SceptreBooks

Watch SceptreBooks